THINNING THE HERD

BOOK ONE OF THE OPHIR RIDGE SAGA

ROB TURNBULL

THINNING THE HERD: BOOK ONE OF THE OPHIR RIDGE SAGA

First Printing: 19th August 2014

Editors: Mark E. Williams, Ken Huss, Brad D. Melichar, LCDR, USN

Beta reader: Scott Chappell

Cover illustration:
Copyright ©2016 Sergey Belyakov @12pixels. Pixel art illustrator and game designer. Creator of the upcoming game Zombie Box®. All Rights Reserved.

Author page: https://www.facebook.com/RobTurnbullTtH

Author's Twitter page: @turnbullr67

TABLE OF CONTENTS

SOMEWHERE IN MEDINA, OHIO

The day after the world went to hell Jim was still trying to grasp the reality of it all. His life was normally a simple daily routine of work, home and sleep which he rarely ever deviated from and knowing that his life would never be simple or ordinary again was crushing his soul. He missed his comfortable couch, his big screen television and his game systems with a longing that was acutely physical. To compound things, he had spent the night hiding in a crawl space under a porch while non-stop violence happened all around him. It was surreal.

There were a bunch of close calls but so far he had escaped serious injury, mostly due to luck. Jim had sprinted, and then later, after he had run more in one day than he had in his entire life, limped away from close encounters with his ex-neighbors and the other crazies. Now he was sore, hungry and confused. Confused about what the hell had happened, exactly.

Deep down he felt guilty that maybe he wished this holocaust into existence. Feeding on a steady diet of zombie movies and games, moping through life with an overall distaste for the direction it was headed, Jim had often let his thoughts wander onto the possibility of an apocalyptic event and the excitement and liberation it would bring him. The freedom from having to go to work, having to pay bills, of population overcrowding, and the general trend of an increasingly impersonal world where people only cared about themselves and theirs.

But the reality of the end of days was much worse than the fantasy of it. In his daydreams Jim pictured himself striding majestically through devastated streets, thin-hipped with a commando-type assault rifle resting against his broad shoulder, a grizzled veteran of countless skirmishes against the sluggish zombie horde. In reality he was an out-of-shape, weaponless, thirty-two year old wimp getting chased by crazy people that were easily capable of outrunning and outfighting him.

Even in his wildest dreams Jim couldn't have imagined that when the end came, it would begin for him with a routine trip out to the mailbox in his robe and slippers. One second he was headed back inside with his junk mail and the next he was yipping and shrieking, clumsily hauling his flabby body down the street in the run of his life.

Two old women and a younger man rushed him after he grabbed his mail from his mailbox. Jim had noticed them standing on the opposite sidewalk, but they only merited a quick glance on his way out to the curb. It was when all three loudly whooped that he focused on them, confused about their behavior and appearance: They were bloody and enraged and the man appeared to be swinging a doll over his head like a war banner. Shocked into inaction by the bizarreness of the whole scene, Jim stared at them dumbfounded. It was only after he recognized that the doll was a bloody, ripped apart baby that he decided to beat feet.

Even in his initial dash to freedom he remembered thinking to himself that it took exactly two seconds for dignity to go out the window and a mad panic to come in and take over. That mad panic ran the show for the next several hours. In fact, even now after he had calmed down and sort of accepted the reality of his new situation, Jim still had trouble remembering most of what had transpired since he began running twelve hours ago. Everything was a blur of chases, escapes, blood, and terror.

By random luck he happened under a porch crawlspace in front of a house he was hiding near. As he lay there, he took a mental breather and began decompressing. The wood above felt solid and reassuring, an impenetrable blanket, and for the moment he was safe and in no hurry to leave the sanctuary it provided. But he was also hungry and sore. He lost his slippers early on; all he had on now was a ripped bathrobe over soiled underwear. His feet, legs, arms and face were a mess of cuts and bruises and he had actually shit himself at some point. He was bothered by it, the flaky itching of it more than the smell, but the thought of getting jumped on with his drawers around his ankles in order to void properly was more frightening than the embarrassment of being seen with dirty underwear. Besides, the chances of meeting a hot chick under these circumstances only happened in books and movies. The hot chicks in this new world were probably the first to get decimated, torn apart as they minced down the street in their too tight pants and designer high heels, all the while texting their BFFs for help.

His stomach rumbled and Jim decided his number one priority was food. He wasn't used to skipping meals and he was feeling weak. He glanced down at his belly, half expecting it to be magically thinner now that he had gone a while without any calories but the familiar sight of his still large gut made him sigh and look away in disappointment. Nevertheless, he was hungry and tired and needed a better provisioned hiding spot, maybe one with cheeseburgers, clean water, and some real clothes.

Over the span of the last several hours Jim had heard a lot of screams and had seen countless people being chased and attacked by what he called "crazies". Since he was also being chased he wasn't in a position to help anyone. One encounter stood out for him: Last night he was running from some of them and went past an alleyway as a blonde woman wearing only one shoe emerged from it. She briefly ran alongside him as their separate packs of pursuers merged behind them. Neither wanted to be caught and they both picked up their speed in an effort to outrun the other.

Jim came very close to losing that race. His breath came in large gulps and he was leaking tears of failure, when luckily for him the blonde woman had a blowout and slowed down to a fast hopping gait. He glanced back long enough to see her clutching the back of her leg as the pack caught up to her and overwhelmed her. He felt ashamed that he chuckled at her misfortune, but he still smiled the better part of ten minutes at the image of her looking over at him seconds before she pulled a hammy, the sneer of victory on her face right before it was replaced by a look of surprise, horror, and agony.

In the last few hours the screams had become more infrequent but the number of crazies running around seemed to increase. It was still only early morning and Jim wasn't keen on popping out into the bright daylight and announcing his presence. His only option was to lie there on his stomach in the dirt, peering through the wooden lattice covering the crawlspace entrance. From his position he could only see the side of the house next door along with a few tree trunks. He wanted to get to a wider angle so he could look out into the street, maybe even find an escape route, but there was a dead body about five feet out from his hiding spot that was obstructing that view.

Jim tried to think of a good place to go once he left the crawlspace. For sure, any house he went into had a high probability of having crazies in it, either trapped inside or in there hunting for living people. Same with businesses and every other place he could think of. From what he remembered, he didn't recall any of the crazies doing complex movements, like opening windows or doors. They only chased. He wasn't going to bet his life on that, but if they could pick locks or plan coordinated searches he was in for a long haul.

With his limited options Jim concluded that his best choice was to get a car and drive to a place that had fewer or no crazies, but could still offer shelter and provisions. He needed a safe place while he figured out something long-term. Again, though, getting a car meant getting keys, which meant going into houses. He didn't want to do that, but it made sense that the only way to match a key to a car would be by entering a house with a car in the driveway.

Jim's stomach growled again and he broke wind. In the stagnant air of the crawlspace the smell had nowhere to go and did little for his morale. He continued to watch and wait, hoping for a golden opportunity to drop into his lap. If nothing presented itself Jim was willing to stay where he was until at least dusk.

When his opening did come, it wasn't golden, but terrifying. The quiet morning had lulled Jim into a lethargic half-sleep when the loudest noise he had heard in hours brought him to full alertness. A cell phone in the pocket of the body outside his hiding place was blasting a country music ringtone into the relative silence. The response was immediate. From seemingly nowhere, a crazie loped up from behind the house next door, making the throaty whoop-whoop sound Jim had already learned to hate and fear.

The crazie had once been a middle-aged business woman. Her practical suit was ripped and bloody and her purse dragged behind her from a broken strap as she reached the dead body and began jumping up and down on it, distressing it into weird flopping postures. She began to claw at the corpse's head and neck, flinging stringy bits of scalp, flesh and hair in all directions.

The phone stopped ringing and the crazie calmed down and sunk into a squat on the corpse's belly. Jim was holding his breath, willing the thing to go away when his stomach growled. The crazie turned in his direction and locked eyes with him through the lattice. At that moment Jim reverted back a million years in evolution and did what came natural to him. He panicked.

In an instant business suit lady lunged right at the crawlspace and smashed through the lattice work. All of a sudden Jim's cozy little hideaway was cramped and full of activity. He squealed, the crazie gave a muted whoop-whoop and then the game was afoot.

Having zero experience with physical altercations saved Jim's life. As soon as the crazie got into the crawlspace with him, Jim's first instinct was to leave it to her. The fastest way out of any conflict is to flee, and as improbable as it was Jim tried to stand up in preparation for a sprint, the crazie still clinging to his back.

The deranged woman was raining down devastating punishment to his head, neck, and upper back and when Jim lifted up, the full weight of his big panicked body cracked the crazie's head against the wooden support beams of the porch above.

The fists stopped beating on him as the woman on his back went limp. Jim sank back to the ground but the body stayed up, its head impaled on some nails sticking through the floorboards. Weeping softly, he waited for more of the crazies to come running to finish him off but it seemed that they were otherwise engaged. He looked out of his crawlspace hole and saw that with the latticework gone he was no longer hidden, just trapped, so he crawled out of the darkness and into the sunshine.

…

Now that Jim was exposed and out in the open his first priority was to get back into cover, preferably a better and more permanent protection than the crawlspace offered, and although he didn't want to, Jim had to chance entering a house. During the several hours he had spent hiding in the crawlspace he hadn't heard any noise from the house attached to the porch so it became the obvious choice. Besides, Jim reasoned, one house was as good as any other house, and this one was close and probably empty.

He crouched down and crept his way along the side of the house to the back, attempting to be as inconspicuous as possible. He made it around the corner without incident and tried the back door. It was locked. He flipped the door mat over hoping the owner might have stashed an emergency key there but it was empty underneath. Jim cursed to himself. The longer he stayed crouched where he was, the more danger he was in. He briefly considered smashing out a window pane to get at the lock from the inside but discarded the idea because the risk of noise outweighed the unwanted attention it might attract. The lesson of the ringing cell phone acting as a beacon was still fresh. Jim looked up to the overhang above the door, thinking that maybe he could shimmy up to it and try a second story window, but he couldn't remember the last time he pulled his own body weight further than to stand up from his recliner. The last thing he needed was to fall and sprain an ankle.

There was a doggie door that Jim briefly considered using, but he imagined himself stuck halfway through the door with his ass presented as a punching bag and shook his head. Besides, even if he did somehow fit through, so could a crazie.

He squatted low and considered his few options. His thoughts kept getting interrupted whenever he breathed in whiffs of himself; he was surrounded by a fecal cloud of his own manufacture and it was distracting. Sighing, he trotted over to one of the back windows and gave it a try without success. The second window gave him better luck and he slid it up all the way up.

With no way of knowing if anyone or anything was inside, Jim had to take his chances and climb in. He jumped up and managed to somehow get his belly over the sill and the sharp edge of it dug into his tender flesh and hurt. Jim didn't have any abs and the impact with the sill whooshed all of the air out of him and pressed into his unprotected organs. He grunted and managed a clumsy roll that flipped his legs over and dropped him onto the floor inside.

Jim forgot to let go with his hands and when he dropped his arms were wrenched behind his back and he almost cried out in agony. He laid there for a while massaging the pain from his shoulders before he stood and quietly closed and locked the window. He looked around his new sanctuary. The room he was in was a small dining area that led into the kitchen to his right, and a sparsely furnished living room was towards the front of the house. Past the living room Jim could see the front door and a staircase leading up. There was no one on the first floor, just him.

A silent fist pump: The house appeared safe. Jim felt some of his tension dissipate. He desperately wanted to lie down and rest but knew that if he wanted to be absolutely secure in his newly found haven he was going to have to inspect the rest of the house. He decided to check the upstairs rooms first.

He tiptoed into the kitchen and grabbed a large knife from the dish drying rack. It looked like a bread slicer. Jim frowned. What he needed a stabbing weapon, or a something big like a bat, because based on what he had seen so far, a crazie didn't look like it would be discouraged by a little slicing. They were maniacs and it would take massive damage to stop them, like a head puncture or a cracked skull. The movies and games Jim had watched or played over the years always showed mutants and crazy people taking more than normal damage and they still kept coming, so to him the logic of massive head trauma to put them down seemed reasonable.

Wavering briefly, Jim considered leaving the upstairs alone and taking a chance that it was empty up there until he was better armed. After all, nothing came running for him when he opened the window so maybe he was safe. He mulled it over. What if he fell asleep and snored and the snoring was loud enough to attract the attention of a crazie upstairs? Could he take that chance?

Wanting to cry, Jim knew that he was going to have to be sure if he wanted to stay alive. He stood there frozen and thought of all of the terrible things that might happen to him in the next couple of minutes. Most of the visions involved a camera-like panning out from his dead and bloody body, sad music playing as he lay there clutching a useless bread knife. It was a far cry from how he pictured the end of civilization for himself, as he mowed down hordes of zombies on his game console from the comfort of his recliner. He sighed and shook his head glumly. He needed some aspirin.

Mentally bracing himself for the worse possible outcome, Jim tiptoed towards the stairs, his ear cocked for sounds of movement. He didn't know if the crazies were able to see or hear any better than when they were normal but he hoped not. He did know from experience that they didn't hesitate. They weren't patient predators and if they saw something they went right after it. It made Jim feel a little better because he had to have made a little noise getting into the house and so far nothing was charging down the stairs after him.

He hesitated at the bottom of the stairs and gave a low whistle. Nothing responded. He gave a second whistle, a little louder than the first. Still, no reaction. Feeling much better about his chances, Jim started up, doing his best to be as quiet as a guy his size could possibly be. At the top of the stairs was a short hallway with three doorways leading off of it. Someone had left all of the doors open and Jim became more confident that nothing was in any of the rooms. He checked and found that he was right; he was alone in the house and for the moment, he was safe.

The three doors led to two bedrooms and a bathroom. One of Jim's first priorities was to wash and find better clothes, and to that end he dedicated several minutes at the sink with a wet washcloth exfoliating dried waste off of his body while he gagged into his mouth. Afterwards, the simple everyday feeling of a clean crack was euphoric and Jim's morale surged from that one simple improvement. He tossed his old stuff and the used linen into a trash can under the sink. It felt awkward to be standing naked in a stranger's bathroom and he slunk into the bigger of the two bedrooms to find something to wear.

After quick search of the dresser drawers for some underwear it was apparent to Jim that all of the clothing belonged to a petite woman. Annoyed, he went to the other room, but it was obviously a spare bedroom because it didn't have that lived in look of the first bedroom and all of the dresser drawers were bare. He tiptoed naked back to the master bedroom for a more thorough search. None of the clothes were even close to a fit for a guy, especially one that weighed almost two hundred and fifty pounds. Jim looked in dismay at the thongs and panties, pulled out a pair and held it at eye level with his fingers in the waistband, and laughed under his breath. There was no way that that was going to happen.

He had better luck in the closet. On a shelf was a pair of pantyhose still in the package, and he found that after he ripped the legs off using his teeth that they actually made a serviceable pair of stretchy drawers. Jim purposely avoided glancing in the mirror hanging on the closet door as he looked for more stuff to wear, then chuckled as he imagined himself in a movie-type clothing montage, trying on outfit after outfit for the audience, pop music soundtrack playing in the background. Most of the clothing didn't fit him, but eventually he found a pair of yoga pants and an over large sweatshirt that weren't too bad. After putting everything on, he accidently caught a glimpse of his reflection. Jim was never one to dress for other people, but a small part of him was glad that anyone who saw him in his getup would be too busy running from crazies to comment on it.

Back in the bedroom he sat on the bed and inspected his feet. Earlier, when he was cleaning them, he noted that they weren't as bad off as he thought they might be, but they did have some cuts and blisters on them and they were extremely sensitive from running barefoot on the asphalt. He didn't relish the thought of running in his bare feet any more, even if it was to save his life. Jim thought how ironic it was that now that he was relatively safe and not fleeing from crazies, his perspective had shifted from just staying alive to personal comfort and appearance. That aside, now was the time to take stock of his situation and think about living past the next moment. He needed a plan. Sure, he wouldn't have to worry about showing up and punching a clock for the foreseeable future, but technically he still had a job, a more difficult and never-ending one with the sole task of not getting stomped to death.

Jim decided that his priorities were protection and defense, followed by food and water. Protection-wise the house he was in was a good starting base. The windows were closed and locked and none of the crazies knew he was inside. As long as he kept quiet and didn't show himself or turn on lights or equipment there was no reason for anyone or anything to investigate his refuge. Although the knife Jim took from the kitchen earlier was better than nothing, he needed to canvass the house while there was still some daylight for a more effective weapon.

Starting with the bedrooms on the second floor Jim double-checked the closets, under the beds, and all the dresser drawers. He even looked under the sink in the bathroom and was about to head back down to the first floor when he spied a ring inset into the hallway ceiling. When pulled the ring activated a retractable ladder leading up to the attic. Excited and hoping for a big score, he momentarily lapsed and forgot what he was doing and yanked down on the ring.

A shriek of unoiled hinges assaulted Jim's ears and he freaked out, letting the panel slam back up into its original position. He froze in place, his arm still above his head with his finger in the ring, and listened intently for a reaction from outside. There was no response that he could hear and after a long time, he relaxed his arm and stood there, thinking about his close call and the chaos happening outside of his temporary stronghold. Jim put the lesson he had just learned into the forefront of his brain and resolved to keep it there; a moment of relaxed vigilance was all it took for the worst possible outcome to occur.

He was wiped, mentally and physically. A full day of being on the run with no food or water, witnessing horrific sights and sounds of violence was telling on him. Having seen so many people being battered to death, ripped to pieces, screaming, crying, trying to escape an awful fate, it all just overwhelmed him and he collapsed in the hallway at the top of the stairs. He didn't cry, but he felt the beginnings of tears, a moistness that filled his eyes that threatened to develop into a deep despondency. Jim couldn't imagine what the next few hours or the next few days would bring and he wasn't really sure he wanted to be around to live through them. Then, despite everything, he slowly sank into a deep slumber.

...

The next morning Jim awoke stiff and sore from a dreamless sleep. The day was bright and sunny. He momentarily forgot where he was and looked around the hallway confused before the memories rushed back. He took a deep breath. With a clarity he didn't possess before he crashed, he began to think through how he ended up in this house and what steps he should take to ensure his long-term survival. He was on the right track the night prior before mental and physical exhaustion muddled his thoughts.

What he needed was food. He was already losing weight, which was good, but he was also losing strength, which was not. Putting his weapon search on hold for the time being he crept back downstairs to raid the kitchen. Once back on the first floor and after a quick recon to make sure he was still alone he began quietly opening cupboard doors until he found something edible. He scored some cookies first and leaned back against the counter and slowly chewed them. They were dry but he didn't care. Jim couldn't remember a time when he had gone without food for more than half a day and the cookies rejuvenated him.

While he chewed he looked through a window over the sink out into the side yard. It looked and sounded peaceful out there; no crazies and no screaming. If he hadn't seen it for himself he would never believe it if someone told him that civilization was now fundamentally changed forever, that the world he knew was gone and would never return.

Jim wasn't a social person. Before things went bad he had worked overnights doing maintenance at an ammonia refrigeration facility. The only people he normally socialized with were other loners like him that worked the same shift. But even that personal intercourse was infrequent. With over 300,000 square feet of warehouse, it was easy to avoid four or five people. It suited his personality; he preferred his own company whenever possible.

He compensated for his lack of social integration with console gaming. Most of the money he made that didn't go towards bills went towards enhancing his gaming lifestyle; a large screen television, a nice stereo, and the latest gaming systems and games. Thinking back on it Jim realized that the way he lived both saved his life and put him in danger.

On that first morning he slept through what he assumed was the worst of it. If he worked a normal schedule in a normal office environment he would have been in the midst of the general slaughter. Instead, he went to bed at around eight in the morning, woke up late afternoon and went out to get his mail. Since then he had been running, climbing and hiding, activities his sedentary lifestyle did not promote. He was stiff and sore and lucky to not have any serious injury.

A raid of the kitchen pantry produced some microwavable beef stew packages. Jim grabbed all three, snatched a spoon from the sink strainer and resumed his post looking out into the back yard while he ate. He relished the taste of the cold preserved meals and felt his strength returning.

After devouring his second package Jim considered what he knew about what was happening outside. Admittedly, it was very little. Since being chased from his front yard he hadn't seen television, read a newspaper or heard a radio broadcast. He also hadn't talked to a single soul. However, he had seen and heard a lot, so he decided to catalogue what that was.

First, what he was calling 'crazies' were people that appeared to have lost their minds and gone primitive. In zombie movies and games people turned into creatures after being bitten or scratched, but most of the crazies Jim saw did not show signs of injury. They also moved differently than normal people; they either stood stock-still or went all out like an Olympic sprinter or high jumper. The only ones Jim had seen lying down looked dead or injured, but what or who caused their injuries Jim could only guess.

He also witnessed several attacks. The crazies could take an enormous amount of mechanical damage. Jim saw one fall from a third floor fire escape and get up into a limping sprint, and saw another get hit by a car and smash through the windshield, only to bounce up onto the front seat within seconds and attack the driver with enraged hammer fists and bites. It was savage. He thought about helping the woman driver getting beaten, but knew instinctively that there was nothing he could do to help her, even if he wasn't petrified beyond reason of even being sighted by one of those things.

A crazie attack generally left little of the victim intact. They stomped, bit, and tore apart whatever they caught, human or animal, and they even destroyed the once living. Jim recalled the attack on the corpse the day before after the cell phone began ringing. He broke into a cold sweat. "Oh, shit," he muttered. Putting his stew down, he quietly went through every room on both floors and unplugged all of the lines leading into the phones. He got a little light headed thinking of what might have happened if someone tried calling the house, or an automated telemarketer rang the phone. One or more of the crazies could have heard and that could have been the end of him. Jim wondered how many people died because someone else called just to check on them. It served as reinforcement that he needed to be careful.

He went back into the kitchen, finished the last of the stew packets and drank a bottle of water from the pantry. Then, his stomach full, he resumed his canvass of the house for weapons or anything else that might be of use. After half an hour of searching he had collected enough loot to cover the top of the living room coffee table. He did an inventory and divided things up into things he would bring with him on the road and things he would have to leave behind.

One of the better discoveries he made was a couple of backpacks in the upstairs closet, one suited for everyday use and one made for hiking. The hiking backpack had a metal frame and a large carry capacity, but Jim decided on the smaller, more practical pack. Also, the hiking backpack was orange and Jim envisioned his chubby body fleeing down the street wearing a large orange target while crazies easily loped after him, latched onto the convenient metal frame, and flip-flop slammed him to death on the pavement with it.

In the first of Jim's two piles, the one going into his backpack, was duct tape, a box of raisins he found in a cupboard, a full water bottle and an empty one, a multipurpose tool, a Maglite, and two walkie-talkies. He had also found some batteries and installed them so that the walkie-talkies and flashlight had fresh power. To make sure the backpack contents were quiet and didn't bounce around he stuffed a windbreaker he found into the top of the backpack. Jim put it on and adjusted it to his larger body before setting it aside. He could tell by the straps before he adjusted them that the last person to wear the backpack was much smaller than he was.

The last item in his to-go pile was a homemade weapon he created with a small aluminum bat, a pair of scissors and some duct tape. After some trial and error on the configuration, he settled on taping the scissors onto the end like an old-time bayonet. He reasoned that he could swing that bat like a club but still poke through a skull or body with the end. He also duct taped a hand guard on the end so it would be less likely to get pulled out of his hand. Looking at the spear-bat, he was impressed with himself for his cleverness. The only thing the bat wouldn't help with was if he encountered more than one of the crazies at once. If that happened he was a goner.

In his other pile Jim had more food, mostly junk like crackers and gummy worms, and the rest of the bottled water. He also found a small pair of binoculars on the back windowsill. Maybe the person who lived there was bird watcher. Jim wasn't sure if he wanted to take the binoculars with him if he had to leave or not. He used them to scan the neighborhood from the upstairs windows but didn't see anyone or anything moving about, crazie or otherwise.

During his check of the house Jim found a door off the kitchen that led down to the basement. He put off investigating it until he had a weapon and now that he had his spear-bat he was ready to go. He did another quick look around the neighborhood with the binoculars before he headed down.

…

The only light in the cellar came through two small frosted windows on the rear wall which was just enough dim light to see shapes and outlines. After waiting at the bottom of the stairs for a minute or so, Jim's eyes adjusted until he was able to see a little better. The basement was clean and open, with everything pushed back against the walls. It was unfinished with a bare cement floor. Jim enjoyed how the cold cement soothed and comforted his damaged feet.

Underneath the stairs was a washer/dryer pair and a sink, and a furnace sat in the corner of the far wall. Next to the furnace was some shelving and Jim started towards them when he was suddenly jerked off his feet. His bat dropped to the floor and clattered loudly across the cement.

Confused, Jim's plans to protect himself and to fight back if attacked were immediately abandoned. He curled into the fetal position and prepared to die horribly. When the anticipated whoop-whoop of a crazie never came, he finally peeked out from behind his hands to find the cellar still empty. Jim looked up and felt idiotic when he saw a clothes line hung between the walls. He wanted to laugh but couldn't. He got up and walked over to grab his bat. Once again he was glad that no one saw him fold under pressure.

The shelves didn't hold anything that he could eat, wear, or use as a weapon. Most of it was board games and laundry supplies. There was a small tool box but no serious tools like a hatchet or machete. The best he could do was pocket a large screwdriver to add to his to-go backpack. He checked the windows to make sure they were locked and headed back upstairs.

With the morning barely gone and the whole afternoon left to kill Jim was already starting to go a little stir crazy. He considered going up and trying the attic crawlspace but was afraid of the noise opening it would make. He decided it could wait and instead went upstairs and sat in a chair next to the master bedroom window to keep watch. Nothing seemed to be happening. There were dead bodies in the street and a few abandoned cars, but no movement. He checked again with the binoculars hoping to find someone like him, someone alive and unchanged.

Starting at the far end of the street he began checking every car, window and roof for signs. Almost every house along the street had the curtains closed, which told him nothing. Some doors and sidewalks had dried blood splashed on them and the fourth house he looked over had a beat up corpse in a flower print dress sprawled on the lawn. On the sidewalk was a crumpled and bloody stroller and bits of baby littered the area. Jim whispered to himself: "That particular scene did not go down easy." He processed it as motivation to not let the same thing happen to him.

Thinking it weird that it only took one day for a pretty normal civilized guy like himself to get used to the savage carnage he was looking at, Jim continued checking the rest of the block. He muttered as he passed each house: "Nothing, nothing, nothing."

"Whoa..."

He backed the binoculars up to the house he had just scanned and saw a hand waving from behind partially opened curtains of a second floor window. Like a dummy, he pointed to his chest, raised his eyebrows and mouthed the words "Me?" But it worked, because the curtain opened up a little more and he saw a face smiling at him. It was a pretty face.

Jim waved back but there wasn't anything else he could do. He wanted to shout to her, or cross the street, but he knew anything he did would be suicidal for him and just as dangerous for her. He didn't want her to leave the window, but he couldn't sit where he was and wave all day. He could see her enthusiasm waning also as she accepted that even though they could see each other, they had no real way of communicating.

He shrugged to her with empty hands to let her know that they were at an impasse. Her response was to hold up a finger, in a 'wait a second' gesture before she let the curtain drop. He watched the closed curtain for a minute or so before she returned holding a phone. Pointing at her phone then at Jim, she motioned that she was going to call him.

Jim waved her off and gave her a shushing. He pointed at his ear and then mimicked the crazies, then shook his head. She understood immediately and disappeared back behind the curtain. This time she was gone several minutes. Although it had only been a short time since Jim had communicated with a normal person, he almost panicked when she didn't come right back. He didn't think that he would actually miss being around others.

When she finally did reappear, it was to give Jim a 'thumbs up', pointing to her handset. He understood that she had disappeared to disable her own phones. Then she held up a piece of paper with writing on it. Using the binoculars Jim could read her message. It said: 'Don't unplug, turn ringer down'.

He grabbed the upstairs phone, turned the ringer down and plugged it back in. He let the cord out and brought it to the window. She did the same and he watched her dial, then she gave the thumbs up and he picked up the receiver.

Her first word was a breathless whisper. "Hi."

"Hi," Jim whispered back. "What's your name?"

"Megan. What's yours?"

"Jim. It's nice to meet you, Megan. Are you okay? Are you hurt?"

"No, no, we're fine. It's awesome to finally talk to someone, it's been so crazy. I've been really worried. How are you doing?"

"I'm alive, which is great considering everything that's happened. Do you know what's going on? How all of this started?"

"No. It seemed like it just happened. I was on my way to work when all of a sudden people started going crazy. They were getting out of their cars and attacking people, killing them. It happened so quickly that all I could do was run. They were all over and because they were blocking the street, I couldn't drive away. I saw that the front door of the house I'm in was open so I got in and locked the door behind me."

"Something similar happened to me, except that I didn't see how it started. I've been running ever since and was lucky enough to find an unlocked window in the back here. By the way, how did you know the phone number to this house? Did you know the lady who lived here?"

Megan gave a soft chuckle. "No, I don't know who the house belongs to. I looked up the number from the name on the mailbox. There's only one 'Hamby' in the phone book."

"Oh, I didn't think of that. Smart thinking," Jim complimented before changing the subject. "So, Megan, what's next? You mentioned a 'we'. Who else is over there with you?"

"Well," Megan said quietly, "When I ran into the house there was a boy in here, in a wheelchair. His name is Tommy and he told me his nanny ran out and left him. Said she was going home to get her family and that she would be back. Tommy told me that when she opened the door one of those monsters saw her and she screamed and ran outside. He saw her get attacked through the front window."

Megan paused and added, "I think I actually saw it happen, right before I came into the house and slammed the door. The thing was mauling and raping her, killing her right in front of my eyes. Luckily for us those monsters didn't try and open the door, because I must have spaced out for a bit. When I finally came to, it was night. I've spent most of the time since looking after Tommy and trying to find a way to get out of here."

Jim gave what she said some thought. Finally, he whispered "Megan, is Tommy sick, or is he injured?"

"Sick, I guess, but it's not really sick. He has MS."

"I see. Does that mean he needs to be wheel chaired around and cared for? Can he do anything on his own?" Jim asked.

"No, not really. He has to be fed and changed, and he's also on oxygen," Megan answered.

"That sucks. What's your plan then? What do you intend to do?"

She seemed puzzled. "You mean, about Tommy? What do I intend to do about Tommy?"

"Yeah. He can't fend for himself, right?"

"Unfortunately, no, and I'm not sure what to do about him."

Jim paused. Megan was clearly uncomfortable with Jim's line of questioning. "Listen," he ventured, "I know it sounds cruel, but if you ask me there's no way you and I can survive on the run with him." Then he explained further, pushing ahead before she could protest: "Eventually you're going to have to leave the house. You can't stay there forever, just like I can't stay in here forever, and we'll do better if we team up to find food, weapons, and a more isolated place. I hate to say it, but I think you already know that the kid is a liability. He'll only slow us down. I mean, I definitely want to help you and I need your help too, but I don't want to die because of it."

Megan chirped a "Heh," and hung up abruptly. Jim looked across the street and into her window. She was scowling at him. When Megan saw he was watching her she flipped the bird at him and disappeared behind the curtain.

…

After the call with Megan, Jim thought a lot about what he'd said. He tried, but no matter the angle, he couldn't find a way to escape to a better location while being burdened with a kid in a wheelchair, and a sick kid at that. He supposed it didn't matter anyway. Megan had already given him her opinion of his views and it seemed like she was determined to look after Tommy.

In a way Jim was relieved. He had doubts on his own ability to make it without the added stress of worrying about someone else. Since there were still things left to do before it got dark he was able to push Megan to the back of his mind. Her mention of the phone book got him to thinking. He didn't know where he was exactly. To figure that out he needed the address of the house he was in and a map of the area.

He learned the address by going through some old mail sitting on the kitchen counter. Jim also discovered that the woman who owned the house was named Gladys Hamby. Based on the advertisements and bills she received, she was retired, divorced, and owed the water company ninety six dollars and fourteen cents. She also owned a two year old Lincoln Town Car that was due for an oil change and recommended tune-up. Jim looked around for the keys to the car and found them on a hook inside the back entrance. He added them to his to-go pile.

Gladys Hamby lived on 412 Highland Drive. Jim didn't know the neighborhood well since he had rarely deviated from his routine travel routes of work, food and game stores. He found the Yellow Pages in the top drawer of the telephone table and inside the front cover were four pages of maps. He ripped them out and spread them out on the kitchen table. He was looking for Highland Drive when he heard a loud commotion outside.

Remembering to keep very quiet, Jim rushed to the upstairs window and looked out into the street. He didn't see anything although he could hear the whoop-whoop of a several crazies close by. If he didn't know better he would have suspected a pack of gorillas escaped from the zoo and were running around outside. Then a woman's scream came from a few houses down in the direction he was looking. Using the binoculars Jim saw a group of five people rush out from between houses and into the street. An overweight woman was lagging slightly behind the rest, and she was the one screaming.

Once he saw what was chasing them Jim almost screamed himself. There were at least a dozen crazies in pursuit. They overtook the screaming woman and swarmed her. Jim watched as the pack pulled, bit, punched and stomped their hapless victim only fifty yards from where he watched.

In less than thirty seconds there was little left of the woman that resembled anything human. Most of the crazies left her corpse and resumed the chase. The other four people had made it across the street and were disappearing between houses and into backyards. One of them, a man, was struggling to keep up. Jim figured he would be the next one to get mauled.

The guy must have sensed the same thing, because instead of continuing with his group he dove into a thick hedge growing alongside one of the houses. The pack still hadn't rounded the corner of the house and he wasn't spotted.

Jim knew from experience how scared the guy must be because he had been in that very same predicament just yesterday. The crazies were relentless and outnumbered normal people by a large margin.

The guy hiding in the bushes was well hidden and the main pack rushed right by, never suspecting he was there. The crazies that had stayed behind were busy eating and flinging into the air what was left of the woman. A few others rutted near the remains, whooping occasionally.

Jim took everything in. He was determined to survive so he tried to learn some lessons from what just happened. Although he had seen the crazies bite people before, he didn't know they also ate them. Maybe they were too dumb to forage for food like he was doing, by going into houses. Also, they usually seemed to hunt in packs. From the way they ran by the older guy in the bushes, he now figured that they probably didn't have any enhanced senses, or at least a heightened sense of smell. He catalogued this new information for planning purposes.

It was starting to get dark. Jim took a last look around. The guy in the bushes hadn't budged, and if he was smart he wouldn't for a while. Jim was willing to help him, but only if there was absolutely no risk to himself. He checked Megan's window and was surprised to see her there, watching him. When she saw him looking at her, she made the phone sign again. Jim nodded and went over to pick up the telephone.

"Hi," she whispered. "Sorry about earlier. I didn't understand then, but I do now. You were right about Tommy but I can't just leave him. He's only a little boy and he's unable to take care of himself." Her voice quivered slightly. "He'll die."

Jim sighed. "I know what I said earlier made me sound like an uncaring douche, but it's the truth and I think that maybe now you realize it. You know what you have to do. You have to leave him and it's bothering you, and that's totally normal. It should bother you," he told her, "but Tommy won't make it even if we could take him with us. There isn't a civilization anymore, there's only survival. It's sad, but he's not meant to survive." He paused and asked her, "Even non-handicapped people are dying. Did you see what happened to that woman?"

Sobbing noises came from the other end. Jim felt slightly bad. After a time Megan answered.

"I saw it. It frightened me more than anything in my life. But leaving Tommy, I just don't think I can do it. Besides, even if I could, where would we go?"

Jim briefly outlined his plan to her. He wanted to take the Town Car and run for a mega store or someplace like it. He asked her if she knew the area. It turned out that she only lived a few blocks away, so she knew the neighborhood well. She said she would think about some more places and they could go over it in the morning.

Before hanging up, Jim told her about the guy who ditched his pursuers and was hiding across the street in the bushes. Then they made plans to talk about Tommy again in the morning and said good night.

…

After the phone call with Megan Jim ate some food from his 'stay here' pile and took a deeply satisfying dump in the downstairs bathroom. He didn't dare flush it down because the noise might bring something running, so instead he lowered the lid quietly, closed the door, and went back upstairs. He ended up sleeping in the spare bedroom. He tried the bigger bed in the master bedroom first but the pillows smelled of old lady perfume. Inhaling a stranger's scent gave him the creeps. Anyway, the smaller bedroom gave him a better view of the street.

Jim woke several times during the night to screams and crashing noises, but each time none seemed too close so he went back to sleep. Even with the interruptions he still slept well. He almost felt guilty about getting to spend the night in the relative safety of the house while the loner in the bushes spent a more terrifying evening. Almost. He had no idea how many people just stood by in safety and watched him get chased when he was on the run. It was a smart move to not endanger yourself for a stranger, to put their life before your own, and Jim felt comfortable with his reasoning.

He rolled out of bed the next morning, ambled into the bathroom, and found an unopened toothbrush in the medicine cabinet. He brushed two days of funk from his teeth and was amazed that the little things he used to take for granted now seemed magical. Fresh breath, for instance. Then, wanting to get clean but not wanting to risk the noise of running water, Jim lifted the toilet lid, kneeled down and sniffed the water in the bowl. It didn't smell awful, like his toilet did back home, it actually smelled kind of fresh. He shrugged, cupped his hands, ducked his head and wet his hair. He grabbed some hand soap and lathered up, then gave his head a good scrubbing. He rinsed off and used a small decorative hand towel from the rack over the toilet to dry off. Clean teeth and hair. He felt renewed and thought that if only he could find some man clothes to wear he would feel more like his old self.

He slipped quietly down the stairs and grabbed a couple of snack bars from his stay-here pile and washed them down with some more of the bottled water. The nourishment gave him optimism for what the day would bring.

Jim headed back up to his roost did a quick scan with the binoculars and saw that Megan was already at the window waiting for him. She looked exhausted and she wasn't smiling like she had been the day before. After she made a brief phone signal and disappeared behind the curtain, Jim went over and picked up the phone.

The line was silent. Jim whispered "Hello?" into the handset.

"Hi," she replied, followed by a long silence.

"Hey, is everything alright? You don't sound good. How's the kid?" Megan was starting to bum him out. He was having such a great morning, too. He never understood why women felt compelled to act so mysterious. A guy will tell you what he is thinking straight out, but for some reason girls liked to make everyone guess what was in their heads.

When Megan finally spoke, her voice husky, weepy. "We won't have to worry about Tommy slowing us down anymore."

Her meaning was clear. "Uh, okay. Wanna talk about it?" Jim asked, hoping she wouldn't.

"No. In fact, I never want to discuss it again."

"Sure, I understand." Relief swept through Jim; he didn't have to waste time and effort with an uncomfortable discussion. He wondered how long he would have to wait to bring up a topic that really mattered, like getting better weapons or finding someplace safer. The line went silent again, for a longer period this time. Jim waited, not wanting to be first to break the silence.

Megan finally spoke, and when she did, her voice was almost back to normal. "I thought of some places we could go," she said. "There are several big stores nearby, but I'm assuming we don't want to go to a place with a lot of windows or other easy ways in. Have you ever heard of Klimps? It's a big wholesale store. There's one a few miles from here off of Commerce Drive."

"Yeah, I know it. Do you think it was open when the attacks started?" Jim got excited. A Klimps would be perfect. Food, clothes, cement walls and with just a couple of entry points. It was built to resist break-ins, too, so those crazies had no chance once he and Megan got in and closed the entrances down.

"It's not far, not really, but I'm worried about those things attacking us on the drive there. We won't have much time out in the open once they find us," she advised.

Jim was starting to appreciate her analytical mind. She was thinking like a survivor. "You're right, Megan," he agreed. "The hardest part will be getting from the car and into the store. Not only that, but we don't know what shape the store is in, like, if it's wide open and those things are inside, or if it's been ransacked, or if other people had the same idea and won't let us in."

"True, true," she muttered back. "I thought about that. The back-up plan is to try the National Guard Armory near Mellert Park. It's a little farther, but if it hasn't been raided we can use the weapons there to help us find someplace else. Plus, it's fortified too, so we'll be safe while we work things out."

"How do we get in, though?" Jim queried. "We would have to fight those things off while trying to find a way in. I'm positive the armory is locked up tight so I vote that as a last resort."

"Okay, I guess you're right. It's just that I saw what happened to that woman last night and I never want that to happen to me."

"Yeah, I hear you. But force alone won't get us through this. The guy that hid in the bushes across the street showed me that they aren't superhuman and that they can be tricked. They're just fucking crazy and mean. Besides, I have to be honest. I'm not in the best shape. You know, physically." He paused, and then added, "I was a pretty good couch potato."

"I'm not in tip-top shape myself. That means that what we have to do, what we have to rely on, is being smarter than they are, use what they are against them."

Jim could only agree, especially since it was his idea. "Yep. I also think we could use some help, starting with the guy hidden in the bushes. After I grab you, I'm going to stop and see if he'll get in."

"Wait. To do that you'll have to turn around and go in the wrong direction. Swing by him first, then come and get me. I'll run out and get right in. Don't stop, just slow down."

"Okay, sounds like a plan. Are you ready now?"

"Yes. Are you? Do you know if the car works?" She asked.

"Oh, yeah. Uh, I have a quick question for you. Can you see the car from where you are? I don't have a window on the driveway side, so I don't even know if the car is there or not." He couldn't believe he forgot to check before now. He had to stop being so stupid.

"Umm, it isn't in the driveway. Good thing you asked or I would have been watching you getting killed next." He saw her open the curtain a little wider and she tried for a different angle. "Hey, there's a garage though. Maybe the car is in there."

"I'm not too happy with that idea either. I don't know how long it would take for me to get into the garage, and if the car isn't in there, I'm basically fucked. Hang on a second, Megan, I'll be right back." Without waiting for her response he set the phone down and went to the bathroom. He remembered seeing a window there that looked out into the back yard.

At first Jim couldn't see much. The window was small and was higher up than a regular window. It was annoying, but Jim supposed most people didn't want others to look in and see them using the toilet. He stood on the lip of the fiberglass tub and got a good downward view, but the angle didn't let him see into the garage windows.

"Fucking detached garages," Jim whispered aloud.

He really didn't want to, but he had to crack the window to get a better look. He unlocked it and slowly slid it up a few inches, listening for any reaction. Nothing. He slid it up far enough to slide his head out sideways and looked down into the window. The car was in there.

"Bingo!"

From directly below the window Jim heard a confused grunt. He looked down as a crazie looked up and they locked eyes. They both recognized each other's presence at the same time. Jim's eyes registered shock and panic while the crazie's eyes lit up in excitement.

"Whoop-whoop-whoop!"

"Fuuuuck!" Jim squealed as he lowered the window, immediately breaking out into a cold sweat. He ran back into the bedroom and picked up the phone.

"I'm screwed!" he shouted into Megan's ears. "I need to go now! I'm so fucked!" and he threw the phone down onto the bed and ran out into the hallway. He checked himself, ran back in, picked up the phone, and yelled into the mouthpiece: "Be ready, I'm coming for you!"

Jim ran back into the bathroom and looked outside. He saw a few crazies converging on the back yard and he figured more were probably coming from other directions.

Not sure yet how he was going to get out to the garage and then into it, Jim grabbed the car keys, his backpack and the bat-spear and looked out the front door window. Empty, at least for the moment. That meant that the only crazie that was close right now was the one he saw from the upstairs window. If he hesitated he was done for. He went out the front door. The street was clear, but Jim could hear them all around, making that stupid noise. Thinking back to his conversation with Megan, he tried something he thought might work on someone that acted only on instinct. He went to the front side of the house opposite from the garage and thumped the side of the house, loud enough for the crazie in back to hear.

The response was predictable and immediate. The whoop-whooping crazie came barreling around the corner of the back of the house on that side, intent on doing Jim harm. When the goon was fully committed to coming around after him, Jim ran back across the front of the house and into the driveway towards the garage. Luckily, the crazie continued to take the long route around the house, gifting Jim a buffer of a few extra seconds to get to the garage without being overtaken.

Trying his best to sprint on his damaged feet while carrying a bat-spear and a backpack and also fumbling for the door key of the garage side entrance, Jim didn't feel like he was running fast enough to make it. He decided halfway up the driveway that stopping to unlock the side door was going to get him killed, so he concentrated on looking for the car key instead.

Grateful that Gladys had a newer car, Jim pointed the remote at the garage door and heard the 'bleep bleep' of the Town Car unlocking. He somehow managed a wide, awkward turn, generated some momentum, and rammed his shoulder into the side door of the garage and hit it so hard that it splintered open and his body flew past the car and into the far wall. Yard equipment and a trash can bounced along the concrete and made a loud ruckus.

After he recovered Jim went around and opened the driver's side door and tossed his stuff into the front seat. He slammed his door shut, locked it and put the key into the ignition. The crazie from under the window finally bounded into the garage through the open door and Jim knew he needed to escape the garage immediately.

He yipped with relief as the car turned over on the first try. He threw the gear shift into reverse and punched the gas. The crazie jumped onto the trunk and began punching on the back window.

The large luxury car had no problem tearing through the garage door, scraping his unwanted passenger off in the process. The crazie rolled over the top of the car, bounced off the hood and then smacked onto the driveway as Jim accelerated into the street. Jim wasn't surprised when it hopped right back up and began the chase anew.

Not wanting to waste time, Jim continued in reverse across the asphalt and onto the lawn of the house across the street. He got as close as he could to the bushes and hoped the guy hiding in there got the message. Jim mentally counted to three and was about to take off again when the guy popped up and ran to the back door of the car.

The guy screamed at him and slapped at the back window, "Oh my God! Unlock the fucking door!"

Oops. The door must of auto locked after he put the car into gear. Jim reached over and clicked the "Unlock" button on the door panel.

The guy immediately jerked the door open and dove into the back seat. "Go, go, go!" he shouted, but Jim was already moving, spinning the car tires on the manicured lawn and kicking clumps of grass and dirt into the face of a crazie that had run up on them from behind. The car noise and the yelling continued to attract a lot of attention as more of the crazies ran out into the street. Jim did a quick double-take at a crazie that looked at least ninety years old pumping along on thin legs. The oldster was easily overtaken and knocked over by the others in their frenzy.

Cutting left, Jim raced over lawns on his way to the house Megan was in, obliterating toys, flower beds and a metal flagpole. The town car took to four wheeling like a champ. Jim saw Megan up ahead and got pissed when he saw she had wheeled little Tommy out with her.

He yelled into the back. "Hey, dude, don't let that kid into the car!" Jim glanced into the rear view mirror and saw the guy look up from seeing Tommy out in front. The new guy seemed confused by the request.

Jim slid to a stop and to his surprise, instead of grabbing Tommy to bring him with her, Megan gave the wheelchair a push down the front walk towards the street and ran for the car. The guy in the back opened the door for her and she got in as Jim watched the wheelchair roll down into the street. It toppled over and Tommy spilled into the street, cracking his head on the curb. The little boy didn't move. To Jim he looked to be dead already and it became clear to Jim why Megan didn't want to talk about it.

Megan slapped the back of his head and he snapped out of it. "Go!" she yelled into his ear. "Drive!"

Jim pressed the gas and headed back onto the street. He gave Tommy a last look through the rear view mirror and saw most of the crazies, about ten of them, veer off from their pursuit of the car and attack Tommy's body. Jim watched as they worked Tommy's corpse over pretty good. The few that were chasing the car fell back as the Town Car gained speed and left them behind.

ON THE MOVE, MEDINA, OHIO

"Turn right at the next corner."

Jim drove and Megan navigated. She climbed over the seat and into the front, transferring Jim's stuff into the back. Beyond Megan giving directions, nobody else had said anything yet.

The crazies emerged in large numbers from backyards, open houses, and side streets but the car was traveling too fast for them to intercept. Once Jim and the others were sure that they were safe as long as they continued to move, they relaxed a small amount and began introductions. Megan smiled at Jim, shook his hand and said, "Hiya." She looked into the back, introduced herself and asked the new guy his name.

"I'm Jim. Nice to meet you, Megan. And thanks to both of you for picking me up. I thought I was going to die in those bushes."

Both Jim and Megan let out a small laugh. "Backseat Jim, you got a nickname?" Megan asked. "You two boys share the same name and I already know my Jim as Jim."

"Yeah, no problem. I'll go by my last name. I was in the military so I'm used to it. Call me Vickers."

"Thanks, Vickers, it's nice to meet you too. We're headed to the Klimps on Commerce Drive. Hopefully, once we're there we can get better acquainted. We're close now, about a minute out." She looked over at Jim. "We need to be ready. Those things are following us and we won't have much time." Peering back over the seat at Vickers she asked, "Do you know if the Klimps store is safe?"

"Sorry, I wasn't over this way. What I can tell you is that those things are everywhere, so getting in if it's closed is going to be tough, especially without weapons."

"I guess we'll know soon enough," Megan replied, turning back to Jim. "It's the next right."

Jim turned the corner and saw the Klimps ahead and off to the left. "Holy shit," he mumbled, "What the fuck happened here?"

A muted "Wow" came from Megan. Vickers could only stare.

The parking lot was filled with hundreds of bodies, over two hundred at least. Cars, trucks and SUVs were randomly parked or crashed everywhere. It was like a scene from a war movie where a bomb had exploded in a busy parking lot. Jim stopped the car at the lot entrance. He wasn't sure he wanted to drive over dead bodies, he didn't think he was ready for that yet. Some of the bodies showed signs of the brutal attacks of the type the crazies inflicted, but most of them looked like they had no visible injury.

From the backseat Vickers slapped the roof of the car and told the two in front, "Hey, we have trouble. The pack is catching up and we need to move."

Jim looked in the rearview mirror and saw a few dozen of the crazies loping down the street, headed their way. He wasn't squeamish, especially not after what he had seen lately, but there were dead women and children laid out in front of the car. He couldn't imagine running over them. He froze.

Megan was speaking to him, telling him to go, and he could see the worried eyes of Vickers in the mirror pleading with him to move. He could also see that the crazies had made up some distance on them and were now only fifty feet away and gaining fast. Still, his foot wouldn't press down on the gas pedal. His eyes blurred, everything seemed to shift into slow motion and he bowed his head into his chest.

He knew that this was his test. This one moment defined whether he was going to survive or if he was going to die horribly, and also condemn people that were depending on him to the same fate. "Jim," he said to himself, "C'mon! You can do this. You need to do this."

Jim looked up at the dead bodies then to his two companions. "Let's live," he declared.

...

Once Jim got used to it, running over the bodies became more of a messy chore than anything else. The first few were tough, as they popped or flattened under the weight of the big Lincoln, but Jim quickly mastered the quick, random jerking of the steering wheel as it cleared the grisly obstacles. The car skewed through viscera and spun out occasionally, but at least it was moving forward. He avoided the larger piles, afraid of getting hung up on the bodies.

The going was slower than he had hoped and the crazies gained some ground. The bodies were a hindrance to them too, though. Some of the crazies peeled off in ecstasy at the availability of bodies, picking random corpses to defile. The main body remained about twenty strong and Jim felt the specter of defeat looming. His passengers hadn't said a word, but he could feel them mentally urging him on. Megan was clutching the dashboard in front of her with both hands.

Suddenly the driving became easier. He chanced upon a path through the bodies made by another vehicle. Much like walking in someone's footprints in the snow, Jim was able to follow the marked path and increase his speed. He could see that the driver that came before had tried different routes but had backed up and reset several times. Jim was grateful since it allowed him to drive non-stop around the wrecked vehicles and through the carnage.

They were finally close enough to see the entrance clearly and when they did spot it their hearts collectively sunk. The grate was down, which meant that it was locked. By the time they got to the door and started to prize it open the crazies will have had enough time to catch up to them. There was no way they could take on the group chasing them with just a spear-bat while at the same time forcing open an industrial strength security door.

In resignation, Jim was about to turn the car around and make a run for the parking lot exit when suddenly the gate went crashing up and a group of six people armed with handguns and machetes came out. At the same time, shots rang out from the Klimps roof. Jim looked in the mirror and saw a crazie drop. They were being rescued.

...

Jim pulled the car out of the field of fire and stopped. He didn't think it was safe to get out with all of the shooting and the closeness of the crazies. He intended to wait it out and was about to tell Megan and Vickers that when Vickers excitedly grabbed the spear-bat from the back seat and got out to help the group at the Klimps entrance.

Megan and Jim looked at each other, not sure now if they should also get out now that Vickers was joining in on the fray.

"Wanna get out and help?" Jim asked her.

"Uh, not really," she replied. "Vickers took the only weapon, unless you have a couple of guns you didn't tell me about. I'm not good enough to go hand to hand with one of those things."

Jim thought she made perfect sense. "Yeah, guess you're right. Not too happy Vickers grabbed my weapon without asking, but now that he has, we're more of a liability out there than in here."

They watched the rest of the battle from the relative safety of the front seat. It turned out that Vickers never even got the chance to use Jim's bat-spear. The rescuers were accurate with their shots, and Jim saw two snipers on the roof firing every couple of seconds. Within a minute, all of the crazies were down and the parking lot was quiet.

Vickers was already introducing himself to the new group before Jim and Megan exited the car and headed over. They could hear Vickers thanking the people for saving their asses. He pointed at Jim and Megan and named them.

As Jim got closer, he yelled over to them, "Now I understand why the parking lot looks like it does. Thank you. You have no idea how good it feels to be safe again." Megan echoed his thanks and they quickly introduced themselves.

A man in a camouflage jacket stepped forward. He was short and rugged looking and had a full black beard that only partially covered a heavily acne-scarred face. He seemed to be the leader. "I'm Saul," the man said as he put his hand out for all of them to shake, "and this rough bunch behind me and up there on the roof is what's left of the Klimps overnight shift.

Saul pointed to each of the rescuers in turn. "That's Cindy. She is, I mean was, the night shift manager." Cindy was a large blonde woman with freckles. She smiled and waved her fingers at the newcomers. "That's Chuck and Jack, the overnight stockers. They were college students up until a few days ago."

The two young men nodded their heads and smiled. Jim noted that they were both fit and tall and in their early twenties.

"Next here is Suresh, he's some kind of engineer or professor back home in India, but here in America he works with me operating the forklifts." Suresh bowed his head slightly. Saul concluded the introductions with, "Last, the old-timer there is Ray, and he was the day manager, came in early that first day. He's also the best man with a pistol we have." Ray, a paunchy fellow with white hair and a goatee, smiled and nodded. "I'll introduce the two on the roof after we get inside. We should probably head in. No sense antagonizing the locals."

Saul turned and began corralling them back into the store. Out of habit, Jim turned back to the car and beeped the locks down, which elicited a few laughs from the group. Megan punched him in the arm and smiled, and Jim let out a light "Ha-ha," before following everyone in.

KLIMPS MEGA STORE, MEDINA, OHIO

The first thing the newcomers noticed was that the lights were on. After just a few days without using electricity, Jim never expected to see artificial lights working again. Saul noticed them looking up the lights and chuckled. "Yeah," he explained, "we should be good for a long while. Klimps has a pretty good redundancy system, on account of all the stock in the freezers. According to Ray, the generators should run for weeks. Eventually we'll have to worry about another fuel source, but for now we're good."

Ray spoke up. "Let me show you new folks around. Afterwards we can all sit down and get to know each other better." He led them to a golf cart and told them to hop on. "Nice little cart, isn't it? I figured Klimps wasn't going to be selling much of anything anymore, so I liberated it." They got on and Ray pressed the accelerator.

"First things first," Ray began, "let me show you guys the essentials, like the ways in or out and the restrooms. You'll be happy to know we have showers here, and, unless Cinderella here," Ray pumped his thumb at Jim "prefers looking like a tranny on steroids, we have a huge selection of clothing that might be more appropriate for our present circumstances. No offense, Jim."

Jim felt like blindside punching Ray's neck but held back, not wanting to get kicked outside after being somewhere safe for the first time since this whole thing began. Instead he faked a smile and said "None taken. We appreciate you guys taking us in."

"Well, to be honest we probably wouldn't have yesterday, when things were really bad. Once things settled down we figured that there weren't many of us regular people left, and we needed to save who we could."

Vickers spoke up from the back. "It looks like you guys had some trouble inside," indicating the large blood stains they were driving over.

"Yeah," Ray answered. "Most of that is from the rest of the night crew." The cart squeaked to a stop in front of several large loading bay doors. Ray explained, "Besides the front doors and the emergency exits, these roll up doors here are the only other ways in or out. We welded them shut. The goons weren't able to get in, but a couple of days ago some men were able to force one of them up. They made it in without us hearing it and managed to kill some of us before we killed a few of them and forced the rest out.

Afterwards, we discovered they were able to take one of our members, a girl named Rosa." Ray pointed to where one of the damaged doors had been repaired. Evidence of fresh welding burns showed on all of the roll ups.

At the mention of the girl's abduction, Megan spoke up for the first time. "Did you guys go after Rosa?" she asked.

"No, I'm sorry to say we didn't," Ray confessed. "Some of us wanted to, but Saul talked us out of it. I know it sounds heartless, but after he explained what would happen if we went after her, we relented. It's sad, I know, but going after her would have divided us up, maybe gotten more of us killed, or weakened the force we had inside enough for another group to come in and take over." Ray looked back at Megan and frowned. "We just couldn't risk it."

Megan was sympathetic. "I'm not accusing or blaming your group for what you had to do. We've all done things we wouldn't normally do just to survive." She gave Jim a knowing glance, and he remembered how upset she was earlier that morning because of Tommy. She went up a couple of notches in his estimation, but vowed to himself to never get himself in a 'Tommy' situation, at least where she was calling the shots.

"We're all still learning how to cope," Ray admitted before stepping on the go pedal again. "Let me show you guys where the emergency exits are, in case we have to bug out. After that I'll take you all shopping, and give you a chance to freshen up. No offense again, but someone in this cart needs a good scrubbing." He reached over, patted Jim's knee, gave him a friendly wink, and then floored the accelerator.

...

After hot showers and fresh clothes for the newcomers there was a group meeting in the old employee break room. Almost everyone was there; only Cindy and Suresh were missing. Saul explained that everyone took turns on the roof to keep watch for survivors or gangs like the one that broke in the day before yesterday.

Saul began the group meeting by stepping to the front of the room and clearing his throat. "I want to start things off by welcoming our three newest members: Jim, Megan, and Vickers. If you all wouldn't mind, tell us a little about yourselves, maybe what you did before all of this, any talents or skills you have that might better us as a group. We all pitch in around here, so anything you can do to help would be great."

Megan stood first. "I know I speak for my two friends when I say thank you guys so very much for saving our asses earlier. We were at the end of our rope and I didn't think we were going to make it." Her voice quivered a little before firming up. "Up until all of this started I was a nurse at Bethlehem Memorial Hospital. Besides nursing the only other thing I'm really good at is skydiving, which doesn't really count for much anymore."

While she spoke Jim took the time to give her a good checking out. Up close, she was older than he first thought when he saw her from across the street yesterday. Instead of being in her twenties he put her age closer to forty, if not on the other side of it. She had red wavy hair and was petite in that small efficient way women who took charge always seemed to be. Jim guessed that she rarely stood still or lacked for something to do. He could easily see her in a hospital ward, managing patients, doctors and other nurses. She was the exact opposite of Jim, who liked to decompress as much as possible whenever he had the opportunity.

Ray spoke up. "I'm sure your medical skills will come in handy, Megan. If you wouldn't mind looking to a few of us after this meeting, I would appreciate it. Nothing too bad, just minor cuts and stuff." Megan nodded her assent and sat down.

"Jim, how about you go next." Saul said.

"Sure," Jim replied. "I'm afraid I don't have any survival type skills, like combat or whatever. Ever since high school I worked in a place kind of like this, but much bigger. In fact, my warehouse probably supplied this store. What I can do is drive a forklift and service the freezers in here to keep them running. I can also work on generators and stuff, if the right kinds of tools are in here somewhere." Jim shrugged. "Beyond that, I can pitch in on any general work that needs to be done."

Jim looked around at everyone at the table. He already knew who Chuck, Jack, Saul and Ray were, but there were two new faces. A young-looking, pretty black girl, and a chunky white teenager that could easily pass for Cindy's little sister. They must be the two from the roof, he figured. It was hard to imagine the two girls at the table as the marksmen who saved his group with their deadly sniping, but that was the only explanation that made sense.

Vickers took the silence as the signal to go ahead and introduce himself. "I'm Jim, but please call me Vickers. I'm not from here; I was on my way to visit my sister in Cleveland when everything went crazy. By the way, I know Jim calls those things crazies, but what are you guys calling them?

Ray spoke up. "I think with us, the general consensus is goons. One of us that didn't make it, John, was an avid hockey fan. He started calling them goons because of how aggressive they are and the name just stuck. But we can call them anything; no one here is stuck with a certain name."

"I think we should all call them the same thing so that in an emergency we are all speaking the same language," Vickers answered. He looked at Jim. "Do you have any objections to calling them 'goons', Jim?"

Jim was annoyed at being put on the spot, like it mattered what the monsters outside were called. Vickers seemed to enjoy pushing his buttons, first with taking his weapon and now, by patronizing him in front of the new people. "Sure, whatever," was all he said in reply.

"Cool then" Vickers responded. "Anyway, like I said I was on my way north on the interstate when traffic slowed, then it stopped. At first I thought there was an accident, like a pile up. Some of the people started getting out of their cars. It was weird, because they weren't opening their doors; they were climbing out of open windows, or kicking their windshields out, like they were trying to escape something. It took me by surprise," Vickers confessed. "Then they swarmed, attacking everything and everyone within sight."

Saul spoke up. "It took all of us by surprise," he said, indicating the rest of the people around the table. Murmurs and head nodding followed this statement. "Sorry, keep going."

Vickers continued. "I'm a recently retired Army Master Sergeant. I spent a few tours in the sandbox, err, I mean Iraq and Afghanistan, and have seen a lot of combat. Even so, that didn't prepare me for the goons. They ignore damage, even devastating injuries like amputations and broken limbs. At first I tried to disable them, thinking they were real people, but they were relentless. Plus, they were incoherent, making that monkey noise." Vickers paused, reliving his first moments after the change. "I reverted back to my training. To me it looked like some kind of chemical attack so I knew I had to leave the area. I didn't stick around to help anyone. I just took off."

"You think this is a chemical attack? Like a terrorist attack or something?" Megan asked.

"I can't say for sure," Vickers replied. "In the Army we get drilled on chemical and biological warfare, especially if we're headed over to the Middle East. My best guess is that it's biological, but whether it's a deliberate attack or something gone wrong I couldn't guess. It's all the same in the end anyway. So," Vickers wrapped up, "my skills are combat and survival, among others. However, I want to point out that Jim here is amazing in a pinch. He saved my ass at great risk to himself, and got Megan out of trouble too."

The unexpected compliment took Jim by surprise. Maybe he was being too harsh on Vickers.

Saul stood back up and addressed the whole group. "I don't think we could have rescued a more capable group. We lucked out. I wasn't going to mention this, but we considered letting you guys fend for yourselves. After the ambush we lived through a couple of days ago we had a lot of heated arguments on what our responsibilities were to others. There are some bad people out there, but also good people that are just desperate and scared. It's hard to know the difference and impossible to know what the right decisions are. When this shit went down there were a lot more of us working in here. To see friends and coworkers turn on each other, on us, to suffer the loss and the violence of those first hours was difficult."

Saul leaned forward onto the table. "With that said, even though we accept you as part of our group, we want to make some things clear. First off, I'm in charge. We voted on it early on and I'm sorry you guys weren't here to chime in, but that's how it is. Second, everyone pitches in. For now, the plan is to keep this store and its contents safe. That means keeping watch on the roof, cooking, keeping the equipment running or whatever else it takes." Pausing, he looked at Jim, Megan and Vickers. When there were no objections, he continued. "Do any of you have loved ones that are unaccounted for?"

Jim and Megan shook their heads. Vickers nodded. "My sister and her family. I tried calling and texting a couple of times before I lost my phone but I didn't get an answer. She's over forty miles away so I know there's nothing I can do for her right now. Eventually, once there's a handle on all of this, I need to go to Cleveland and find her."

"Which brings me to why I brought it up," Saul explained. "One of us, Zoe, has family out there, within reach. But first, let me introduce the remaining two members of the group. Zoe" he said, pointing to the black girl, "was a cashier, and Sandy," he indicated the chubby blonde "is actually Cindy's little sister. She was here to pick up Cindy and was lucky enough to make it into the store that first morning. Zoe's brother Owen was still at home when she left for work."

Ray added, "And now that you three have joined us we can consider an expedition to go get him and bring him back here." Everyone around the table was looking at Jim and his two companions. What could they say? Jim looked around the table, trying to pretend he didn't hear what Saul just said and Megan appeared to be mulling it over. Then Vickers stood and smiled and said "Count us in."

...

Jim wasn't a fan of heading back out to help rescue strangers. He finally felt safe for the first time in days and wanted that feeling to continue. Maybe after he got some rest and some food he would feel differently but at the moment he was enjoying a nice hot meal and relishing the comfort of practical clothes and shoes. Ray and Vickers went up on roof patrol but everyone else was seated around picnic tables the group inside the store had set up.

Food consisted of burgers with all of the fixings, stale doughnuts and various snack foods. It was Chuck's turn to cook and even though technically using a grill indoors was a no-no, in a building with the indoor space as large as the superstore, no one was worried.

Jim looked around. This was now what his life was. A bunch of strangers holed up in a warehouse, defending it against others, both human and goon. Looking to the future, Jim saw no relief in sight, but in a moment of epiphany, he realized that he truly didn't miss much of his past life. He had been in a dead end job, had few friends, and spent his spare time marking time without purpose. Had his life stayed on its previous track he would have just rolled on to his death, slowly becoming oblivious to how sad he was. Even though the events of the past few days shocked him out of his life stupor, and he was glad of that, he wasn't ecstatic with the new scenario. He had played hundreds of video games and watched thousands of movies, and, according to them, people in situations like the one he was in rarely fared well in the end, especially when they left a safe zone to wander around in the dangerous areas outside.

"It's weird," Jim thought, "how the rest of the people sitting around the picnic table can still laugh and chatter on as if everything is going to be okay. Either they're wrong or I am. I hope it's me." Still thinking these thoughts, his head slowly dropped down to his chest and he dozed. He began snoring, oblivious to the looks it generated.

CELL BLOCK NORTH, SUMMIT COUNTY JAIL, AKRON, OHIO

Ten miles to the east of the small city of Medina, where Jim's small group of survivors was trying to strengthen their foothold, the denizens of the Summit County Jail in Akron were also trying to cope with the event. The jail was only twenty years old, built to replace an overpopulated older structure called the "Workhouse". When the jail was built it was meant to accommodate a much smaller inmate population than it currently held but in the intervening years the demand for jail space increased exponentially, easily outpacing new construction. The subsequent overcrowding meant inmates eventually went from having their own cell to being triple stacked in the same amount of space. The men were crammed in beyond capacity.

It was a mad house. Whatever was happening inside the prison blocks seemed to change more people than it left alone; the first hour in the cell blocks were brutal. The best chance for survival was to be locked in with two other people that hadn't transformed, however none of the inmates were that lucky. In cases where only one turned, the other two usually prevailed, but even then, the ferocity, the extreme rage, and the way those that changed ignored pain made it an even match.

Prisons exist to cache trouble away from the rest of society, a society that deems some people are meant to be incarcerated; people that are intrinsically violent and lack empathy for others so they rob, murder and rape. These dangerous types of individuals are typically not society's overachievers, only tending to excel once placed in a prison environment. Finn, a slight and nerdy young man, was not one of those frightening people, but his two cellmates were.

John and Justin were large men, veterans of multiple physical altercations. They typically spent their yard time benching weights the size of manhole covers and squatting even more. When Finn showed up as their third, both his newbie status and his smaller size made him an automatic bitch. It was quite a large adjustment for Finn, who found his switch from hetero to homosexuality painful and humiliating. One of the things Justin told Finn while he tearfully serviced both men was "Don't worry boy, prison gay ain't real gay." That particular incident stood out for Finn, kneeling in front of Justin as both of his cellmates and the men from the surrounding cells laughed at his humiliation and submission.

On the morning of the change, the three cellmates were marking time in their cell as usual when John leapt from the top bunk down to the floor. Finn saw the large man drop past. He didn't think anything unusual about it, he was just grateful that he wasn't going to be used again. In fact, judging by the sounds coming from the bottom bunk, it sounded like John and Justin were going to have a go at each other. While Finn had never known the two to hook up before, he felt relieved despite having to listen to the unpleasant grunts coming from below.

When the grunts turned to screams and blood arced in a fountain four feet high to splash against the far cell wall, it caught Finn by surprise. He shrieked in fear, jumped down from his bunk and ran to the door in a flee response. Similar commotions began all over the block in a riot of screams, cries, roars and primal whoop-whooping.

Resigned to his role as a victim, Finn didn't know what was causing the uproar but knew instinctively that help wasn't going to come in time to save him. He turned back and got a good look at his cellmates. John was bent over and holding Justin's head down with his right hand while his left hand was shredding flesh from Justin's neck. To Finn it looked as if John was mimicking ripping weeds out of a garden.

Justin was doing his best to defend himself. Finn knew from spending time in Justin's rack that the huge prisoner kept a shiv under his pillow, which he was now using to punch holes in John's side, chest and neck. Finn had no idea how Justin was still alive; his face was gone. Pieces of nose, lips, eyes, and hanks of hair coated nearly every surface inside the cell, and blood was pouring out of both men, soaking and splashing the mattress and spilling onto the walls, floor and even reached all the way over to where Finn was cowering at the cell door.

SUMMIT COUNTY JAIL, CONTROL CENTRAL IN THE QUAD

In the jail's control center, or C2, things were not going any better. Correctional Officer Josh Ritter, less than two months on the job, had just returned from his rounds through the south cell block and swiped back in to his post when the majority of the prison population and staff turned. With over seven hundred inmates and one hundred staff inside the complex Josh should have known right way what was happening, but because the control center was soundproof he never heard the screaming or any of the other commotion; a more experienced officer would have scanned all of the monitors before settling in, but that was a habit Josh hadn't yet developed and now never would. As a consequence, the slaughter was already minutes old before he happened to glance up at one of the surveillance screens. What Josh saw shocked him to the core. In the north cell block the prisoners and the guards on both tiers were engaged in an all-out brawl. More incredibly, the guards were attacking each other as well as the prisoners.

Summit County Jail followed the industry standard layout of four cell blocks arranged in a diamond pattern, with the command facility located in an open courtyard in the center. Operating protocol called for meal and yard times to be rotated through each block individually to ensure that only a quarter of the inmates were free at any given time. Josh engaged the jail-wide panic button to alert the corrections officers in the other blocks to the problem and checked for their responses. There wouldn't be any; the guards appeared to be fighting amongst themselves in the other three blocks also. "What the fuck?" he muttered uselessly at what he was witnessing on the screen.

Josh scanned the other monitors, looking for help. As the most junior corrections officer on his shift, he didn't have the experience to handle what was happening, an event so inconceivable that it was never covered at the academy. He thought about going into one of the cell blocks and helping the other guards, but what training he did have dictated that he couldn't abandon his post. Unsure of what else to do, he sat there and watched.

CELL BLOCK NORTH

Finn heard the riot alarm go off. It confirmed what he already knew, that things were bad. Across the tier opposite his cell, two inmates were ghetto stomping a third. In his own cell the fight between Justin and John was ebbing. Justin wasn't moving and John lay on top, bleeding out. John was alive, making small mewing noises as he burrowed weakly onto Justin's neck, still trying to cause damage by taking small nips at the exposed meat and bearded skin. Finn felt sick. He burped a cupful of bile into this throat and tried swallowing it back down but he couldn't manage. It let go and he added his effluvia to the gore.

Eventually the screams and cries of pain faltered then stopped as the individual personal dramas in each cell played out. The nature of those turned would not allow cohabitation with normal people, so as each conflict resolved, those remaining in each cell were crazy, normal, or dead, and almost all were injured. The cell block echoed with a cacophony of whoops, alarms, and shouts of rage, terror, and pain.

When Finn came out of his daze and slowly recovered from his shock he was at a loss as to what to do next. His cellmates were dead. The enclosed space of the cell smelled like shit, piss, blood and vomit that had soaked into his shirt, and as it dried it adhered to his skin and invaded his nose with a thick coppery smell. The frights, the noise and the gore, all of it was so overwhelming that the only way Finn could escape it was to crawl to the back of the cell and curl up behind the toilet. Within moments, Finn, the cell block's most unlikely survivor, was asleep.

CONTROL CENTRAL

Back in central Josh was coping with the chaos better than Finn could ever hope to. Even though he was only a few months on the job, Josh was trained and capable. On top of that, he was an alpha male, which was part of what initially drove him towards a career in corrections. He liked the regimentation, he liked the discipline and he liked establishing control and order over chaos. Had things turned out differently, these characteristics would have eventually transformed Josh into a seasoned and abusive yard bully, someone who empathized less and less with the inmates under his care as the years passed. It was the established way of things and was evident in the more senior officers he trained under.

Fortunately for everyone trapped in the Summit County Jail that morning, Josh did care. He didn't understand what was going on, not everything, but he knew enough to institute emergency lockdown procedures to make sure that the situation was contained. Going full lockdown transferred control of all systems to him in central and kept everything in situ. No one could enter or leave the containment areas without his say so.

Using the camera system to search for any guards that might still be alive, Josh hoped that one of the more senior officers made it so that control of the jail could be turned over to a person with more experience. Josh was still early on in his training on how to control the many camera feeds and remote door lock system: The jail had cameras in every area, over ninety altogether, and the locks were a complicated mix of manual, automated, and remote, many programmed to various routines and emergencies. Josh needed to master in a few minutes what normally took someone weeks to learn.

In the moment, Josh forgot about the automated locks while he continued to focus on finding survivors that weren't crazy, murdering lunatics, but he could tell by looking at the screens that all of the guards were either dead or turned. He watched as the surviving guards attempted to get at the inmates locked in their cells.

Out of all the areas east block fared the worst. The cells in that block were locked open for morning chow when the attacks began and the crazies caught everyone unprepared. By the time the unaffected inmates figured things out and tried to fight back it was already too late. They were mauled to death, ripped apart and smashed against the bars. The few who survived were the ones who were last in line. They made it back to their cells and hid long enough for the automated doors to shut and lock them safely inside.

Josh was flipping through the camera feeds when it hit him that what had happened in the east block was going to happen again, because every automated jail routine was the same; it always rotated clockwise through the four cell blocks in a north, east, south and west pattern. During meal times the cell doors opened and closed in half hour increments over a two hour period. Josh glanced up at the clock and his heart dropped. It was less than two minutes before the next block, south, was due to open and he didn't know how to stop it from happening.

DAYTON TOWERS, APARTMENT 303, DAYTON, OHIO

Fiona was worried. She was a single mother with two small boys that were hours overdue. The last time she saw them was when they got on the school bus earlier that morning, waving to her from their seats as the bus pulled away. When Fiona heard Ronny, her youngest say "Bye Mommy," through the open window, she never suspected that it would be the last time she ever saw them. Her boys were her life, her everything.

The afternoon deepened into dusk. She sat for hours in her chair by the window, crying and thinking about how scared they must be facing the day's horrors alone, without the protection and comfort of their mother. Fiona desperately wanted to go outside and find them but her maternal drive could not override the terror she felt when she imagined herself exposed to the lunatics outside.

"Don't worry, Momma's going to come and get you," Fiona whispered as she gently rubbed the two little faces in the photograph she clutched to her bosom. The frame had "Mommy's Little Treasures" written in crayon font along the top. Fiona sent constant prayers and promises of rescue to her boys ever since the people in her building and up and down the block started going crazy. She had caressed the faces behind the glass countless times, always with a promise that she was going to leave the apartment and search for them, yet she never budged, not even to pee.

She watched most of what happened that morning from her apartment window overlooking the street. The first signal she got that something bad was happening came from a man screaming on the street below. Fiona lived on the third floor and the apartment windows were open to let in the fresh spring air. The scream she heard was primal and robust, a raw exclamation of pain and terror. Puzzled, she thought there might have been an accident even though she hadn't heard squealing brakes or the sound of an impact. But Fiona was never one to ignore drama. She set down the dish she was drying and used the towel to dry her hands on the way to the front of the apartment.

Halfway there the screaming rose in intensity and was joined by the din of fighting and running footsteps. She hurried. Fiona had witnessed street fights in the past and from the sounds of it, a lot of people were fighting right under her window. Her apartment was right in the middle of Sherwood

Projects, a subsidized area in the low income belt of Dayton, Ohio, so she was used to the sound of people running towards a fight, either to cheer somebody on while they doled out an ass kicking or to join in on the fray. This time the running and the yells sounded different than the usual, more like people were running away in fear than running forward in excitement. People in her neighborhood didn't scare easily so she knew immediately something bad was afoot.

When Fiona arrived at the window, she couldn't immediately comprehend what she saw down in the street. "What the hell is this?" she muttered beneath her breath. She tilted her head sideways, as if canting her brain could somehow give the scene more clarity. The scene below looked like a riot, but not a riot. It was bedlam, a flashmob on steroids.

It reminded Fiona of a television show she watched on the reality channel, "When Animals Attack", a scene where a couple of chimpanzees escape a cage at a wildlife sanctuary and turn on one of their keepers. The keeper lost all of her fingers and most of her face before she could be rescued. From the rampage in the streets Fiona knew that there was no helping any of the people being slain. No rescue force in the world could get to them before they were literally torn apart.

It was pandemonium. People were attacking others who were desperately trying to get away or defend themselves, but everything was happening so quickly that nobody had time to get their bearings or arm themselves. The attackers didn't use any weapons, which somehow made it worse for Fiona; the damage they were inflicting with just their fists, teeth and feet was ghastly to look at. The victims were outnumbered four or five to one and were quickly overwhelmed.

A small group of men at the entrance to one of the projects across the street was trying to fight back, to defend themselves from a larger group. Within seconds the smaller group was swarmed and violence visited upon them was awful to witness. Heads and chests were caved in and arms and legs were snapped to pieces and twisted off, to be raised overhead in triumph before being flung into the air. The discarded trophies were soon everywhere; on fire escapes, on top of cars and draped across the branches of the few scraggly trees that lined the street.

Fiona couldn't look away, even when a small child was swung repeatedly by her feet into the side of a fire hydrant, flopping and shredding apart. Pieces of the little girl's body disengaged to fly into the crowd, coating hair and faces and slathering nearby walls with innards. The lunatic, an elderly woman, soon tired of her sport and dropped the body on the curb, where it slithered slowly into the street. The sprightly old woman moved like a woman sixty years younger. Fiona watched as the hag Olympic-hurdled a shopping cart before vaulting over a chain link fence in search of more prey. She sat slack-jawed and witnessed one horrific scene after another. Once, there was a commotion out in the hall as someone was chased down the stairwell by a howling pack of the lunatics. The train ran by her door and then down the stairs but Fiona was afraid to look out of her peephole, worried that one of those things might somehow catch her looking out and come in after her.

The scenes of violence eventually tapered off, but it wasn't because the crazy people grew placated or tired, they simply ran out of victims. Fiona suspected that anyone left alive had found someplace to hide or were locked in their apartments. She herself had no intention of leaving, ever. She knew deep down that she should go out and find her boys but the thought of doing so struck her with a debilitating terror. She was scared for them and broke into weeping fits on and off. She tried unsuccessfully not to think about them, about how scared they must be. Maybe they were injured. She imagined them crying out to their mommy and that sorrow rode on top of her fear and made everything worse.

Just before dark the power went out. Fiona didn't even notice at first because she was preoccupied with her thoughts and the building she was in was quiet anyway; there was none of the usual television noise, loud music, kids running up and down the stairs and hallways, people talking and yelling. Just silence, as if everyone was afraid to make the slightest noise and draw the attention of the crazy people prowling outside down upon themselves. She eventually tiptoed through her apartment when she could no longer ignore the urge to urinate. Afterwards, on the way back to her chair she went to the refrigerator for some water and it was only then that she noticed the lack of electricity. The light inside was out and it registered with her that the slight humming of the compressor was gone.

She grabbed a bottle of water, some bread and processed cheese slices and went back to her post at the chair. As she munched on her cheese sandwich, she scanned the streets and buildings for movement. Nothing much had moved lately except for the crows, which covered the dead in an undulating, sable blanket. Bemoaning the fate of her children and the uncertainty of her future, she cried briefly and then passed out from mental exhaustion.

…

Fiona awoke to a light knocking at her door. She bolted upright in her chair, too afraid to get up and check. Maybe she had imagined it. Then again, what if it was Ronny or Tracey and they somehow made it back from school? She sprang from her chair and quick-walked on her tiptoes to the door. She didn't see anyone through the peephole.

A loud whisper came from out in the hall. "Fiona, open up!"

Puzzled, she angled her view. To the left she saw her upstairs neighbor, Fran, hunched low to the ground. She didn't know him very well, just enough to occasionally say 'hi' to him in the stairwell, but she was desperate for contact. She quickly unlocked her deadbolt and ushered him in with her hands. "Hurry," she urged him softly, "get in here and out of the hallway."

Fran hustled in carrying a backpack and she quietly closed and locked the door behind him. When she turned back from the door she found her face full of fist. The pain was jarring and intense and her broken nose squirted blood out of both nostrils, fanning out from the sides of her face in a thick spray. The last thing Fiona saw before her lights went out was Fran reaching into his backpack and pulling out a roll of duct tape.

PARLIAMENT SQUARE, LONDON, UNITED KINGDOM

"This is BBC correspondent Walter Doucet reporting live from Parliament Square, where the House of Lords and the House of Commons are still in emergency session. This is most assuredly in reaction to recent developments overseas in America, where it appears a catastrophe of global proportions has occurred. There is very little concrete or verifiable information, but speculation has run rampant. What we do know is primarily from disturbing videos on the internet, uploaded from all over the Americas and Canada, of horrific scenes of violence and riots. What exactly is happening, or why, remains unclear. Back to you, Martha." He made a throat cutting gesture and his cameraman, Luis, signaled that the uplink was cut.

Walter lowered his microphone, sighed and leaned in towards Luis. "What the fuck is going on?" he asked emphatically. "Look at this chaos. The world is falling apart." With a wave of his hand he indicated everything and everyone around him. The few people there were rushed by, hurrying past him and his cameraman without the curiosity and attention that a live newscast usually generated.

"Eh," Luis said, looking around. "It's not good, Walt. I'm telling you right that this is going to end badly." The cameraman pulled a phone from his pocket and showed it to Walter. "The wife keeps texting me. She wants me back at the flat." He looked down at the ground. "I'm sorry, but I can't do this with you right now. I need to go home."

The way things were, Walter couldn't blame Luis because he felt the same expectancy, a contagious weighty nervousness that hung in the air. And while he didn't have anyone waiting for him at home, he still felt as if the longer he stood outside the palace reporting, the more time he was wasting. Only the fear of losing his job and the sense of professional responsibility he felt kept him from bolting.

The streets had almost completely emptied in the half hour since his arrival on scene. On a typical Monday afternoon foot and vehicle traffic from the nearby Supreme Court building and Saint Margaret's Church crammed every sidewalk and road near Parliament Square. That was not the case today; instead of usual thousands of people the square only hosted a few dozen. Walter looked east and saw that the Westminster Bridge only had a few cars on it. In his many years living in London, Walter couldn't recall a time when the bridge wasn't deadlocked with traffic. It was eerie.

BBC mobile news teams used to have three people on them: The anchor, the cameraman, and a technician who doubled as the driver. Because modern cameras no longer required complicated lighting or equipment setups, a few years earlier Headquarters made the determination that the expense no longer justified the extra manpower. Luis now did the driving as well as the camera work while Walter did the reporting. Since the change, the two men handled most of the assignments by themselves and in that time had gotten to know each other well.

Luis was noisily packing up the van and getting ready to leave. He raised his eyebrows to Walter. "Coming with?" he asked.

A quick look around the square showed a couple of other news channels reporting from different areas of the lawn, but they also looked like they were packing up their gear and preparing to leave. Walter got the same vibe from the square emptying that he had a minute ago from looking at the bridge; the vibe was saying to leave with Luis. He certainly didn't want to be out here on his own. On top of that, how could he report without a camera man? Walter reached up and loosened his tie. "Okay Luis, let's go. Drop me off?"

"Yeah, sure, no problem," Luis said. "Let's hurry, though. The wife wants me home right now." Then he pointed in the direction of Victoria Street at a convoy of military vehicles heading their way. "That can't be good."

"Wait," Walter hesitated with the van door open, suddenly remembering his responsibilities as a news reporter. "This could be big. Shouldn't we stay and get this?"

Luis jabbed his finger across the seat at Walter. "You can stay and report on whatever you like, Walt, but I'm not fucking around here. I need to be with my family." Luis engaged the ignition and revved the van. "Decide now because I'm leaving either way." He put the car in gear.

Walter took a last look around. Other reporters were being directed to leave by a military foot patrol and barriers were being erected in the distance. The soldiers toted rifles and were unloading sandbags, guns and other gear from the back of large Mastiff fighting vehicles. Walt spent months reporting on the British Army in Afghanistan and was familiar with how a defensive perimeter looked. It was exactly like what the soldiers were setting up in the square now.

The convoy was veering off Victoria Street to surround Parliament with tanks and several platoons of the Territorial Army. Walter even saw the newer special-use Foxhound patrol vehicles as part of the cordon, which he thought were all deployed overseas. This was definitely big. A squad of armed men detached from the main group and headed in his direction. "Okay, then, I'll call it in," Walter decided, swinging into the van and closing the door. "But whatever is going on here, it's important."

Luis accelerated and turned left onto Victoria Embankment. As they headed north, another military convoy went past them headed in the opposite direction. "Must be nice to be a lord," Luis commented. "I wish I could dial a number and have the army come and protect me." He glanced at Walter. "What I don't understand is why they need that level of protection anyway. There aren't any reports of those crazy bastards here in the U.K., so who or what do they think is coming for them?"

Walter thought about and envisioned what was coming. The transformation into madness by half of the planet was just the beginning. Economic collapse, food and water shortages, looting, and every kind of chaos was about to roll onto the rest of the world. "Us, Luis," he said to the cameraman. "They're protecting themselves from us."

KLIMPS MEGA STORE, MEDINA, OHIO

Jim awoke to the sound of a soda can being thunked onto the tabletop. Saul was unrolling a large map and Ray was placing cans on the corners to keep it flat. He handed one to Jim and grinned. "Sorry to wake ya, buddy, but we have some planning to get to."

Jim took the drink and peered around. Almost everyone gathered at the table was watching him. He looked sheepishly at the group; he wasn't used to being the center of attention and wasn't sure if he should wipe the drool from his mouth or make like he didn't know that it was there. Saul solved the dilemma by reaching across the table to offer a napkin, pointing to his mouth and saying "Uh, you got a little, uh, something there."

Quickly wiping his mouth, Jim pretended everyone wasn't watching the interplay and cracked open his soda before ambling over to stand beside Vickers. He and Vickers briefly locked eyes and Jim let out a low "Heh."

"Okay guys, let's get started," Saul began. "I can speak for all of us who know Zoe's brother Owen that we appreciate the offer of help from you newcomers. It's a lot to ask, to put yourself in harm's way for the sake of strangers, but try to think of it as an investment in your own safety. Once folks recover from the shock of what's happened and they start running low on food and supplies, they're going to head here. The more people we have on our side the better off we'll be."

He met the eyes of every group member before continuing. "Everyone here, right now, is one of the lucky ones. That includes our three late additions. We occupied this space first so we get to determine what happens to it. And while we do this as a group I want to say again that I'm the one in charge. Anyone have a problem with that?"

Ray spoke up. "I sure don't, Saul." To the rest of the group: "Speak up if you disagree, now's your chance."

Nods, murmurs of "sure," and "no problems with it here," came back as Ray scanned the group. It was obvious to Jim that Ray had assumed the second-in-charge position, but Jim didn't care. Assuming responsibility for others and taking charge weren't really his thing. Jim gave the thumbs up and muttered "Cool," before he glanced over to Vickers. Jim assumed Vickers would want to step up but was surprised when Vickers announced with a smile, "Sounds good to me, guys."

"Great," Saul said. "Now that that's out of the way let's talk about what's next for us. Before we head out we need to put our heads together and better figure out what it is we're up against." He pointed. "Megan. You, Jim and Vickers are the only ones from our group who have been out there in the wild. All we know is what we've seen inside this building and out in the parking lot, so let's begin by going over everything we know about the goons, because even if we don't know how they got this way, we can at least strategize on how to beat them, or get around them."

Jim spoke up. "Well, we know they aren't zombies. Once you kill them, they stay dead."

The group went silent and when he looked up, Jim saw that they were all looking at him with blank stares. After a few seconds, Saul broke the silence. "Yep, there's that. Uh, okay, anyone else?"

Megan was watching Jim. He had risked himself to save her life and keep her alive and she felt an allegiance to him that would never be supplanted. She noticed how the group's reaction affected him. "Jim's right," she added. "It's important to keep in mind that these crazy people are just that, crazy people. They aren't supernatural or superhuman. They act and react in certain ways, and knowing that they can be killed or disabled is valid information." She met everyone's eyes.

Jim was grateful for Megan's aid, but ashamed that she felt he needed it in the first place. Part of the reason he was a loner was because people didn't understand him. "Well," he thought to himself, "this is why I don't like people. First chance I get, I'm out of here."

"Okay, good point Megan." Saul held up one finger, validating Megan's input while at the same time ignoring Jim's, despite both being identical. "First, we know they can die. What else?"

Everyone started speaking at once. "They're stupid." "They swarm." "They hunt in packs." "They're stronger than us." And so on.

"Okay, okay. One at a time. Let's concentrate on figuring what will help us go get Owen and come back in one piece. "

Vickers spoke up. "The group is right. They are stupid and strong and all of those things. But before anything else the most important thing to remember is to be quiet and stealthy because they converge as one."

There were nods of agreement. To purposely draw attention from the crazies outside was suicidal.

Okay," Ray said. Turning to Saul, he asked, "Think we should probably do a quick run first and get some practice under our belt?"

Vickers, Jim and Megan all spoke up at once, protesting the idea.

"Just a sec." Saul answered, raising his hand. "I disagree with a practice run too, but we need to go over everything carefully. Jim, can you group up with Suresh and relieve the two boys up on the roof? We'll fill you guys in on the plan when your turn watching is done." Saul gave him a friendly clap the back. "Suresh will give you the rundown on things up top."

Jim nodded. He was tempted to ask Saul where the dental care aisle was, to drop a hint to the smaller man about his bad breath, but held his tongue at the last second. Instead, he made a mental note to grab a package of breath mints later and leave them where Saul would find them.

Suresh motioned for Jim to follow and headed to the service stairs near the manager's office. At the top Suresh pushed the roof access door open and after the dimness of the store interior the sunshine seemed glaringly bright. Jim squinted and shaded his eyes.

"Ah. I can't see," Jim said.

Suresh smiled and walked towards the corner edge of the roof. One of the boys, Chuck, sat in a lawn chair looking out over the back and one side of the superstore. Suresh tapped him on the shoulder.

"We're here to take our shift. Can you explain please to Jim on how to do it?"

Chuck seemed like a happy sort. He cheerfully went over the lookout duties with Jim while Suresh walked away to relieve Jack. "First off, you got your binoculars for looking, although right now it's pretty quiet." He handed them to Jim. "From up here you can see all the way to the interstate.

Jim put the strap around his neck and peered through them. Most of the middle ground was cleared. It was mostly just grass and small scrub. Further back and on each side was forest and a small road on the right led back towards the interstate. Jim figured the private access was for tractor trailer direct delivery. The place where he used to work had the same setup.

Chuck pointed to an area about halfway to the expressway. "See there, that pile of clothes and such. Those are bodies. Yesterday, a woman and a couple of dudes were making a run for the store from the woods with a bunch of those things chasing them. Ray was up here and saw the whole thing. He tried taking out the crowd chasing the lady but there were too many of them."

Continuing, Chuck jerked his thumb back at Suresh, who was on the opposite corner relieving Jack of his gun and binoculars. "Suresh ran over to try and help, but he's new to guns and not the best shot." Chuck shrugged and added, "Not sure what else we could have done. Anyways, the idea is to try and kill the goons as far from the store as possible. They can't get in, but Saul and Ray figured that just because we're safe in here isn't a reason to let 'em come close."

Unslinging his rifle and handing it to Jim, he explained the rifle's characteristics. "This here is your basic Remington Model 700. We have a bunch of them for sale downstairs and tons of ammunition to go with them so don't worry about wasting any." He gave Jim a sideways glance. "Have you used the 700 before?"

Jim shook his head.

"Have you used a rifle before?"

"Uh, yeah, just not in real life," Jim confessed.

"Ah, so you're a gamer then. Cool, no problem. It's kind of the same. You point, you shoot. The scope on the 700 is the best scope we have in the store, and the distance isn't too far to have to worry about wind and stuff. It really is just aim the gun and pull the trigger. Any questions?" he asked.

It didn't seem too tough to Jim. "I got it," he said, shrugging. "Shoot things that can't get to me, infinite ammo. Shouldn't be a problem."

"Yep, that's right. Just a couple of things left to go over," Chuck began, pointing to things on the ground. "That's your spare ammo, that's your water and some snacks right there, and that's a walkie-talkie that talks to Saul. And if you need to piss, piss over the side. You need to go number two, call someone up to give you a potty break."

He held his fist out for a fist bump. Jim complied and Chuck headed downstairs, but turned back around after a few steps. "Oh, yeah I Almost forgot. Don't push the safety in. Those 700's sometimes have a problem when you push the safety on and off; it'll stick. It's best to not use it."

"Got it," Jim said, nodding. He wasn't sure where the safety on the gun was and had no plans on messing with anyway.

Chuck went downstairs quickly followed by Jack and then Jim was left on the roof with Suresh. It felt strange to be outside and not needing to flee from the crazy goons. "Or just 'goons'," Jim said aloud, in a facsimile of Saul's voice. He chuckled to himself. "Like it matters what we call them."

He looked over to the opposite corner and saw Suresh sitting and scanning the area with binoculars, so Jim sat down and did the same. Starting with the tree line, he slowly panned left to right, over the open area to the woods on the opposite side. He didn't see any movement. He randomly checked out other areas, like the interstate in the distance and the sky. He checked out the bodies Chuck had shown him earlier, but after seeing so many violent deaths recently he wasn't impressed or bothered. Jim found that he really didn't even care that much. Only the living mattered now.

Within half an hour he was bored out of his mind. He couldn't believe that in less than a week he went from never having to work again to what amounted to working again, only this time he was working for free. Still, deep down he knew that what he was doing now was a little different. At least he wasn't working ten hour overnight shifts and punching a clock. He turned and yelled over to Suresh. "Hey, Suresh, how long do we have to stay up here?"

Suresh dropped the binoculars, faced Jim and yelled, "Do you need to make a bowel movement?"

Confused, Jim waved Suresh off and answered back, "No, no, no, buddy, never mind, I'm fine." He silently vowed to limit his communications with the Indian from now on. He sighed. While he was grateful to the group for the food, shelter and protection, he already belonged to a new mini society, and it only took a few hours for him to be pegged back down once more to his previous station of menial labor.

Resigned, he picked his rifle up and used the scope to scan his area. Still nothing.

CONTROL CENTRAL

Josh watched helplessly on the surveillance cameras as the cell doors in the south block slid open and the violence there began anew. Inmates who had survived the first wave within their cells were now exposed to the former guards and the other inmates who had turned. This time the survivors were aware of what was going to happen, but it didn't change the outcome at all. Vastly outnumbered, they were dragged from their cells and dogpiled by dozens of maniacs and destroyed. Pieces of men sailed through the air and a red rain fell onto the floors and walls.

A few of the tougher or just luckier men made a run for the end of the cell block and pounded on the bars to be let out. With a start, Josh remembered that opening the sally port was something he already knew how to do. He quickly opened the jail facing door and watched the handful of men scramble into it before he shut it again. Now the prisoners were trapped between the jail side door and the exit door of the sally port, but at least they were alive.

Somehow, one of the inmates still in the block survived the gauntlet and made a limping dash for the safety of the sally port enclosure. Josh saw the man a few paces ahead of the pack chasing him, but couldn't risk opening the door and letting him in. He couldn't be sure he would be able to close it again behind the man and keep the lunatics out. Instead, he watched the man make it to the end of the cell block and grip the bars and scream, pleading for protection from their pursuers. Josh and the other prisoners could only watch helplessly as the inmate was clawed and pummeled and his head was smashed repeatedly against the bars. Chunks of hair, skull and brains were flung through the bar openings to splash the other prisoners safe behind the bars just a few feet away. Josh was grateful that the camera feed was video only and that he wouldn't have to hear the ravaged man's piteous cries; even so Josh felt powerless and nauseous, sad for the man's useless death.

He looked up at the clock and was surprised that it had only been three minutes since the cell doors in the south block opened and the majority of the inmates inside there were massacred. He grabbed the stack of operating manuals off of the shelf on the control room wall. Although he hadn't asked for it, he was the only person in a position to do anything for the remaining inmates and if he didn't want to be responsible for more men dying he needed to bone up quickly on the unfamiliar gate system.

Speaking aloud for self-encouragement, Josh flipped through the shelves of operating procedures and manuals looking for the correct volume. "C'mon. You can do this, Josh. You have twenty seven minutes to figure out how to disable this automatic timer and save the rest of those guys. Focus."

CELL BLOCK NORTH, SECOND TIER

Across the quad from the south cell block Finn was oblivious. He sat in the far corner of his cell, hugging his knees and staring at the side of his state-provided metal toilet. Since his imprisonment months ago, Finn had discovered the ability to blank out and ignore his pain and surroundings when he was under severe duress. Typically, it was when his body was being used for someone else's sexual release, but it also served well in his current circumstances. Once, after his two cellmates tormented him on what they had planned for him later in the privacy of their shared cell, he went catatonic in the mess hall and was placed on suicide watch.

Suicide watch meant being temporarily separated from the general population and undergoing psychological review. During his sole interview with the psychologist assigned to him, Finn broke down sobbing and described the physical and emotional abuse he was undergoing. The doctor, an older woman with a permanent scowl but kind eyes, asked him if he went into a trance as a way to deal with his ordeals.

"Yes," he admitted. "I black out while the bad things happen to me."

"Every time?" she asked.

"Yes, every time since the first time."

She patted his knee and said "Good for you, Finn," and left. A few days later he was introduced back into his cell, where he was eagerly awaited by John and Justin, both of whom had missed him very much.

In the cell block around him, the maniacs gathered around the cell doors of the surviving inmates, venting their rage by reaching through the bars and grabbing at those inside or jumping up and down and bellowing in frustration when the inmates kept to the back wall of the cells, safely out of reach. At first, there were some grouped at Finn's door, but his apathy and lack of fear at their presence confused them and they wandered off to find other, livelier prey.

DAYTON TOWERS, APARTMENT 303

An overcast sky dimmed the interior of Fiona's apartment into gloom. Fran walked out of the back bedroom, wiping his knuckles clean with a child's t-shirt he found on the floor. He hadn't expected her to fight so much. Since the change, he had visited three other apartments, using the same trick to get into all of them. So far Fiona was the only one who had resisted beyond a token amount, inciting Fran to the point where he had to beat her until he ran out of breath. She was duct taped to the four bedposts and couldn't defend herself at all, and Fran had accidently over-beat her until she blacked out from the pain. Because Fran wasn't a fan of forcing himself on an unconscious woman, he was waiting for her to come to so he could properly terrorize her.

Fran was an elite class of vicious, a hyper-predator. At least that was how he identified himself. He practiced and was accomplished in all forms of bad behavior. He did it for fun and for the same reason a computer hacker broke into secure systems - because he could.

Even though Fran was just an inch under six and a half feet tall and immensely built, he excelled at portraying himself as smaller and weaker. He perfected his speech, dress and mannerisms in full length mirrors, pretending to be effeminate, friendly and disarming. Women fell for it the easiest, but he was nearly as good at his tricks with men.

To see Fran on the sidewalk, in line at the grocery store, or in the hallways of his apartment building, one would never guess that what he showed the world was a ruse, that he was actually an ex-con and a sexual deviant. He was always careful, calculating, and had a genius level IQ, so he was able to get around the normal roadblocks someone with his past normally had.

For example, when he was released from prison five years ago, he was required to register as a convicted sex offender. After he filled out the paperwork with his parole officer, he monitored the state's website that disclosed the address and identity of people like him. He was very pleased to note that it took eight months for his paperwork to make its way through the system. Eight months before he showed up on a map.

After that, he moved every six months. He complied with the conditions of his parole and filed the required paperwork with his parole officer, but he never showed up in a search of his neighborhood while he was still living there. In fact, over the previous couple of years, the gap lengthened to over eleven months. He often chuckled to himself when he thought about it. He was a level-five offender, which meant he was considered a threat to all demographic types: women, men, and children, black, white, everyone, and despite that, he still had almost a year grace period every time he changed his address. It was as if the system was giving him permission to do whatever he felt like doing, even encouraging his deviant behavior.

That morning when the world changed irrevocably, Fran recognized immediately the enormity of what had happened. The government oversight he operated under before now no longer existed and the irrevocable changes to the system of order now worked to his benefit. A world without law didn't scare Fran in the slightest because he was finally free to do as he wished, and what he wished to do was impose his will and his dominance over everyone, like a king. He smiled to himself. King Fran. He liked the sound of that.

Fiona awoke. Her moans of pain emanated towards the front of the apartment where Fran was looking out of the window. He broke out of his daydream, the fantasy where the rest of the world bowed to him. The newly self-proclaimed King Fran grinned in anticipation and headed to the back bedroom to resume his work.

RIVER THAMES, WEST BANK, LONDON

The news van sped north up Victoria Embankment and Walter was grateful for the empty roads. Luis drove the news van fast and recklessly, taking advantage of the lack of traffic. Every intersection they left behind was manned by military checkpoints facing outwards, but since they were leaving what Walter assumed was a secure zone around the city's government sector, they weren't harassed. At each strongpoint, the armed soldiers there moved the barricades to the side and waved them through.

Luis stopped the van before the Hungerford Bridge. Up ahead was the largest contingent of soldiers they had seen so far, busily running about and setting up gear. Semi-permanent structures and military equipment filled the road from curb to curb.

On a normal day the embankment was cramped with tourist buses and vendors but today they were conspicuously absent. Luis and Walter had driven south on this same road to get to Parliament Square less than two hours ago. Then, it was business as usual; the sidewalks were crowded with tourists and buses were bumper to bumper. Looking east over the water, Walter saw that the Ferris wheel on the Millennium Pier was uncharacteristically still, empty of passengers.

Luis voiced what they were both thinking. "This feels like an episode of the Twilight Zone." Walter nodded and Luis proceeded to the checkpoint. Armed soldiers moved the barricades and waved them through, but Luis slowed and stopped. He rolled down the window and waved a soldier closer. "Hey mate, we're with the BBC. Mind telling us what's going on here? What's with all of this?"

There was an immediate reaction. The soldier raised an arm and shouted, "Open hands! Covered wagon!"

Dozens of rifles came up and pointed at the van, and from the side mirror Walter saw soldiers or police in riot gear double time in formation to the rear of the van, preventing the van from backing up.

The soldier Luis had addressed pulled a pistol from a leg holder and went into an aiming stance, the barrel pointed directly at Luis. "Sir!" he shouted through the vents in his facemask, "Proceed through the checkpoint immediately or you will be neutralized. This is your only warning!"

Unlike Walter, Luis had never been to a combat zone and had never held a firearm in his life, much less been the target of one, so his immediate reaction was to comply without hesitation. He punched the gas and they zipped through the route laid out through the armed encampment, never slowing down once. At the end of the camp was another barrier, but it was already open for them.

"Jesus H.!" Luis swore, sweat breaking out and running down his face. "What the hell was that all about? All I did was ask a question and they were going to shoot us!"

"I'm not sure that announcing ourselves as members of the media went over with them very well. I've seen that same reaction before when I was in the Middle East. Contrary to popular belief, flashing press credentials isn't always a magic ticket."

"Yeah, but I never thought that would happen here."

Walter shrugged. "It was a sign that things are as serious as they can be. The government must be pretty worried."

Luis nodded and kept driving. Since leaving the last checkpoint, the streets ahead were beginning to get busy. Cars, buses and crowds of people were milling about. To Walter it looked like people were fighting each other. In the distance small fires threw smoke into the air.

"Hey, Luis, how do you want to handle this," Walter queried, looking over at the cameraman.

Luis looked visibly shaken. His run-in with the soldiers and now the disturbance up ahead was starting to unnerve him. Trying to calm him down, Walter reached over and placed his hand on his friend's shoulder. "Let's make a plan, Luis, get to your family."

"Look at all those people. I live all the way over on the other side of the fucking city Walter. I fucking told you we should have left earlier. Now I'll never get to them, not through this mess." He turned to Walter and roared in frustration.

Bits of spittle landed on Walter's face and he recoiled, as much from the grossness of it as from unexpected outburst. The two men had been in some hairy predicaments in their time, but Walter had never seen his cameraman act this way. He switched tactics from cajoling to feigned outrage in an effort to snap Luis out of it. "Man, calm down!" he shouted. "You'll never get to your family by acting this way."

Apparently that was the wrong tact because Luis backhand punched Walter in the throat. Walter grabbed the dashboard with both hands and gasped for air. He turned to Luis, who he was sure would be immediately apologetic, but instead of helping him the camera man opened his door, came around the front of the van and yanked open the passenger door. Still trying to get in a full breath, Walter could only watch helplessly as Luis reached across his lap and fumbled for the seatbelt latch.

The seatbelt clicked open and Walter sagged forward. Luis grabbed Walter by his jacket collar and his hair and flung him from the van. Walter's head cracked against the side of the curb and he briefly saw stars. As he lay there trying to recover, Luis closed the passenger door, got back in the van and sped off.

Eventually Walter got his breathing under control and was able to sit up. He did a quick pat-down check of his body. The only injury he found was a small lump on his head. It was bleeding a little, but didn't hurt much. "Could have been worse, I guess." he said aloud. "Fucking nutter punched me in the throat. Who does that to a friend?"

He stood up and looked in the direction Luis had gone and saw that his cameraman wasn't able to get very far. The van was stalled about a hundred meters down the road, having only made it a small way into the crowd before Luis abandoned it. Walter could see the open driver's side door, but didn't see Luis anywhere. A dozen or so people were on the passenger side, rocking the van in an effort to tip it over. Walter couldn't fathom why they did it; it seemed like a waste of effort to him. He made up his mind to avoid crowds for the foreseeable future.

He brushed himself off and checked his head again. The bleeding had already stopped. He took a last look in the direction Luis had disappeared to and thought about his next move, and since he had no idea what exactly was going on and the full scope of it, Walter decided that the first order of business was to gather information. He checked his pockets for his phone and remembered that it was still on the van's dashboard when Luis yanked him out. The van was now on its side so retrieving it was out of the question, especially since the same crowd that had tipped it over was now setting fire to it. Walter shook his head and sucked in air. "So no phone then, I guess."

Where Walter was standing looking at the mob destroy his company van, he was facing north. Next to the road on his right was Victoria Embankment which ran north and south and up ahead the embankment curved right, following the River Thames as it wound through London. His apartment was to the north, on the other side of the rioters. Since there was nothing in his apartment he needed anyway, and lacking any better ideas, Walter decided to try for the BBC Television Centre in Shepherd's Bush, roughly six kilometers to the west through the London streets. Traveling that far unescorted was not something he looked forward to, but he had nowhere else to go.

Resigned, Walter turned left and began walking, hoping that by using the roads closest to the military zone he would run into less trouble. More and more smoke appeared on the horizon to the north. He heard the pop-pop of gunshots but couldn't tell if it was the military or if someone else had gotten a hold of a gun and was shooting. Up ahead he spotted another checkpoint. Walter had no doubt that the soldiers that would shoot him if he approached too closely, so he turned right towards Trafalgar Square.

Before he hit the square he passed a pub on Craig's Court with the odd name of Walkers of Whitehall. Walter had eaten there before and recalled that they served a mean bangers and mash. He heard voices from inside and decided to give it a go. He was surprised to find the door unlocked when he pushed it. A man standing behind the bar and two women seated in front of him turned away from the television and looked Walter over.

The man, burly and grey haired, spoke first. "We're closed, mate. I'm not serving today, or didn't you notice?" He reached under the bar and pulled out a small cricket bat, which he placed on the bar for Walter to see. The women said nothing, content to just watch the interaction. They had aprons on, so Walter figured they were waitresses or servers.

"Yes sir, I understand. I'm not here to bother anyone, but I need to know what's happening." Walter held his hands out towards the television, palms facing up in supplication. "Please?"

The man grunted and frowned, but waved Walter forward. "Sorry. There are riots everywhere," the man explained. He used his chin to indicate the television mounted over the end of the bar.

Walter approached the screen. It was showing a mob scene, shot from a helicopter. He grabbed a stool and bent to sit.

"Wait." The bartender pointed at the pub entrance. "Lock the door behind you."

Walter operated the deadbolt and returned to his seat at the bar. On the screen the helicopter had ascended and showed London from a wider angle. It was worse than Walter figured. There were dozens of fires throughout the city and smoke obscured much of the skyline. He couldn't believe that the city he was seeing on the screen was the same one he had driven through so casually that morning.

He looked over to the bartender who was drawing a Guinness. As a reporter, Walter was used to being the most informed person in the room but right now he felt lost, out of the loop. "What else is happening?" he asked. "Can you fill me in?"

Placing the draft in front of Walter, the bartender looked from the television to Walter and then back up again. "I think we're witnessing the second Dark Age, friend."

CONTROL CENTRAL

It took Josh ten minutes to find the right manual and just a few seconds to punch in the sequence disabling the automatic door timers. While he was proud of himself at the way he handled things he was also upset that most of the men in the south cellblock had perished so horribly because he wasn't quick enough.

From what he could tell he was the only living guard left in the entire facility and even though he was the most junior officer, he knew enough to realize that the manuals weren't going to be much help with the current situation. He had training on riot control, but what was happening was not the typical riot. Still, it was up to him and he was confident that he was level-headed, intelligent and capable enough to figure out the problem he now faced.

His first priority was to the inmates under his care. Grabbing the microphone, he clicked to the setting that broadcast to the entire prison. He felt weird using the broadcast setting because of the number of times he was told to 'never, ever touch it', but he wanted to let the prisoners know what he was up to. He also needed their cooperation in order to clear the cell blocks.

Josh keyed the mike. "Uh, listen up everyone," he began. He could see in the monitors that his voice coming through the speakers sent the lunatics into a mad frenzy; they leapt for the ceiling speakers and jumped up and down on the bodies strewn about. He continued: "My name is Josh, err, I mean, I'm Corrections Officer Ritter in Control Central. I'm not sure what's happening exactly, but from what I can tell some of you guys and some of the guards have gone crazy and a lot of you are dead. I'm sorry to the guys in the south block, but I couldn't stop the timers from opening the cell doors. I'm glad at least some of you made it to the sally port okay."

He unkeyed the mike to gather his thoughts before getting back on. "I think I'm the only guard left alive that didn't go crazy, so that means you guys need me. Believe it or not, I want to get those of you that are left out alive and in one piece." He saw the inmates between the sally ports cover their ears and back up as far as they could. The lunatics were throwing themselves at the bars trying to get to them, enraged by Josh's voice on the loudspeaker. "And while I want to get you guys out I don't want to die doing it, either from those things, or from you. I'm pretty sure that if help was going to come from outside the jail, it would have been here already, so you need me. As far as I'm concerned, once I let you out, you can go wherever you like, you won't have a problem from me." He unclicked then reclicked the mike again. "I hope that's clear. I am not the enemy here. Good? Okay, give a few minutes to figure this out."

Josh also decided to try and reach someone outside the jail for help. There was an emergency checklist next the phone so he picked up the phone and began dialing. He tried the warden's office, the warden's home phone and then went up the chain of command until he got the Ohio governor's office. Not one single pick up. He decided to try calling home. His father was at work but his mother might be there, if she wasn't out shopping.

The other end rang three times before his mother picked up. "Oh my God!" she whispered. "You just killed me."

"Mom?" Josh asked. "Mom, is that you?"

He heard the phone drop on the other end, and glass breaking. "Mom?" he tried again.

Josh heard maniacal whooping and it only took Josh a moment to figure out that it must be the crazy people, clamoring excitedly as they cornered his helpless mother. He heard her weeping, then pleading. "Nooo," she cried, "please!" The whoops intensified, but underneath Josh could hear the sounds of flesh striking flesh, of things breaking, and his mother's whimpers as she was beat to death.

Josh sat frozen while his mother's protests turned to gagging and moaning as she expired. The beating continued, however. The sounds of fists smacking into his mother's body made Josh weep. It was his fault. He called her and the ringing of the phone brought those lunatics into the house. Somehow, she had survived the first onslaught, either by running or hiding, and he had doomed her because he didn't think things through. He had led them right to her.

He put his head down on the command console and cried it out. He hated those goddamned things. In his anguish, he wondered how many other people he had doomed just by going down his phone list. He imagined secretaries hiding under desks as he was on the other end of the line, letting the phone ring dozens of times hoping for a pick up. How they must have cursed him, and his stupidity, as the monsters smashed down doors and flipped over desks to get at them. Josh wept anew at the thought that his mother's last thoughts were to regret the day he was born. In her final moments, as the fists and feet crushed her organs and snapped her bones, how she must have hated Josh.

CELL BLOCK NORTH, SECOND TIER

In the northern cell block Finn was coming out of his self-induced trance. While he was in his daze his mind had prepared him for what he might see when he opened his eyes. Blood and bits of flesh were spattered everywhere. Josh saw that his arms and hands wore a coating similar to sawdust on them, but it wasn't wood fiber, it was dried gore. From his position on the floor he could see a long stringy bit of something bloody hanging off of the toilet flusher and he gagged a little.

He thought back to how he ended up in this particular nightmare, a convicted felon and a fuck toy of brutes. Finn wasn't a career criminal, a bad person predestined for prison. He had a normal childhood and generally considered himself a nice person. He had a decent job and was planning to finally move out of his parent's basement when a friend approached him with the opportunity to make some easy money. Finn was suspicious at first, but all his friend needed him to do was to set up and run an eBay site for his friend's buddy.

It was really easy work for Finn. He was able to figure out how to automate listings so there was very little hands on. After a while, he was offered even more if he helped out on the weekends, mailing packages out to the buyers. Within four months he had earned enough for a security deposit on a nice place and several months' rent and was in the process of moving out when federal agents burst into his basement. They smacked the box he had just finished packing out of his hands and manhandled him to the floor.

Finn remembered screaming, thinking he was under some kind of terrorist attack. Papers were shoved into his face, which he was unable to read with his face planted into the cement and a knee grinding into the back of his neck. When he heard the words 'FBI' and 'mail fraud' Finn was actually relieved. He was about to tell them about the terrible mistake they were making, how they had the wrong house, when 'eBay' and 'theft ring' came up.

That was his moment of clarity. Small details that hadn't made sense before suddenly came into focus. For example, why was the business run out of the back room of someone's house? Why were there multiple people doing shipping runs? Why was he always paid in cash?

Face down in his basement, discussed like he wasn't there and having all of his possessions rifled through and thrown about the room scared Finn worse than he had ever been in his twenty two years. After his parents posted his bail, their lawyer showed Finn the surveillance video of him shipping stolen goods across state lines, and informed him that he was facing minimum of seven years in prison. After that Finn went from scared to being outright petrified.

After Finn's trial the lawyer shook hands with him and declared how lucky Finn was. Due to funding issues and overcrowding he wouldn't be going to a federal prison, but would be housed in the next county over, only ten miles from where his parents lived. Before his lawyer left, he patted Finn comfortingly and said, "Glass half full, and all that. Good luck, Finn." Finn nodded and was led away handcuffed to the sound of his mother's weeping.

Finn recalled the lawyer's attempt at optimism during his first night in prison, as he was bent over the bottom rack, his face full of sheet that reeked of man sweat while he was violently deflowered. His glass had been empty ever since, and a day didn't go by without him cursing a penal system that put people who mailed packages across state lines into the same cell as rapists, murderers, and every other kind of degenerate filth society wanted to hide.

His parents had visited him at first, but Finn was usually so despondent and distant that they stopped coming. He understood why and suspected that they had some idea of what he was enduring, but their inability to change his circumstances made them feel guilty and useless. He could have called and asked them to visit more often but it was easier for everyone if he didn't.

Snapping back to the present, Finn stood and stared down at the two bodies on the bottom bunk. He expected to feel ecstatic about what had happened to his former tormenters. After all, he had often dreamed that they would meet a violent end; a fire, a shower stabbing, maybe ground-up glass in their food. But instead of joy, he felt nothing but a desire to be out of this cell, this jail. He didn't belong here.

Finn was startled out of his pity party by a touch on his arm. He turned to the cell door and saw that one of the creatures was trying to grab him and pull him close. He jerked his arm back, grateful that he hadn't strayed six inches closer to the bars before the thing tried to grab him. The lunatic began whooping and others came running. Within seconds a crowd of them formed.

The longer they raged at him, the less his fear gripped him because the cell meant to imprison him also kept him safe. Finn edged closer to their reaching fingers and looked at them. The men on the other side of the bars were all familiar to him. They were the guards who had escorted him to and from chow and the yard. Once in a while one of them would put a sympathetic hand on his shoulder as he passed, or give him a pity smile or a smirk. He knew that they knew what was happening to him in his cell because nothing in jail was a secret, yet not one of them had tried to stop it or help him.

He studied their faces as they roared their frustration at him, at his staying just out of their reach. Their faces were almost the same as before but their eyes were not. The pupils were enlarged and black and where their normal eye colors should have been a variety of blue, green and brown they were all dark grey and the surrounding sclera was dark pink and bloodshot. Every eye was intently focused on Josh, even as the mouths whooped and grunted in extreme rage and flicked spittle everywhere. Josh saw bits of meat in some of their teeth.

He waved his hand in front of their hands, fascinated as every reaching finger collectively followed it like a shiver of sharks seeking prey. "What the fuck is going on?" he asked out loud, and his talking drove them into a more intense rage.

Finn thought that maybe if he stood there long enough the intensity of their rage would die down, but it didn't. Five minutes passed, then ten, and still they showed that they wanted to rip him to pieces with the same fury as when they first got there. Eventually, though, even the most frightening conditions tend towards normal if one is exposed to it long enough. Finn's immediate fear of them waned. Even so, looking around his cell at the amount of blood and flesh splashed everywhere he reminded himself that he still needed to respect them. He couldn't let them get a hold of him or he was done.

The bodies of his former cellmates had bled out and lay on the bed, one on top of the other. Justin lay on his back, his left arm draped over the side of the rack. His hand was touching the floor palm up and the back of it was glued down by a morass of drying blood and vomit. Finn looked at what was left of Justin's face. The damage was bad. Finn remembered a story from right before he was arrested, about a guy who snorted bath salts and ate a homeless guy's face. He imagined that when the cops pulled the bath salt zombie off, the homeless guy's face must have looked a lot like how Justin's face looked.

He actually bordered on the verge of feeling sorry for his cell mates, but then Finn remembered the pain and humiliation the two men had reaped upon him and how the guards had been in a position to help but had stood by and done nothing. Spying the shiv in Justin's right hand, Finn leaned over and pried it out of the clenched and stiffening fingers and examined it. The shiv was about six inches long overall and obviously homemade, probably from an old metal bedpost. The handle was round, about half the length and inexpertly knurled. The blade itself was shaped more like an icepick than a knife. Finn remembered watching Justin carefully sharpen it on the concrete floor. Justin was always mindful not to make a pattern on the concrete; the guards were trained to look for sharpening marks.

Justin would spit on the floor behind the toilet and slowly drag the blade across his rude whetstone. He did it late at night with nary a hint of noise. He was so quiet that Finn didn't even know Justin was doing it when he got up one night to take a leak and saw Justin crouched down with his hands busy behind the toilet. Afraid to ask what Justin was doing, and not wanting to pull his junk out and pee only inches away from Justin's face, Finn did an about face and headed back to his rack.

Justin had whispered for him to come back down. Petrified but well-trained, Finn did what he was told. Beckoning him close, Justin showed Finn the shiv he was making and explained the lethality of it. "See this?" he said, pointing to the slim length of the blade. "You don't want a flat blade, little man, because it might get stuck in a bone. You need it short sticker like this so you can…" Justin made piston-like punching motions in Finn's direction, jabbing at him but stopping a few inches away from his stomach. Finn figured Justin could easily perforate him ten or fifteen times within a matter seconds.

Justin continued the lesson. "A shiv doesn't hurt much at first but whoever you poke will slowly bleed to death from the inside. They say it's the worst pain in the world." Justin was short of breath, excited at the prospect of pain. He gave Finn a menacing look. "You won't tell anyone about this now, would you?"

Finn looked down at the shiv, just inches from his stomach, then back up at Justin's face. In the low light in the back of the cell Justin's face took on a monstrous aspect. The shaved head, the neck and face tattoos, the bulging muscles. Finn couldn't even speak. He could only shake his head emphatically. "That's what I thought," Justin sneered and pointed at the bottom rack. "Now get your pants off and your ass up."

Finn complied. He knew that to resist was much worse than to submit. Even so, Justin was hyped up and the raping Finn took was particularly brutal. To further demonstrate his superiority over Finn, Justin set the shiv down next to Finn's face while the abuse went on, knowing that Finn had been thoroughly broken and would never reach for it. What Justin didn't know was that Finn had already retreated into the special haven in his head that he had created to withdraw from the pain and humiliation. Despite his detachment, deep down Finn knew what was happening to him and from that night forward he never again left his rack at night to use the toilet, no matter how urgent the need.

The noise outside his cell snapped Finn back out of his thoughts once more and he blinked several times, shaking his head to clear it. The shiv fit comfortably in his hand; the weight, the grip, and the balance were perfect. As he looked down at the bloody bodies on the bed, Finn finally felt like he was ready to strike out at his former tormentors.

After hesitating for the briefest of moments, he stabbed down into Justin's body. It wasn't as gross as he thought it might be, possibly because there wasn't enough blood left to make the stabbing messy. Finn stabbed down again, then smiled and whispered, "You were right, Justin, this does go in easy." He stabbed again, then again. He picked up speed, his arm like a sewing machine needle. Stick, stick, stick. He adjusted his aim and peppered Justin's face, but not really caring where he struck. The small three inch deep holes created dozens of little face craters, pockmarking it completely. Eventually, the amount of holes Finn put in Justin's face caused it to cave in, reminding Finn of a jack-o'-lantern left on the porch too long.

Breathless, Finn's confidence soared and he felt like a bit of his old self was reemerging. He had a weapon now and he vowed that no one was going to hurt him again. He lurched from his wet work on the bottom bunk and went over near the bars. The lunatics reached for him as they roared and whooped in frustration and a primordial eagerness to stomp, bite, pummel, and kill. Finn roared back. He screamed his frustration out at these things, these monsters that wanted to harm him. Yelling obscenities he lashed at the hands with his shiv, ripping and shredding palms and fingers. Bits of flesh and blood splattered every surface anew, adding a shiny new patina to everything, red-on-rust. His attacks drove the lunatics into a mad frenzy. Those he injured with the shiv redoubled their efforts to seize him.

Finn swung and impaled a hand above the wrist. The shiv got stuck between the arm and wrist bones, stopping his momentum short. Immediately, other hands grabbed his wrist. Finn screamed again, this time in abject fear. He jerked back as hard as he could and broke the lunatics' grip, stumbling back and slipping on a blood puddle. Before he was knocked unconscious, he had time to marvel at how much higher in the air his feet were compared to his head.

CONTROL CENTRAL

Josh had seen the battle at Finn's cell on the camera. He wasn't sure what was happening inside the cell, but from the camera's vantage point it looked like someone was putting a hurting on the maniacs. He saw how the monsters reacted to their injuries; how they cried out and redoubled their efforts to get at the man or men inside the cell. Josh was glad to see that someone was fighting back and that the monsters could be injured, although pain seemed to madden them further.

DAYTON TOWERS, APARTMENT 303

Fran was ready to move on. He had dedicated most of the late afternoon to Fiona before finally growing bored with her and smashing her head in with a toy truck he found on the floor. Afterwards he ransacked her small apartment looking for jewelry and other valuables but all of her jewelry was fake or cheap so he left it. He robbed her purse and was disappointed, but not surprised, when her wallet only had a little more than forty dollars in it. He pocketed it anyway. He was pretty sure that money was useless in his new existence, but just in case things weren't as bad as he thought, he figured to amass as much as he could.

While going through Fiona's wallet he saw a picture of her with her two boys. He checked them out. "Good looking kids you have there, lady," he said to the body on the bed. "Too bad they weren't here today. I could have shown them a great time." He chuckled to himself. He threw the wallet at Fiona. It made a small slapping sound as it landed on her face but she was past reacting.

Fran sat on the bed and turned on the television. He was surprised that there were still regular shows on. He grabbed the remote and started flipping through channels, looking for news on what was happening, but there weren't any live reports, only prerecorded talk shows, cartoons and movies.

With no idea of how bad things were, how much of the state or country was affected, and exactly how much more he could get away with, he had to plan small. No sense getting his kingdom set up until he knew the full picture. In the meantime he was having a blast doing what he was doing. He reached over and patted Fiona's lifeless foot. "Good times ahead. Isn't that right, lady?" He laughed aloud and stood up to get dressed. He had places to go, people to torture, and he was eager to get started.

KLIMPS MEGA STORE

Jim startled awake, fell out of his chair and knocked his rifle onto the rooftop. Suresh was shooting at something. Ashamed that he had dozed off while on watch, Jim glanced around to make sure no one had seen him before hitching up his pants and picking up the rifle. No one else was up on the roof besides the two of them, and Suresh seemed like he was paying attention to his sector instead of worrying about what Jim was doing. "Ha!" Jim joked to himself. "I got a free nap out of this deal." A quick scan at his area of responsibility showed that the back and side of the store he was responsible for was clear.

Suresh was still popping off shots, so Jim jogged over to the far corner to see what was going on. When he got there, he saw that Suresh was doing a terrible job of trying to save a woman being chased by a pack of goons. Suresh aimed and fired again. A small dot appeared in a car door about six feet behind the entire goon group.

"Have you hit anything yet, Suresh?" Jim asked.

"No, no, I'm trying," Suresh said, popping off another shot and scoring another miss. "These things, these goons, they run and I miss."

"You have to lead them. Watch me." Jim put his Remington up to his shoulder and found the goons in his scope. He adjusted his aim to a few feet in front of the lead runner and squeezed the trigger. The goon, a young woman, pitched forward and landed on her face. Her momentum kicked her feet up so that they tapped the back of her head, knocking the baseball cap she was wearing into air.

Jim put his fist out for a Suresh fist bump. "Ha-ha, classic scorpion. Pound the potato, bud."

Suresh looked at Jim's fist and looked up, confused. "What potato are you speaking of?"

Jim shook his head. "Forget it. Anyway, now you try. Remember to lead your target."

The woman's screams were more frantic now. She was starting to tire but the goons were relentless. "Hurry up, Suresh," Jim said, raising his own gun to help in the rescue. He aimed and fired, dropping another one.

The door to the roof opened and Saul, Vickers, Ray and a few others rushed out. Saul yelled out "What's going on?"

Jim turned to him, and pointing at the woman below, said "There's some chick down there getting chased. Suresh and I are help..."

Suresh fired, cleanly dropping the screaming woman, silencing her.

"ing…her. Oh. Ah. Yeah."

Suresh quickly placed his Remington on the ground and backed up. Jim filled the awkward silence. "Anyways, we were helping that chick. The plan was to save her." He shrugged. He glanced down into the parking lot where the woman was getting a thorough whupping, obviously dead. Everyone one the roof except Suresh lined the roof edge and peered down at her.

Saul turned to Vickers. "Mind taking over for Suresh?" he asked.

"Sure. No problem."

WALKERS OF WHITEHALL, CRAIG'S COURT, LONDON

Walter sipped his stout and licked his lips appreciably, giving the bartender a nod of thanks. He rarely drank this early in the day but felt the circumstances allowed for it. He held his hand out and introduced himself. "I'm Walter Doucet, live action news reporter for the BBC. I was trying to make my way there when I stumbled onto your lovely joint."

The bartender shook his hand. "I thought I recognized you. Weren't you in Parliament Square just a bit ago?"

"Yeah, but it's an armed camp now. The army has it set up proper; sandbags, artillery, fighting vehicles and platoons of soldiers." Indicating the screen, Walter asked: "Any updates on what's going on?" The girls broke off from watching the television to listen in on the men's discussion.

"Well, they say some kind of solar anomaly hit that whole side of the planet. The BAA called the flare in earlier this week, said it would disrupt communications. The usual stuff we hear all the time and ignore."

The girl sitting closest to Walter, a petite blonde, spoke up. "What's 'BAA' mean?"

Walter was familiar with it so he filled her in. "It's the British Astronomical Association. It's over in Piccadilly. They're the lads that let the BBC know when something weird is happening, astronomically-speaking. Since it isn't terribly exciting stuff most people pay it no mind." He gave the bartender a wink and said, "For example, did you ladies know that Princess Kate has a new puppy?"

The girl's faces lit up and they smiled. "Oh, yes," the second girl, also blonde, chimed in, "it's a setter. Kate named him Mosh. It's so cute." The first girl nodded in agreement.

Walter turned back to the bartender. "There you go. Topics like the royal puppy are more interesting than real news. So what happened with the flare?" he asked.

Shaking his head, the bartender continued: "The news says it turned out to not be a typical solar flare, at least not by itself. Something about how the radiation got changed somewhere on its path between there and here. The scientists say it might have passed through dust from a meteor tail, but so far it's all speculation." The man's face registered deeper seriousness and he leaned towards Walter conspiratorially. "What really matters is what it did. It fried peoples brains somehow, did something to it to make them go crazy."

"I saw that!" the second blonde blurted out. "My cousin sent me a link but I didn't think it was real at first. People were killing each other. It was gross." She grabbed her phone and started looking for the link in order to show everybody.

"Yeah, I saw it too, and it looked too crazy to be real." The bartender tilted his head towards the blonde. "I forgot to introduce us properly. I'm Mack and this is my place. The girl with the phone is Imelda, and Grace is the one in pigtails." Imelda was still busy with her phone, but Grace got up and came over with her hand out.

Walter shook it but couldn't meet her eyes. He was stunned at the size of Grace's breasts. They looked artificially large. Grace noticed his stare and laughed at him. "Yes, these are my two girls." She squatted to meet his eyes, to draw his attention back to her face. "I don't mind you looking. They are quite obvious." Her comment made Mack chortle from behind the bar.

Imelda turned to the group and held her phone out. "Look, here it is. It already has over a million views, just since this morning." It was hard to see every detail on the small screen, but it was obvious to Walter that a mob had surrounded a car and was jumping up and down on it and pounding it. The driver opened his door and tried to flee, but he was quickly mobbed. Other attackers went in through the open driver's side door and began pulling out the car's remaining occupants, two older children, a girl and a boy, and a woman. The woman fought hard to protect the children to no avail. The violence visited on them was so unreal that if Walter hadn't known better he would have guessed that the video was a movie clip from some over-the-top shock horror movie. But it was real, and it was difficult to watch.

The clip, obviously taken from the safety of a high vantage point, ended with the camera being turned back on the person filming it. The screen warbled and then refocused on a black face, a young teen with a thin moustache. The teen spoke into the camera, eyebrows raised in excitement. "Daaaamn, did you all see that? Shit just got real. Coming to you from the 2-1-3 Dogpound, straight outta Compton niggaaz!" The video ended suddenly.

No one spoke for a few seconds. Walter glanced up at the television and saw one of his co-workers anchoring instead of the same riot footage. He turned to Mack. "Can you turn this up? I know her." Mack nodded and complied, filling the bar with the sound of the news woman's excited but professional voice.

"...and authorities are currently putting those measures into place. Once again, martial law has been declared throughout the entire United Kingdom. A curfew has been put in place in all major cities. Stay tuned to this channel for further details regarding the martial law restrictions. We go now live to Army Headquarters in Andover, where Chief of the General Staff, General Sir Leonard Joseph Fells has called an emergency press meeting.

The feed switched from an interior shot of the BBC headquarters news desk to a brightly lit room with a podium. On the front of the podium the yellow seal of the British Army, with the crossed swords, lion and crown were the only splash of color. The camera picked up stray noises of people off-screen; shuffling paper, low talking and coughing.

Everyone in the bar stood rapt, watching the empty podium on the screen, both anticipating and dreading what was going to be said. Walter's left hand absently searched for and found the seat of a bar stool, and without taking his eyes from the screen, he slowly scooted over and slid up onto the stool. Mack spoke to the television. "Well? Bloody get to it."

The rustling got louder and the camera panned left to catch several army officers striding toward the podium. Leading them was an older gentleman in full military regalia. His shoulder boards, braiding and thick belt were all bright gold, which contrasted starkly with the red stripes on his pants and cap. His stride and demeanor denoted that he was the most important person in the room, despite his relatively short stature and thick waist.

He stepped up to the podium and adjusted the microphone while the staff officers arranged themselves behind him. He cleared his throat before speaking. "Thank you all for coming. What I am about to say is unprecedented and quite shocking. Please ensure my announcement gets the widest possible dissemination." He removed his military cap and placed it on the podium, then leaned in to the microphone again.

"I'll keep this short and sweet. From all possible resources available to our country, be it military, civilian or otherwise, there is every indication that the United States, Canada, and all countries in South and Central America have ceased to exist as sovereign states. This includes any island nations in those regions as well."

He continued over the sudden talking his announcement generated. "Our best estimates put the population loss in the western hemisphere at close to nine hundred million souls lost. That equates to nearly one seventh of all the people on the planet." Hands shot into the air, reporters began shouting. A few of the officers behind the general stepped forward, anticipating trouble. The general waved them back and put his hands out in front of him at head height with a lowering motion. The crowd noise died down and people resumed their seats.

"There's more. When I say they 'ceased to exist,' I also meant that most of the population ceased to exist in the way we generally consider people to be people. They appear to have transformed into a primitive state. Those that were not changed are now fighting a battle for survival. I believe everyone in this room has seen video coming out of the area. It's all very disturbing and upsetting, horrific."

Indicating a tall thin man behind him with his hand, the general introduced a man who stepped forward slightly. "Surgeon Vice-Admiral Raffaelli will brief everyone on the medical aspects of this catastrophe when I'm done here. He and his staff have a lot of work to accomplish over the next couple of days." The surgeon inclined his head a bit before stepping back.

The general beckoned one of the other officers forward, a major, and the two of them held a short, whispered conversation. The major nodded several times then took out a small memo pad and a pen from his uniform jacket and wrote some things down. He then saluted the general and hurried off.

Resuming his place at the podium, the general resumed his briefing. "I apologize for that. Moving on, I would like to announce that as of eleven thirty five today, I have assumed de facto leadership of this country and all of her territorial possessions. This is to be confirmed in a closed session of the Prime Minister and his Cabinet within the hour." His face somber, the general leaned forward and spoke slowly. "I have declared martial law. I want the following information to be clear to every citizen, and it is to them that I am speaking to now. In addition to curfews, I am suspending civil law, civil rights, and habeas corpus. From today and this moment until the termination of my authority, all civilians are subject to military law and military justice."

The reporters again erupted. Shouts of "You have no right!" and "This isn't legal!" were caught by the camera's microphone and transmitted. The general let it go on for half a minute before he roared, "Sit down and be quiet!" Plainclothes guards stepped from the perimeter of the room and directed people back to their seats.

His face softened. "As difficult as this is for everyone to accept and understand, these measures are being put in place for everbody's benefit. The economic and geopolitical fallout from this calamity is severe, long reaching and indefinite. We are all going to suffer and the only way to see ourselves through this difficult period is by the calculated steering of the country through it."

The general turned to his staff, held his hand out and one of the men stepped forward and placed a folder in it. Ignoring the rest of the room, the general opened the folder and perused it for a while. He then held it up and showed it to the room. The front was stamped with 'Operation Ophir Ridge' in large red letters, with the caveat 'Eyes Only' at the top and bottom. "What I have in my hand is a contingency plan drawn up by a joint commission that included the United States, Great Britain and France. Normally a document like this would never see the light of day, much less be shown to a room full of reporters. But today is a day like no other."

"The exact devastation that hit the United States could not have been predicted, but by random chance what has occurred there could have easily occurred to our great country and the rest of our hemisphere instead." General Fells elaborated. "What Operation Ophir Ridge is, when you boil it down, is a living will for the three joint countries. It outlines specific military and political actions the surviving countries should take in the event one or more of us could not operate effectively as a government." Looking up, he asked "Are there any questions before I continue on with the outline of this plan?"

Hands shot up and dozens of questions were shouted at once. General Fells tried to pick out individual questions but it was impossible through the clamor. He waited for it to die down, and when it did, he pointed to a woman in the front row. "Yes, young lady, what is your question?"

She stood up. Even though she was dressed smartly, she looked tired. Her blonde hair hung in greasy strands and she had bags under her eyes. But when she spoke her voice was strong and clear. "General, I'm Regina Ross, an American reporting for Fox News. I think I speak for all of the American citizens who are still over here when I ask, 'When can I go home?'"

General Fells gave a sad smile. "Thank you for bringing that up, Regina. I intended to get to that point next actually, so it's appropriate that it's the first question." Waving his arm to indicate the entire room, he asked, "How many of you are from the Americas, Canada, or the Caribbean Islands?" Regina's hand went up and it was joined by another twenty or so.

The general looked at all the hands. "It's you folks, and all the others currently here in Britain from the areas I mentioned, that I speak to now: Your countries no longer exist. I am deeply sorry. In adherence to this document," he pointed to the Operation Ophir Ridge doctrine on the podium, "you are all, as of this moment, citizens of the United Kingdom. On behalf of every one of us, please accept our condolences on all you have lost."

Murmurs throughout the room as this information was absorbed. General Fells waited politely for the din to die down before he continued. "With the enormity of the global repercussions of what has happened, everyone should be prepared for significant hardships. Many of the issues we will face as a nation were anticipated and have been outlined in the Ophir Ridge plan." The General looked to his staff and nodded. The uniformed men and women pulled folders from a box on the stage and began walking through the room distributing them.

"It doesn't make sense for me to recite what is in this plan, we simply do not have the time. Even though it goes against standard security procedures, the Intelligence and Security Committee and I agree that the widest possible dissemination of the operational document I have before me is paramount to its success. Let's cover some of the highlights together."

He waited until everyone had a copy, then, flipping open the cover, he said, "Let's skip to page six, shall we? Third paragraph down, please. It begins, 'In the event one or more of the three nations participating in this agreement suffers an event so catastrophic such as to render its government or peoples vulnerable to hostile occupation or subjugation, the remaining nation(s) will union with that nation, annexing it and treating it as an extension of their own nation(s). All citizens are to be assumed into the gaining nation(s) as full citizens. In addition, all surviving properties and land are to be considered property of the gaining nation(s).'" The general paused and looked up. "France has deferred primary control to Britain. The exact logistics of that, and much more, still needs to be fleshed out. Unfortunately, as we speak, nations unfriendly to the United States, France, and Great Britain are mobilizing for a hostile takeover and occupation of the Americas, a possibility we absolutely cannot and will not allow. Now is the time for sacrifice and solidarity. If we fail at that the world falls with us." Taking a deep breath, the General referred to the plan again. "Let's continue. We have a long evening ahead of us."

KLIMPS MEGA STORE

After turning his rifle over to Vickers, Jim returned downstairs to the store proper. Maybe it was from sitting up on the roof in the full sun that was causing it, but he felt a fever coming on. He was normally an inside person and wasn't used to being outside for such long periods. He was looking for a cool spot to lie down when he saw Cindy racing by on the golf cart. "Hey!" he yelled out.

Cindy screeched to a halt, the cart's small tires locking up and sliding for a couple of feet before catching. She looked back at Jim and went into reverse. The little warning tone beeped a few times before she pulled up alongside him. She had a peevish look on her face like she was angry. "What can I do for you? What's so urgent?"

Jim looked at her thumbs tapping impatiently on the steering wheel, then up to her unsmiling face. "Uh, sorry I bothered you. Never mind." He put his hands in his pockets and started walking away. Keeping the cart in reverse, Cindy backed up again and blocked his path, almost hitting him.

"Seriously. Why did you stop me?" she asked.

"No big deal, but I was wondering where the medicine is. I'm not feeling well." He shrugged.

"Saul had us gather up all the medicine and lock it up in the manager's office. He has the keys to it so you'll need to make your case to him if you want anything."

"What do you mean I'll need to 'make a case'?"

"Saul thinks the medicine should be rationed. At least that's how he told it." Cindy explained.

Jim protested, "There's what, ten or twelve of us? This store must have had tons of medicine, enough for everyone for a long time."

Cindy grew serious. "Are you going to be a problem, Jim?"

"Whoa there lady, how am I a problem? I'm just asking. I thought I was part of this group."

She put the cart back into drive. Before taking off, she looked at Jim and said, "If you were part of this group, you would know my name isn't 'lady'."

Jim watched her go, wondering what in the hell had just happened.

Instead of seeking out Saul for permission to have an aspirin, Jim wandered around the store a little, going up and down each aisle seeing what was where. The store really did have everything. He saw the empty shelves where the medicine used to be and there were also empty shelves where the batteries had been. The cases and lockers for the guns and ammunition were also cleaned out.

He heard the cart approaching near the end of the aisle he was in before Cindy zipped past, never looking in his direction. He watched as she slid to a stop at the entrance to the restrooms and scuttled towards the women's bathroom. Jim smiled when he saw her walking with her cheeks bunched together, and her hand in her ass crack, as if she were trying to prevent an accident.

As soon as she went in, Jim ran to the cart, hopped in and took off. He drove it along the back of the store until he figured he was at the farthest spot from where Cindy got off, than he parked it and left it there.

The small act of defiance restored Jim's mood and he found his headache had disappeared. He decided to head back to the group's operations center in the break room and see what was going on. When he arrived there Saul, Ray and a few others were talking. They all turned to him at his entrance and Saul smiled and waved him over. "Jim, come on in. We were just refining our ideas for the rescue before sharing it with the group." He had a map pinned up with different routes leading to Zoe's house marked on it. "We tried to pick streets that would typically not be busy as our routes in and out." He turned to Jim. "You've been out there. After looking at this do you have anything to add?"

Jim checked out the map. Since he didn't go out much he didn't know some parts of the city. He pointed to one of the lines. "What's along here? I'm not familiar with it. Are these like stores, or houses, or what?" He looked up at Saul. Saul's face registered a dawning realization.

"Damn, didn't think of that," he said. He called Zoe over and asked her to go over the route to her house where they hoped her brother might be hiding. They all waited as she mentally went over the route she took every day to get to work. She took a sharpie and started drawing on the map, sectioning it off. "Here to here, and here to here, these are all houses, regular neighborhoods. Nothing special. This whole section," she drew a large rectangle, "is strip malls, banks, supermarkets, that kind of stuff." She scribbled the rest out. "Everything else is country, nothing."

"Okay, then," Saul spoke up. "It's roughly three and a half miles to Zoe's house. About half of that is countryside. The rest is either business or houses." He turned to Jim and handed him a sharpie. "Okay, buddy, explain to everyone why you asked that and tell us what to look out for."

Jim mentally reviewed his first day on the run. He tried to pick out things that were significant in terms of where the goons hung out or where people went to get away from them. "First of all," he started, "anyplace where people can hide and the goons can't get to them is a goon magnet. They're stupid, but if they don't have anything better to do, like chase a new victim, they'll hang out in the last spot where they cornered someone. It's possible they might wander off, looking for more prey, but if they do it won't be far. I've seen people get tricked by that, thinking the goons left, when they really only went a little ways away. I watched people die for assuming that and I almost died myself before I learned."

"Okay, anything else?" Ray asked.

"Yeah. We can't go by how busy a place was before all of this started. We have to look at this map with the eyes of where we would go if we weren't home when this happened. Where would we hide? That's where the goons will congregate. That's my guess, anyways. So I guess that means the goons are probably near the strip malls and business areas and that most likely there are people trapped there." He turned to Saul and grimaced. "Sorry, but I just remembered something. I wouldn't call people on the phone, the ringing sets the goons off, alerts them and drives them apeshit. It's like a dinner bell to them."

"Damn it, Jim," Ray said. "I wish you would have told us that earlier. I've called everyone I know at least a dozen times and let it ring a long time just to be sure." He gave a glare in Jim's direction. "I should beat your ass."

Saul stepped in between them. He looked at Jim and said, "Ray doesn't mean it. He's just worried about his family and friends." He turned to the older man. "Isn't that right, Ray?"

"Yeah, yeah. Sure. No offense."

Meeting Ray's eyes, Jim responded. "Sorry I didn't say anything earlier. It never came up."

Ray nodded his forgiveness, but the simmering anger that Jim saw in his eyes did not reflect it.

DAYTON TOWERS

For the first time in a long time Fran felt at peace with his life, as if a rift in the world's natural balance had finally been restored. He stood on the roof of his apartment building, ten stories above the street, he spread his arms and screamed his primacy into the wind. If he noticed the mobs of crazy people perk up at the sound of him yelling from the rooftop, he didn't show it. Some of them wandered in the direction of his building, trying to pinpoint the source of the sound, but when he didn't repeat his shout, they lost focus and resumed prowling where they had left off.

After a top to bottom scourge of every apartment on every floor looking for more victims, Fran found an elderly woman in apartment 702 who was blind and confused. Fran suspected she suffered from dementia or Alzheimer's disease. Going along with her false hope that he had come for her, Fran pretended to be her son. She prattled on about nonsense Fran didn't care about while he ransacked her place. Occasionally he would answer her questions to prolong the joke, but by the time he was ready to move on her voice had started grating on his nerves.

Smiling, he had landed a roundhouse punch to her face in the middle of her asking how her grandchildren were. The impact nearly tipped her wheelchair over backwards. She began crying, confused and unable to see what was going on, suddenly deathly afraid of the man she thought was her son. "Please, Patrick, why are you doing this?" she wept, spilling gobbets of blood down her chin. "What's happening?" Still grinning ear to ear, Fran leaned in close and whispered, "I'm doing this because I don't love you anymore." Then he tweaked her left nipple, hard.

At the invasion of her private area, she shrieked, a shrill noise which Fran could absolutely not abide. She was still weeping when Fran picked her up and stuffed her out of the small bathroom window, the only opening in the apartment without bars on it. Afterwards, Fran thought about how even in those last moments, even when everything left to her had been taken from her, she still tried to live. She latched onto the window sill with the tenacity of a wildcat, making it somewhat difficult for him to push her through. He finally reached a hand out and snapped both of her brittle arms above the wrists, taking the fight out her and enabling him to finish the job. He thought she would scream on the way down and was slightly disappointed when all he heard was a small thump as she landed on the sidewalk seven stories below.

After that, he wasn't in much of a playful mood. He found a few more living residents and used the same trick that had worked on Fiona to get into their apartments. Most were dispatched easily enough, but the last victim, a burly biker type, fought back vigorously. Fran might have lost his battle with the biker, but the man hadn't made the transformation yet from civilian to survivor. He had held back just enough for Fran, who had never held such convictions, to fight at a different, more primitive level and prevail.

Before he left the apartment Fran thought that it was a shame he had to kill the biker. Like all kings, he needed an army, men and women willing to do what it took for him to carve a kingdom out of the new landscape, people willing to follow him and do his bidding. When Fran looked down into the street he didn't see destruction and death, he didn't see savages looking to cause more suffering. What Fran saw was potential, the opportunity for him to realize his destiny.

There was an almost overwhelming urge to begin immediately, but a lifetime of discipline in predatory patience pushed the impulse back. The time for action was soon, but running out into the street without a plan would just get him killed, regardless of his belief in his innate superiority over the creatures and everyone else. What he needed was a core, a seed. A few well-armed men practiced in violence willing to follow him, and to do what was necessary to convince others to do the same.

The city of Dayton was spread out before him, ripe for the taking. Fran took in the view from his rooftop perch and pondered. Normally the law was something to be avoided as a matter of practicality, but the way in which the plague or whatever it was had struck it didn't spare anyone in particular; either a person turned or they didn't. So far Fran hadn't seen a person who had changed recover, or person who hadn't changed later turn into one of those things. That meant that the police were down to about twenty percent manned at best; most likely a lot less than that. The transformation was so sudden, anyone who stayed normal that was caught in the open either fled from the mobs or they died on the spot. Fran knew cops and had never seen one run from trouble, so he concluded that any that were exposed fought and died. He doubted that enough of the police had survived to effectively reorganize, so if he acted quickly the police station armories would be his.

Cloaked with his renewed sense of purpose Fran headed back downstairs. He didn't normally employ guns when he worked but he understood the changing times called for a change of tactics. Before he went out to gather his army he needed real weapons with legitimate stopping power. Gun laws in Ohio were very liberal and allowed almost anyone over the age of eighteen to own one or more. Since he was an ex-felon, Fran wasn't allowed to and didn't possess one, but he was confident that at least a few of the apartments below should contain at least a handgun. He stood a better chance of making it to the police station if he was armed.

The apartment search produced a decent haul. By the time he hit the bottom floor Fran had two pistols, a rifle and a shotgun. He wasn't a firearms fanatic, so all he knew about the guns he found were the name inscribed on them. The rifle was a Bushmaster, the shotgun was a Moss, and the handguns were both Berettas. Each of the guns had ammo, or at least he thought so, since the ammo was found with the guns. The pistols also had holsters, one for the shoulder and one for the hip. King put the ammo in a duffel bag, along with multiple prescription bottles of Percocet, Oxycontin, Vicodin and others that he had found while looting medicine chests. At first Fran stuffed the drugs he looted into his pockets, but soon there were too many to fit and he didn't want to leave any behind; he had a feeling that drugs would be the new currency and would go a long way in establishing his new kingdom.

The rifle had a sling and he slung it over his shoulder and both pistols were snapped into holsters. In one hand he carried the shotgun and the other held the ammo bag and drugs. Fran felt just shy of being overloaded as he walked to the front door and looked out the window. There was a district police station only a few blocks away. Fran knew this because he was methodical when researching new neighborhoods before he moved into them; he also knew where all the homeless and battered women shelters, schools, and drug corners were, but those places were of no use to him at the moment. He laughed aloud to himself when he thought about breaking into a police station. The last place he figured he would ever intentionally seek out was a place where cops normally congregated.

CONTROL CENTRAL

Saddened over the death of his mother but determined that her death would serve as a lesson both to be careful and to think ahead, Josh decided that as penance for her death he would save and keep alive as many people as he could, starting with the inmates under his charge. The practice of keeping people locked up for their crimes had suddenly become obsolete and Josh had no intention of trying to keep the inmates prisoner. As far as he was concerned they were free to go, but he needed to press one final duty on them before their release. He hoped he wouldn't have any difficulties securing their cooperation since doing so was primarily for their benefit; the only thing Josh gained from staying and risking his life to get them out of the cell blocks was the absence of guilt if he did otherwise.

He got on the jail-wide intercom again and made his announcement. "Hey everyone, I'm back. First, I want to say again that I have no intention of holding any of you to your obligation to the state of Ohio. As far as I'm concerned, you are all free to go with time served. Second, I am your one and only hope of getting out. I am releasing you because it is the humane thing to do and regardless of what any of you have done to be locked in here, those of you with family need to go to them. I've already lost my mother this morning and I can only imagine the frustration all of you must be feeling." Josh paused to collect his thoughts and fight back tears before he continued.

"My plan is simple. I am going to free you guys in the west block sally port first. Not only am I going to free you, but I'm also going to arm you with weapons from the armory." Josh leaned in to the mike for emphasis. "I only ask that you help me clear the north block afterwards. There are still some men alive in there but they're trapped in their cells. It goes without saying that I have to trust every one of you to not kill me as soon as I let you out."

"Stand by while I get things ready. For those of you in the north block, be patient; we'll get to you as soon as we're able." Having a plan and actually doing something about it raised Josh's spirits.

The armory operated a double lock system; it had to be unlocked from a console in the command center as well as with a physical key. Before pressing the button to release the electronic switch, Josh flipped through the many camera views until he found the inside of the armory. It appeared empty of people, crazy or otherwise. Satisfied that it was safe to do so, he actuated the release to open the remote lock and grabbed the armory key from the lock box before heading over.

Firearms were normally secured in the armory because it was standard procedure for guards to go unarmed in the presence of inmates; the jail relied on both a system of door interlocks and strict movement patterns for enforcing order instead of weapons and the threat of force. Prisoners and guards could only enter and exit the cell blocks via the sally. In the event firearms were ever needed, a designated response team was supposed to muster at the armory and get a brief situation report before having their weapons issued to them.

Josh arrived at the armory entrance and used his key to unlock the door and then locked it again behind him. He turned on the lights and looked around. He had only been in the armory once before, during indoctrination, but he remembered the simple layout and quickly found everything he needed. He donned a full kit of specialized aramid and ceramic riot armor. The armor looked relatively new and Josh remembered being told by his training officer that the gear was only about four years old and had never been deployed in a real world situation, only for training exercises.

When he was done gearing up, Josh was covered head to toe in a tough but maneuverable exoskeleton. He flexed and punched down on his shoulder pads to test their strength. A normal kit also came with a riot shield specially designed to be interconnected by a line of defenders to prevent flanking. With just one person a shield would cumbersome and near-useless, so Josh left it behind. He also left the gas mask and tear gas, at least for the moment, but grabbed several extra boxes of ammo and a taser just in case.

He unlocked and slid the chain free that was strung through the trigger guards of the 12 gauge shotguns and undid the lock bar keeping them upright in the rack. As part of his training he was shown that the guns were maintained combat loaded, so all he needed to do was transport some of them to the door entrance so the inmates could arm themselves as soon as they came out. He grabbed twelve plus his own, which was a few more than the number of survivors, but he felt it was better to be safe than sorry.

When Josh was finished, he relocked the armory and went back to central to close it electronically. If the inmates, or newly former inmates, decided to turn on him, they had no way of knowing about the armory door interlock and they wouldn't be able to get in there and grab more weapons. "Small compensation for my life," Josh acknowledged to himself. He decided to leave the extra ammo in central also, but kept the taser with him.

He buzzed the west block's external sally port door open and the men trapped in there hurried out. Josh left central to meet them halfway.

When they came around the corner Josh raised his arm in greeting and was relieved when most of the men did the same. He made sure to keep his shotgun pointed down and away from them in a demonstration of trust. Josh flipped the visor of his helmet up and smiled. He waved in greeting and yelled out as they approached. "Glad you're all alive. I'm Josh."

WALKERS OF WHITEHALL PUB, LONDON

Walter stayed glued to the television until the general, his staff and the reporters finished discussing and disseminating all of the information contained in Operation Ophir Ridge. Mack served up food while they watched and the girls occasionally napped, but Walter took it all in. He was impressed with the level of detail the plan contained. The global impact of the loss of the United States was covered using graphs, maps and charts; the total loss of the continent was obviously considered 'worst case scenario'. Details of phased actions and reactions were outlined in categories of economic, military and reconstruction. The stage the world was currently in was labeled in the plan as 'Phase One Alpha – Initial Stabilizing Actions'.

The newsman in Walter respected General Fells' decision to make the plan public. The simple act of explaining the rationale behind declaring martial law and the heavy military presence had lessened the rioting significantly. Citizens went from scared to informed, and with that change many of them came to realize the negative consequences of their behavior and disbanded peacefully. There were still the usual troublemakers, but without the numbers of the previous hours to mask their looting and lust for violence the police were able to identify and detain them.

The bar was quiet for most of the press briefing as everyone absorbed the information. Mack finally broke the silence. "I am just starting to realize what Americans must have felt on Nine Eleven. Things will never be the same." Walter and the girls could only nod in agreement.

BBC broke from the scenes of the riot control and mop up operations and went back to the news desk. Walter recognized the anchor woman. Her name was Aiswarya Patel. As one of BBC's foreign correspondents she was usually out of the country and Walter was surprised to see her broadcasting domestically. He had never personally worked with her as she was always on assignment, but he knew that she had a reputation of remaining calm in difficult circumstances. She had been publicly molested and beaten a few years ago by several men during a Syrian uprising, all of it caught on camera. After the attack she not only resumed broadcasting almost immediately, she even accompanied the police as they hunted down her molesters and she identified them face-to-face. Walter remembered the public respect she earned as she covered the men's court trials for the BBC. Afterwards, she attended the public lashings and then the hangings in the central square in Damascus.

Aiswarya was a cool professional and Walter was glad her presence might serve to help further calm public tensions. Still, even given the circumstances, Walter felt a small pang of envy, then guilt. Aiswarya was going to have a 'moment', the golden nugget of the news profession. Clips of her news delivery at such a momentous time in history were going to be viewed millions of times for years to come. Her face and name were going to be forever linked with the voice that emanated reason during chaos. Even given his jealousy, though, Walter still wanted to hear what she had to say.

"Good evening, I'm Aiswarya Patel with the foreign desk reporting on developments here at home and abroad." She shuffled papers on the desk in front of her and looked off camera a moment as if listening, then nodded. "Secondary and tertiary effects of the Americas calamity has hit global proportions. The world economy is in a tailspin despite every attempt by the European Union to stabilize it."

A graphic popped up behind her showing an older man with white hair and glasses standing at a podium. Aiswarya continued: "So far seventeen of the twenty seven permanent members of the union have withdrawn their support, and fifteen of those seventeen have declared the European Union defunct and frozen their international union assets. The President of the European Council, Janssen Vermeulen of Belgium has denounced their departure as 'incalculably damaging to the survival of the human race' and 'recklessly short-sighted'. The remaining union members are in emergency session and sources say that they are in talks to form a new union, one that incorporates military and regional security alongside the previous economic foundation."

Camera footage of military mobilization replaced the picture of Vermeulen. "Scenes like the one featured behind me are occurring in almost every developed nation. Militaries around the world are on high alert in preparation for what General Fells has declared 'the largest land grab in world history'. We go now to our pundit on military affairs, retired general John G. Cleve." A video window appeared to the right of Aiswarya. In it, a bald man in a business suit was putting a hearing bud in his left ear.

"General Cleve, can you hear me?" Aiswarya asked.

"Yes, yes, I can hear you. Go ahead, please."

"General, can you fill us in on what you know of the current global military picture?"

"Yes, yes, of course, Aiswarya. What we know is that at the moment most of the world's remaining governments are recalling and arming all available military assets. Whether that mobilization is being conducted out of fear, aggression or opportunity depends on the nation. For example, England and her allies are mobilizing in defense of both home and in defense of the unprotected territories hit by the disaster. It's going to take an enormous effort to complete both missions simultaneously, but we are committed to this endeavor."

"General, for the people watching, our country is already under strife and I know they are asking themselves and each other: "'Why not just do as much as possible to protect the homeland? Why invest resources and put our soldiers in harm's way merely to protect the Americas, primarily the United States, when they have ceased to be a country by any reasonable definition?' In other words, why split our forces and our efforts?"

"That's a very good question, Aiswarya. I understand that mindset completely and in normal times I would be asking the same question. But these are extraordinary circumstances and it's vital that we grasp the bigger picture here, the disastrous implications of what's possible. In fact, not just possible, but what has been assessed with a ninety nine percent certainty as likely. Our intelligence assets have determined that there are currently several nations with intentions to capture and hold some or all of the Americas. Among those nations are China, North Korea and Iran. That must not happen. While some of those nations, in fact most of the nations, that we have deemed aggressor states are small and relatively weak offensively, once they establish a foothold in any of the affected areas they will be extremely difficult to dislodge. That goes doubly so for China, the most effective force-capable of the aggressor states."

General Cleve sat up and leaned into the camera. "Right now nearly thirty percent of the world's land mass is up for grabs. I would like for everyone to ponder that for a moment and consider whether or not they want the North Koreans or the Iranians to have possession of roughly one third of the world's real estate and resources. In addition, from what we know, the majority of the physical assets are unharmed and functioning, which includes the nuclear arsenal of the United States."

"That's very disturbing," Aiswarya replied.

"Indeed. From General Fells and the leaders of the remaining members of the European Union, I would like to pass on a message to the British people and to all people who relish and enjoy freedom: We must stand together in this. What happens next is what will define us as a people and determine the future of the human race. I hate sounding melodramatic, but it is that serious, and more." The general stood up. "Thank you for having me Aiswarya, and God Save the Queen."

"Thank you, General Cleve." Aiswarya faced the camera again and pressed her ear bud again to receive instructions from off-screen. She waited silently a few moments and then was handed a sheaf of papers. She blatantly ignored the journalist's unwritten rule that said there should never be empty air during a broadcast while she read what she had been handed.

After a full minute, she looked up and addressed her audience once more. "There are some new developments. General Fells has issued a national call to arms. Within twenty four hours there will be recruitment and screening centers established throughout the country. At the moment, the call is for volunteers of all trades and specialties. Stay tuned to BBC for more information as it becomes available. In addition, we have just received word that General Fells has relaxed curfews. We are to remind everyone that martial law is still in effect." She pressed her ear once more. "Motor traffic is still restricted to military vehicles only and food and water is being protected and rationed by the army. We will provide more details on food centers as they become available."

...

The news began repeating everything and Walter knew he should get going back to BBC Headquarters. Still, he sat and mentally evaluated all of the new information processing it. "World economy gone," he mumbled to Mack. "Conflict on a global scale. Monsters running around killing people." He looked up. "Is it all bad, Mack?"

"Not all bad," was the reply. Mack placed a pint glass under the Guinness tap and pulled it. "Least not until this runs dry." Walter gave a small smile and turned to look at the two girls, but they just stared back mutely.

"I'll be seeing you then, huh?" Walter said as he stood and headed for the door.

"Sure. Good luck Walter."

"Take care, Mack. Ladies."

Walter stepped outside and although it was early evening and the sun was already settling into dusk, the outside light caused him to squint painfully. He looked around through narrowed lids and shaded his eyes with his hand. The usually busy street was eerily silent. Walter had worked and lived in this area of London for most of his career and he couldn't recall a time when it was quiet. Without the sound of cars or crowds of people, or even aircraft arriving and departing Heathrow Airport to the west, the street had a somber and eerie mood to it. Despite that, as Walter resumed his journey he felt oddly energized and hopeful.

KLIMPS MEGA STORE

"Can't believe we're going back out there," Jim said, as he geared up.

Megan was tying her new sneakers. Like Jim, she had decided on speed over any possible tactical advantage boots might provide. "Well, I'm not terribly happy about it either," she answered. "I'm thinking long-term though, at how things could be better with more people."

"Better how?" Jim asked.

"First of all, less time up on the roof. Second, more people means more safety. Plus, the more of us there are the easier it will be to hold this place against anyone who might want what we have."

After pondering what Megan said, Jim nodded in agreement. "I suppose that as long as we're careful about the people we let in it should be okay. Keep in mind that the more people we let in the more chance there is of one of them messing things up. I already had a run in with that Cindy chick earlier. She acted like I was a problem."

"Do you get that a lot, Jim?" Megan looked at him, eyebrows raised quizzically. "I mean, people disliking you right away?"

"Usually, I guess, although I'm not sure why. Do I give off some kind of vibe or something?"

Megan shrugged and looked away. "Beats me. I like you just fine. Anyway, screw them. You saved my life, and you saved Vickers too. Neither of us would be here if it wasn't for you." She smiled at him.

It was Jim's turn to look away. "Yeah, okay." He reached up and stretched, arching his back and grunting. He was starting to get the feeling that she was a little sweet on him but he wanted none of that. She wasn't his type at all: Too old, too confident, and too smart. "Let's get this over with."

They walked together toward the store entrance where the rest of the group was already starting to gather. A large pile of gear was laid out on the ground and Vickers was inspecting and loading pistols, long rifles and shotguns. He looked up and nodded to Jim. Cindy was kneeling on the ground doing something with cell phones. Jim noticed the cellular service counter when he came in and he guessed that the phones were taken from the kiosk and activated by Cindy somehow.

Trying to smooth things between them Jim sauntered over to her and asked "Who gets the phones?" then added "Um, Cindy." She turned from her task and gave him a withering look. "Everyone gets one," she sneered, "even you." She went back to what she was doing. Jim got the message and shrugged to himself. He had no idea what her problem with him was but he wasn't going to waste his time trying to be nice. Instead, he just stood there and loomed over her annoyingly. He could tell it made her uncomfortable, especially since he wasn't saying anything. The only noise he made was his breathing and a slight shuffling of his feet. He watched her hunch up and when he sensed when she was about to explode he quickly spun around and went over and watched Vickers, who was busy arranging guns and ammo into different piles.

After putting the spare ammo into the side pockets of everyone's backpack, Vickers put bottled water, energy bars, a first aid kit, and a survival knife inside each. Jim was impressed at the tactical efficiency of Vickers and asked him, "How do you know what to pack? Did they train you for an event like this in the Army?"

Vickers looked up and smiled. "Nah, not technically. But you'd be surprised at how many military people are preppers. It kind of goes along with what we do."

"So did you have a bug out bag and everything?" Jim wanted to know.

"I had one in my trunk, but when everything went haywire the truth is that I didn't grab it. I actually forgot all about it. I'm some prepper, huh? I panicked and ran just like everyone else did. In a way though, not having it with me kept me alive. During those first few hours my bag would have slowed me down, and speed is what saved me. I ran like I've never run before. Eventually, I met up with others and traveled with them." He turned away and went back to his packing, slumping a little. "Since I'm in a confessing mood, I'm going to admit that part of the reason I hung around the other people was that I was using them as a buffer. Most of them were slower than me, both physically and mentally, so I felt that unless I was unlucky I was going to survive, even if it was at their expense."

"Like how a pack of wolves single out the old or the weak as their victims?" Jim inquired.

"Exactly," Vickers nodded. "Survival of the fittest."

Jim's estimation of Vickers went up even more. "Man, I should have gone into the Army. I could have used some of that knowledge."

"To do what?" Vickers asked. "Stay alive? Dude, you did that. Plus, you saved two others. Even with all my training, I was sure I would die in those bushes, or get trapped in the open when I got too hungry or thirsty to stay there. Give yourself some credit. Megan and I are counting on you, a confident you, to help us get through this."

Jim smiled at the unexpected compliment. He had never really been in the position of savior before even though he had daydreamed about it often enough. "Okay. I'll work on that. I'm glad you and Megan are on my team. Sort of like a secret alliance within the group."

Looking concerned, Vickers looked around to make sure none of the others were listening in to their conversation. "You're right. These are some good people but I think we should hold off on getting too close to them, at least until we see how things work out here," he said, jerking his thumb towards the store entrance and the world outside. "The biggest reason some of these people in here are still alive is because they were in this huge store when it happened. And they had access to weapons. We both know being out in the open is a whole different story, so we should wait and see how they handle themselves when their lives are on the line before we render our final judgment."

Nodding his head emphatically and sucking air in between clenched teeth, Jim could find no reason to disagree. He also vowed to himself to learn everything he could from the Army sergeant.

Vickers continued. "When we get out there keep my tactics in mind and try to not get separated from the group. Personally, I don't think we'll find Owen. Whatever this thing is that's happening, it turned almost everyone. Out of those that didn't turn, a bunch more got fucked up by those goons. So I'm thinking there's less than a one percent chance we'll find him alive. Worse, we'll probably lose some of the people going out with us before we get back, if we get back."

Jim became angry. He accused Vickers in a loud whisper. "Mother fuck! If that's what you think why did you volunteer us to go back out there?"

"Shh, shh, hold it down and think about it, man. What choice did we have?" Vickers stood up from his squat and gestured at Jim to stand up also. He leaned in conspiratorially. "From your talk of alliances, it sounds like you were a fan of reality shows. Think of our situation like that. You do what you have to do to get through another day. While we're out there, we do some intelligence gathering, watch the others and pay attention to which of the people seem to have their shit together. Those are the people we need in our 'alliance' group. Also, look for defendable fallback positions, places to get supplies, how these goons think and act, things like that. "

Jim looked worried. "Think we'll need a fallback position? I mean, look at this place." Jim held his arm out and indicated the vast indoor space. "There's over a hundred thousand square feet of space here, packed with anything we could ever need. Why would we ever want to leave?"

"You're right, absolutely right. There's enough stuff in here to never have to leave. And do you know who's going to want what we have, Jim? Everybody. This place is going to be a survivor magnet. Everyone still alive is still like everyone we used to know before this shit happened: Good people, bad people, greedy, mean, and worse. It's a given that anyone who has made it alive to this point is some combination of tough, crafty or lucky. And while some might be perfectly content to share, the rest are going to want it all, and that's something we have to be ready for."

"We should tell Megan about this," Jim replied. "I mean, I wasn't really thinking that way but what you said makes perfect sense."

"I basically filled her in while you were on watch up on the roof. She's onboard." Vickers smiled. "Do me a favor and help me finish loading these packs, would you?"

Jim nodded and put the gear in the way he saw Vickers do it. First aid kit at the bottom, then the bottled water and the energy bars. The knife went on a lanyard on one of the pack straps and the side pockets held spare ammo and a paper map of the area. Jim unfolded one of the maps and saw that someone had taken the time to circle their location at the store, Zoe's house where they hoped to find her brother Owen, and the proposed route. A few other locations were circled. Jim brought the map over to Vickers and asked if he knew what the circles were for and was told they were places of interest, like a car dealership that sold Hummers, and a medical supply store. "Thanks," Jim told him, then went back to finish packing.

Soon after the packing was done Cindy came around handing out cell phones. She had taken the time to program the number of each person in the group into everyone's individual phone. As she handed them out she warned to keep the ringer off. "Vibrate only please," she repeated to everyone who got a phone. "Apparently the ringer drives the goons wild, makes them attack. Latest information." She gave Jim a sideways look as she said the last bit. As she handed a phone to Jim, she made sure not to come into direct contact with him but looked directly into his face. Raising her top lip she said, "Thanks for the timely info, Jim."

Jim put the phone in his pocket. He suddenly realized that his tip on not using the phones had actually damaged most of the group's opinion of him. "What the fuck?" he thought to himself. His mind took things a step further and he strongly suspected that if Zoe's brother ended up dead or missing that he might get the blame for it, even though he agreed with Vickers that most people didn't make it no matter what the circumstances.

While in his past life he would never have even considered doing so, he wanted to confront the group that was gathering by the door preparing to head out. Saul was there waiting for everyone to muster up. "Let's go, people," he shouted. "We're wasting daylight."

Although not everyone was leaving, all of the group members crowded around Saul. Jim could tell who was going by who had a backpack. The six who had backpacks were Saul, Vickers, Megan, Chuck, Zoe and himself. It made him happy to know that he was picked to be part of the team to go out, even though he had zero desire to do it. He was also glad to see Zoe included in the rescue effort since it was her brother they were attempting to rescue.

Jim looked at those being left behind. There was Ray, who was in charge in Saul's absence, Jack, Cindy, Sandy, and Suresh. Jim was glad Suresh wasn't going. The guy was useless and the general consensus was that Suresh was as likely to shoot one of them as one of the goons. Since being relieved on the roof earlier, Suresh had kept his head down and done very little talking. Having been on the outside of groups for most of his life, Jim felt a small amount of sympathy for the man. Not enough, however, to give him a gun and invite him to come with.

Saul gave a short pep talk. "To the folks going out, let's be as quiet as possible. I know we all have guns, but they're a last resort. The first shot you fire is going to bring the goons down on us, and we don't have enough ammunition to kill them all. The intention is to stick together, but after talking with our three new group members, I realize we may get separated. There are two locations marked on your map with blue circles. Those are rallying points. If you get lost, try and fall back to one of those two points and we'll do our best to come and get you." He held up his phone to the group. "The phones are also for emergencies only. I suspect we'll all be busy just trying to stay alive and get to Zoe's brother in one piece, but don't be fucking around on the phone."

He looked at everyone. "Anyone have anything else?"

"Yeah," Vickers chimed in. "Don't be fooled about how few of the goons are out there. This store is out of the way, but when we get closer to town there are going to be a shit ton of them and you need to be ready for that."

Saul nodded. "Good point. Don't panic. Stay with the group. We know from earlier in the parking lot that they swarm, so if you run, you better keep running. Make your way to a rally point and text everyone where you are. And don't just text Vickers or me, we might be dead. Make sure to text everyone." He turned to open the door.

Jim cleared his throat and held up a finger. "Wait a sec," he said, and pointed at Ray. "Hey Ray. How many times did you try and call everyone in the days before we," and here Jim pointed at himself, Vickers and Megan, "showed up?"

"Quite a few probably," came the response. "Why?"

Jim glared at Cindy. "Because I get the impression I'm somehow being blamed for not notifying you sooner, about the phones." He raised his voice a little. "Maybe even get blamed if things don't turn out okay on this rescue attempt." Zoe and Cindy both backed away a few steps. He stabbed his finger in Cindy's direction, then at Ray. "I better not get blamed if that happens." He turned back to Saul. "Is that understood?"

Saul raised his hands up in mock surrender. "Take it easy there, Jimbo. Nobody's blaming you for anything so calm down. We're all hoping for the best." He looked like he was smiling behind his thick beard but Jim couldn't tell. "Are you done? Can we go now?"

Suddenly embarrassed, Jim deflated. "Uh, yeah. Sure."

"Okay then, gang, let's go," Saul said to those heading out before he pushed the button to raise the galvanized steel door up. It slowly rattled up to expose the brightly lit world outside.

The group was immediately overwhelmed by the stench of rotting bodies. They recoiled, retching and gagging. Taking baby steps, Jim tried to shield his eyes from the sun's intensity and hold down his nausea as he retreated. He tripped over Zoe, who was on her hands and knees heaving, and landed on the back of his head with a loud crack, hard enough that he bit his tongue and voided a tiny squirt of urine into his underwear.

Someone hit the switch to close the door and Jim heard shots ring out from the roof. Groaning, he struggled back to his feet, careful to keep his back to everyone as he did a quick spot check on the front of his pants. Everything looked good, but he could still feel the rapidly cooling area where he had let loose. He sighed and looked at Zoe, hoping maybe for an apology, but she paid him no mind as she got up and grabbed a mint from a plastic container Megan was passing around.

Saul addressed everyone. "Guess we should have expected that. Take a minute and grab what you can to help with the smell, but it's going to be with us for a while. Plus, I guess the noise from the security door going up got some attention. We need to use a quieter exit."

Jim joined the gaggle headed for the store interior. Saul was talking to Jack on the roof, asking about conditions outside. "Uh huh, that's good," he heard. "How's the service entrance look? Clear? Good, good. We'll be heading out that way in a few minutes. Let me know if anything changes."

Putting the phone back in his pocket, Saul let everyone know that the mission was still a go and for everyone to meet at the side service entrance in three minutes.

Deciding not to bother with blocking the stench of the corpses outside, Jim followed Saul. Vickers caught up to him and together they were the first ones at the door. Megan soon followed and the three of them chuckled at the rest of rescue party wrapping bandanas around their faces or spreading toothpaste under their noses. "Noobs," Jim chuckled. He noted that Saul was the only one of the others to forego a mask. Having smelled the short man's breath, Jim doubted he even noticed the smell of the rotting bodies outside.

In short order, everyone was lined up along the wall leading to the exit. Saul dialed the roof and asked "All clear?" then "Good, thanks." before hanging up. "C'mon, let's go," he ordered, then pressed the push bar on the door.

The smell on the side of the building was less intense than in the front, where the majority of the killing and fighting had occurred. The six stepped out and the door quietly clicked shut behind them. Zoe and Chuck watched it latch closed, a look of trepidation apparent on their faces.

Saul noticed. "Don't worry guys. We just need to call the store on the way back and someone will be waiting there to open it. For now let's focus on what we need to do. Vickers, do you mind taking the lead?"

"Sure, I'll take point. Everyone stick close and no talking unless it's an emergency. No shooting unless I give the go ahead. Remember the fall back positions, okay?" He waited a few seconds for objections or questions and got none. "Good."

The store was surrounded by a narrow lawn, then forest. Vickers headed directly for the trees. He went in a semi-crouch and the rest followed suit. When they got to the cover of the trees, Vickers took out his tanto knife and gestured for everyone to do the same.

"Everyone get comfortable with the idea that you're going to have to stab someone today, actually kill someone. Maybe even someone that isn't a goon. Think about that as we move along. Anyone that hesitates puts the rest of us in danger."

Jim looked around. He personally had no problem with the concept. Thinking back on it, he had already killed and never even given it a second thought. Looking around at the others he saw a mix of emotions. Saul, Vickers and Megan looked a combination of determination and anticipation, but Zoe and Chuck appeared all fear and jitters. Jim didn't know them very well; there hadn't been enough time. He hoped that they could carry their own weight. Of course, they were also in the same boat because they had to trust in him, basically a stranger, to watch their backs and to not get them killed.

Vickers stepped out again, trying to move quickly with a minimum of noise. The trees they were traveling through were not thick, so they could see a good distance in all directions. Saul had drifted to the back of the line to make sure Zoe and Chuck didn't straggle. Jim was third, behind Vickers and Megan.

Up ahead the trees thinned out even more and Jim could see the road ahead. It was the same road that led to the store that they had taken earlier. Vickers saw it also and adjusted his path to parallel the road from about fifty feet in. The parts of the road they could see were empty; no cars, no corpses, and no goons. The only sounds Jim heard came from the six pairs of feet lightly tramping through the undergrowth and the chirping of birds from their safe perches high in the trees. For some reason, Jim was getting annoyed at hearing the birds happily going on with life as normal, that it made no difference to them that the world had fewer humans on it. He glared up at them and frowned.

After a few more minutes they hit the end of the tree line and Vickers stopped again. There was a large field of knee height growth ahead. They squatted and scouted the field for anything moving. Vickers called for a huddle and cautioned them: "Just because you don't see anything doesn't mean that there aren't any goons out there. They have to eat and sleep just like any other wild animal. If we stumble on one you have to keep it quiet. They call to each other and I know you've all seen what happens then. Zoe, Chuck, I'm not picking on you two, but are you guys okay with this?"

"Yeah, sure," Chuck responded.

Everyone looked at Zoe. "Yeah, I think I'll be okay."

With a look of concern, Vickers pointed at Jim. "I want you partner up with Zoe here. Megan, you stick with Chuck. Saul, keep covering our rear." Motioning forward, Vickers turned and crouch walked across the field, keeping the road in view as before.

As they went, Jim studied Zoe. He thought she was pretty even with toothpaste caked under her nose. She had a nice face and a thin athletic body. In better times, when the pickings were a little better, Zoe would never have given a tall doughy white guy like him a second glance. Now, however, with most of the competition out of the running, Jim liked his chances. He checked her out again, and she caught him looking. He pretended to be looking past her into the distance and she pretended to ignore his creepy behavior. As soon as he could without being too obvious, Jim swiveled his head forward again and got back to business.

Vickers halted and held his arm up vertical with a closed fist. A veteran of countless hours on the virtual battlefield, Jim knew what it meant and reached over to stop Zoe. She froze in place.

Nobody moved. Vickers slowly lowered his arm and pointed off to the right. About ten feet away a man and woman wearing blood stained clothes were sleeping in a nest made out of field grass. Vickers made a 'shh' signal and then a throat slitting motion. He aimed his index and middle finger at Megan and Chuck and pointed to the guy, then did the same to Jim and Zoe and pointed to the woman.

Vickers made a chopping motion and the four designated adjusted their blades and crept forward. A slight breeze rustled the grass and covered the noise of their progress.

The two goons continued to sleep. The four of them snuck within eight feet, then six. At four feet the man's eyes flew open and he jumped up. The woman also woke, but before she could stand Jim and Zoe rushed forward.

Jim launched into the air and double kneed her in the gut. The momentum forced her tongue far out her mouth in a 'bluhh' as her lower ribs cracked. For his follow-up he punched his knife down at her head but the goon's frantic wiggling caused him to stab the ground instead. Zoe's foot shot out and connected with the goon's temple, stunning it and allowing Jim to punch his knife down into her cheek. The blade's tanto tip did its job and penetrated the right orbital bone, sinking in about two inches. Jim withdrew his blade for another strike when Zoe's own blade came down and sunk to the hilt into the goon's left eye socket, killing her instantly. Jim was breathing hard from the excitement of the battle and his hands were covered in dark red blood. Still straddling the goon he looked over to see how the others were doing.

The male goon was down and Chuck was punching his blade over and over again into its chest. Blood spurted in high arcs, most of it coating Chuck's face, chest and arms. The only sounds were that of the knife hilt hitting ribs and the young man's gasping. Jim glanced over at Zoe and saw that she appeared calm, in mute juxtaposition to the young man's almost nervous release of violence.

Slowing down and finally stopping, Chuck sagged and rolled over onto his back next to the goon he had just killed. The group crouched around him, watching him as he gulped in air. Vickers reached over and patted Chuck's chest, then nodded in approval to Zoe. Saul put his hand around her and gave an affectionate squeeze.

Jim wanted to let her know he thought she did a good job and leaned in to whisper it to her, but when she saw his face incoming she quickly scuttled away a few feet. Red-faced, he pretended to inspect the goon and clean his hands on the grass while the rest of them that witnessed the interaction faked ignoring his awkward recovery.

After giving everyone a breather, Vickers made a 'follow me' motion and led the group away.

DAYTON TOWERS

Looking out the window of the apartment building's front door showed Fran a street empty of the living. There were bodies everywhere; draped over car doors, in piles in the street, and some were just pieces of bodies. Fran even saw a woman's body hanging by one foot from a third floor fire escape. He imagined her rush to escape the beasts when she miscalculated a rung and slipped her foot through, only to get caught there and beat to death as she struggled upside down, helpless.

"Waste of a good woman," he muttered to himself.

Fran knew that he was also trapped. There was no way he could survive out there long enough to make it to the police station. If he tried he would be caught and overwhelmed, no matter how well armed he was.

He thought through several possible escape scenarios. If he had left anyone alive, maybe he could have used them as a decoy or as bait, but he had already eliminated everyone in the building. He thought maybe he could drive away, but he remembered the way people were ripped from their cars. Besides, he didn't have any keys, and the cars outside that were being driven when the attacks began were badly damaged or stuffed full of decaying corpses. Unfortunately his apartment building didn't have an underground garage where he might safely score a working vehicle. Personally, he never owned a car; the required paperwork made it too easy to be tracked.

Frustrated, he decided to go back up to the roof and see if there were any opportunities up there. Maybe he could jump over to an adjacent roof to a building where the possibilities of escape were better than where he was. Better yet, a different apartment building would have fresh victims.

Still carrying all of his gear, Fran retraced his steps back upstairs. Climbing to the roof with his guns and the heavy duffel bag soon tired Fran out and he made several stops to catch his breath. Once there he unslung his holsters and dropped everything into a pile. He desperately needed something to drink so he went back down one floor and grabbed a bottle of water from one of the open apartments.

Returning to the roof he went to the ledge and looked at everything below with new eyes. He chuckled and wondered, "What the fuck was I thinking, that all I needed was a few guns and a bag full of drugs to survive?" He checked the buildings lining the streets and it occurred to him that nothing had been looted. Everything had happened so fast that no one had time to do anything but flee or fight. That was a plus, anyway.

The perch on the roof had a great view in all directions and confirmed Fran's initial assessment from the front door, that not only were those things still around, there were a lot more than he initially thought. At first he didn't see that many because they weren't moving around much, but when he trained his eyes to detect the slight swaying motion they made as they stood in place he saw they were everywhere. "Shit," he cursed softly. "I need to get the hell out of here." He sat down with his back to the roof ledge, sipped his water, and thought.

Like all apex predators, Fran was a specialist. He didn't rely on speed or power, like a cheetah or a lion. Fran's skills and abilities were more akin to a spider's, based on patience and cunning that allowed him to detect and exploit weaknesses in others. He was given several aptitude and intelligence tests in prison and was told that his IQ was extremely high. Had he decided to pursue a different, more productive role in life he would have done very well for himself, but he had an innate disdain for others and perceived everyone else as weak and stupid, and therefore as deserving victims. Fran looked down on the creatures below and recognized that they were predators much like him, but with a major difference. They represented devolution and barely maintained the basic instinctual functions of detection, attack, and a reliance on mobbing their prey. He, on the other hand, was normally selective and precise.

Fran considered the best way to capitalize on his advantages over his predatory inferiors. He got up and circled the rooftop, hoping for access to a different building, something that would take him closer to more concrete safety. He found that only one side had another building close enough for him to jump to, but it had a rooftop that was three stories lower. He briefly considered a makeshift rope made out of sheets. Scanning the lower roof, he noticed that the door into the building was like the one he used to access the roof from the internal staircase in his building, and his door had been locked from the inside.

So that was out. He wasn't going to go through the trouble of rappelling to the next building over only to be locked out. If he had a tool that he could pry the door with, something like a crowbar, he would be able to get in. Fran went back inside to check the apartments again.

A search of the top floor resulted in useless tools. The best he could come up with was an extra thick broom handle and some butcher knives, but he doubted they would do the job. The next two floors were equally unproductive.

Despite his initial enthusiasm, Fran was growing dispirited again. In one of the fourth floor apartments he found some cereal bars and ate two of them as he ransacked the rooms. Having spent most of his life either in prison or moving frequently from apartment to apartment Fran had no idea where a person might keep tools even if they had them. He checked drawers and closets but kept coming up empty. He found scads of remnants of personal lives that would never resume, and a lot of it was extremely interesting to him. Normally he would have reveled in such unattended access to people's most private and intimate matters, but he reminded himself that there would be time to indulge in all of his sordid pastimes once he was finally safe and secure.

Even so, he found himself drawn to places where a crowbar wouldn't reasonably be stored, like dresser drawers and night stands, looking for filth and things kept hidden from prying eyes. In another apartment, he spent minutes taking out one by one and arranging on the bed an impressive display of sexual toys he found in a box in the closet. He was contemplating the type of person who had lived there when he heard a staccato of gunshots coming from the street outside. The sharp crack of the guns discharging was accompanied by unintelligible shouting coming through a loudspeaker.

Fran dashed out of the apartment and down the four flights of stairs to the front door. He pushed the curtain aside and saw a military vehicle, a Humvee, traveling very slowly down the street. It had a turret on top and a soldier in a camouflage helmet was peeking out, firing short bursts at targets outside of Fran's range of vision. The lead vehicle was trailed by several open bed troop carriers with armed men standing around the sides. They occasionally fired bursts into people rushing pell-mell at them.

The loudspeaker crackled again. Some of the message was drowned out by gunshots, but Fran was able to fill in the missing pieces. "Citizens, listen carefully or you risk being shot on sight. This is Colonel Mark Slater of the United States Air Force, Wright-Patterson Air Force Base. We are here to rescue you. Come out slowly waving your hands over your heads. We will protect you while you make your way to the vehicle." The message began again. To Fran it sounded like it was on a loop.

Not sure if he should risk going out in the open or not, Fran watched for a few seconds more. He knew he had little time to decide what to do. He watched as a shirtless fat man wearing ripped jeans hobbled out on crutches from a building across the street, headed for the second vehicle in the convoy. Following the broadcasted instructions, every couple of steps the man stopped and waved the crutches over his head. Two of the soldiers on his side of the truck motioned him forward, yelling at him to hurry.

What made up Fran's mind was the protection the man received as he slowly limped his way to safety. Emboldened by the sight of live prey, half a dozen of the beasts came from the alleyways on both sides of the building and rushed the fat man, whooping and screaming. The soldiers reacted quickly and calmly, picking off the attackers with practiced precision. The man made it to the truck and was hauled in by other citizens. He leaned over the truck railing and pointed towards his crutches still on the sidewalk, but the soldiers ignored him.

Emboldened, Fran opened the door to his building and stood on the top of his stoop, waving his arms and yelling "Hey, hey, over here, over here!" Several soldiers motioned him forward and he jogged down the steps.

When he got to the sidewalk, one of the men pointed towards the following truck and yelled "Get in the next one, we're full!"

Looking left Fran saw at least a dozen of the troop carriers in the convoy, all manned like the first one. By the time he got to the next vehicle, he saw another carrier join the line, turning right onto the main road from a side street. It was an impressive display of order and might, something Fran never expected to see again.

Hands reached down to help him into truck body but he ignored them and easily clambered in. Once he cleared the lip he saw half a dozen people of all different types and ages. Many directed smiles in his direction which he ignored. He sat down next to a soldier and leaned back against the side of the truck breathing a sigh of relief. Recalling how just a few minutes ago his situation was as bleak as it could get and how quickly his fortune had changed, Fran let a small smile creep onto his face. His rescue was self-confirmation that he was meant for bigger things.

As he sat congratulating himself on his luck the soldier he was seated next to kicked him with the side of his boot and yelled down over the noise of the gunfire and speaker. "Move over you fucking idiot. Can't you see I need room?" Fran looked up. The man was athletic, white and in his early twenties. His helmet hid some of his features, but not the sneer he was giving Fran. "Civilian douchebag," he spat, unnecessarily booting Fran in the side again.

One of the other soldiers, an older Hispanic with lots of stripes on his arm yelled "Hey Clark, secure that shit. The colonel told us to treat survivors," here he paused and shot at something Fran couldn't see, "with TLC. I'm not telling you again."

"I got it. Sorry, sergeant."

During the exchange between the two Fran relocated himself to the opposite side of the carrier to a spot clear of soldiers. He took a good look at his surroundings. Besides the four military men and Fran, the six other people sitting on the truck bed were an older woman with wild hair and wearing a blood stained dress, a girl in her mid-twenties, and a balding black man. The other three were all white men wearing plastic riot cuffs. Judging from the bruised and bloody condition of their faces, Fran assumed they resisted getting the cuffs put on them.

He leaned over to the closest one and asked "What did you do?"

The man looked straight ahead and didn't respond, but one of the others did, an older man with grey hair and a neatly trimmed goatee. "Fuck off," he growled.

The sergeant yelled down at Fran. "Leave those three assholes alone. They're in deep shit and you don't want anything to do with 'em!"

Fran sat back and didn't do or say anything more as the announcement blared the same message over and over and the gunfire continued. A few more people joined the group in the carrier, squeezing everyone together. The girl ended up next to Fran and although he was tempted he glanced at the men in plastic cuffs and decided he didn't want to join them in the naughty boy corner. He noticed the old woman looking at him knowingly, like she could see the evil beneath the surface, but he ignored her.

The convoy made several lefts and then picked up speed. The announcement was turned off and the shooting stopped. The sergeant announced to the carrier's occupants that they were "RTB, ETA fifteen mikes."

Once or twice they slowed down while the military vehicles pushed or scraped by obstacles in the road before finally stopping at and passing through a double set of security fences.

The trucks parked and shut off and the sergeant yelled "Everybody out. Welcome to Wright-Patterson Air Force Base, your new home. Form up on the sidewalk for processing."

Hopping out Fran saw that they were in front of a big tent with an American flag flying in front of it, guarded by men with rifles. He queued up near the front and looked back. The line was long; it looked like at least a hundred people had been rescued.

The three men in cuffs were a few people ahead of Fran, escorted by the sergeant and Clark from Fran's carrier. As the line advanced into the tent he could see long rows of tables. Grim faced soldiers were seated behind the tables, interviewing the newcomers and typing information into laptops. More armed men and women flanked the tables.

As people finished getting processed they were handed a bundle of goods and shown to a side flap in the tent. Some, especially the infirmed and the elderly, were escorted to the right side flap. Others, all younger or fit people, went out the left flap. When it was Fran's turn, he was escorted to a seat in front of a young Asian woman with a severe hairdo. Her hair was pulled back so tight Fran witnessed a strand pop out of a follicle on her forehead to join several others that had suffered a similar fate floating in a wispy tangle over her head.

He had eavesdropped as he got closer to the front of the line, so Fran knew they wanted his name, occupation, and other personal information. He had time to formulate fake answers to hide who he was. When he sat down, the no-nonsense woman said, "I'm Airman First Class Seguan. I need to gather basic personal information from you. What is our name please?"

"Fran King," he answered. He watched her type it in.

"Occupation?"

Fran's real-world occupation was 'serial opportunist with a specialty in human misery'. He certainly couldn't disclose that, and having surmised that people with useful skills would be put to work on the base somewhere, Fran decided gave his best vague answer. "Entrepreneur," he said.

She looked up and met his eyes. "Entrepreneur?" She looked past him at the long line and back to him. "Okay, entrepreneur it is." She gave her head a small shake but typed it in.

"Education, highest grade," she demanded.

Again, not wanting to get put to work, he low-balled it. "Ninth grade."

She sighed and typed it in. She knew what he was doing and let him do it.

"Any special skills, Mr. King?"

"None," he answered. "I was a businessman before all of this started."

"Okay Mr. King. That's all I need from you right now. Please wait here." The Airman got up and went to one of the armed men flanking the table and spoke to him in a low voice, turning to point at Fran. The man nodded.

She came back and sat down. "Mr. King, your processing will continue shortly. Please head out the exit there," she said, pointing to the left flap. Fran stood up and headed that way, but became a little discouraged when the three handcuffed men were hustled out of the same exit just before he got there.

Not sure what to expect on the other side of the flap, Fran slipped through the canvas slit into a fenced enclosure with more armed military in it. All of the people he had seen go through while he was waiting were in there either ambling around or sitting down against the fence. On the far side of the fence was a large metal hut with a metal door in the center. Fran recalled seeing similar looking buildings in old black and white war movies.

He turned to one of the guards. "What's going on? What am I doing here?"

Fran had only been exposed to the military for a short time and so far most of his interactions had been negative. They all either acted aloof or were extremely formal; certainly not friendly. He was surprised when the soldier grinned at him and leaned in conspiratorially. "Don't worry buddy, everything's good. I'm not allowed to say anything about what's next, but it's not bad, trust me. We're just waiting for everyone to process through."

"Why should I trust you or anyone here? So far from what I've seen, none of you guys like civilian people."

Sighing, the guard shook his head and said, "Okay, fine, don't trust me. I was just trying to be nice."

Fran frowned and wandered to an empty spot inside enclosure. Once again he was in a situation where he had no control, like his time in the penitentiary. He sat down in the corner against the building and tried to get some perspective.

He closed his eyes and thought about his grand plans for carving his own realm out of the chaos. It seemed like the military had their ideas on what the new world should be like and they were in direct opposition to his ambitions. Fran remained calm and decided the best course for the time being was to follow directions and get along. He needed arms and men and what better place to recruit people and arm them than a military base? He fell into a light doze while his mind worked.

He knew he made the right decision when he opened his eyes and directly across from him were the three men from his carrier, still handcuffed but no longer guarded. All three were taking in their surroundings without trying to appear like it, but Fran saw how they checked the fences, assessed the guards, and whispered to each other, colluding. He knew because he sensed that they were his kind of people, fellow predators. Of course, they were closer to the bottom of the food chain than the top, but they were prime material for recruitment.

The enclosure area was getting crowded with newly processed men and women. They stood around, a lot of them with their arms crossed and with apprehensive looks on their faces. They ignored him and each other, which Fran didn't mind.

Nonchalantly, he stood up and made his way over to the three men. They watched his approach with curious eyes but disinterested faces. Sitting a few feet away, Fran checked the guards and saw that they were chatting with each other and ignoring everyone else; they were not expecting any trouble from their charges. Besides, the enclosure area was getting so crowded that it would have been impossible for the guards to keep an eye on everyone.

Fran assumed that the guy from the trio who told him to fuck off earlier was the leader. He looked at the man and didn't say anything. It was a method he used to get people to talk; stare at them long enough and they will usually blurt something out. The technique worked.

"We didn't do anything wrong," the older man spit out in a low voice.

"Of course not," Fran replied, smiling. He was happy. Not only was he sure he was smarter than the three men since they broke so easily, he knew they could be manipulated. Things were looking up.

To get them to open up more he asked a few simple questions. "Do your cuffs hurt?" and "did the soldiers beat you when they caught you?"" to which they answered "no" and "yes". After all three started replying to him Fran dug in a little bit. "You know, there's no more government anymore so technically what you guys did isn't even illegal. They don't have the authority to detain you like this no matter what you did."

"Damn right" and ""Fuck them, they ain't got no right" were the replies.

"So what did you guys do? I might as well know, since technically I'm on your side, defending you," Fran added.

"Well, you gotta hear the whole story before you judge. It was a complicated situation." The older man was relaxing, easing into a submissive role without even realizing that he was being socially engineered.

"Sure, it always is," Fran urged.

"Okay, here's what happened. Loomis," he pointed to the man next to him, a doughy muffintop wearing tight bicycle shorts and a tank top, and sporting a wispy fu manchu beard, "and Gunter," he pointed to the third man, a skinny biker type with balding white hair pulled back in a ponytail, wearing all denim and beat up motorcycle boots, "told me about this thing they thought up. What they wanted to do was…" Fran was leaning in a little, interested despite himself, when an air horn went off making everyone jump or yell.

The same Hispanic sergeant that had yelled at the soldier for kicking Fran was standing at the tent flap with his arm extended. He was clutching an air horn and chuckling at the reactions his noise caused. The other military men and women laughed with him.

"Sorry about that," he said, before slipping back into his military persona. "Listen up and pay attention. I am First Sergeant Lopez, the senior enlisted person on this base. In addition to search and rescue operations like the one just conducted to get you to this place and time, one of my principal tasks is to provide the base commander, Colonel Mark Slater, with a mission ready enlisted force prepared to execute unit missions." He paused when someone near the front of group raised their hand. "Please hold your questions until I'm finished."

"I feel some background information is necessary for what I am about to disclose to all of you. As you are all aware, we are in the midst of a world changing event. The base population on the day of the event was twenty eight thousand people, spread out over nearly twelve square miles. The best we can calculate, nearly ninety percent of that population changed into what we have termed LCBs, or "Lesser Cognitive Beings." There was some mumbling and a few derisive snorts from the crowd.

Someone asked loudly "Why in the fuck are we still PC after all that's happened? Why not just call them what they are? They're crazy fucks!" This got some "hell yeahs" and "true thats" from the other rescued people. Fran didn't say anything but agreed with the crowd. So far he didn't vibe well with the way the military did things. Getting cataloged and then locked in a cage was not what he envisioned when he ran out of his apartment building to be rescued.

Fran nudged the old man from the trio and suggestively whispered to him. "Why are we locked in a cage without food and water? Why are we being detained?"

Fran was pleased but not surprised when the man nodded his head and spoke up, loudly yelling the same questions Fran had just implanted.

The questions had the desired effect. The other detainees picked up on the vibe and started adding their own discontented voices. The soldiers perked up and brought their weapons to a more ready position.

The sergeant held his arms up for quiet but was ignored. He held the air horn over his head and gave it a blast. Again, people jumped at the blast of noise and the uproar eased to a more conversational level. Acting as if none of the disruptions had occurred, Sergeant Lopez resumed his brief where he had left off. "I repeat, the LCB transformation occurred to roughly ninety percent of the population. Those of us on this installation were fortunate. We have access to military hardware and all of us have combat training. In the right circumstances and environment, LCBs are easy to contain or terminate. However, that's not to say it was easy. We lost many of our cognitives during the initial outbreak. Out of nearly twenty eight thousand people we have been whittled down to just two thousand cognitives that are mission capable."

Sergeant Lopez had anticipated the question and held up his hand for silence. "A cognitive is us, you, people who didn't transform and can still think rationally. I know I tend to do a lot of military speak but I promise that you will all get used to it." He lowered his hand and resumed his briefing. "I know all of you have your own horror stories and must be wondering why I'm holding you all here, making you listen to this."

He turned and nodded to his men and they all went into tactical formation, forming up around him. Fran had a feeling that what the sergeant was about to say wouldn't be good.

"In light of this national emergency, and by order of the installation commander, Colonel Mark Slater, you have all been selected for conscription into the United States Air Force, effective immediately."

Now Fran understood the sergeant's desire for protection. The majority of the people in the enclosure protested vehemently with shouts and raised arms, many with an upraised middle finger on it. Confused, Loomis turned to Fran and asked "What's 'constriction' mean?"

Fran relaxed into his role as their leader. "He said 'conscription'. It means is that you belong to the military now."

"Oh," was the only reply.

Fran held up his finger and made a circle motion a few times, indicating himself and the three others. "Don't worry. If we all stick together we'll be okay." They nodded in agreement.

The air horn sounded again. "You are all awarded the rank of Conscript in the United States Air Force and as such you are subject to the Uniform Code of Military Justice. That may not mean anything to you at the moment, but it will. Once you are sworn in every one of you will be provided with uniform items and everything else you need to carry out your duties, as well as several documents detailing your position. I suggest you study all of the material because you will be held liable for the content. Those of you identified as military veterans may eventually be awarded your previous rank and duties and if so, will be exempt from the Conscription Act."

He pointed behind the group at a door opening up into the large metal hut. "Proceed through the door to your rear, and welcome to the Air Force. That is all."

The eight men jogging up to Josh were a mix of race, size and age. Josh knew that inmates didn't normally embrace diversity. They tended to keep to their own kind and it was lucky for him today wasn't a normal day. Today the eight men seemed unified in their desire to survive, and he hoped they weren't also unified in their desire to hurt one of their former captors or he was in trouble.

As the men reached him he felt that it was the moment of truth. If they wanted to kill him they could easily overpower him even though he was armed. Instead, and to his relief, the men practically hugged him and nearly broke his wrist with their vigorous hand pumping. For the first time since everything went to shit Josh felt optimistic. Everyone quickly introduced themselves as Josh tried to remember their names. Some he already knew, the rest he decided he could get better acquainted with after the rest of the prisoners were freed. It was weird for him to hear the men reference themselves by their first names; the prisoners were always referred to by the corrections officers by their surnames.

After the men grabbed up their shotguns Josh addressed them again. "First of all, does anyone need to be shown how to use their firearm?" Laughter exploded, startling him.

"Good one" and "Ha-ha, you're funny" and similar comments were voiced. He grinned and pretended he meant it as a joke as he watched the men inspect and heft the weapons with practiced ease. Josh made a mental reminder that these were inherently violent men, and that that fact should never be far from his thoughts.

"Great. From what I can tell there are about half a dozen more men trapped in the north block. The good news is that whatever happened to the guards and other inmates that changed seems to have robbed them of their ability to reason, at least for now. The way I see it all we have to do is open up the sally port and let them come at us. We shoot them through the bars until they're all dead."

"Seems simple," said one of the men. "Why didn't you just do it? You don't need us for that."

For a split second Josh was about to defend himself but he knew that the men in front of him wouldn't respect that. He went on the offensive instead.

"True. I could have also saved myself some trouble by leaving you guys to deal with those things in the block, but I didn't. Look at our situation. Does it look like anyone can lone wolf it anymore?"

The man gave a grin. "Aww man, I was just joshing you Josh. We got your back." The man turned to the others. "Right guys?"

The men were solid in their agreement and Josh felt like he had just passed an important test. "Cool. Give me a sec to open the outside door to the sally port and we can go," Josh told them before headed back to central. The men followed.

To prevent the men he was leading from seeing the door code, Josh made sure he got to central first and shielded the keypad with his body while he quickly typed it in. He knew that it was essential that he learn to trust the inmates, and he did a little, mainly because they didn't attack him the moment they met up, but the code to get into central wasn't something he intended to share right away.

The men waited outside at a respectful distance. Apparently years of conditioning to avoid that particular building didn't go away in one morning, regardless of the circumstances. Josh was glad for it. Once inside, he used the mouse to remotely expose the sally port in the north block. On the cameras he could see the beasts turn and move towards the noise of the opening door.

He exited central and waited for the security door to close and lock behind him before heading to the north block. The men grouped up behind him. It was finally starting to occur to them that they were free. Free for the rest of their lives. Knowing that seemed to lift their moods and they began chatting and even laughing with each other. Josh smiled inwardly. He could empathize with them. Even considering the circumstances, everything that was happening felt a bit like an adventure. The future was no longer predictable and that made it kind of exciting. But first they had to rescue the last of the inmates.

As they approached the door they could hear the whoop-whoop of the creatures and the occasional yell for help from the inmates trapped inside their cells.

The man who had tested him earlier said aloud, "Oh, boy, this is going to get messy." And it was.

After the last creature was gunned down, Josh jogged back to central to open the inner sally port door. He thought back to the violence he had just witnessed and participated in; Josh had never killed anyone before, and even though the people rushing the sally port were changed, for the most part they still looked like people. Josh knew every one of them; they were all guards he had worked with. He knew their names, their personalities, which of them were married and had kids, all of the intimate details men sharing dangerous work disclosed to each other. Then he killed some of them, brutally, by short range shotgun blasts to the head. It bothered him more than he thought it might. Josh looked back on the person he was just a short fifteen minutes ago, a guy who saw all of this as an adventure. He didn't see it the same way now. He had lost some of his enthusiasm and was a little sick to his stomach.

He pulled out a pen and some paper. The cells inside the north block would have either beasts or people in them and he wanted to open the correct ones. To prevent a mistake from happening Josh wanted to write down the cell numbers of which doors to open.

The group had already done the work of moving the bodies away from the sally port entrance. He expected rancor from the former convicts when they confronted men who were their former keepers, but there was none. If anything, the men treated the dead officers with respect. Josh noted that when he looked at the bodies there was no trace of their former beast-like selves. When they died the bestial aspects of their appearance were erased, which made their deaths seem a sad waste that didn't need to happen.

One of the inmates spoke up. "Why did some of us change and some of us stay the same? Why were all of these poor bastards picked?" No one answered but Josh could tell by their expressions they were all thinking the same thing.

With the bodies cleared the group entered the main cell block and immediately an outcry from the cells started. The whooping from the cells containing the beasts intensified the longer they were denied the opportunity to rend and rip the men walking by just yards away, and the noise drowned out any cries for help from survivors.

Safe from harm by the bars separating them, Josh and some of the others got as close as they could and looked at the former humans. The most apparent change in the imprisoned beasts was in the face. Their eyes were extremely bloodshot and their skin was bunched up around their eyes and forehead in a permanent grimace. Spittle flew as they roared and whooped in excitement and an unfulfilled desire to get at the men standing just inches from their fingertips.

The man next to Josh tried talking to one of them. "Is anyone in there?" he asked, snapping his fingers a few times. The only response from the creature in the cell was a banging as it rammed its body at the steel bars in a renewed effort to get at the man. Everyone turned and watched as the beast ignored the damage it was doing to itself. Within moments it had opened several long gashes on its forehead deep enough to show bone. Sickened, Josh turned away and the men followed suit.

By unspoken consensus they regrouped in the middle of the common area, as far from the cell doors as they could get. There were several tables there and Josh found one relatively free of blood. He decided to make it the command table.

He needed help getting the cell numbers of the men to free. Looking at the men grouped around the table he asked, "Okay, which one of you guys is the leader? I need help with something." They all looked at him with blank looks. One of them stated simply, "Uh, you are, I think." The rest of them nodded or looked at Josh with raised eyebrows, like he had missed something obvious.

"Oh," was all he could say initially. He was uncomfortable with this but knew that if he didn't step up one of the others would, and he was even more uncomfortable with that. "Fine. Let's free the survivors and then we can come up with a plan for afterwards. I need the cell numbers of anyone alive so I can open their doors remotely. Can a couple of you run up to the second tier and yell them down to me?" Two men dispatched themselves and ran up the stairwell on either side of the block as Josh headed out to gather the numbers from the ground floor cells.

CELL BLOCK NORTH, SECOND TIER (FINN)

When Finn heard the door open outside the sally port he couldn't believe his ears. He thought all of the guards were dead. But his hearing must have been accurate because the crazy people around his cell door took off at a loping sprint towards the first floor. Shortly afterwards the shooting began and that was when Finn saw that the predatory instinct to kill overrode the monster's sense of self preservation. No one in their right mind ran towards gunshots.

Eventually the shooting stopped and in its absence Finn's ears rang. The beasts still trapped in their cells whooped and screeched but without the larger number of them out on the walkway they weren't as loud as before. He heard talking from down below in the common area.

Not long afterwards an inmate ran by Finn's cell, then put on the brakes and ran back.

He looked at Finn and gave him smile. "We'll get you out in a second, buddy," he said then looked above the cell door and yelled down "2D, we got one in 2D." Then the man took off looking for other survivors.

Excited, Finn climbed up to the top bunk where John used to rack. It was the only time he had ever been up there voluntarily. He could still smell the dead man's musky scent wafting up off of the sheets and it gave him goose bumps. He shivered and shook it off with a mental effort.

At the head of the bunk he threw John's pillow aside and put his head to the bars. By craning his neck he was able to look down into the common area and had his first positive emotion since his imprisonment.

All of the beasts outside the cells were dead. Tears rolled down Finn's cheeks when he saw the scattered piles of bodies. The biggest heaps were at the sally port, where the light from outside was reflected by the wide pool of blood that leaked from the bodies and formed into a large puddle there.

He quickly squelched his low weeping and wiped his face free of any evidence of it. Tears in prison were like a pheromone to the other inmates and he didn't want any rebound relationships; it took some kind of unbelievable freak of nature event to get him out of his last one with John and Justin.

Yelling came from below as the men communicated with each other. He heard the man who had briefly stopped by his cell yell down, "2J, we got a live one in 2J, but he's fucked up pretty bad." Finn saw a second inmate running along the opposite tier also checking for the living. He noted that the man across from him was careful not to get too close to the cells; the beasts had their hands and arms out and were attempting to grasp him as he did his survey.

CELL BLOCK NORTH, COMMON AREA (JOSH)

Down below, as Josh passed the cells with normal people in them he found them overjoyed at their impending rescue. Hands came out to shake his and they pleaded, "Boss! Boss! Please! Get me out of here."

"It'll only be a minute, I swear." he assured them.

The men from the tier above yelled cell numbers down and Josh wrote them on his sheet. When the muster was complete he looked at his list and was dismayed at how few numbers there were. Only seven men in the whole block made it. There were three from the first floor and four from the second.

The runners reported that a few of the survivors were seriously injured and Josh nodded in acknowledgment. The infirmary was right off the quad and he had access to it, but he still didn't know whether it was occupied or not.

"After we free these guys we need to clear the infirmary next. Anyone here have medical training? I know basic first aid, but that's it."

None of men did. "Well, maybe one of the guys in the cells can help out with that. You guys wait here and I'll be right back."

Back in central Josh pulled up the menu to disengage individual cells doors. He quickly punched in the numbers from his list before jogging back to the north block.

CELL BLOCK NORTH, SECOND TIER (FINN)

Finn saw one of the men in the group below, a CO, separate from the rest and take off running. He thought it odd that the man seemed to be teamed up with the inmates and was puzzling over this when all of a sudden his cell door opened up.

Half an hour ago Finn was expecting to die in his cell and now he was free. Bracing himself he stepped out onto the walkway. He had transversed this same piece of concrete hundreds of times since his arrival without thinking about it, but today it felt like conquering a new land. It was safe territory. He relished the feeling of the smooth cold concrete on his bare feet. He looked down.

"Oh, forgot my shit."

He rushed back in and grabbed his prison-issue coveralls and shoes and hurriedly put them on. On his way back out he checked once more to make sure the two men on the bottom bunk were dead before jabbing his middle finger in their battered faces. Through gritted teeth he whispered "Fuck you assholes. I hope you both rot in hell." Subconsciously, Finn felt a sudden fear that his enmity might revive his dead cellmates, so he jerked his hand back and quickly exited the cell once more.

Back on the walkway he looked over the side and saw about ten men in the middle of the common area. One of them was fudging with the television, flipping channels, only finding screens filled with colored bars or static that meant the station was off the air. The men noticed Finn watching them from up on the second tier and yelled out to him. "Come on down, it's safe," and "Woohoo, another live one."

Inmates were always segregated by their blocks so when Finn joined the group downstairs he only recognized a few of the men. The rest of them were strangers. He felt some trepidation at being around them even as their congratulatory slaps smothered his shoulders and back.

Since his first day of incarceration, Finn was what the men in prison termed a 'pussy boy', a man so weak and scared that he let others use his body for sexual gratification in exchange for their protection. According to the prison pecking order he was near the bottom rung, ranking only above snitches and sex offenders. Finn had no misgivings on exactly how he was regarded, and even though he welcomed the positive attention he was getting for having survived, he wondered how long it would be before they all figured what he was and shunned him, or even worse, withdrew the group's mantle of protection.

The slaps petered out and the men grew contemplative. Most of them were now looking at Finn, regarding his value beyond that of just another number to add to their group. They sensed his discomfort, their prisoner antennas zeroing in on his scared vibe. It was the moment he most dreaded.

Suddenly a shout erupted from an enormous black man. "What the fuck is happening out there?" he demanded, startling them out of their introspective thoughts on Finn. "Why did all these mother fucks turn into crazy shits and start killing everybody?" He looked around at the faces in the group. "Anyone have a clue?"

A lot of head shaking and "No idea, Ben," and "Wish I knew because this is fucked up."

"Well then, just like the CO said, it's best we stick together," he told the group. "We're going to need all the men we can get. So stop sizing each other up and get with the program."

CELL BLOCK NORTH, COMMON AREA (JOSH)

When Josh met back up with the men they were gathered around two inmates laid out on the large gaming tables the cons used for dominoes, cards and chess. He took a look at the injuries and recoiled, surprised that the men on the table were still alive. They had obvious broken bones and had lost a lot of blood from bites, gouges and scratches. One of them was worse off, with chunks bitten out of his face and scalp. Josh could see the man's teeth and tongue through a large hole in his cheek. A muscular prisoner, a black man wearing tiny round spectacles spoke up. Josh remembered that people called him by the ridiculous nickname of Ben Franklin. Ben said, "These two are fighters. Both of them killed a pair of those things locked up in the cell with them."

It was clear to Josh that defeating two beasts single-handedly earned the injured men enormous respect. Josh was also impressed but understood that 'respect' meant something different to the group gathered around him than it did the average person. In prison, respect was currency; the more respect an inmate had, the better he was treated. Josh supposed that in that regard respect on the inside was much like money was in the outside world. What it meant in this situation was that the broken men, useless to the group, had paid for special treatment. They would not be left behind unless completely necessary.

"Let's get these guys to the infirmary, see what we can do for them" Josh told the men.

"Okay Boss," one of the men said, out of habit.

Josh turned to him, but addressed the whole group. "Listen, guys, my name isn't Boss, it's Josh. There are no more jails, there are no more bosses, and there are no more laws, which means that you guys aren't inmates and I'm not a CO. We need to start thinking in this new moment or we won't survive." He smiled at them. "Is everyone good with that? Good."

Ben spoke up again. Apparently he was stepping up to fill the middleman role between the ex-inmates and the old establishment that Josh represented. Josh admired the easy way he had with the men and that he seemed to understand that the group would only survive by acting as a unit.

"You heard the man," Ben said. "Let's get these poor bastards to the infirmary." Setting the example for the others, he turned and addressed Josh by his name.

"Okay, Josh, how do you want to do this?"

Grateful for the bridge Ben was building and the assurance it gave him, Josh straightened up and spoke more confidently. "Let's get the men over to the infirmary building. We may have to clear it first and it'll be harder this time because they might come charging out. I looked on the camera, but I can't tell if there are any of those things in there, so be ready on my signal."

The moaning, damaged men were hauled across the quad by some of the other prisoners and then set down in the shade of the infirmary building. Josh was back in central by then looking out the window at them, watching them prepare. A quick look at the monitor showed nothing right inside the entrance. He didn't have a view of what was further in. Due to strict privacy regulations, in Summit County an entrance camera was all that was legally allowed inside a jail medical facility.

Almost all of the able-bodied men were now armed and a dozen shotguns were pointed at the infirmary door. Ben raised his arm to let Josh know they were ready and Josh disengaged the door lock.

The men slowly opened the door and when nothing charged out at them they relaxed a little. Glancing down at the monitor Josh didn't see anything either. Even so, there were no volunteers for going in first.

Sighing, Josh grabbed his shotgun and headed out to them. Somehow he had ended up as the leader of his small group of unlikely allies, even though he had no idea why they picked him. Now, he supposed, it was time to earn their trust and respect. He would have to go in first.

CRAIG'S COURT, LONDON

After stepping out of the pub and checking his surroundings, Walter headed north up Charing Cross Road in the direction of BBC London. It was a little over three kilometers, normally a few minutes by car, but since he was hoofing it he figured to be there in less than half an hour.

It took him almost three hours. Every few blocks he was held up while his credentials were verified and he was allowed to pass through. The martial law restrictions in effect required civilians to proceed only in the direction of their residence and Walter was going the wrong way. He gave the same explanation, that he was a BBC correspondent reporting to work, to the same wary-looking soldiers at every checkpoint.

Somebody must have gotten tired of hearing his name relayed up and down the network. At the Oxford Street gate he began telling the sentry who he was and where he was headed. The soldier held up his hand for silence, handed Walter a plastic placard, and opened the barrier without saying a word. He ushered Walter through the checkpoint and directly through to the other side.

As the barrier was lowered behind him, Walter looked at the placard. At the top was the seal of the Lord High Steward of the United Kingdom Provisional Government. He did a double take. In a matter of hours the standing government had peacefully changed hands to the contingency commander.

The placard was a travel pass. Underneath the seal were the words 'Unrestricted Travel' and a brief statement that read 'The following individual,' and then 'Walter Doucet, BBC' was typed in a space for that purpose, 'has been deemed essential personnel and is allowed unrestricted access for zones Green and below. Questions or concerns are to be directed to the Adjunct Staff Officer of the Provisional Government using secure channels HOTEL or OSCAR.' It was signed 'Major-General Ethan Thornber for the Chief of the General Staff, General Sir Leonard Joseph Fells, Lord High Steward of the United Kingdom Provisional Government.' There was a black magnetic stripe on the back.

From then on Walter made good time. All he needed to do was hand over his driving license and his placard. The sentry on duty would then swipe his pass through a handheld reader and he was allowed through the checkpoint.

Despite the inconvenience Walter was impressed at how quickly measures were taken to limit rioting and control movement through the city. Even though he saw many people outside their houses and apartments as he passed through, he did not see a single instance of violence or looting. He could tell by the way people were congregating on corners and the front of their buildings that they were still concerned.

He finally made it to the BBC broadcasting house on Portland Place and found it guarded by a large military contingent, more than Walter expected. When he showed his placard he was allowed through the barrier but then asked to wait just inside.

Within a few minutes a smiling army officer approached and put out his hand. Walter shook it. "Mr. Doucet, a privilege to make your acquaintance. I am Major Tim Steeds-Nelson. Sorry about all the bother, but I'm sure you understand we have to take precautions." Then the major gestured to the entrance of a large command tent that had been set up to the right of the main door. "Would you mind?"

Walter looked at the near-century old statue of Prospero over the BBC's main doors and briefly wondered what the buildings designers would think of it serving as a backdrop to a military encampment. Glancing into the dark interior of the tent, Walter saw banks of computer screens manned by military operators.

Resigned, Walter shrugged. "Sure," he said, and preceded the major into the tent.

The only illumination inside came from the glow of LCD screens, and the only noises were the muted communications of the operators as they spoke into headsets and the soft clicking of keys as their fingers worked their keyboards.

The major took the lead and walked towards the end of the tent where several office cubicle partitions were set up. To Walter they looked oddly out of place, not very military like at all. He kept his thoughts to himself, however. He had no idea why he had been waylaid and didn't want to say anything until he did.

Walter and his escort ended up in the last cubicle. The only furniture it contained was a folding table and a matching set of four chairs. On the table was a pitcher of water, some glasses, and a manila folder. Still smiling, Major

Steeds-Nelson pulled out one of the chairs for Walter and said, "Please, sit. Can I get you anything? Water? Coffee?"

"No, Major. I'm fine, thank you. Could you please tell me why you pulled me in here? What's going on?"

"I promise you Mr. Doucet, this will only take a few minutes. I'm certain you are well aware that today is an unusual day and that standard operating procedures have been placed on hiatus for the time being. I have been instructed to brief members of the media on those changes."

"What changes?" Walter asked.

"Did you have the opportunity to view General Fells' press conference earlier?"

Walter nodded. "Yes."

"Great. The general mentioned portions of a contingency plan called Ophir Ridge. During his briefing the general gave the simplified version, something the people could understand. But the plan is actually incredibly detailed and thorough." The major paused to pour himself a glass of water and sip it. "So detailed in fact, that if you saw the whole plan printed out it would be a stack of paper about this high," the major held his hand out flat next to his belt."

"Excuse me Major, but what's your point? That the plan has many pages? What does that matter?" Walter put his hands palms-out in supplication and raised his voice. "Tell me why you're holding me here. Why can't I report to my work?"

Two armed sentries came to the cubicle entrance and looked to the major. The major shook his head and they left, but only so far as to take station right outside the cubicle entrance.

"Mr. Doucet, I apologize for my roundabout way of conveying to you the gravity of what I am about to ask of you. Clearly you are a man who prefers brevity, so I'll get straight to the point." The major reached down and grabbed the manila folder from the table and opened it while shielding the contents from Walter's view.

"Please sit down Mr. Doucet."

Walter sighed and sat in one of the folding chairs. "Okay. Now please tell me what all of this is about."

Major Steeds-Nelson sat down across from him, held out the folder, and smiled. "It would be my pleasure, sir. Right after you read and then sign off on this Non-Disclosure Agreement."

Walter looked at the folder. It was standard policy for BBC reporters to not sign Non-Disclosure Agreements, or NDA's as they were commonly called, especially without them first being vetted through a very involved and complicated legal department screening. Walter was about to say so when the Major held up his hand and said "Before you refuse, look at the memo, please."

Opening up the folder the first thing Walter saw was the letterhead of the BBC Director-General. The memo was short. The subject read "Notice of Cooperation to All BBC Employees and Affiliates." and the contents were to the effect that all employees under the purview of BBC were to cooperate fully and in any capacity with the provisional government. It was signed, in ink, "William Anthony Graves, Baron of Glenstock and Commander of the Order of the British Empire."

Walter subconsciously straightened up in his chair. "Okay, Major," he said. "You have my attention. What do you need me to do?"

Reaching across the table and flipping the memo over to expose the paperwork beneath, the major pointed to the NDA. "Thank you, Mr. Doucet. You're doing the right thing. It's standard boilerplate. Feel free to read through the entirety of the document if you need to." Flipping the page, Steeds-Nelson said, "Pay special attention to the penalties. Normally, breaking the trust on something with this security level would land you in Her Majesty's Prison Belmarsh for all of your remaining life. As of today the punishment is a bit more expedient and permanent." The major smiled humorlessly. "Death, I'm afraid." Still smiling, he pulled out a pen and placed it next to the folder. "But I'm getting a little ahead of myself, Mr. Doucet. I'll give you some time to read it."

Standing, the major left the cubicle. On his way out he leaned in and told one of the sentries in a low voice, "Come and get me after he signs."

A muted "Yes, sir," came back to Walter as he began reading. It wasn't a complicated document and only took him a few minutes to finish it. 'Operation Ophir Ridge' was stamped in big red letters at the top and bottom of every page. There were several section headings such as Disclosure, Aiding the Enemy, and Sabotage that defined particular crimes. Walter noted that the punishment for violating any part of the NDA was universally 'death', without the benefit of due process.

The last page of the NDA was for signatures, already typed out with both his name as the 'Member' and Major Steeds-Nelson as the 'Duly Authorized Witness' under the signature lines. Picking up the pen, Walter thought about what signing it meant.

Never in his life had he ever doubted his loyalty to anything. He just always assumed deep down that once one committed to something, whether it was an employer, a partner, an ideology or anything else, that the commitment was true and binding. He was born British and had lived his whole life identifying himself as British, and while he wasn't the most patriotic citizen in the United Kingdom he was certainly a proud one. Walter decided that since the thought of betraying his country never once crossed his mind, the consequences for doing weren't an issue. He jotted down his signature and closed the folder.

When the major returned Walter was in the middle of pouring himself a glass of water. Major Steeds-Nelson picked the folder up and quickly flipped to the back page, signed it and handed the folder out to one of the sentries. The sentry tucked it under his arm, saluted and left.

"Welcome to the team, Mr. Doucet," the major beamed at Walter and shook hands with him. "I want you to know that we are very glad to have you with us. I was told that you were personally picked to join this operation by General Fells himself."

"What? Why? That makes no sense," Walter exclaimed.

"Well, I can't tell you the why of it, but I can tell you the what."

"Okay then, what's the 'what'?"

"In accordance with the Ophir Ridge operations plan, the BBC has been militarized and is now a special branch of the provisional government. Baron Glenstock has been authorized the rank of Lieutenant-General. What's more..."

"Wait, wait, wait," Walter interjected. "Can General Fells even do that?"

"I'm afraid so. His provisional mandate is absolute. He has been charged with protecting British peoples and British interests by any means necessary.

The assimilation of the BBC is only one of the measures that have already been put in place." The major paused. "But I'm getting off track again." He met Walter's gaze and dropped his military persona for a moment. "Mr. Doucet, everyone else inside the headquarters building was briefed en masse before you showed up, and they all reacted much like you are doing now. So believe me when I say that I understand that what's happening is a bit of a paradigm shift, particularly for someone so heavily entrenched in the concepts of personal and public freedoms."

Walter was confused. "What 'paradigm shift', exactly."

"Let me give the context. Make no mistake that today is the beginning of a long struggle for our country and our way of life. All of us, every single person, will have to make sacrifices. To aid the struggle for our side we, the military, are going to have to fight, and kill, and take from other people. Take everything from them if we have to. General Fells has named you and a few others within the BBC for special consideration because of your extensive experience covering military conflicts. Are you familiar with the British principles of war?"

"Probably not like you are," Walter confessed. "Please elaborate."

"Sorry. I promise this is leading somewhere so bear with me a moment longer. The master principle of war is this: a single, unambiguous aim." The major tapped his finger on the tabletop with the syllables as he emphasized his next sentence. "A single, unambiguous aim. That aim is the preservation of the British people and free peoples everywhere. Sacrifice and effort are necessary to achieving this aim so we must put aside the things that don't matter. You, sir, must put aside the things that don't matter in order to aid in this struggle. Are you ready to do that, Mr. Doucet? Are you ready to commit to this effort and put your entire being, your soul, behind it?"

Silence from Walter. He thought about the consequences if the British endeavor failed. He knew that the rest of the world was gearing up to invade the Americas, especially the northern continent. If the wrong country, or even the wrong group or person gained a foothold there and had access to the American's nuclear repository, then England would fall soon after, or simply get nuked out of existence. He imagined his country governed by a greedy despot or religious extremists and he broke out in a cold sweat. He would give all he had to make sure that it didn't happen; he had no choice but to dedicate himself to the effort.

"Yes. Without reservation," Walter answered. "I can't stand by."

Major Steeds-Nelson pushed his chair back and stood. Walter saw him dismiss the guards stationed at the cubicle entrance by nodding at them and Walter sensed that had he answered in the negative they would probably be leading him away instead of simply leaving.

"A small team of military and civilian experts are being assembled at the Wellington Barracks and you're to join them. I am your liaison here at BBC to facilitate your operational needs, but you report to Lieutenant-General Glenstock."

"You make it sound like I'm going somewhere. And what team of experts? What is it I'm expected to do?"

"I'm not in the loop on that. You leave shortly for Wellington Barracks for your operations briefing. I'm sure they'll fill you in there," Major Nelson-Steeds explained. He motioned for Walter to stand and guided him out of the cubicle and to the tent entrance. "There is one more thing, Mr. Doucet. To better facilitate your mission the decision was made to award you a commission in the British Army. The paperwork to that effect will be forwarded to the barracks. Congratulations, sir."

Completely taken aback, Walter asked, "What's my commission?"

Major Steeds-Nelson laughed and shook Walter's hand. "You now outrank me, Mr. Doucet. Excuse me. I mean Lieutenant-Colonel Doucet." At the shock on Walter's face, the major grew serious again. "A military commission and spot promotion to Lieutenant-Colonel is very uncommon, even with the times as desperate as they are. Whatever your assignment is, I'm sure you'll find the rank necessary."

A jeep was idling outside the tent entrance and a soldier stood by the open passenger door. The major pointed to the jeep and said, "There's your ride. Good luck, Colonel."

MEDINA OHIO, NORTH OF SAVANNA TRAIL

Jim trusted his small group more after the encounter with the sleeping goons, especially Zoe who seemed to have gained confidence by her first kill. She wasn't glancing behind and all around as much as she did when they first exited the super store. And even though Chuck had acted with a nervous energy, at least he had acted. It could have gone worse and Jim was certain that more tests lay ahead. Eventually the group was going to hit an open area, a place without cover and without a nearby sanctuary. When that happened he was going to take Vickers earlier advice and buffer himself with the three former Klimps employees, because even though he was definitely sweet on Zoe, he valued his life way more than he did hers.

The group continued on their way through the woods, keeping the road within sight and as the trees thinned out their visibility distance increased. Occasionally, they passed signs of previous struggles, places where the ground was torn up and blood and flesh coated the grass. After passing a few of these, Vickers circled his finger in the air for a group huddle.

After they gathered around Vickers spoke in a low whisper. "Anyone notice anything strange about these blood circles?"

Megan was the first to speak up. "Yeah. No bodies. Almost always when those things attack people they leave the corpses alone. That means that someone or something is cleaning up after them."

"That doesn't make sense," Zoe hushed back. "No one in their right mind would come out here and move bodies. Maybe nobody died and they just moved on."

"No way," Megan replied. "If that were the case, with this much blood there would be goon bodies. Those things don't retreat."

Jim followed the discussion. He wanted to agree with Zoe to score some points with her, but Megan made the better argument. He was going to add his opinion but Vickers spoke up first.

"Let's keep going. If anyone sees anything else weird, let me know."

Jim stood and took his place in the formation behind Zoe. Within a few minutes the road curved to the left and away, which was the direction they needed to go. There were bodies in the road and Jim wondered idly if any of them were goons that chased the Town Car earlier. He turned his eyes back to the front and contemplated Zoe's butt, mesmerized by its rhythmic swing as the denim stretched and released over the twin bumps of her rump with her every step.

His stomach grumbled and he thought about grabbing a chocolate chip energy bar out of his backpack the next time they stopped. Musing on how he might even be able to get one out now and unwrap it quietly, he felt a thump on the back of his neck. He almost yelped. He snapped his around and found Megan frowning at him. She leaned in and whispered in his ear. "Pay attention. Look around you instead of at her ass."

He nodded and felt his face get hot as he blushed. Jim was pretty sure Zoe heard the comment because she reached back and pulled her shirt tail down to cover as much of herself as much as possible.

Soon the group ran out of deep grass and light forest. They had finally reached the outskirts of Medina. Vickers stopped at an abandoned backhoe and everyone ducked into the shadow of the large construction vehicle's tires.

"Saul, you're up," Vickers said.

The little bearded man put his hands around Megan and Chuck for an impromptu huddle and the rest aped him. "Here's the plan: Once we cross the state road here we hit a bunch of subdivisions. Zoe's house is almost directly behind the row on the other side." He made a leaping motion with his hand. "I think going through the yards along this road would be suicidal, so we're going to skirt them around the left side. If we get split up, let's make her house the new rendezvous point." He gave a few seconds for any questions and got none. "Let's cross the road in singles, it's less conspicuous."

Leaving the safety of the backhoe's shadow the group made their way as stealthily as possible to the ditch lining the highway. Saul was climbing the bank to the road surface to cross when Jim spotted a large culvert about thirty yards away. "Wait a sec," he whispered.

Saul looked back and everyone else turned to Jim as he pointed left and said "Let's try that first. We can use that drainpipe to crawl under the road."

"Ah, didn't see that. Good thinking," Saul whispered back. He crept off in that direction with the rest of them close behind. Halfway there Saul held up a closed fist and turned his head, listening. He pointed to the road about ten feet above them.

They heard the discord of whoops a few seconds before they heard the sound of a car engine coming towards them from the direction they were walking. Everyone fell flat with the exception of Chuck. He stood a moment longer, contemplating the sounds coming from the road before he realized that he was the only one still upright. When he finally dropped down next to Megan she shot him a dirty look. Jim hoped Chuck knew how he had just put everyone in danger.

Twenty seconds later the car drove by. From the sound of the mechanical chugging noises it was making it was either running out of gas or the engine was failing. As it passed a woman's voice could be heard screaming for help, but then her voice was drowned out by the bestial cries and slapping footsteps of the dozens of goons in pursuit.

Megan tapped Jim's shoulder, pointed to the drainpipe and started low-crawling to the entrance. Saul was already headed there. Jim turned and let Zoe know before moving. Halfway there he began breathing weird, like he couldn't get a full breath. The main pack of goons was close above on the road, and he was stuck either crawling for the drainpipe or staying in the ditch out in the open. He went on autopilot and his body seemed to move on its own. He felt himself crawling forward, the physical sense of moving closer and closer to his goal, but at the same time his mind was screaming at him to get up and run.

After he made it to the pipe the helping hands of Megan and Saul pulled him in. He struggled to get a deep breath but couldn't. He heard Megan whisper to Saul, "He's having a panic attack," before his fingertips began to go numb and his head buzzed. "Panic attack?" he thought to himself. "That's not right, I never have panic attacks." He felt Megan swing around behind him and embrace him, her arms folding over his chest. She whispered softly into his ear from behind: "You're okay, Jim. Calm down, everything's okay, shh, shh. Calm down. Relax."

His gasping gradually slowed and he began to breathe normally again. He looked around to see everyone staring at him with looks of concern. Everyone except Chuck. Jim vaguely remembered passing him on his way to the drainpipe entrance and assumed that Chuck would follow him in. Apparently he hadn't.

Vickers peeked around the corrugated lip of the drainpipe and motioned for Chuck to crawl to him. He turned to the group, shook his head and whispered, "He's lying there frozen. Won't move."

"We'll wait here for him until all the goons have passed, then go and get him," Saul said, speaking low through his beard. Jim watched the short man lean back and grab an energy bar out of his backpack. Saul folded open the aluminum seal of the wrapper and went to take a bite when a scream filled the air. The whooping of goons was suddenly much closer.

As a unit the five remaining members of the group went into a crouching run to the opposite end of the pipe. Jim was behind Megan again and he felt Zoe bump into his backside a few times in her rush to get as far away from what was happening outside as she could. He felt a sense of relief when his earlier panic symptoms did not re-emerge and he could do his part in the exfiltration from the pipe. He hoped he never had to live through that feeling of helplessness again. Had he been alone it could very well been him outside in the ditch getting ruined instead of Chuck.

Jim thought that they were just going to wait inside the pipe until the goons left but he found himself outside with everyone else, running for the cover of some trees about fifty feet from the pipe exit. He risked a look back and was relieved that the road was clear. Chuck's inaction and subsequent death had served as the distraction the group needed to get out of the dire situation they were in. Of course, if Chuck hadn't of locked up in the open they still would have probably been safe.

All of the stress of the past fifteen minutes had served to put Jim back into the survival mode he was in during the time right after the change. He felt himself settle at the higher plateau and the thoughts of panic he had dissipated. He mentally felt his mind going into better focus.

Everyone made it to the trees without alarming the goon swarm on the other side of the road. Squatting and catching their breath, nobody said anything for a few minutes. Finally, Vickers quietly asked, "What just happened sucks. What lessons did we learn from it?"

Jim wanted to show the group that he was back in the game mentally, to restore their confidence in his ability to add value to their survival. "Well," he said, "we know they're bad at multitasking and are easily distracted."

For some reason this caused everyone to laugh, albeit softly. Jim hadn't seen Zoe even crack a smile up until this point, but she was laughing the loudest and had to be quieted by Megan's hand on her arm. "Okay, Jim, good point," Vickers admitted. "What else can we use from Chuck's sacrifice?"

Zoe spoke up, proving that she had made it through the gauntlet of her second encounter with more confidence and the capacity to capitalize on what she had learned. "We need to keep moving if at all possible. Those goons are unpredictable. Also, I don't want to be trapped out in the open again like that."

"She's right," Saul added. "We need to figure out a better, safer way to travel out here in the wild. Learn a better way to scout. To be honest, I have no idea what better ways there might be."

"Agreed," Vickers said. "Let's all keep that in mind. Think about what's going to keep us safer when we're out here. Now get your maps out and let's cover the route again while we can."

Some light rustling as maps were pulled out and unfolded. "Oh, and that reminds me. We should be using kneeboards out here. I'll set that up when we get back and explain what they are after." He pointed to their location on the map. "The plan is still the same. We head to the next road, which is Reagan Parkway, circling north around these housing developments, and only go house to house once we hit Zoe's street, which is on Hillview Way. Jim and I have gone house to house before, and although I wish there was some kind of tactic or method to do it safely and easily I don't think there is. Do you agree Jim?"

"Yeah, it sucks," was all Jim could add. "Plus, once we get there we have to go inside." He looked over at Zoe and said, "Your brother is either in there or he isn't, but we need to be ready to fight once we get inside."

Thinking about what Jim meant, Zoe nodded and replied with a simple, "Okay."

"Alright, back to silence from here on out unless it's an emergency," Saul ordered, and led the group out of the trees.

WRIGHT-PATTERSON AIR FORCE BASE, DAYTON, OHIO

Fran and the others were formed into lines and corralled into the metal hut at the end of the fenced-in enclosure. Inside, there were tables set up on each side of the line and unarmed soldiers stood behind them asking the new conscripts questions before handing over items. By the time Fran got to the tables half of the people were already through with their issue. He could see them, in the large open area at the end of the tables, being yelled at by armed soldiers. It was far away but it looked like everyone was being forced to undress. His thoughts were interrupted by a short, pockmarked woman on his right. "Shirt size?"

"Oh, large I guess," Fran answered. He was promptly handed two camouflage long-sleeved shirts. He continued down the tables and was issued the rest of his gear: boots, camouflage pants and hat, toiletry kit and a manila folder labeled 'Conscript Rules and Regulations'. He also had his blood drawn and had to answer some basic medical history. The entire procedure was fast and impersonal and to Fran it felt a lot like the in-process routine he went through in various jails. He definitely did not enjoy the feeling but knew that now was not the time to act. He was already at the end of the line of tables and the shouting he had heard earlier was now being directed at him.

"What the fuck are you doing, asshole?" was screamed into his ear from a distance of about six inches. "Can't you hear me? Get the fuck undressed and don your gear!" and then he was shoved forward into a mass of confused former civilians, all trying to change into their new military-issue uniforms as fast as possible. Fran almost fell but was held up by a hand on his arm. It was the older man from the trio. "Gotcha, Boss. C'mon over here with the rest of us."

Fran allowed himself to be led. Soon he was with familiar faces and the chaos seemed to mitigate. The three men were now free of their cuffs and already outfitted in their military garb. Fran noticed that the uniform changed not only their appearance but also their mannerisms. They seemed more comfortable being allowed to blend in; with their military uniforms and hats on they looked like everyone else.

The men stood guard around Fran while he changed. With his bearings back and the buffer his men were providing keeping the shouting soldiers off of him, he was able to get everything done without harassment. He transferred what he had collected from the apartment building from his old clothes into his new ones. He didn't remember sticking them in his pocket but he still had a handful of prescription drugs, about fifty pills, most likely Vicodin or Percocet. It really didn't matter since both were now valuable currency. He also had a folding knife and a bunch of money. He threw the money onto the ground but kept the rest of his stuff. His men initially made to lunge for the money out of conditioned instinct but stopped themselves once they remembered that money no longer had any value. Fran was happy to see that like him, they were able to quickly reprogram their impulses to different situations.

The soldiers were soon outnumbered by the number of conscripts and the intensity of their shouting became diluted by the mass of humanity squeezed into the space at the end of the hut. Fran saw one of the soldiers hand a large broom to a conscript and point to the piles of clothes scattered around on the floor. The last thing Fran felt like doing was menial work doled out arbitrarily so he gathered the men together and pointed to the back of the hut, away from the soldiers.

When they regrouped Fran told the older man "I know Gunter and Loomis, but I never got your name."

The older man said "Name's Bill. Bill Crystal. What's your name?"

"Wait. Did you say your name is Bill Crystal?" Fran asked.

"Yeah, yeah, and it's because of that dickbag actor I had to change my name from Billy, like I used when I was younger."

"Heh. Good call, Bill. By the way, I go by my last name. It's King."

The men nodded at that, like it made sense. "I have a plan," Fran told them. "I figure that if we have any chance of making our circumstances better, we've got to stick together from here on out," He tried to impart urgency into his voice because he suspected that he didn't have a lot of time to cement his role as the leader of their new foursome. The other three men were nodding in agreement. "Great. Do I have everyone's word on that?" He looked each of them in their eyes. "Can we make a pact?"

"Fuck yeah," and "Sounds great," were the replies as the air horn blasted again.

"Done," Fran said and shook their hands to seal the deal.

People were milling about, unsure what the air horn meant. Most of them were uncomfortably out of their element, having been shuffled from one terrible situation to another, before finally being forced, at gunpoint, to serve in the military. They hadn't had time to properly process the loss of loved ones, the fact that their previous identities were meaningless, and that the civilization that had been protectively wrapped around them their whole lives was gone, replaced with a horror-twisted version of it.

Once again the soldiers stepped in. They pushed people into a general semblance of a military formation. To Fran it was interesting that the gaggle of people in the fenced in enclosure earlier had somehow been transformed in less than an hour into a semi-organized and uniform looking unit. He felt that there was a lesson in that and mentally recorded the process. If he was to gather forces to himself, he needed discipline similar to what he was witnessing with the soldiers.

Soon it grew quiet. Sergeant Lopez handed his air horn over to one of his men and addressed the assembly. "Everyone raise your right hand and repeat after me."

Although he didn't want to, Fran raised his hand and his men followed his example.

"I, 'state your name', do solemnly swear…," the sergeant began, waiting for the response. When it came he continued, "…to defend the Constitution of the United States," again a pause. Fran didn't even pretend to mouth the words, but he understood the value in making people swear an oath. He planned on instituting the very same practice when he gathered enough people to himself. The oath continued, with swearing to follow orders, to be subject to the Uniform Code of Military Justice and so on. When it ended, everyone put their hands down.

Fran noted that some of the same people who were bitching earlier about being pushed around by the military were now smiling and shaking the hands of those around them. Half mocking, he turned to his new men and shook their hands, saying "Welcome to the group Gunter," and "you too, Bill, and Loomis." The men caught the sarcastic flavor of his comments and smiled back knowingly.

"Same to you, King," they replied.

The room was quieting so they stopped talking and turned back to the front. Sergeant Lopez snapped upright and yelled out "Conscripts, Attention!"

Most of the room understood the command even if they executed it poorly. In front, Fran saw a non-remarkable man in a formal blue uniform approach Sergeant Lopez. The sergeant saluted, his fingers quivering as it came to a stop at the brim of his hat. "Ninety one conscripts ready for duty, sir!"

"At ease Sergeant, thank you," the man replied. Then to the group: "At ease, everyone." There was a rustling of stiff clothing as the conscripts relaxed. "Good afternoon, I'm Colonel Mark Slater, the installation commander," he said. The colonel's voice was strong and confident, an indicator he was someone used to being obeyed without question. Fran studied the man: His oratory, his mannerisms, and his assumption of authority, and catalogued these traits almost without realizing it. Later, in private, he would work on emulating and adapting the Colonel's style to his own.

Using a hand microphone the colonel looked out over the crowd gathered in front of him. "I know that all of you must be wondering why you're here." Some mumbling, but the colonel's amplified voice rode over it. "I also realize that some of you may be upset with your current situation." The mumbling increased in volume as the colonel nodded expectantly, like he was asking the questions deliberately to get these exact reactions. "A quick show of hands. How many of you were in dire need of help when my men rescued you?" Almost every hand went up. "How many of you would have survived out there on your own?" All but two hands lowered. Fran was careful to drop his hand. Even though he was confident that he would have survived, he didn't want to draw any attention to himself.

The Colonel noted that two hands stayed up. He turned aside and spoke to Sergeant Lopez, who in turn yelled out "You two with your hands raised, step forward." An average looking man and a fit looking woman stepped forward and stood in front of the Colonel. "You two are now the section leaders of this flight, designated as India Flight. You will receive additional instructions on your new duty assignment shortly," the Colonel informed them.

To the group, he added, "India Flight is the ninth group of conscript inductees gathered since the cataclysmic event that tore this country asunder. As I believe that understanding the mission is imperative to good conduct and successful mission completion, I will briefly cover your role in this installation's efforts to curtail the chaos outside our gates. As you may or may not know, the current catastrophe is localized to our hemisphere. The other side of the planet suffered none of the effects that we have all witnessed."

"We are almost certain that what happened was caused by a freak occurrence of residual radiation from an asteroid, interacting with microorganisms in the upper atmosphere," he explained. "It's actually much more complicated than that, extenuating factors include the superstorms of late and climate change, but in any case it has been determined to be a singular event. It was just our bad luck to be in the path of the sun when it happened. Had it been night it would have never occurred, at least to us."

The Colonel moved from the front of the formation and began walking around and through the lines of the formation, meeting the eyes of the new conscripts and placing his hand on random shoulders. "So why am I telling you this?" he continued. "Do I think we cognitives are the lucky ones?" He paused for a moment for the conscripts to mull over his question. "Well, I can't answer that for everyone, but I can tell you this: You men and women of India Flight are now part of a grander purpose than mere survival. There are larger forces in play and helping you understand them will strengthen your resolve to contribute to your mission."

"While we stand here there are several unfriendly nations mobilizing to occupy what was once the United States of America." He paused while the formation broke into whispers but he didn't stop the chatter. He slowly walked back to the front and waited for quiet before continuing. "So what's to stop them from coming over here and conquering what's left? Us? Our few military numbers and the new flights of conscripts? No. That's not going to stop them. There are other military pockets like us, spread out across the country, but even if we could combine forces and coordinate a defense, it would be a futile effort."

Colonel Slater pointed his finger up to the sky to emphasize his next point. "So why are you men and women here if we can't stop what's going to happen? I'll tell you. We have assistance. Our friends the British are coming. That's right, the British are coming. Our nation's closest ally is executing operational plans as we speak, to recover and preserve our nation's properties and assets. Your role," he pointed at several people in the front role indiscriminately, "is to help set the stage for their arrival."

"I'll leave the rest of your instruction in the capable hands of Sergeant Lopez and his crew. Sergeant Lopez," he concluded, and began walking away.

"Conscripts, Attention!" Sergeant Lopez shouted.

After the Colonel disappeared the sergeant brought the two new section leaders up and spoke to them. Then he handed them blue rope loops which they clipped onto the right shoulder of their uniforms. The section leaders came back and the woman yelled "Fallout!"

Nobody moved at first. Then, a few people moved, or looked around at everyone else knowing that they were supposed to be doing something, but unsure exactly what it was.

Sergeant Lopez watched with a slight smirk before interjecting. "Everyone is dismissed. Leave through the gate to your rear and remain with your section leaders. One last item: I'm issuing a warning to you all. If you leave your flight area without proper authorization, or you assist others in leaving, you will be held accountable." He then added, "And you won't like what happens then, I can promise you."

Again Fran found himself in a circumstances beyond his control. He processed all that he had seen and heard since his rescue as he overheard snippets of conversation from the rest of the conscripts; complaints, worries, and excitement pervaded. Turning to Bill and the others, Fran told them, "Believe it or not, we're in the best situation we can be in right now. We're protected. We have information. I think we should stay here and regroup until we figure out the best time to make our move."

Loomis asked, "What move are we talking about?"

Gunter jumped in. "The world is our oyster, idiot. It's all out there waiting for us. Right, King?"

"That's right," Fran answered. "But now is not the best time to talk about it. Hush up."

The four men fell silent and walked along with the other conscripts until they hit an open area with rows and rows of large tents set up. "Holy shit," Bill said. "There must be a thousand tents out here."

"Six to a tent," shouted the woman. "Let's go, six to a tent." She was directing groups of six into tents as they followed her along.

Fran and his crew followed along and made sure they ended up in the same tent. Two others joined them, a man and a woman, who, as soon they got entered, grasped each other with ferocity. The woman sobbed lightly while the man consoled her by rubbing and patting her back.

Gunter watched the interplay and his reaction was immediate. Grabbing the man by scruff of his jacket, he dragged the consoler to the entrance and flung him out. "Get the fuck out of here you pansy piece of shit." He rubbed his hands together as if washing his hands of the man, then turned to the woman and said nicely, but with a leer, "I took the trash out, but a nice piece of tail like you can stay if you want."

She whimpered and scrambled outside. Loomis smacked her on the behind as she passed and said, "Bye-bye sweetie. Come back soon."

The inside of the tent erupted in laughter. Fran joined in, but only on the surface. On the inside he was studying his men, judging their character traits for more weaknesses or motivational inroads. At some point he might need to play one off of the other so it was good to know as much about them as possible. On the flip side, since these three men were to be the core of his new empire, he would be remiss if he didn't realize their strengths as well.

After the laughter subsided the men took a look around their tent. There were six cots, three to a side. Fran took the middle cot on one side and told the other three to use the opposite side. As he expected they deferred to him without argument or hesitation.

In his past, Fran normally didn't work with others. He preferred to minimize his personal risk by controlling every aspect of a situation and so he had never led a team. What he did have was an uncanny aptness for reading people, and the mental awareness and acuity to manipulate and control them. It was when he had his epiphany on the apartment rooftop that he knew he could scale his ability to form a personal army that assumed most of the personal risks. In this new world, where most saw only disaster, loss, and pain, Fran saw opportunities.

INFIRMARY ENTRANCE

The men stood by while Josh spent a long moment looking into the darkness of the infirmary interior. He had been in there many times as he did his rounds and he was familiar with the layout, but never having been in there when the lights were out added a level of complexity, and with the potential for those things inside, a sense of fear and trepidation. With the help of the sunlight from the open door he could see a long hall with closed doors off to either side. At the end, he knew, was an open area used for processing and triage. After that there were several more rooms for inpatient care.

It was eerily quiet at the doorway, but just because nothing came charging out at him didn't mean that the infirmary was clear of the crazy people. Josh squinted but he couldn't see past the second set of doors.

He looked back at the men. Ben Franklin and the others were shooing him forward and giving him low words of encouragement. "If I don't move soon they're going to start losing respect for me," Josh thought.

Taking a deep breath he lunged through the doorway and hugged the wall. He brought his shotgun to the ready and sidestepped his way towards the triage area, bypassing all of the rooms with closed doors. As far as he was concerned they could stay closed. He was pretty certain they contained nothing of use anyway.

By the time he got to the end of the hall he had regained some of his confidence. He found the wall switch for the lights and turned them on. As soon as he did, a few of the doors he had already passed and some of the closed inpatient rooms erupted with whoops and pounding from the inside.

"Get in here guys!" he yelled. "I'm not sure how long these doors will hold them!"

Suddenly the hallway was filled with the men from outside. The barrels of their firearms were pointed everywhere and Josh had to yell at a few of the men. "Get your guns out of my face! Point them somewhere else!"

Ben Franklin stepped up again, calming the men and dispatching them to the noisy doors. That was when Josh decided to make Ben his second in command. With the two of them working in concert Josh was certain they could lead the men to safety.

The men knew there was no reason to open the doors to kill the crazy people. The creatures were violent and dangerous, but they were also predictable and stupid. Leveling their shotguns at the weak interior doors, the former inmates let loose and fired multiple rounds, which shredded the thin veneered wood as well as the occupants pressed up against them on the other side. When the firing stopped there were no more whoops.

With the infirmary secure it was safe to bring the two injured men inside. Ben and the others went out to get them from where they were stashed in the shade of the building, but only one came back. It was the man with the missing cheek and scalp. Ben shook his head in the negative at Josh's questioning look about the one left out front.

Josh was amazed that man they brought in and placed on a gurney had outlasted others whose injuries didn't seem as severe. He lay there fighting for breath and moaning with his eyes closed, hands clenching and unclenching. Many of the men found it hard to look away.

"Does anyone know this guy's name?" Josh asked.

Someone spoke up. "Yeah, that's Murph. He's a tough son of a bitch."

Josh said, "Yeah, he's tough all right." Then: "Okay, we don't need everybody in here." He pointed to the nearest man and said "You, stay here and help me." He turned to Ben. "Take the rest of the men and see what you can salvage. We need food, supplies and quieter weapons if we're going to survive on the outside. We should also clear the commissary. Can you check it out, see if it's clear?"

"Sure thing Josh," Ben replied. "I'll take care of it."

To Josh it seemed like Ben felt the same positive rapport developing between them that he did. He hoped it was genuine on Ben's part, but he couldn't be sure because prisoners tended to be very good at manipulating others. A consequence of being locked up with very little to do in an environment with a very rigid social hierarchy was that it forced everyone to hone their interpersonal skills to a high degree. In fact, part of Josh's training at the academy was dedicated to the topic of how to avoid prisoner and CO entanglements. He was taught that there was no such thing as an uncomplicated CO and inmate relationship and that the only method proven one hundred percent effective was abstinence. As reinforcement, newly graduated correction officers were placed under a mentor at their first assignment and it was the mentor's primary duty to guide the new officer through the traps set by inmates until they mastered the skills themselves. Josh's mentor was gone now, killed in the initial wave that morning, but he remembered his mentor's motto: 'Be aware, take care'. He supposed the motto was still appropriate.

To the man he had picked to stay behind, Josh said, "Guess what? You're a medic today."

INFIRMARY (FINN)

Finn was uncomfortable being singled out for anything so when the CO, Josh, pointed at him and told to him stay behind and help, he wondered at first if he had done something wrong. He just stood there.

"What's your name?" Josh asked him.

"Finn, uh, sir," he answered.

"Ha! I'm no sir. Call me Josh. Would you mind giving me a hand figuring out where the bandages are, Finn? We need to patch this guy, um, Murph, patch him up. Also look for the dispensary. This guy is going to need a hell of a lot of painkillers and antibiotics."

Finn moved. For some reason he felt immediately comfortable around Josh. They were around the same age and under different circumstances they might have been friends. All of the other survivors were rough seasoned inmates, insensitive at best, but Josh seemed like he belonged on the outside. Finn relaxed a little and helped enthusiastically with the search.

Cabinet doors flew open as the two men looked for useful medical supplies. On the third cabinet Finn found a bunch of gauze and tape along with stitching kits. "I think I found some stuff we can use," he announced.

"Great," Josh said after he walked over and looked. "Grab what you can and bring it over to the table."

Finn mustered up the courage to look over at Murph on the table. Even though the man was unconscious, his jaw worked up and down. Finn could see the tongue lolling about inside Murph's mouth as the exposed tendons and muscles contracted and relaxed. Bloody drool leaked out of the cheek hole and formed a large pink splotch on the sterile white medical paper covering the table. That wasn't the extent of the injuries. Part of Murph's scalp was missing too, and his left leg was gouged and swollen from the knee down. Finn suspected there was other damage, but the man's blood coated everything and it was hard to tell.

Finn grabbed everything from the cabinet in two trips and set it on a side cart, in case any of it could be used to patch the injured man up. Josh was still opening doors looking for the drug supplies so Finn joined him.

Josh started talking to him in an easy, conversational way. "Thanks for helping me out Finn, although I'm not sure Murph is going to make it. It might be more humane to just let him go, but I know how important it is to you guys that he survives. Was he a friend of yours?"

Finn couldn't help himself. "What? No, the guy's an asshole and I can't fucking stand him. He tormented me more times than I can count and I hope he fucking croaks."

"Whoa. Okay buddy, sorry I asked," Josh said, smiling. "I was only joking. I know who you are. It's the reason I kept you back, to give us a chance to talk." Josh's face turned serious. "Listen, Finn, let me know what you want me to do here. These guys are listening to me, at least for now anyway. I know how you were treated but there was nothing I could do to stop it before. I'm trying to make up for it right here. Tell me what you think your best possible option is."

The weight of the horrifying morning, the anguish of the past months and this one simple act of compassion were too much for Finn. His face wrenched up in anguish and he broke down. He covered his face and his hands were immediately soaked with tears. He cried for a few minutes as Josh stood patiently by. Eventually, his wracking sobs subsided and he regained control of himself. Finn squeaked out a limp "sorry" to Josh and got a comforting pat on the shoulder in reply.

"Better?" Josh asked.

"A little bit, thanks. Sorry about the waterworks. If I did that in front of any of them," and pointed towards the outside of the building, "I would be in real trouble right now."

"Hey man, I totally get it," Josh told him. "I don't know how I would have survived if I was in your shoes. I give you tons of credit for still being here. But we don't have a lot of time left before they come back. Tell me, what do you want to do? How can I help you out?"

"I honestly have no idea. There's no way I could last out there on my own. I need the protection of the group." Casting his eyes down, he confessed, "I guess I also need protection from the group." Looking back up at Josh he asked, "If you don't mind, I'll just stick close to you until I figure it out."

"Sounds like a solid plan," Josh replied.

Feeling both relieved and emotionally spent, Finn tagged along with Josh. They discovered the drugs locked in a cabinet behind the doctor's desk and Josh used his tactical knife to pry the metal doors apart enough to grip them and bend them outward.

"I'm glad we found these before the others did," Josh told Finn. "Last thing we need is to introduce hardcore drugs into the situation."

"What should we do?" Finn asked. "They'll be back soon."

"Here," Josh answered, pulling bottles of pills out and collecting them in the crook of his arm. "Grab these and hide them in the ceiling panels in one of the other rooms. I'll keep just enough for Murph."

Finn grabbed the doctor's "in/out" baskets from the desk and dumped its contents on the floor, then took the pills from Josh and filled the baskets. There were bottles of Vicodin, Percocet, Roxanol, and Phenobarbitol, among others. Finn couldn't believe the fortune of medication he was given and was tempted to sneak one of the bottles for himself for insurance purposes, but the implied trust that Josh had in him and their recent bonding made him rethink it. Finn decided that he would trust Josh and see where it took him before he resorted to other means. He took the pills into an empty examination room and hid them in the ceiling.

He rejoined Josh who was busy at Murph's bedside, reading the dosage instructions on the liquid morphine. Murphy was still unconscious, and even though Finn hated the injured man immensely he still couldn't help but feel a little sympathy for Murph's condition.

"Says we need to put four drops under his tongue every hour," Josh read. He looked at Finn. "Mind holding his mouth open while I drip it?"

Looking down at Murphy Finn said, "Not really. Can't you just drip it through that hole?"

"Sure, why not," Josh laughed and put the dropper over the cheek hole. He squeezed out the correct dosage under Murph's exposed tongue.

They both watched speechless as the tongue wiggled. It seemed to seek out the liquid and suck it in. Finn got goose bumps, hunched his shoulders, and shook his head side to side. "That's fucking gross."

"This dude's a goner," Josh replied. "There's no way in hell he's making it, not with all that damage."

Finn heard someone coming through the infirmary entrance. "They're back."

INFIRMARY (JOSH)

Josh was glad he was able to reach out to Finn and that he was in a position to offer the guy some protection from the other men. He would try and do what he could. They were standing next to Murph, Josh still holding the medicine dropper, when the inmates returned from their scavenging run. Ben Franklin's bulk filled the hallway as he marched in and walked up to Josh. The rest of the men spread out and started pilfering the clinic. Josh noted that there weren't as many men compared to the number that left.

"How did it go, Ben?"

"Good and bad, Josh. I'll tell you the bad first." Ben looked over at Murph and turned away, wincing. "First thing we did was go to the commissary to see about the food situation. We cleared the main galley and the food prep areas easily enough because they were empty. Then, I guess because no one was in there, some of the fellas relaxed. And guess what?" Ben asked, and then answered his own question. "They opened the walk-in. Just opened it without checking to see what might be inside."

Ben shook his head. "There were three of those motherfuckers in there. Came barging out and attacked us." At this, Ben held up his arm and pulled his sleeve up. There were several large semi-circular bruises on it. They were puffed up and leaking blood. "One of them bit me through my shirt." He put his sleeve back down. "Here's the bad news. We lost four of our guys. None of us are trained to fight as a unit, so these crazy assholes panicked and shot wild. They did some of that friendly-fire shit." Ben shook his head in dismay as he recalled the battle. "There's more. Three more guys kept their guns and took off. They pulled the ambulance over next to the wall and jumped over. Said they couldn't wait and were going to look for their families on their own."

"Man, I wasn't expecting that," Josh said. "We might still be okay, if nobody else leaves."

Ben thought a moment. "Yeah, maybe, but I want you to know I'm not a babysitter. I'll try and keep things going with you, but some of these men have their own ideas."

"Ben, I don't hold you responsible. We're all lucky to just be alive and I totally appreciate what you're doing." He paused. "Shit. We just lost seven men. That didn't take long, did it?"

"Nope," was all Ben could say.

Josh perked up. "Oh, wait, you mentioned good news. What is it?"

"There are two walk-ins in the commissary. Since the power is still on all of the cold food is okay. There's enough meat and frozen goods in those coolers to feed a prison full of people for a while and there's less than ten of us left. Not only that, the stockroom is full. That means if we stay here we can last a good long while. Even if the power goes, we can still survive on the dry goods."

"Huh," Josh said. "I never thought about it that way, just staying here. Makes sense. The walls and fences can keep people out just as easily as keeping them in."

He put the syringe down and declared, "We need to have a meeting. Gather up the men."

INFIRMARY (FINN)

Finn wasn't too upset when he heard that seven of the men were gone. With the social structure of the prison gone, he hoped that the remaining guys would start to see him more as a person than as something to be despised. To that end, he would do his best to contribute and hope to fit in. Finn felt lucky in one regard: None of the men from his block made it back from the commissary. Whether they were dead or they jumped the wall, he didn't care. It only mattered that they were gone because the fewer people who personally knew who he was before, the better off he was. Murph was the only one left who had actually witnessed and contributed to Finn's humiliation and at the moment Murph had other, more serious, issues to worry about. The rest only knew or suspected second-hand, which might be enough to make a difference.

Josh and Ben walked over to the where some of the men were sitting against the wall, having ransacked the clinic without finding anything they wanted. Finn heard that Josh and Ben were getting ready to call a meeting to decide what happened next and he started walking that way too. On the way by Murph's gurney he noticed the syringe Josh had left lying next to the injured Murph. Finn looked up. Josh and Ben had their backs to him and no one else was paying him any attention.

In a sudden surge of self-preservation Finn grabbed the syringe and jammed it through Murph's open cheek hole. He depressed the remaining Morphine down Murph's throat, quickly set the syringe back down where he had found it, and walked over to the others as quickly as he could without seeming obvious. He caught up to the two men as Josh started speaking.

Just then Murph started struggling for breath, loud enough for the whole room to hear. Murph was sitting upright with his mouth opened impossibly wide, gasping like a fish. Josh hurried over followed by the rest of the men and Finn was pulled along. He watched as Josh reached the table, looked down at the empty syringe, and palmed it. No one else saw the cover-up.

Sweating with relief Finn joined the others in watching Murph die. The faceless inmate was clearly suffering. One of the men whispered, "Poor bastard." Murph turned towards the voice, causing the men to back up. His eyes were bulging and his fingers clenched spasmodically.

The wheezing for air stopped suddenly and Murph died, contorted and frozen in a bizarre human 'L' shape. Ben reached over to check his neck for a pulse as Murph's body leaned away and spilled over onto the floor.

The sound Murph's head made as it imploded on the floor broke the spell the men were under. Most of them jumped back yelling "oh shit" and "aaah!" afraid that some of Murph was going to splash on them. A few laughed despite themselves, which triggered a contagious response. Within moments everybody's head was tipped back in laughter and they were roaring and slapping each other on the backs.

Finn wanted to laugh despite being the real reason Murph was leaking out onto the floor. He looked over to Josh who was laughing as loud as any of the others, even mimicking a wide-eyed Murph tipping over, creating new outbursts. When Finn caught Josh's eye, all Josh did was shrug in a 'what can you do' gesture and kept on laughing. Finn finally joined in. He couldn't remember the last time he had laughed and he did it hard and loud.

Eventually the laughter eased. Tears were wiped away accompanied by the catching of breath. "Oh, gosh," Ben muttered. He took off his glasses and wiped them on his shirt. "That sure was some crazy shit." Everyone agreed.

"Well, now that Murph's gone, let's get back to it. Team meeting," Josh said.

He walked back to the meeting area and the rest followed. The men were grabbing chairs, subconsciously arranging them in a circle. Finn grabbed his and when he went to squeeze in, the men on either side made room for him without complaint and without dirty looks. The simple gestures of acceptance went unnoticed by the men that made them, but to Finn it was huge. He put his head down and smiled to himself. He was being accepted.

INFIRMARY (JOSH)

Josh saw the men accommodate Finn and decided that from now on he would only intervene on the guy's behalf as a last resort. He seemed to be doing fine on his own, the combination of the day's events and changed circumstances working in the young man's favor.

Everyone was looking at him expectantly so Josh got started. "I'm sure you guys know why we're having a huddle. There are only seven of us left in the entire prison and we need to decide what we're going to do next. But first, show of hands from everyone that intends to stay with the group." Josh put his arms out a placating gesture and said, "No one is going to say anything if anyone wants to go out on their own. It's just better if we all know we can count on each other. If you want to go, we'll load you up with whatever you need and nothing bad will be said about it. So, who's staying?"

Josh looked around and grinned. Everyone's hands were up.

BUCKINGHAM GATE, LONDON

The car trip from the BBC Broadcasting House to Birdcage Walk where the Wellington Barracks were located took less than ten minutes. A lack of traffic and being waved through checkpoints were contributing factors to the speedy transit. The route took Walter past an eerily empty Hyde Park and he figured that it would be some time until people starting freely enjoying themselves again.

Before turning right onto the barracks grounds Walter thought it ironic that he could see the very spot where he and Luis had set up their broadcast equipment earlier that morning. It wasn't even nightfall and he had somehow been transformed into a mid-rank army officer on his way to a high-level operational briefing. He smiled to himself. Despite the circumstances he was more excited than he had been in years; in the past he had been scared while on many of his assignments, but rarely was he excited.

The driver spoke up from the front. "Sir, I have to let you off at the designated debarkation area and you'll have to walk in."

"Thank you, that's fine," Walter replied. Being formally called "Sir" was new to him too but he supposed he should get used to it. He looked ahead at a massive staging area. Tanks, trucks, and soldiers were everywhere. It was strange to see actual troops because the barrack's grounds were normally packed with sightseers there to see the ceremonial guards.

The car stopped at the military checkpoint turnaround and Walter opened his door before one of the soldiers could perform the courtesy for him. He stepped out and was met by the checkpoint commander, a young Second Lieutenant with a rifle slung over his shoulder. From his time covering the military Walter recognized the rifle as the standard issue SA80. The young man saluted Walter and said, "We've been expecting you, Colonel. This way please."

Walter had never saluted in his life so he didn't return the courtesy, but nodded instead and said, "Thank you, Lieutenant."

He stuck close while the man wended left and right around tents, troops and vehicles. They eventually ended up at the simple columniated entrance. The lieutenant spoke with the soldiers manning the access post and turned to

Walter. "Colonel, these men will take you from here. Good day, sir." He saluted again and was gone.

The man who greeted Walter this time was a major. He smiled and did a semi-formal salute before extending his hand. "It's a pleasure to meet you, Colonel Doucet. I'm Major Ackerman. I'll show you inside to the briefing. I've been temporarily assigned to you to facilitate your transition into the military. I hope you don't mind."

"No, I don't mind at all. I welcome it," Walter smiled back.

The major handed him a belt wrapped bundle. "This is part of your new issue, Colonel. Let me know if you need any help with it," he offered.

Looking down at the bundle Walter saw that it was a pistol and holster. He was expecting one of the older Browning nine millimeter pistols, or maybe even its replacement, the P226 SIG Sauer, but instead the major had handed him the very newest issue, a Glock 17. Walter whistled. They had only been put into service within the last six months.

Walter smiled. "Very good. Thank you, Major Ackerman."

"You're welcome, sir." The major returned the smile and indicated the front door. "Shall we proceed?"

Nodding, Walter put the holster around his waist and buckled it on while they walked. Before he holstered the new firearm Walter held it up to the light and admired the weapon's clean lines and its new gun oil smell.

The major kept a brisk clip and Walter had to increase his gait to keep up. The hallways they traversed were packed with men and women, both in uniform and not, moving gear or having loud discussions. The noise and level of activity was infectious and Walter felt his adrenaline spike. By the time the major led him into the barracks auditorium he felt more alert than he had been in months. The last time he had felt this way was during his latest assignment overseas, serving in Afghanistan as an embedded journalist. Being around tense and motivated people was contagious.

The auditorium was crowded with small groups talking animatedly amongst themselves. Walter overheard snippets of conversation and everyone was discussing the recent crisis. The major led him down the front to one of the groups and presented Walter to them. "May introduce Lieutenant-Colonel

Doucet, the new General Staff Adjunct for Information and Public Affairs. Colonel, this is your new staff."

A group of three men and a woman wearing military uniforms nodded at Walter. "I apologize that we don't have time at the moment for proper introductions," Major Ackerman apologized, glancing at his watch. "The presentation is set to start. We should rendezvous at your office after the briefing, Colonel."

Just then a high pitched squealing came over the speakers. On stage, a nervous young man in a suit and tie wrestled with a microphone mounted on a podium. A few more short squeaks of adjustment and the ear wracking noise quit. The young man hurried off stage while everyone in the auditorium found seats.

The lights dimmed and a projector beamed a slideshow presentation to a large screen at the back of the stage. Walter smiled at the barely contained groaning from the audience; it was the universal reaction for the agonizing, slide-based presentation method. The intro screen read "Operation Ophir Ridge - General Staff - Eyes Only" in large red block letters.

For several minutes nothing more happened and in the interval the audience chatter picked up again. Finally, a mousy looking man in an ill-fitting lab coat walked out to the stage from the left. He carried an armful of papers and a round white object, which he set on the podium. He adjusted the microphone, lowering it several inches, before pushing his glasses up on his face and looking out into the audience.

Walter was close enough to see the small man gulp as he took in the size of his audience. The scientist was clearly not used to addressing large groups of people. After rifling through and rearranging some papers, the man started speaking.

"Uh, good evening everyone," he began. His voice was high pitched and weak. He coughed to clear his throat and read from a sheet of paper. "My name is Doctor Oberast Kurgen. I am the lead researcher at Cambridge University's Neurosurgery Unit. General Fells has tasked me with giving a short briefing on some recent discoveries linked with the hemispheric event." The doctor shifted his feet nervously. "Before I get to the main content, I would like to apologize in advance for my lack of presentation polish. This brief was compiled in pieces over the last several hours, largely because we've been constantly uncovering new information. It's quite groundbreaking, actually."

The more Doctor Kurgen spoke, the faster he talked. He was obviously excited about something and the listeners picked up on it. They began to lean forward, waiting for him to get to the point. "First slide please," he said to someone off stage.

Using a laser pointer the doctor highlighted the picture of a cruise liner. "This is the passenger ship Adriano, operating out of Oranjestad, Aruba. Her manifest listed a combined four thousand and eighty crew and passengers. Shortly after the event, her captain issued a mayday and activated a distress positioning beacon." He paused, adjusted his glasses again, and looked up at the audience. "Eleven hours ago she was found dead in the water, roughly three hundred nautical miles east of Nassau, by the HMS Illustrious Expeditionary Force."

Doctor Kurgen sighed and pushed his heavy glasses back up. "When the military boarding party hit the deck it was immediately attacked by what are now being called 'LCBs,' or Lesser Cognitive Beings. After a brief firefight the bridge was cleared, and a remote assessment of the status of the liner's remaining passengers was conducted via the ship's closed circuit system."

More slides appeared of the liner's passageways and decks filled with dead bodies or living LCBs. "It was determined that the entire ship had been overrun and that no unaffected, or what we have termed 'cognitives', survived."

He flipped to pictures taken on scene of LCBs in nets and in restraints. "The boarding party captured twenty seven of the LCBs and flew them directly to our Cambridge facility, where they have been undergoing intense anthropological and neurological study by myself and my team."

Doctor Kurgen signaled offstage and two men in lab coats wheeled out a cage containing a naked teenage boy. The boy was an obvious LCB; his face was tight and his brows were furrowed with a fierce intensity. The boy fixedly studied the members of the audience.

The captive looked clearly angry but was placid, and Walter wondered how they kept him calm. From everything he saw and knew about the LCBs they went crazy at the sight of regular people. Walter turned to the major and whispered, "They must have it sedated," and the major nodded back in agreement.

The doctor continued. "I know what you are all thinking. I must have lobotomized this young man because he isn't enraged and trying to attack every one of us, but that wasn't necessary. I won't bore you with the all of painful details, but the control group we captured contained seventeen males and ten females with ages ranging from prepubescent to elderly. This young man in the cage is one of only two LCBs we captured under the age of puberty. Coincidently, those two are the only LCBs that don't exhibit enraged behavior."

The boy in the cage continued to stare at the audience. At one point he looked directly at Walter. The boy's intense stare made Walter uncomfortable and he didn't know exactly why except that it was a vague feeling of being scanned and analyzed. Walter broke the stare, deciding to focus on the podium instead.

The doctor continued. "Before moving on I have been directed to announce a caveat and a caution. First, LCBs have been given the classification designation, 'Hostile Combatant: No Restrictions' by the military, a special category created specifically for beings affected by the event. As such, limits normally in place to legally protect captured combatants have been relaxed."

Appearing contrite, the doctor spoke softly into the microphone. "That was the caveat. Now here is the warning: Many, if not all of you, are going to feel uncomfortable with what I am about to show you, but please keep in mind that everything from this point on has been deemed morally, ethically and legally justified. It is vital that we understand what we are dealing with before we enter any of the affected areas."

The slide transitioned forward. There were pictures of autopsies, exposed body cavities, removed organs, sawn off skulls, and more. The audience gasped and some people yelled outright. Doctor Kurgen stood at the podium and waited. The noise eventually waned and he began speaking again. "There were some surprising insights when we conducted our studies of the LCBs. Our original mandate was to investigate what caused the transformation of these former cognitives and to possibly reverse its effects. The challenge was intriguing, because besides some obvious outward changes to their appearance, primarily in the face, LCBs could pass as normal cognitives."

He held up the white object he had brought out with him. It was a human skull. The doctor detached and removed the top half. "This is a normal human skull," he explained, tilting the open cavity towards the people seated in front of him. "Without going into detail, the brain is divided into two hemispheres joined by a bundle of axons called the corpus callosum. In cognitives, it normally looks like this."

A new slide showed a normal looking brain joined by a smooth pink feature, vaguely tongue shaped. "In LCBs it looked like this." A picture came up that initially looked like the same thing, but it wasn't smooth. It was split and ruptured in places. It resembled a microwaved hot dog.

"As you can see here the corpus callosum has undergone extreme gyrencephalization, a process similar to cortical folding. Unfortunately, the corpus callosum is comprised of tissue that is too rigid to survive the process intact and when it ruptures it destroys the pathway between the two hemispheres of the brain. The rupture, from what our early research indicates, also damages the neocortex, which controls functions typically associated with intelligent behavior. In essence, it transforms the people affected into raging, instinctual brutes, incapable of reason."

The crowd got noisy as people discussed this with each other. After half a minute, the briefing continued.

"Yes, they become beasts, operating only on instinct. But," the doctor held up a finger, "there is one more discovery, which leads me to this young man here," he said, pointing to the boy in the cage. "I mentioned that we had two children; this one and a girl. Sad to say, the girl was ill and passed away shortly after arrival from a burst appendix." He looked up and shrugged.

"During her autopsy we did a cranial extraction and made an amazing discovery." A slide popped up showing three brain cross sections. "Look here," the doctor said, using his laser pointer. "This is a normal brain, with a normal smooth corpus callosum connecting the two hemispheres, and here is an adult LCB brain with the ruptured connection."

Everyone was leaning forward to get a closer look at the third cross section the laser was highlighting. "Notice that something extraordinary has happened," the doctor said, "to the smaller brain from the girl LCB. Do you see where the corpus callosum is slightly enlarged and has folded over into itself multiple times, increasing the surface area exponentially? Also notice the extreme cortical folding and encephalization of the two hemispheres. It opens the bandwidth, so to speak, of the neural pathways by several factors from what we here sitting in the audience currently enjoy. Even in this dead brain we can see enhanced connections forming as the brain accommodates. In this girl's brain we have determined that the encephalization quotient, or EQ, is nearly thirty, roughly four times that of a normal human. Speaking plainly, they have quadrupled the analytical thinking and advanced reasoning potential of everyone in this room, us normal cognitives."

He put the pointer down. "I cannot conclusively say what this portends, but what we are seeing here is essentially a whole new species of human. Right now we aren't certain where on the evolutionary tree the new species falls; lower, laterally, or higher. We think the process is still in the middle of stabilizing. What we do know is that children are not affected by the event in the same way as the adults, and that changes everything. Thank you."

Picking up his papers and his skull, the doctor gestured for his assistants to wheel the cage off of the stage. He followed closely behind them and disappeared from view without saying anything more. Within seconds of his departure everyone was out of their seats, loudly discussing what was just disclosed. Walter stayed seated and thought about the implications of trying to take back the Americas while fighting off both the LCBs and hostile soldiers, but sparing the undamaged children. To him, preserving the children was what was most important. They represented something never seen before.

The lights dimmed and the crowd quieted. They resumed their seats in anticipation. General Fells himself walked out and stood center stage. Without preamble, the general started speaking. "I have assembled all of you here because you represent the core of our reconstruction and defense efforts. Operation Ophir Ridge has outlined the next steps for recovery, but like every operational plan, the further one gets from its roots the more fluid the strategic and tactical goals written down on paper become."

He gestured offstage to where the cage with the boy in it had been rolled off. "While this new discovery puts a wrinkle in how we execute some elements of the plan, our strategic goal, which is to protect our citizens and our way of life, has not budged and it never will. From this point forward things are going to move very quickly, and I fully expect all of you to do your part, and more."

The general stepped away from the podium and began walking around the stage, meeting people's eyes. "The plan calls for the assembly of particular functional areas that align both military and civilian needs and that is why when you look around you, you notice a mixture of both factions. It is a deliberate action that will require some adjustment from all of you and I charge you to make it a short adjustment and move on from it. If you cannot, you will simply be replaced. Every single one of you here was handpicked to be part of my staff corps because of your skillsets and your dedication, but there are others waiting in the wings almost as qualified. Do not let what is happening out there cause you to waver towards our purpose."

Before he departed the general announced, "I'll give everyone a little time for a meet and greet. Branch heads meet with me at 2200 hours for the evening staff meeting." As he turned someone off stage yelled "Attention!" and everyone stood. After he was gone a second command, "Carry on," was issued. Multiple conversations started up at once and people began filing out of the auditorium.

"This way, Colonel Doucet," the major said, leading Walter and the four members of his staff out of the auditorium with the rest of the crowd.

The hallways seemed even busier than before, so it was all Walter could do to follow the major as the man wound his way around groups of people talking and or milling around, or machinery distributing gear and supplies to different offices. They finally arrived at a door identified with a sheet of legal paper and black marker as "IPA Branch Staff".

"Here we are, Colonel," the major intoned. "Information and Public Affairs. Your new home."

Inside five desks were crammed in with a just enough room to squeeze by each one. On top of every desk were two workstations, and every available inch of wall space was covered by flat panel televisions. The televisions were on and most of them showed scenes of military mobilization, rioting, or other scenes of violence.

"The desk furthest back is yours, Colonel," Major Ackerman said. "There's a small conference room across the hall for your shared use, if you have need of it." Pointing to a sheaf of documents on every desk, he told everyone "That should be everything you need to get logged on, as well as where to access the latest operational blogs."

Walter nodded and said, "Okay." Looking at the others, he introduced himself. "I'm Walter Doucet, lately of the BBC Headquarters. I've been an embedded journalist for my entire career, either with the U.N. or with our own troops deployed overseas. My initial understanding of our role is to manage the flow of public information and to maintain international public relations. I've never served in the military so until I get a grip on things, I see myself acting within our group as more of a facilitator and enabler." Pointing to the one woman in the group, Walter asked, "Why don't you go next? Tell us about yourself."

"Yes, Colonel," she answered. She was compact, brown-skinned and unsmiling. "I'm Staff Sergeant Kennett. I am a military media relations expert. Normally, I work for Warrant Officer Smith," and she pointed to the soldier to her right, a balding, thick white man in his mid-thirties.

He stood up. "Oh, yes, how do you do, Colonel? I'm Jacoby Smith, of the Press Corps. Before the event, I oversaw the British Army's press junkets and news feeds. I also edited the Army portion of the 'British Forces News'. Besides Sergeant Kennet I had two other assistants, and I requested that they follow me here: Sergeant Rowbree, translator and IT, and Colour Sergeant Cooper, also a translator as well as media equipment specialist."

The two men nodded and Walter nodded back and smiled.

"Okay then. That will do nicely for now. General Fells mentioned a branch head meeting in," Walter began, checking his watch, "forty two minutes. If you could all catch up on events and give me a briefing at fifteen minutes until, I would appreciate it. Warrant Officer Smith, please dole out the assignments accordingly. I need national and international reactions to the event, open press on military and insurgent activity and recommendations on what gets released to the news outlets. Do your best in the short time we have. I expect we'll get further direction following the briefing." Turning to the major, he asked, "Will you be accompanying me?"

"Yes, of course, Colonel," he answered, smiling. "I am your shadow until further notified."

"Great. Would you mind filling me in on what to expect?"

"Yes, sir. I'd be glad to."

CORNER OF WEST REAGAN PARKWAY AND HILLVIEW WAY, MEDINA, OHIO

Jim and the others huddled next to a backyard shed at the far end of Zoe's street. "Well, that was easy," Saul said. "I guess that car pulled most of the goons out of here."

"Most likely," Vickers replied. "Still, we can't know how many goons stayed behind, especially if they were in the houses. I think the safe bet is still to travel through the backyards because the fences should help block us from view." Turning to Zoe, he asked "How many houses down is your house?"

She thought for a second and said, "I think it's ten or eleven."

"Fuck," Jim exclaimed involuntarily. He looked up and saw everyone staring at him. Zoe especially was giving him the stink eye. "Sorry," he muttered, "but that's a lot of backyards."

Pretending he didn't hear the interruption, Vickers continued. "Everyone clear on the rallying points if things don't work out?" They all nodded. "Great. Let's go."

They headed out in the same order as before, minus Chuck. Vickers looked over the first fence before climbing over. After he disappeared from view, Megan followed and then peeped over and motioned everyone on.

When Jim landed on the grass on the other side he saw an empty doghouse and a dog with a caved-in skull at the end of a lead. Brains and blood were still leaking from it onto the grass. Vickers gestured for them to follow and continued to the opposite end of the yard where they regrouped.

The next yard over was quiet. Jim put his eye to the crack of a fence slat and peeked through. He couldn't see much. Megan hopped up on an overturned wheelbarrow and stuck her eyes over the top. Her hand reached behind her in a thumbs-up and they climbed over all together. They proceeded that way for several more yards until they got to one that had a simple chain link fence wrapped around it.

"That's my yard," Zoe whispered.

Everyone squatted behind some hedges and listened while they took in the surroundings. Jim suspected trouble because the patio door to Zoe's house was wide open and it made sense that if anyone was inside, at least anyone that was normal, they would have closed the door at some point. He looked around and could tell the other four were thinking the same thing. He was all for skipping it, but Saul said, "Well, we didn't come all this way to not know. Might as well check it out."

The relief on Zoe's face was apparent. Jim didn't have any family or friends to worry about, but he supposed that if he did, he would rather know for sure that they didn't make it rather than not know anything at all. Still, it seemed like an unnecessary risk.

Zoe went ahead and leapt the fence, landing silently on the other side. She was followed by Vickers, then Megan, Jim and Saul. They approached the door on their tiptoes. Saul tried to cut in front of Jim, but Jim kept the smaller man behind him with a dirty look and a shake of his head. Saul looked confused, but Jim didn't feel like explaining to Saul that he was buffer bait, something to get stomped first during an attack from behind while Jim sprinted to freedom.

The group took station on both sides of the open door. The curtains were torn down and they could see into the house all the way to the far wall. Nothing moved. Vickers showed everyone his watch and put up two fingers, a sign that they would wait at the patio entrance two minutes before heading in. Zoe sighed and shook her head impatiently but squatted down anyway.

Time passed. Jim's legs were sore from holding a deep crouch and he felt a cramp coming on. He tried straightening his right leg without standing and involuntarily broke wind. The passage of the gas reverberated off the denim stretched across his cheeks and was extremely loud in the afternoon quiet. For Jim, the next few seconds blurred into slow motion and every nuance of his accidental act burned into his brain like a video recording.

First, every head turned in his direction. He saw Zoe's face twist into a deep frown, like Jim had just deposited something foul and fecal into her open mouth; her tongue came out as if trying to push it back out. Vickers and Megan were trying not to laugh, and Saul, who was behind him, instinctively scurried backwards. At the same time, every chirping bird in the area went silent, alert to danger. To Jim the birds did it on purpose to give his fart access to the entire sound spectrum and to acquire an echo. Maybe he imagined the echo, but when he later recollected that exact moment, that was how he recalled it.

Second, his flatulence broke something loose inside the house and a scurrying noise came through an open second floor window. Everyone looked up to see an athletic black guy parkour jump out of the window and into space. He landed into a graceful roll and then was up and sprinting for the back fence.

"Owen!" Zoe yelled to the retreating figure. Jim flinched at the yell, but the man braked to a stop, dropped into a crouch, and looked back.

"Sis?" he asked, smiling from ear to ear. He hurried back to the group. The two siblings hugged.

Dreading the attention Zoe's yell would attract, Jim said "We should move."

Vickers nodded and the group started back the way they had come. They hopped the chain link fence and were almost out of the yard when they heard the noise of a window opening.

"Wait!" a female voice called, trying to both yell and whisper at the same time.

The voice sounded cute, so Jim, who was leading the retreat, braked. He looked up at the window and saw a pretty blonde girl leave the window. Fifteen seconds later she was opening a patio door and running out to them.

"Holy moly! Thanks!" she said excitedly. She had a backpack on and was carrying an aluminum baseball bat. Jim immediately forgot about wooing Zoe and switched his infatuation over to the new girl. After the fart incident Jim was pretty sure he lost his chance with Zoe anyway.

Losing himself in the moment, he was about to introduce himself when Vickers pushed him and said, "Let's go, Romeo."

"Heh," Jim answered embarrassedly and started off again. Having already cleared the yards on the way to Zoe's house gave him the confidence to take the lead, but then he heard the familiar whooping coming from all directions and his confidence ebbed. He had to remind himself not to panic again. It was only luck last time that determined he got lucky and made it into the drainpipe while Chuck died. Jim didn't want a next time.

Since he was in front it was up to him to get the group out of trouble and he wanted to prove to himself and everyone else that he could contribute to the team, that the last time was a fluke event. He also wanted to impress the new girl. He allowed himself a small smile as he thought about how brave he probably seemed to her. To amp it up a little he pointed to Saul and said, "You, little man. Cover the rear."

He turned back to leap the second fence. Behind him he heard Saul mutter, "What the fuck?" in a confused voice. Jim knew he would pay for that remark later and hoped he got enough mileage out of it to make it worth whatever Saul was going to do to him.

Jim knew the trick was to get out of sight before the goons saw them. He scanned the yard they were running through but didn't see any obvious hiding places, like a shed or hedges, so he kept going. He climbed over the next fence a little slower than he climbed previous one. It was taller, but he was also getting winded. Megan hit the ground at the same time he did and his ego bruised a little at how nimbly she landed. Megan was an older woman and she was physically outperforming him.

Then Owen passed them all up and took the lead. He veered off to the side of the next house and motioned for everyone to follow him. He went straight for a large camper parked in the driveway. Jim wanted to cry out that it was probably locked, but Owen reached the camper first and reached under the vehicle's frame to retrieve a key.

Owen quickly unlocked the door and swung it wide. The man went up several notches in Jim's estimation when he held the door for everyone else before piling in himself. Selfless acts like that would only help Jim out in the long run, because selfless now equaled dead.

Once in everyone sat on the camper floor to catch their breath while outside the whooping and the growling increased in volume. No one spoke for the several minutes it took the goons to swarm the area looking for them. Eventually the goons lost interest or forgot why they were there and wandered off. Vickers called a huddle.

"This area is reinfested now, so we have to be careful. By the way, it's nice to meet you Owen, and thanks for bailing us out. You're a quick thinker."

Owen smiled at the compliment. Zoe was holding his hand and she brought it up to her lips and kissed it.

Vickers turned to the blonde and asked, smiling, "What's your name, new girl?"

"Bettina," she answered, still a little out of breath. "Nice to meet you guys. You sure saved my bacon back there. I ran out of food a few days ago and thought I was a goner."

Everyone quietly said their names and shook hands with the new girl. When he introduced himself, Saul gave Jim a dirty look and said, "Hi, I'm Saul, the 'little man' of the group. And I don't shit my pants like some people," he added, jerking his thumb at Jim.

Bettina looked at Jim's reddening face, confused at the inside comment. Everyone else except for Owen seemed amused.

"Low blow, dude," Jim whispered.

"Now we're even," Saul replied, patting Jim on the back.

Vickers let the moment happen, and then said, "Glad to see you guys work things out, but now we need to get out of here and back to the store. If we can, I think we should find a truck or car, unless someone has a better idea."

"A car or truck would just lead them back to the store with us. We should try and avoid that," Megan advised.

"She has a point there," Saul added.

"What store are you guys talking about?" Bettina asked.

"The Klimps superstore," Zoe answered. "A bunch of us used to work there. It's safe"

"Awesome. I've been stuck in that house since this whole thing started. A superstore full of food sounds like heaven," the blonde said, looking up at the camper ceiling dreamily. Then she realized that there might be food supplies in the cupboards, and became distracted, quietly opening the lower doors looking for a morsel.

While her attention was elsewhere Jim checked her out. She had a nice body but was a little young, maybe in her early twenties. She also seemed a little fluffy in the brain, but to Jim that just meant he had a better shot with her because intelligent women were normally repelled by him. Megan was the only smart woman he could recall that ever showed an interest, but he chalked that up to her age and the fact that he had saved her life. He kept hoping that Vickers would step up and claim Megan for himself, but the former soldier hadn't done so yet. Maybe Vickers had a wife somewhere or was gay.

"Hey. Jim." He heard finger snapping and came out of his daydreaming. He noticed that he was still looking at Bettina's ass and probably had been for a while with everyone watching. Owen laughed softly and Jim reflexively checked his mouth for drool. Zoe shook her head and Jim knew that he now definitely lost any shot with her he might have had. He was left with no choice; he had to go all in on Team Bettina.

The afternoon waned while the group rested and thought of a way out.

At one point Zoe asked Owen "How did you know that there would be a key to the camper under the door?"

Owen smiled to himself, but dropped it when he met Zoe's eyes. "Mrs. Snyder," he said by way of explanation.

"Who? You mean Derek's mom?" Zoe asked, confused. "Why would she show you the key to...," then went quiet as she and the rest of the group mulled over Owen's affair with a woman they had never met.

Finally, Owen spoke up. "We can't sit here forever. Those things aren't going away and we'll just rot away in here."

"He's right." Saul said. "We'll move when it gets dark. Goons can't see any better than us. I think we should go to one of the rendezvous points. They're closer than the Klimps and we'll have more options there."

"Which one were you thinking?" Megan asked.

"The car dealership. It's possible that ..." he paused, then held up a finger. He took out his phone and put it to his ear. "What's up?" he asked whoever was calling. "No, Ray, we're fine. Well, kinda, but we will be fine. Yeah, everyone except Chuck, but don't tell Jack that yet. I'll break it to him when we get back." Silence while Saul listened, then "Okay. That's good. Yeah, we got Zoe's brother. Plus, some girl Jim likes." Saul smiled at the horrified look on Jim's face. Bettina looked up from where she had nodded off and said, "Huh?"

"Okay. See you when we see you," Saul signed off. He put the phone back in his pocket, looked at Jim and said, "Oops. I guess I let that slip out."

The rest of the group chuckled, even Bettina. Jim decided that the only way to get along was to go along, so he pretended to enjoy the moment. He was glad he did when he glanced over and saw that Bettina was checking him out. She smiled at him and he blushed.

Dusk came and darkness soon followed.

"Saul, are we about ready?" Vickers asked.

"Yeah, but before we go everyone grab a drink or a bite to eat or do whatever else you need to do. Use the toilet if you have to, but no flushing and no stinkies unless you're going last."

"I'll go last," Megan quickly volunteered out of the grey darkness.

"Okay, let's get to it then."

Almost everyone used the restroom before Megan went in. Before she did her business, Megan whispered out to everyone, "Apologize in advance."

Jim ate an energy bar while Megan used the restroom. He thought about the difficulty and embarrassment of dropping a deuce in front of people you just met, maybe even someone you liked, all the while maintaining stealth so you didn't piss off a bunch of raging former humans who would love nothing better than to catch you with your pants around your ankles.

Zoe watched Jim eating to the sound of voiding bowels with a look of disgust on her face. Then she almost lost it when Bettina leaned over and asked, "Can I have some, Jim? I'm starving here," and took a bite when he offered it to her. Both Saul and Vickers smiled and shook their heads.

Megan came out and quickly shut the door behind her. "We should go now," she said in obvious embarrassment. "Seriously."

Vickers helped her out. "You heard the lady, time to go."

The door opened outward on quiet hinges. Jim hadn't realized how stale the air inside the camper had become until fresh air rushed in. He breathed it in, instantly refreshed.

The night sky illuminated the door frame. Vickers spent some time at the camper entrance listening for any sounds of movement. Finally satisfied, he stepped out and waited near the back of the camper for the other six to do the same.

Some of the streetlights were still on, removing the option of easier traveling along the streets and sidewalks. They headed towards the backyard strung out in a line; Vickers, Jim, Bettina, Zoe, Owen, Megan and Saul. Vickers scouted the yards over the fences before climbing over, followed by the rest. Twice, when the fences were too high to peek over, Jim got on all fours so Vickers could stand on his back and check things out.

They got to the end of the street without a problem and breathed a collective sigh of relief when they saw that the lights on Reagan Parkway were out. They turned left back the way they had come and took to the center of the road. Off to the right were large empty fields while the left was lined with cramped houses, an area they avoided earlier. Up ahead in the distance and on the right of the road Jim could see stadium lights marking where the car dealership was.

It was strangely quiet. The world seemed empty of life even though it wasn't. It was just different. Not even worse, at least to Jim's way of thinking. It was without a doubt more dangerous, but along with that it was more exciting too.

Before the group got close enough to be seen in the light given off by the dealership, Vickers led them off the road and into the fields. The going was a little rougher. Sometime recently a farmer had tilled deep furrows into the earth and the lack of rain made the peaks and troughs solid and difficult to navigate in the near total darkness. Jim walked along the tops, stepping into the footprints made by Vickers.

They were coming up along the rear of the dealership when a scream came from deep inside the housing on the opposite side of the road, immediately answered by a muted whooping emanating from the same area. From somewhere close by Jim heard brush snapping and the answering whoops from goons further away. Goons were cutting across the fields to meld with the fray brought on by the scream. Jim and the others dove to the dirt and for the next minute the field came alive as goons in singles and small groups raced across the open space and crossed the road, anxious to vent their rage on a living victim.

One of the goons ran by about fifteen feet in front of where the group was hiding and it must have caught sight of them because it slowed and looked to turn back when a fresh wave of whoops caused it to change its mind.

Without a second glance it resumed its previous course and redoubled its speed before it finally disappeared over the road.

After a minute the noise subsided and Vickers stood up. He looked back and whispered, "Run!" and took off.

When Jim arrived at the back of the dealership with the others, he looked around to see what they had run from. "Was something chasing us," he asked Vickers in a low voice.

"No, I wanted to use whatever distracted them to get us here before they wandered back."

"Okay," Jim replied.

"Good call," Megan added, then asked "So how do we get in? This place must be alarmed. If we set if off, those things will be here before we could escape or get inside."

Saul started chuckling and everyone turned to look at him, wondering what he found so amusing. "I'm sorry. It's not funny. It's just that we should have thought of that before we picked this place. I should have thought of that. I feel like an idiot." He slapped his palm on his forehead and muttered, "Doh."

Owen was looking at all the circuit boxes mounted to the back wall. He grabbed and tugged experimentally at one of the thick cables that fed into them. "Can we cut the power?"

"Nah, that won't work," Saul replied. "If this place is anything like Klimps, and I suspect that it is, cutting the power will set off an alarm also."

The group spread out looking for another way in when Saul called them back in a low voice. "Wait. Just a sec."

When they regrouped, Saul said "I'm right, but hopefully I might also be wrong. I'm pretty sure that if we cut the power, it will set off an alarm. But, what if it sets off an alarm at the police station, or at the alarm company that monitors it and not an audible alarm right here."

"How sure are you about that? Are you one hundred percent sure?" Vickers asked.

"Nope, I'm not one hundred percent. I might go sixty five or seventy. I'm just putting it out there. Plus, we don't actually have to go inside, we can always just keep going."

"What if we just steal a truck from the front?" Zoe asked. "I mean, that's why we're here, right?

"The keys are most likely inside the building," Megan explained. "There's no way to hotwire one of these newer cars. And I bet all the cars are alarmed too, so we definitely need the keys."

"I have an idea," Owen volunteered. "I run the hundred meters in under eleven seconds." He pushed Zoe's hand down as she tried to stop what she thought he was going to do. "You guys took a huge risk coming to get me, so let me take one for you all. Everyone hide in the trees over there," he suggested, pointing past the fields behind the dealership, "and I'll pull the power. If an alarm goes off, I'll be gone in a flash." Owen snapped his finger to emphasize his point.

"No, Owen, it's too risky. You heard Saul, it's only seventy percent. Please!" Zoe begged and turned to the others. "Please don't let him do this. I just got him back."

Vickers spoke up. "Zoe, everyone here took chances to come and get Owen and it's his call if he wants to help this way. If it makes you feel better we could have a vote anyway, to see if getting inside is worth the risk. What do you think, Saul?"

"If we get a vehicle we could be back to the Klimps in less than ten minutes, versus dodging these goons all night and maybe into the morning," Saul explained. "I'm not saying Owen should pull the power, I'm saying that if we could get in and get a hold of the keys to a truck my vote is 'yes'."

Jim, Megan and Vickers agreed with Saul. Zoe was opposed. Bettina abstained. "I don't know," she said. "I'm new to the group so maybe I shouldn't have a vote. I think I'll vote nothing."

"Bah," Saul said. "If you're with us, you vote. You can't be here and not contribute." He gave her a dirty look.

She pouted and gave Saul duck lips. "Fine, then. I vote 'whatever'."

"You can't..." Saul started, getting spun up, but he was interrupted by Megan. "Leave her alone, Saul. I'll have a talk with her later."

Owen grabbed at the cable again. "So we're good? I take care of the power and split if the alarm goes off?"

Saul shrugged. "Sounds like a plan." He looked around. "Unless there's a better idea."

Only Zoe responded. "This is bullshit," she said, loudly. "He shouldn't have to do this!"

"Fucking hold it down Zoe!" Saul hissed through cracked and rotten teeth. "You're going to get us all killed if you don't zip it. It's his call and we all voted. That's how things work now."

Zoe was seething, but nodded before shaking her head. "Not happy," she muttered under her breath.

Jim saw Vickers slowly and quietly slide his tanto knife back into its sheath and knew that Vickers had been prepared to go Rambo on Zoe if she hadn't quieted down. When Vickers noticed that Jim had seen him, the former sergeant smiled and shrugged. Jim shrugged back.

Owen was pulling on the thick cable, testing its tensile strength. "Okay. You guys go hide," he instructed everyone. "I'll give you a few minutes before I snatch this bitch from the wall and we ride out of here."

Megan had to put an arm around Zoe's shoulder and pull on her to get her to leave her brother. Saul and Vickers both gave Owen a pat on the back and Jim gave him a fist bump. Bettina shadowed Jim and gave Owen a fist bump too, then surprised Jim by grabbing and holding his hand as they headed for the tree line.

It only took a minute for everyone to find a hiding spot where they could still see the back wall of the dealership. Owen was hidden in the shadows. They waited.

The huge arc shower caught them all by surprise. For a brief instant Jim could see Owen in the flash, aiming the exposed power cable away from his body like a roman candle. Then, a loud pop, followed by complete darkness as all of the primary lights at the dealership faded out before the dimmer, battery-powered egress lights activated. After a few seconds it was apparent to everyone that there wasn't going to be an audible alarm.

Zoe was the first one up and running for the rear wall, anxious to see to her brother. Even though he had only met Owen that afternoon, Jim liked the guy and hoped that he made it okay. He was a useful addition to the group.

A bright four foot arc sparked along the wall where Owen had been, forcing everyone to shield their eyes. Jim was looking right at it and was temporarily blinded. Through squinted eyes he saw an electric finger lick out from the live power line and tap Zoe on the shoulder. After he clamped his eyes shut to clear them the ghost images of her spasms remained.

He heard an "Ah, shit" from in front of him. Then he smelled it. Singed hair and a semi-appetizing scent similar to processed cheese dripped onto a red-hot toaster element. His gorge rose when he realized what it was.

When he was able to see again he saw Zoe's body curled up in a fetal position about twenty feet from where the cable came out of the ground. Her right arm was distended and malformed. It looked like she was pointing back in the direction they had just come from and Jim resisted the urge to look. After a few seconds he looked anyway, but Zoe wasn't pointing to anything exciting, just an empty field with some footprints stamped into it.

Owen was bent over her body, sniffling and softly weeping. Megan was clearly upset too, but Vickers and Saul were looking away in an effort to not be seen not being very upset. Bettina let go of Jim's hand and was going to go over and ogle, but Jim pulled her back and whispered, "Don't get any closer. You might get shocked, too."

Her eyes went wide and she made an 'O' face that Jim could just see with the aid of the emergency lights. He almost felt guilty when he smiled, but his newfound infatuation with the blonde girl swamped any feelings he had about Zoe's demise.

Saul was the first to get impatient with Owen's continued sobbing and headed off to look for a way into the building. Vickers looked back and forth between the two and set off after the short bearded man to see if he could help.

Feeling useless, Jim followed them and Bettina grabbed his hand and went along. Before swinging wide around the wire, Jim went over to Owen and said, "Sorry, man."

Owen nodded and muttered, "Thanks."

Megan sidled close, wrapped her arms around the grieving man, and urged him to stand up with her. "C'mon, Owen. We should go before the goons come back."

"But what about my sister?" he asked. "We can't just leave her here."

"I know it's not right, but we have to leave her. For now," Megan said, trying to reason with him.

"Oh, God!" Owen wept anew, his eyelids drooping. He grabbed at Megan's hands. "What was she thinking?"

Jim hurried away. He wasn't good at feelings. He could hear Megan whispering "Shh, c'mon, let's go," to Owen as she tried leading him away from his sister's body. Jim looked back as Owen pulled away and said, "You go. I'm staying here with her."

Megan sighed, shook her head in frustration and stalked off. Jim stood there holding hands with Bettina as she strode by, head down. When Megan went past she muttered, "Jim, grab your little girlfriend and let's go."

Jim wasn't very practiced with women, but he knew when they were angry, and Megan was angry with him. Maybe it was because he was with Bettina and not her. Maybe, but he didn't know for sure.

"Wow, did you hear what she just said?" Bettina asked, looking up at Jim and smiling. "She called me your girlfriend. Am I?"

"Heh. Yeah, I guess you are, if you want to be" Jim confirmed, realizing that it took the world ending for him to get his first real girlfriend. She nodded enthusiastically. "She isn't the smartest," Jim thought, "but she's pretty, she likes me and that's good enough for me."

They followed Megan around the back corner. Saul and Vickers were trying to jimmy the service door open with their knives. "All of the other ways in would mean breaking some glass," Vickers explained. "But if we can force this door open we can get inside without being too loud."

"Why not just tap these hinge pins out?" Bettina offered.

Everyone turned to her in amazement. In the soft light of the moon and the emergency lights, Jim saw the 'duh' looks on their faces. Saul took his knife out of the door jam, put it under the top hinge pin and popped it up with his palm. It came out easy. Too easy. It flew up into the air and would have landed with a metallic clang, but Megan casually reached her hand out and snatched it before that could happen.

"Nice thinking, Bettina," Megan whispered. "How did you know how to do that?"

"Easy. When you've been homeless for as long as I have you pick up some things," she confessed.

"Homeless? I thought that was your house we found you at," Megan said.

"Nah. I don't even know who lived there. I broke in when everyone started freaking out and killing each other."

"Guess you got lucky then when we came by," Megan retorted, somewhat derisively. She gave Jim a knowing look, like he was an idiot to be with the blonde, a worthless homeless girl, instead of her, a capable, educated and mature woman.

Jim just shrugged and gave Megan a lopsided smile. He wasn't looking to marry Bettina. Besides, technically, everyone was homeless now.

While they exchanged words, Saul and Vickers finished removing the other two pins. "Okay, I need help. This door is metal so it can't land on the ground when I pop it off the hinges," Saul said. He squeezed up against the door and grabbed the handle. "Wedge your blades under the door and guide it out of the jamb when I wrench it loose, and don't let it hit the ground."

Bettina didn't have a blade, so she stood to the side while Jim, Megan and Vickers squatted and pressed the tips of their blades between the door and the sill. "Go," Vickers said, and Saul lifted up and away slightly. The plan worked perfectly and the door bolt popped out of the latch hole. "Okay," Saul instructed. "Let's put it back on. Bettina, I need you put the pins back in when we get it lined up."

While everyone worked in sync to line the heavy metal door back in place, Bettina dropped the pins in and Saul unlocked the door using the inside handle.

"Thanks, all set," Saul said, then asked: "Hey, where's Owen?"

"With his sister," Megan answered. She put her hands out palms up. "What can I do? He won't leave her."

"I'll see if he's ready," Vickers volunteered. "If he isn't, he's getting locked out. We can't take any more risks tonight." Everyone nodded in agreement and headed in while Vickers went back for Owen.

"I'll watch the door and wait for them to get back," Jim offered. Saul said, "Cool," and led the women down a dimly lit hallway. Jim alternated looking outside watching for Vickers and Owen, and looking down the hallway at the rest of the group. Just before Saul and the women disappeared from view, the two women broke off and went into a room together. Jim assumed it was the bathroom and hoped Bettina would be okay alone with Megan. He didn't want problems between the two and he especially didn't want Megan to scare his new girlfriend away. Shortly afterwards Owen came in and Jim clapped him on the back as he went by. Vickers followed and shut the door behind them. "Let's go, Jim, this door's secured."

Jim nodded and looked at Owen's retreating back. "How's he doing?"

Frowning, Vickers shrugged. "Okay, I guess. We need to keep an eye on him though. Grieving people do weird shit sometimes. I knew a guy who ripped his friend's ears off in a bar when he found out his girlfriend passed away. Just pulled them off and threw them into a corner, laughing. Anyways, if Owen flips out and puts us in danger, we'll need to take him out."

"Take him outside?" Jim asked, not sure what Vickers meant.

"No, fucking, you know, out." He made a hand pistol and fired it. "Like 'Out' out," the former sergeant said without any emotion, before following Owen down the hall.

Not sure how to respond to that, Jim kept his mouth shut and filed the information away. He double checked that the door was locked and went after Vickers.

SUMMIT COUNTY JAIL, INFIRMARY

Josh looked at the small group seated around him. It was disheartening considering the number that had been alive that morning. He considered that only seven men left in the prison was both good and bad. Good because there was plenty of food, water and weapons to go around but bad because defending the large prison compound was a task normally done by a team of twenty highly-trained men. Josh wasn't quite sure how to best go about setting up the defenses anyway. Luckily Ben Franklin seemed smart on a wide variety of topics and was able to offer some solutions.

After the team meeting everyone went together to take a tour of the prison walls. Josh's indoctrination and training included memorizing many of the facility's specifications. He quoted them to the former inmates. None of them had ever been closer than twenty feet to the outside walls except for the day of their arrival. They laughed amongst themselves as Josh freely gave them previously denied knowledge. He closed his eyes and recited from memory: "The walls are twelve feet high topped by a railed catwalk. There are two external fences, also twelve feet high, topped by razor wire. Both fences are equipped with vibration sensors monitored by the computer control system located in Central. They are calibrated to ignore anything rabbit sized and smaller. Access into and out of the prison is restricted to the main gate, also controlled from Central..."

"That can't be right," Ben Franklin said.

Josh looked confused. "What do you mean?"

"I mean the guys who took off over the wall earlier. If there are two fences, how could they leave?" Ben asked.

"Oh, shit," Josh said, realizing what Ben meant. He sprinted for the catwalk access in one of the corner towers. He got to the door and it was locked. "I bet they're trapped between the fences. Don't yell to them, it might attract those things. This door is operated electronically so I have to run back to central and unlock it. I'll be right back."

Josh dashed to Central. Halfway there he heard footsteps behind him and looked back to see both Ben Franklin and Finn keeping pace with him. "What are you guys doing?" he whispered. "Stay with the group."

"Nuh-uh," Ben said. "If something happens to you we need access to that room. Finn here says he's a computer wiz, so you need to fill him in on how everything works."

Josh stopped at the door to Central. "I don't know," he said, hesitating. "It seems weird."

"Look, Josh, either you trust us or you don't," Ben said matter-of-factly. "But if you don't, none of us are going to make it through this, including you."

Josh looked at Finn, who was just standing there with one eyebrow raised in a facial question mark, then to Ben who implored, "So what's it going to be Josh?"

There really was no choice. "You're right, Ben. We're all in this together." Josh beckoned them over and showed them the combination and how to unlock the door. The door clicked and Josh swung it open, giving the former inmates their first look inside the prison's central control system. "I have to be honest," he told them. "It feels good to share, to shed some of the responsibility."

"That's why we picked you to lead us," Ben reassured Josh. "Now let's get to learning how this shit works."

They all piled in and Josh showed them the various screens and the basics on how to manipulate the different monitoring and control functions. Finn impressed Josh by how easily he absorbed the information. Ben on the other hand was scratching his head after the first minute. "Computer work isn't my strong suit," he announced. "Let me get back out there and stay with the men, keep them out of trouble."

Neither of the two young men replied because they were absorbed in going over the different computer operations, fingers flying and discussing things in a syntax Ben had never learned. Ben smiled as he closed the door behind him, happy for Finn. He would make sure that all of the men waiting at the tower understood the value the young man added to their group; Finn had finally found his prison currency.

Back in Central Josh found the surveillance camera that covered the fenced in area where the men went over earlier, but the men weren't there. Finn gently pushed Josh aside and took over. He was able to work the cameras with more finesse and rapidly switched through all of the external views. Finn found the three men trapped between the wall and the security fence. The nasty looking razor wire prevented the men's escape and they were unable to retreat back the way they came because the inside wall was too high. Worse, they had attracted some unwanted attention. Several of the maniacs prowled the outer perimeter fence looking for a way in.

"Damn," Josh said. "We need to get them back inside and kill those things out there before they bring more, and we need to do it silently." He looked at Finn, eyes glued to the monitors, busily assimilating the various systems and tools. "Finn, would you mind staying in here and running the show?"

"Not a problem. I can handle it."

"Cool," Josh replied. "Here," he said, handing Finn a walkie-talkie.

Finn took it and set it down on the console. "Got it."

Before he left Josh grabbed the rest of the walkie-talkies from their charging stations. They had built-in belt clips so the men could have both hands free. He trotted back across the yard and met back up with Ben and the others. "Finn's running the show in Central," he told them. "Plus, I got everyone one of these," he added, handing out the small communication devices. The men didn't have belts so they stuck them in their pockets. Somehow Josh forgot that prisoners weren't allowed belts or other looping articles of clothing.

"The three guys that went over are along the back wall, but there are seven or eight of those things outside the fence and even though they can't get in, I'm afraid that they might attract more. We need to take them out as quietly as possible." Josh looked around. "I'm going out. Any volunteers to help me?"

Again, Josh was surprised at the support he got from the men. All of their hands went up and it made him smile. "Wow, thanks guys. I'll need some of you to stay behind and make sure nothing gets in."

Keeping in mind that he needed to trust his new companions, but really trusting Ben the most, he didn't pick the large black man to accompany him outside. Instead he picked two others and left Ben inside with the other two men, just in case.

One of the men he picked said, "Hey. We only have guns. We need some other weapons. Something like knives if you want this done quiet-like."

"Sure. Follow me." Josh and the two men trotted over to the armory. He got on the handheld: "Finn, buzz me into the armory."

As he reached the armory door Josh heard the electronic click of the door, then used his key to undo the second lock. "Alright guys, let's arm up." He flicked the lights on and the other men piled in after him, grabbing and donning body armor and helmets. They also armed themselves with tactical knives and whip batons. Because of their lethality the whip batons were normally reserved for catastrophic-level prison events. The metal weapons were very high on the 'use of force continuum' and were more likely to cause lasting or fatal injuries. Josh had only ever practiced with one a couple of times, during his academy training.

The men swung the batons around and tested them on the metal lockers placed around the circumference of the room. The ball ends of the whip caused impressive damage to the steel doors. They all laughed and yelled, "Fuck yeahs," and "Holy shits," as they whipped the weapons back and forth. Josh grabbed extra knives and batons and the other two snagged spare armor kits for Ben and the rest. They stopped by Central to give Finn his gear and Josh told him to be ready on the main gate switch. Finn nodded and reluctantly pushed himself away from the console to put the armor on.

One of the men with Ben gave a low whistle of surprise when Josh and his team approached. All of them appreciated the better chances for survival combat gear gave them over their normal prison denim. They were flexing playfully and thumping each other lightly with the batons. "Be careful with those," Josh warned. "They pack a wallop."

Ben grabbed one up with an oversized hand and gave a sloppy salute. "Got it, sir! And hey, don't go taking any crazy risks out there."

"Roger," Josh replied. Turning to the armored men behind him he asked, "Ready?" They nodded and he raised an arm in the direction of Central.

The solid iron door retracted silently into an opening in the brick wall. When there was enough room to squeeze by he dropped his arm and the gate stopped in place. They slipped through the opening.

The fence in front was clear. Josh clicked his mic on. "Now the two fence gates." The gates didn't retract, they only clicked, signaling that the locks were deactivated. Josh swung the gates open about a foot and they all squeezed through. After going through the second fence Josh studied the looks on the men's faces as it came to them that they were technically free to go. Giving them time to process the fact that there was nothing keeping them from running off, he hoped they would decide that staying was the safest option. While they mulled it over, they looked from the open field and back to Josh, who stood there patiently. When neither of them made to leave, Josh finally asked, "Are we good?"

The men chuckled softly and smiled knowingly, nodding their assent and whispering "Yep," and "Yeah, I suppose." Josh nodded back and led them at a trot along the fence line, around the side, and towards the back wall where the maniacs were last spotted. Before they rounded the last corner Josh stopped and pulled the other two around him.

"Let's be as quiet as we can," he warned. "Hopefully we can surprise them and take them out without any noise." Josh crouch-jogged stealthily around the corner. In front of him there were eight crazy people clustered at the point outside of the fence closest to where the three former prisoners huddled. The harassers were clutching the fence with bloody fingers, trying to pull the fence down. Above them Josh could see gobbets of flesh stuck to the razor wire where the single-minded creatures had tried to scale it. Blood dripped down or coated the chain links where bloody hands had touched it.

Josh's group crept up behind the occupied crazies and cracked the three nearest ones on the top of their skulls with the whip batons. All three slumped to the ground noiselessly. The tactic was so effective and quiet that the remaining five never even alerted to the plight of their brethren, and the men dropped them silently as well. All of this was done in full view of the inmates trapped inside the first fence. Josh put his index finger up to his lips and signaled them to silence, then waved for them to follow. He led them back to the main gate and met them inside.

"You guys okay?" he asked.

One of them spoke up, careful to keep his voice low. The other two were shaking the hands with the members of his team. "Yeah, but I guess we didn't think things through when we went over. I'm Alan. Thanks for the rescue."

"Sure. We couldn't leave you guys out there like that. Besides, you were drawing too much attention to the rest of us." Josh pointed to the outer gate, which was still ajar. "You guys are free to go, if you still want."

"Thanks," the man replied. He looked back at the other two. "Brad and Stretch, you still want to leave?"

Brad and Stretch both nodded. "Yeah, me too," Alan said. By way of explanation, he told Josh, "We have families to see to."

"I understand." Josh put his hand out and the men who were leaving shook it. "Good luck out there," he said. "You run into trouble, or if you find who you're looking for, come back and we'll let you back in." Then he presented his baton. "Here, take this. It's quiet and it's lethal."

The gesture of protection and friendship was unexpected. Alan nodded. "That's much appreciated, man." The other two men with Josh also handed over their hit sticks.

Josh half expected one or both of the men he came out with to leave too, and was surprised when they reentered the prison gate with him. They looked wistfully back at their last glimpse outside for a while and Josh let the moment linger for them before he signaled Finn to "Close it up" over the handset.

There was a small celebration when they regrouped with Ben and his two men. The minor victory was cause for high fives and was a huge morale booster. Josh decided at that moment that he was going to trust the remaining men wholly. All of them had many opportunities to get rid of him without any effort and had instead placed their trust in him. If his small group was going to survive he really had no other choice than to surrender his previous conceptions about their pasts and start seeing them as equals in purpose as well as in stature.

The men must have sensed his change in perspective because they clapped him on the back without the same slight reservations they had before going outside the fence. For the first few seconds Josh's training and conditioning to rebel against prisoner contact almost regained control, but he consciously pushed it back down and it disappeared for good.

"You know what?" Josh asked.

"What's that?" Ben answered.

"I'm fucking starved. How about you guys? Could you eat?"

"Fuck yeah, we could eat," and "Damn right," were among the answers.

The group's mood of camaraderie even encompassed Finn, who came out of Central to join them. One of the guys gave him a bro hug and said "Thanks, man, good job," and for the first time since he was imprisoned Finn held his head up and kept it there.

Everyone headed to the commissary for some chow, happy that the long hard day was headed into a better night.

WELLINGTON BARRACKS

Walter and Major Ackerman walked across the hallway to the conference room to discuss the upcoming branch head meeting. Walter was beginning to feel a little out of his element. Besides his sudden 'battlefield' promotion, a monumental event on its own, roughly one half of the civilized world was transformed into a primitive condition, with huge population losses and all of its assets up for grabs by the survivor nations. Worse, the turmoil and backlash was just beginning to be felt and comprehended. Walter took a deep breath while Major Ackerman patiently waited for his superior to regain his bearings. Eventually the moment passed.

Walter had attended operations briefings in the past in his capacity as a BBC reporter, but as a civilian he had never been privy to high-level military meetings. The major filled him in on what to expect: "Keep in mind that even though it's called a 'meeting' it really isn't. It's more of a way for General Fells to give direction. Of course, he stills expects you to be on top of your game and he may ask questions or want clarification on something. I guess the only good piece of advice I can give you is that that you should be in receive mode and speak up only when called on." The major spent the next ten minutes educating Walter on as many of the other protocols and requirements as he could in the short time they had. When he was done they both stood.

"Got it," Walter said. "That's really helpful. Thank you, Major."

"You're welcome, Sir. If you don't mind, I need to touch base with my unit. I'll be back in time to escort you."

"By all means, and thanks again. I'll see you shortly."

Walter walked back to his office while the major departed down the hall. Sergeant Kennet met him at the door. "Sir, Warrant Officer Smith is ready to give his preliminary report." She pointed to one of the monitors that had a graphic on with the words "IPA, General Staff."

Everyone else was standing along the back wall, so Walter joined them. Warrant Officer Smith stood a little apart and used a wireless clicker to start a slideshow. The first was an infographic that showed the countries affected by the event, broken down by an estimation of population changed and population lost, critical governmental assets, and domestic resources affected by import and export. "As you can see Colonel, we have a global tidal wave of unrest looming. Every single supply chain coming or going from nearly everywhere is broken due to loss of production, transportation, shortages, spoilage, hoarding, and so on."

"One of our mandates is to liaise with foreign governments, as well as publicly spin a positive and beneficial stance in order to minimize friendly nation damages," Warrant Officer Smith continued. "But more on that in a second, sir." he clicked to the next slide.

"A moment," Walter said, putting his hand out. "Let's figure out how many of those people are potentially changed, including those like the boy from the briefing, and add that to the infographic."

The warrant officer raised his eyes at his assistant and she nodded, breaking off and heading over to her desk to do research as he continued. "Sir, this slide shows what information sources we have for data mining and avenues for dissemination, broken down by open source and classified sources."

The screen was filled with tight columns of text so small Walter couldn't even read it. "Warrant Officer Smith, let's focus on the higher stack initially, the information that has already been analyzed. We don't have the staff for that and we should concentrate on providing data that has the most value to General Fells. Your first slide is a good example," he concluded.

"Yes, sir," Smith replied, pushing to the next slide. Seeing it filled with more minutiae, he skipped it and the next several. He finally stopped on a slide that encapsulated the governmental and non-governmental reactions, prioritized by threat and scope. "Colonel, this is a multi-source document that reflects the mindset of what you just mentioned. It captures the ranking threat and assistance entities in areas of the planet still functioning. As you can see, non-governmental organizations, or NGO's, have all but disappeared as the contributing nations pull back to focus domestically. Of course, the United States was one of the largest contributors, and they no longer exist, at least in ways that matter. The remaining data is a matrix of reactions by the various governments, broken down into groups by aggressive and passive. The hostile nations are further delimited by whether or not they are a threat to us domestically or in conjunction with Operation Ophir Ridge objectives, and then finally by threat level."

Using a pointer, Smith highlighted the upper left corner of the matrix and said, "There are three countries in the 'red', sir, that are both hostile and capable: China, North Korea, and Iran."

"That looks pretty dire," Walter said. "Please capture the first slide and this one and package it up with a third slide for me to bring to the meeting. Differentiate somehow between open source and classified information sources, like green and red text or something. Also, we should provide recommendations in the areas of information and public affairs to the General Staff. Let's spend the next ten minutes putting our heads together developing them."

After a rapid fire brainstorming session the team came up with several talking points in case the general asked for recommendations. Major Ackerman returned to pick up Walter and suggested he bring Warrant Officer Smith and Sergeant Kennet along, as it was both normal protocol and because they could take notes. The others stayed behind to man the desks and flesh out the team strategies.

Walter was looking forward to and dreading the meeting at the same time. He had spent years observing and reporting on military operations from the perspective of an outsider, never dreaming he would be privy to the full disclosure of information that went on behind closed doors. Conversely, he was nervous because he felt like a military imposter on the stage where the future of the world was decided.

They arrived at the same theater that they used earlier. Smith went up and handed a thumb drive to a soldier manning a laptop on the stage, then came back and sat down while Major Ackerman guided Walter to a different set of seats. "Colonel, you sit up in the front row. We'll be back here if you need any support." Walter walked up front where a smaller group of men and women stood around talking. They all introduced themselves and gave him a quick rundown of the briefing order and what to expect. There was some small talk for a few minutes before attention was called and General Fells stepped in from the side accompanied by several of his aides.

The general sat down on the end of the first row and waved his hand for the meeting to commence. Everyone sat, the lights dimmed, and the briefing began. Walter absorbed all of the information: troop deployments to the United States, border enforcement and domestic security measures, logistics, maritime efforts, and so on. When Walter's turn came he reviewed his three slides, the last of which contained several recommendations.

Walter came to the last item on the list, the one dealing with a change in the official information disclosure policy, and he briefly outlined the thinking behind it. "General, it's clear that our resources are stretched thin and that we must economize our efforts. At this stage there is very little return on producing anything for international consumption and I recommend all efforts be focused on two fronts: The first is ensuring that our public gets their information in a way that steers them towards our purpose, a combination of pacification through having a well-informed citizenry, and goal-enhancing through the careful manipulation of what and when to disclose."

"The second front," Walter continued, "is to develop a plan to do the same in the western hemisphere, with priority going towards North American survivors."

General Fells spoke up. "So, Colonel Doucet, are you recommending a combination of propaganda and psychological operations?" he asked, tilting his head.

When General Fells used those terms, it sounded pretty bad to Walter even though it was exactly what he was proposing. The question caught Walter off guard and he immediately looked up at his staff for rescue. The general saw the move and laughed good-naturedly. "Relax, Colonel. We can be frank in this setting. In fact, we must be. But there's no need to answer my question, I know the answer," he said, smiling. "And I agree. Many of the liberties we have taken for granted in the past must be put on hold if we are to succeed. I'm glad you came to that conclusion so quickly. It justifies your position and the trust placed in you by your superiors, particularly since your recommendations differ so radically from your own personal opinions. Thank you, Colonel, you may sit back down now."

Walter sat. He felt his armpits soaking through his shirt and he had trouble focusing on the rest of the presenters. Nobody seemed to be paying him any attention despite his having choked at the first question he was asked, but Walter was doubting his promotion and his ability to handle his new responsibilities.

After the meeting broke up, he stood and met back up with his team. They were almost back to the IPA office when a man jogged up behind them and cleared his throat. "Colonel Doucet? A moment, please."

They all stopped and turned around. A man in uniform stood there, slightly out of breath. Recognizing his rank, Walter asked, "Can I help you Lieutenant?"

"Thank you, sir. I'm, ah, Lieutenant Pelka. I have an orders change for you." He handed Walter a folder before continuing. "General Fells would like me to relay to you that he concurs with your recommendations and would like you to personally spearhead them, starting with dividing the focus of effort between here and North America. With that, I'm here to relieve you, sir."

"What?" Walter exclaimed, flustered. He flipped open the folder and read the contents quickly, reading the last part out loud: "You are hereby ordered to Royal Air Force Station Northolt, South Ruislip, London at zero six hundred hours for immediate departure to Wright-Patterson Air Force Base, Dayton, Ohio, former United States of America." Looking up, he asked the lieutenant, "What of my staff? I've only just met them."

"Your staff and Major Ackerman will accompany you. It's all there in your orders, Colonel. Your office is being absorbed into General Fells' deployed staff as its organic Information Management branch."

Walter looked at his watch, then at his team. "That only gives us seven hours. Not a lot of time. You can all go home or make whatever arrangements are necessary. Meet back here at five thirty."

Warrant Officer Smith relayed Walter's orders and simultaneously amended them. "Make it zero five hundred, sergeants."

Recognizing the gentle rebuke made Walter remember he was in the military now and had to respect the chain of command. When possible he should pass everything through his second-in-command. "Thank you," he said.

"Yes, sir," Smith replied, nodding, pleased at Walter's quick adjustment.

Lieutenant Pelka was dismissed and everyone else except Walter and the major departed to get ready. Walter looked at the major and asked, "Don't you need to clear up your affairs? I suspect we'll be gone for a while."

"I don't have any distractions, really," came the reply, "and I packed my gear hours ago, suspecting I would be deployed. What about you, Colonel?"

"I have an apartment but there really isn't anything there I need. I was tempted to go back for some clothing, but I think that instead I'll wear a uniform. The sooner I integrate, the better."

Major Ackerman smiled. "That's the spirit, sir. I'll take care of that right now, it won't take long. All I need are your sizes and a few hours. Is there anything else I can do for you?"

"No, thank you. I think I'll stay here and familiarize myself with the different information streams," Walter told him, jotting down his sizes on his notepad and handing the sheet over.

"Then I'll leave you to it." The major folded the paper, nodded, and departed down the hall, quickly disappearing from view as he navigated around the crowded activity in the hallway.

Walter walked back to his desk and sat, logging into his computer for the first time. The screen was filled with links to various unclassified and classified information sources. Some of the information was so sensitive he would have never even have suspected its existence. Just yesterday he would have loved to have the type of access he was now privy to, but in light of what happened he would have gladly refused it all to have everything back to normal.

The enormity of his circumstances suddenly became real. The world was altered and would never be the same again. He recalled a random conversation he had with Luis just a few days ago. He was bemoaning how dreary and boring it was to be back in London, covering domestic policy and routine press announcements. Luis had no complaints. He said he liked going home to his family every day, the predictability of it. Walter asked him, "Don't you miss the adrenaline, Luis? The bullets, the rush, all of the chances we took?"

The cameraman had given Walter a strange look and said, "No. What I remember is hoping to God that I wouldn't die in some desolate shithole far away from home and my wife and kids. I don't miss that feeling at all, not even the tiniest bit. You say you want excitement, but you ought to be careful of what you wish for Walter, because you just might get it."

MEDINA, OHIO CAR DEALERSHIP

Everyone gathered in the center of the darkened dealership showroom. Saul had already done some preliminary scavenging and because of it everyone was standing around a pile of vending machine food eating snacks and drinking soda.

Jim grabbed a package of toaster pastries and ripped the shiny wrapper off. He hadn't eaten his favorite food in what seemed like forever and he devoured both pastries with half a dozen bites in twice as many seconds. He swallowed most of it barely chewed before he realized he must look like a glutton to Bettina. When he glanced over at her he expected to see a look of shock and disgust on her face, mouth agape at his piggishness, but she was too busy stuffing her own face with one hand while simultaneously opening a soda with the other. To Jim she didn't look at all concerned about how she looked to him so he opened another pastry package. Megan noticed, though, and whispered with a chuckle, "Jim, the toaster store called and they're all out of pop tarts."

Those that had witnessed his manners laughed at the small joke and despite his grief even Owen grinned. The mood lifted slightly. Everyone spent the next couple of minutes stretching out or going to the restroom. "Remember, no flushing, dude. We need to stay quiet." Saul cautioned Jim when he got up to go.

Dismissing Saul with a wave, Jim went into the bathroom and found a stall. He yanked his pants down and prepared to use the toilet, but looked down in time to see that someone else had already visited this particular one. With his pants around his thighs he hopped over to the next stall, found a pristine bowl, and sat. After a minute the motion-activated emergency lights dimmed and then faded out completely and Jim still sat there with his elbows on his knees looking into black space, trying to go. He grew bored and nodded off.

A light slammed through his eyelids and he jerked up, smacking the back of his head on the tile wall behind him. He heard Saul tell someone, "Here he is, passed out on the crapper," and then a woman's soft laughter. Megan.

"Okay, Saul," she said, "I'll have the others call off the search." Her departing footsteps were accompanied by the sound of the bathroom door opening and shutting.

"C'mon, get that light out of my eyes," Jim cursed. "I can't see. And give me some privacy, Saul."

"Sure. You need to hurry though. We grabbed a pickup and it's loaded up and ready to go. We're just waiting on you. "

Speaking to Saul over the stall wall Jim asked, "What's the hurry? I thought we were going to sleep here, get some rest."

"We did, buddy. You were in here for hours."

"Shit!" Jim replied.

"If you say so," was the retort before the door opened and closed and Jim was alone again.

After Jim finished his business on legs numb and tingling from sitting so long, he went out to the showroom and was greeted with mock applause by everyone gathered around the open driver's door of an oversized, four door pickup truck. Jim could see the trees lining the road in the distance, visible in the light of the false dawn that came through the large plate glass windows.

Vickers summarized the plan to Jim, who been absent from the meeting earlier. "The only way to get the truck out is to drive it through the windows. Normally they rotate the vehicles on a turntable after they open a gap in the retracting windows, but since we destroyed the electrical panel last night there's no power for the window controls." Jim noticed that Owen winced a little at the mention of last night and the reminder of the loss of his sister. "We don't want to risk smashing the glass and damaging the truck," Vickers explained further. "So we decided you and Owen need to break the windows and then hop in afterwards."

"Are we still headed back to Klimps?"

"Yeah, but not all the way there. We're going to stop on the empty road near the woods where we came out and park the truck there, then hoof it in."

"Okay," Jim said. "Are we ready now?"

"Yep."

Everyone but Jim and Owen got into the pickup. Saul sat behind the wheel, waiting for the windows to shatter before he turned the engine on. Jim and Owen each grabbed a chair and on the count of three hurled them full power at the window. First Owen's, then Jim's chair bounced off the thick glass with a heavy thump and a clank. It was the loudest sound any of them had heard in a long time. They both tried again, whipping around and throwing the chairs harder this time, but the result was the same.

The external response to the noise was immediate. Some goons wandering by in the nearby fields were the quickest to react, sprinting around the front corner of the building, whooping and rushing at the plate glass windows. Jim was shocked at how attuned to the noise of human activity the goons were. The rage-filled faces were just a few yards from where he stood mutely holding the chair. Somehow the goons locked onto a primordial seed of fear deep within his subconscious brain and rendered him incapable of action.

Owen wasn't affected the same way. Instead of paralyzing him, the goons struck a reciprocal chord of rage with the young athlete. He shouted a battle cry at the growing crowd pounding at the thick glass and hurled his chair a third time, even harder than before. Fortunately for the group trapped inside, the missile still lacked the impetus to break through, because if it had it would have created an opening large enough for almost a dozen of the goons to rush through.

Everyone was yelling at them to get in the truck and somehow the pleading voices got through to Jim and snapped him out of his daze. He was angry at himself for freezing up again, but with the repeated encounters he began to understand his reactions to the goons with more clarity. With every experience he was becoming more and more desensitized to the goon's effect on him. He flipped them off through the window and got in the back seat next to Bettina. Saul closed the door and turned on the engine.

Frustrated because Owen was still at the window, Vickers got out of the truck to get him. Unlike Jim, who recovered from the proximal confrontation with the goons relatively quickly, Owen was still locked in a rage state, pounding on the glass at the goons while the goons pounded back; each wanted a piece of the other. When Vickers approached Owen from behind, grabbing the young man and yelling at him to calm down, Owen turned and floored Vickers with a right cross to the face.

Jim expected the army sergeant to get up and work Owen over because the former Army sergeant was definitely not somebody to mess with. Except that it didn't happen. Instead, Vickers lay on the ground unconscious, gushing blood out of his nose.

Owen recognized who it was that he hit and immediately calmed down. He rushed over to Vickers but Megan had already hopped out and was there first. She pushed the young man away and yelled at him. "You're an asshole, Owen! Fuck off!" She kneeled down next to Vickers and slapped his face lightly. "C'mon Vickers, wake up. Wake up!"

By the time everyone else had piled out in order to help get Vickers into the truck, he started coming around. He was groggy and was only able to get to his feet with Megan and Bettina's help. Owen hung his head and moved several feet to stand alone, a temporary outcast. As Vickers staggered to the truck with the assistance of the two girls, Owen tried to follow, but Megan pointed at him and yelled, "You stay where you are!" Owen retreated without argument.

Megan gave Saul a sharp look. "I don't want him coming with us, Saul. He can't be trusted."

Before the short bearded man in charge could reply, Vickers picked his head up and turned to her. Still oozing blood from his nose he coughed in a weak, nasally voice, "No, Megan. We need him. Now's not the time to leave people behind."

"Fine! He can come, but he better not come near me."

The group of goons at the window had doubled and then tripled in size in the time between the confrontation and Vickers getting back into the truck. Megan pulled the injured man into the front seat with her, Saul got back in the driver's seat, and Jim, Bettina, and Owen piled into the extended cab seats.

"No choice now, we're going to have to chance driving through the glass," Saul yelled, trying to make himself heard over the noise of dozens of hands slapping the large plate glass windows and the accompanying whooping noises. He put the truck into drive and floored the accelerator.

The tires had difficulty getting traction on the shiny, buffed display floor. The engine revved and the tires spun, but the only thing that happened was the formation of a large cloud of exhaust and rubber dust that slowly filled the room and enveloped the truck. Saul slapped the steering wheel, yelling "Move!" while Megan pleaded with him to let up on the gas.

Finally, the truck began to pick up traction, but it didn't take off the way Jim anticipated it might. Instead, it crawled forward slowly, the tires swimming in a thin rubber soup that had formed under them. The tires gradually worked their way out of the morass and went forward the twenty feet needed to hit the window, but instead of a high speed getaway they barely had the momentum to break the glass and clear the metal sill of the turntable.

The goons switched their attention from the window to the truck and because of the slow start they had no difficulty keeping abreast of it, denting the doors and the bed with kicks, punches, and head butts and causing the vehicle to rock erratically on its suspension. Jim looked at Bettina, who sobbed as she stared at the slavering maws just inches from her face, coating her window with phlegm and spittle and they roared in frustration at their inability to get inside at her. She had never seen them close up like she was now. Owen was between Jim and Bettina, but he either didn't notice or didn't care that the girl was having a hard time of it. He just stared straight ahead.

Before the truck group hit the pavement the windshield was cracked and they had accumulated several additional passengers. Saul noticed there were goons in the truck bed and they were trying to get in through the rear sliding window. He swerved, accelerated and braked erratically in a bid to dislodge them but the goons were tenacious and stayed put.

From his position in the back seat Jim noticed them at the same time and dug his pistol out of his backpack. He slid the small window open, put the barrel of his pistol through, and fired off a quick succession of shots. The swerving vehicle caused all of his shots go in random directions and it was only by chance that he actually hit two of the invaders, knocking them to the road. Three remained: a middle-aged, skinny male goon with a large belly, and two very scary looking older women with grey hair and wearing the remnants of heavy makeup.

The two ladies had lost their balance and were down with their backs against the tailgate, but the skinny-fat man was spry. Before Jim could withdraw his arm to reload the pistol the goon did a primitive karate kick. The goon's sneaker smashed into Jim's fingers and knocked the gun out of his hand.

Jim couldn't believe the accuracy of the strike, or at least the incredible luck involved. He withdrew his hand and nursed it while his gun skittered around in the truck bed.

"Fucker kicked me," Jim announced to no one in particular, which caused Owen to laugh and point at him.

"That shit was funny as hell, man," Owen guffawed, throwing a mock kick in the limited space of the back seat area. "Ki-yaa!" The act made Bettina laugh with him. Jim shook his head at how they were acting.

Vickers had finally recovered his senses and was back to normal, holding his shirt tail to his nose to stem the bleeding. "Stop the truck Saul," he said. "There aren't any goons nearby and we need to take care of the ones in the back." He reached down and pulled his pistol out of his holster while Megan copied his action. Saul skidded to a stop and everyone got out with their pistols, except Jim, who took his knife out. Within seconds the goons were down, plugged by five or six bullets each.

Megan lowered the tailgate and began pulling one of the old ladies out. Bettina helped and they dropped the body onto the road. Jim and Owen grabbed the other woman and did the same while Saul reached over the side to retrieve Jim's gun for him. Vickers grabbed the last goon by his ankle and ran with it down the truck bed, flinging the small man past the shoulder of the road and into the tall weeds beyond. The body was thrown with such force that it went head over heels twice before coming to rest. By some weird trick of physics one of the goon's shoes came off and bounced back to the road, landing near Jim's feet.

"I guess he wanted you to have a souvenir," Owen quipped.

That broke the tension they were all under and once again Jim felt like the butt of the joke as everyone had a good chuckle at his expense. He kicked the shoe back into the weeds as everyone got back in the truck. Bettina grabbed his hand and pecked him on the cheek. "Don't be a sourpuss,' she giggled.

Mostly because of the kiss, Jim let her lead him to the truck. He found his mood lifting. Maybe things weren't so bad after all. He had a pretty girl, survived another night, and just participated in a wild escape worthy of an action movie. Thinking back to his time at the dealership, he was a little proud of himself. While he had initially panicked, he persevered and seemed to be getting a better hold on his attacks. As the truck started going again, he told everyone, "I want to apologize for freezing up back at the dealership, but I think I'm making the adjustment in my head to everything that's going on. I got over that last one pretty quickly and I'm sure that it's getting better."

A few nods. Vickers spoke up with a few words of encouragement, but Megan warned, "That doesn't mean you're out of the woods yet, Jim. Saul and I talked, and he's going to let me raid the pharmacy when we get back to try and find something that might help you."

"Okay, fair enough," Jim answered.

"Wait a sec," Bettina interrupted. "You guys have a pharmacy?"

Megan was quick to jump on her. "Yes," she said in a scathing voice, "but I'm not going to give you painkillers, or whatever else you're craving."

"Hey! Fuck you!" Bettina shouted. "What the fuck do you think I am? Just because I was homeless that means I'm a druggie or some kind of crackhead?" She started sobbing. "I'm diabetic, you dumb bitch. And I'll have you know I was homeless because I didn't want to be my stepfather's 'girlfriend'. Is that crackhead enough for you?" She put her face in her hands and bawled. The inside of the truck was uncomfortably quiet.

"Stop the truck," Megan said.

Not wanting to worsen the situation or complicate things beyond having a crying girl on his hands, Saul didn't say a word and veered over to the side of the road. There were fields on either side that gave a good view of their surroundings and it appeared clear and safe. Everyone piled out for a second time.

When Bettina got out Megan grabbed her hand and pulled her over to the side of the truck. When Jim tried to follow Megan gave him an exasperated look and told him to go away. Shoulders slumped in dejection, he joined Owen, Vickers and Saul on the other side of the road.

"Figure we're close enough to just leave the truck here?" Vickers asked Saul.

"Yeah. When they're done," he answered, jerking his thumb at the women on the other side of the truck, "we'll just head in the same way we came out. We cleared the way once so hopefully we won't have as much trouble this second time through."

Jim looked through the door windows and watched Megan talking to Bettina in a low voice. Megan had Bettina's hands in hers and when the girl had another sobbing outburst Megan pulled her in for a tight hug. Jim had heard the comment about Bettina's stepfather and as he thought about it he made a dookie face. It was always his luck to either like girls who didn't return the sentiment, or find ones that liked him but that had some kind of daddy issue or some other problem, like low hygiene standards or excessive weight.

Having to deal with someone else's problems was not something Jim was anxious to do and he almost wrote Bettina off except for two reasons. First, she was much better looking than his limited, but previous standard fare. No way in different times would Bettina give him a second look, homeless or not. Second, Megan was now on Team Bettina so there was no chance she was going to let Jim walk away and make things worse for the damaged girl. Resigned to his fate, he tried to bury deep the mental image of her making out with some scruffy-bearded, middle-aged alcoholic stepfather and vowed to try and see the positive in her.

"Could be worse," Jim muttered to himself.

"What?" Saul asked, breaking off from a conversation with Owen and Vickers. "Hey, are you paying attention? We're talking strategy here, lover boy, so get your head back in the game."

Jim pretended offense and used the opportunity to back up out of range of Saul's breath, which smelled faintly of decaying meat. "Huh? I'm paying attention."

Just then Megan and Bettina came back holding hands. Both looked like they had shed tears but they were smiling. "Okay, we can go now," Megan announced.

"Cool," Saul said. "Let's grab our shit from the truck. We're walking from here."

Everyone pulled their backpacks out except for Bettina and Owen, who didn't have one. Zoe still had hers on, and Jim supposed her brother hadn't been interested in maneuvering it off of her body and using it. As he pulled his own backpack on, Jim wondered idly if the energy bars inside Zoe's backpack had been cooked or the bullets in her gun were still good after the current had hit them. He was tempted to ask Vickers, but remembered the knock out potential of Owen's right hook and decided to put the question on hold for a different time.

The group cut across the road and entered the far field in single file and headed directly into the woods. From this approach the woods didn't look familiar to Jim, but Saul was on point and the short bearded man seemed to know the area well. Once they hit the tree line Saul stopped and whispered.

"Same as before, we pair up. Megan, you're with me. Owen, take Bettina. Jim, it's you and Vickers." Saul picked an opening between some heavy brush and disappeared and they followed him in. They moved quickly but quietly.

The route back took them past the spot where they had ambushed the sleeping goons, but the bodies were gone. Saul paused and gathered everyone together. "What do you think happened to the bodies?" he asked.

"No idea," Vickers responded. "Let's keep going, though. I don't like this one bit. Whoever or whatever took them might still be close."

Saul nodded and resumed walking point and Jim noticed there was urgency to his pace that hadn't been there before. Another ten minutes brought them to where the trees thinned out and they could see the side of the wholesale store. Vickers turned around to keep rear watch and Jim copied the action. Saul got out his phone and speed dialed.

"Ray, I need to you open the side door pronto. We'll be there in thirty seconds." A pause, then "Cool." He stuck the phone back in his pocket and turned to everyone. "We're going to sprint. Ready?" All nods. "Let's go!"

The little man got up and broke into a sprint for the side door and everyone followed. Saul was remarkably spry and he remained out in front of everyone except for Owen. The tall, lean athlete made it to the door first with a lead of several yards. He was so fast he actually made it to the door before Ray had a chance to open it. Jim was impressed. Owen wasn't even breathing hard while he himself was huffing and puffing and couldn't even catch up to Megan or Bettina. And while he wasn't in the best shape, he consoled himself by at least being able to keep up with the others. Being on the run from post-apocalyptic beasts was the best exercise program Jim had ever been on.

The door opened and Owen ran through first. Saul waited and gestured for the girls to go ahead of him. Vickers and Jim turned to check the woods one last time when both of them saw it. It was a boy, standing at the tree line. That in itself was strange. Jim couldn't remember seeing any children since the day the world went crazy. Except for Tommy, of course.

Now that he thought about it, where did all of the kids go? Vickers made to run over and grab the boy to bring him into the store but was stopped short when several dozen goons came up from behind the child, walking in a skirmish line. The goons didn't whoop or leap like they typically did, and not only were they not molesting the kid, they actually halted as one unit when the boy spread his arms out in a "stop" gesture. To Jim, it looked like the goons were obeying a command. In the silence of the moment, the boy just stared at the men outside the door, before looking around at the building: The walls, the roof, and the surrounding grassy open area.

"Holy shit," Jim heard from behind him as Saul witnessed the same thing. "What the fuck is going on?"

"I don't know," Vickers said.

"It's like he's their leader," Jim added.

As if to emphasize Jim's point, the little boy lowered his arms and did an about face, and the crowd of silent goons parted for him. He walked through the gap and back into the woods and as he went past, the goons turned and trailed after him.

Fifteen seconds later the woods were empty again and the three men looked at each other in puzzlement. Jim shrugged and Vickers shook his head. After they went in Vickers made extra sure that the door was shut and locked tight behind them.

CONSCRIPT ENCAMPMENT, WRIGHT-PATTERSON AIR FORCE BASE

Fran and his men spent the night looking over the paperwork they were given when they were mustered in as conscripts. Most of it was useless to them, like the history of the Air Force and the base commander's biography, but some of it was enlightening. Fran had the men study the base map. They memorized the locations of the airfields, the armory, the barracks and other vital infrastructure. There was also information in the packets that explained how the conscripts fit into the organization and the type of work they would be doing.

With the pending arrival of the British armed forces and the influx of new personnel, the conscripts were being used as manual labor, mostly in constructing new barracks, hangars, and airstrips. It was made very clear that no matter the circumstances, conscripts were the lowest ranking personnel on base, and would continue to be so even after the British arrived. The only way out of being a conscript was meritorious promotion into the regular enlisted ranks, earned through superior service.

Fran discussed the information on promotion with the other three and they all agreed that even becoming enlisted was a form of indentured servitude. Their only option was to escape the base. Fran was not one to waste time and before long he came up with a rudimentary plan that involved stealing weapons and supplies, causing a distraction, procuring a vehicle, and leaving.

"We need to be gone before the British arrive," Fran said. "After they get here the base will be better manned and it will be harder to escape. Tomorrow we need to keep our eyes and ears open and try to find out how much more time we have to flesh out our plan. The more we know, the better off we are."

"What about after we leave?" Gunter asked. "Where do we go? The crazies out there, LCBs, whatever, are going to be the least of our problems, especially if we want to carve out a piece of the country for ourselves. This area is going to be crawling with military."

"I grew up in Columbus; it's about fifty miles from here. That should be far enough, right?" Bill offered.

"Yeah, but what's in Columbus?" Gunter asked. "Why should we go there instead of somewhere else farther away?"

"I don't know anybody there," Loomis added. "But even if I did, they're probably dead anyways. Columbus is as good as anywhere else, if you ask me. What about you, King?"

Fran was thinking. He looked up and asked, "Why were you guys cuffed when I first met you?"

"Why is that important?" Bill wanted to know.

"Because it matters to me, that's why. I need to know what drives the men in my crew, what makes you guys tick." Fran stood up. "I know what I want, but what makes you guys happy? We should find a place that everyone wants to go to. So tell me why you were arrested or we're through. It's that simple."

"Okay. Sorry, King, I didn't realize you were serious," Bill apologized. "I should have known you were asking for our own good. Alright, I'll tell you, but it's ugly."

Fran shrugged palms up. "Eh," he told Bill dismissively, "everything's fucked up at the moment, it couldn't be that bad."

Encouraged by King's nonchalance, Bill got right to it. "These two," he said, pointing his thumb at Gunter and Loomis, "came to me with this idea. See, the world was basically ending, well still is, really. Anyways, they came to me and said 'Hey, let's catch us one of them crazy ladies. There isn't anything wrong with their bodies and there aren't any cops to bother us', so I say hmmm, sure, why not. Let's grab up a pretty one and give her a checking over."

Loomis interrupted. "There are a ton of them out there. So we were real careful and found one off by her lonesome, one that was sorta pretty, and we jumped on her. She made that whoop-whoop noise and tried to bite us, but she didn't even bother to scream." Loomis got a faraway look, lost in his story. "Gunter threw some duct tape on her mouth to keep her quiet and did her hands up behind her back and we carried her into an empty apartment."

"She kicked like crazy," Gunter took over. "She booted me in the belly and my face and damn near killed me, 'til we taped her legs together. Chick was fucking crazy, I'll tell you. Then we finally got her set up right and took turns with her. But we had only gone a couple of rounds when the Air Force guys showed up. When we went outside to get in the truck, dumbass here," he said, pointing to Loomis, "forgot to tie her down. She came hopping out after us, pants around her ankles, and those soldiers figured out right away what we were up to."

"It wasn't my fault. No one put me in charge of tying her up." Loomis explained to Fran. "Those Air Force guys weren't too nice to us when that bitch came running out, tits flopping and with her mouth duct taped. They beat us and kicked us around the back of that convoy truck. I saw stars." He shook his head at the memory.

"Well, that's all there is," Bill said. "You aren't pissed, are you King?"

Fran had to work really hard at not smiling. These men were his type of people, but he had to remain aloof if he was going to lead them. He acted like he was thinking it over while he got his smile under control. "No, I'm not mad at all. This is a new world. You fellas see your opportunities and I see mine. I don't expect you to judge me for my quirks so you should expect the same from me."

There were some shouts of "Woot" and "Hell yeah, to each their own" from the trio and they smiled at Fran, grateful for his approval, or at least at his overlooking their unusual ways.

"This is a good goddamned team right here," Loomis said, making a circle motion that included everyone in the group. "Unstoppable."

"That's right." Fran added. "And it shouldn't be a problem to get LCB women from anywhere, clean them up, and then you guys can do whatever you want with them. At first I was thinking Cleveland, but we might as well try Columbus, since it's only half as far. I have a feeling travel is going to be real difficult anyways with those LCBs trying to kill us."

"You think they have tanks here?" Loomis asked.

"What a dumbass!" Gunter laughed. "This is the Air Force. They only have planes, which none us of can fly. Besides, even if they had tanks, we wouldn't be able to steal it. Fucking thing goes like three miles an hour tops. They could walk after us. Jesus Christ, you're fucking stupid!"

Everyone had a good laugh, even Fran. Loomis moped for a few minutes, but got over it when the topic of food was brought up.

"When do we eat?" Bill wondered. "I'm fucking starving."

"Yeah, I could eat," Loomis chimed in.

"Can you go find out where we can get some food, Loomis?" Fran asked. Ordered him, really.

"Sure, King. I'll be right back," the fat man responded, hopping up and disappearing from the tent.

The men relaxed while they waited for Loomis to return with the information. With little else to do, Fran kept reading. He picked up a pamphlet titled 'Conscription: Duties and Responsibilities' and perused it. At first it talked about how honorable it was to serve as a conscript, how the nation appreciated it, how one should be proud to serve, etc. In smaller print near the bottom were bullet points and when Fran started going through them, he bolted upright. It was sobering information. The pamphlet stated that conscripts were considered an auxiliary force, a status below any armed service person, no matter the rank. They were also not allowed arms, received no compensation beyond room and board for their labor, and were subject to summary execution without a trial. When he read that last part Fran got the attention of the others.

"Listen to this, you guys," he said, and explained what he read in the pamphlet.

"Holy shit," and "the hell with that," they responded.

"Yeah," Fran muttered. "That puts things on a whole other level."

Just then Loomis came back and told them how they were supposed to eat. "I asked that lady they put in charge," he said. "She told me that we weren't allowed to gather in groups of more than ten except for morning chow or when we're on a work detail, and nobody gets to go to the cafeteria until tomorrow. She said to check under the cots, everyone has ready to eat food in packets there. That's what we're supposed to do. Work, and then come back here. That's it."

As Loomis was talking they all tipped their cots up and found cardboard boxes labeled 'Meal, Ready-To-Eat'. There were twelve to a box and each cot had three boxes under them.

"Hot damn! MREs!" Gunter yipped. "These things are great. I used to eat these all the time on the ship."

"What ship?" Fran asked.

Bill answered for him. "He used to be in the Navy, until they kicked him out and put him in the brig with a Dishonorable Discharge. Rape, wasn't it?" Bill queried Gunter.

"Yeah, but that was all bullshit. That lady was asking for it," Gunter replied. "But unfortunately for me, she was also the senior chief's wife."

Fran filed that little nugget away before he changed the subject. "Okay, so you've eaten this stuff before. How do you cook it?"

"You don't. Well, you do sometimes, but it looks like they didn't give us something to heat these up with. Open one up and check it out. Try the chicken with buffalo sauce. It's my favorite," Gunter instructed.

Unsure, but hungry, everyone grabbed the chicken MREs and ripped the packages open. Fran was surprised at what the bag contained. It had a full meal: chicken, bread, cheese spread, cheez-its, blueberry cobbler for dessert, condiments, and some kind of chemical packet. It had been awhile since Fran last ate and his stomach growled at the prospect of food.

"What's this chemical thing?" Loomis asked.

"Dunno, never seen this before," Gunter answered. "Oh, wait a sec; it says it's a built-in food heater. Hang on."

Gunter quickly read the package and cut the top off. He filled it with water and stuck his meal in it. "Do like I just did. Twelve minutes and this is supposed to be a hot meal." Everyone followed the instructions and sat on their cots eating their desserts and watching the food heat up. When it was finished, Fran grabbed his food and tried it. He was surprised at how tasty it was.

While they ate, Fran explained the pamphlet to Loomis and reminded everyone: "We need to get out of here. Being slave labor isn't part of my plans and neither is getting executed."

"You're right, boss," Bill said. "We need to figure this out quick. Tomorrow after we do some scouting we can find the easiest way out of here."

“I’m taking all of this shit with us,” Loomis said, indicating the MREs. He began poking around his box for a different flavor, preparing to eat some more. “I’m loving it.”

Fran agreed with him, though not because the food was great, but because it meant they could travel without the risk of stopping for supplies. As he thought back on what he learned from his day, Fran decided to formally bind the men to him. “Alright,” he told them, “tomorrow we get info on escaping, but right now, I want to have a serious talk with all of you.”

Fran drug one of the empty cots over to the middle of the tent where the others were sitting and eating. “I have big plans and I want to take you three along with me. I’m willing to bring you all in on the ground floor and give you a piece of the action but first you have to swear an oath to me. Not like that phony oath you gave earlier, because they made us do that, but a real one that you take freely.” He looked each of them in the eye. They looked back at him with rapt attention, wholly absorbed with his speech and by his manner. It made Fran feel almost god-like and he wondered if it was how the colonel felt when everyone in the room snapped to attention whenever he entered a room.

“It’s very simple. You guys swear to me that you’ll follow my orders without question and in return I’ll promise to reward you with everything you want or need. Sound good?” They all nodded. “Great! Now stand up.” They obeyed.

“Do you guys swear to follow my orders?” he asked.

“Yes,” they all responded in unison.

“Without question?” he probed them.

“Yes,” they answered again.

“Okay. You three are the first recruits in my army. Congratulations.” He shook all of their hands. “Your first reward is rank. I’m the general, of course.” He picked up one of the sheets from his indoctrination packet that outlined Air Force ranks and looked it over. “Bill,” he said, scanning down the various insignia, “You are now a Colonel, second in command.”

Bill smiled ear to ear and did a fist pump. The other two looked a little disappointed and were about to speak up, but Fran overrode them with an upraised finger. “Ah, ah, ah, let me finish.”

"Loomis, Gunter, you two are now majors and answer only to me and Bill. Welcome to King's army, gentlemen," Fran said with a formal air.

Loomis let out a long "Yessss," but Gunter shook his head and said, "Wait. Can I be something else, King?"

The others looked at him, wondering what he was up to. "Like what?" Fran asked him. "Major is pretty high up there. Look." He showed Gunter the sheet with the ranks on it.

Gunter said, "I know, but I don't want an Air Force rank, I want a Navy rank. I want to be a Senior Chief."

"Is that higher than being a major?" Loomis asked suspiciously.

"No, it's lower. A lot lower," Gunter answered, shaking his head emphatically and making his long white ponytail flick from side to side.

"Okay," Fran conceded. "Senior Chief it is."

Gunter's wide smile at his 'promotion' revealed a surprisingly perfect set of straight white teeth. It looked odd on the man, standing out in stark contrast to his weathered face and beady eyes.

Fran shook everyone's hand again. He was pleased with how he had manipulated the men with just a little sweet talk and granting them a meaningless title in his made up organization. It was not his usual way, dealing so intimately with others, but today he found that he had a talent for influencing people on a larger scale than he previously operated in. He needed more practice of course, but he was sure his skill would only improve with time.

Before they turned in for the night, Fran pointed at Gunter's teeth and asked, "Hey, no offense, but the rest of you looks pretty worn out except for your teeth. Are they dentures?"

"No offense taken, King," the man replied, tapping his top teeth with his knuckles. "These are as real as they get. They're a gift from Uncle Sam and the U.S. Navy. One of the reasons I joined was to get them fixed up. They may have screwed me out of my benefits by railroading me out like they did with those false charges, but one thing I can say for sure is that the Navy took good care of me. Good food, good health care, and good pay."

Fran doubted the man's claims of innocence but as he drifted off to an exhaustive sleep he recognized that he had learned another facet of being in charge, which was: "Take care of your men and they'll stick around." It was pretty simple, really. What Fran didn't realize was that his next lesson, discipline, would be learned the hard way.

...

The next morning the four men were rudely awakened by the sound of trumpets blasting over a loudspeaker system. Fran momentarily forgot where he was and jumped out of bed, disoriented.

"What the fuck?" Bill roared. "Shut that shit up!"

Gunter was laughing. "That's reveille, asshole. It means 'Get up and get dressed' so they can put us to work."

The trumpets ended and Sergeant Lopez's voice replaced it. "All flights, you have fifteen minutes to get up, get dressed, and use the facilities. Muster at the chow hall, in formation, by zero five fifteen. Carry on." At the sound of the microphone clicking off Fran could hear the camp coming awake and bustle with activity. Everyone was already dressed, having slept in their uniforms, so they left the tent.

"Where's the bathroom? I gotta piss like a biotch in this biotch," Loomis joked.

"Follow the crowd," Fran said, pointing to the large flow of people all headed in the same direction. Some of the people were sprinting. He stepped out into the flow and merged with the throng.

After going a short distance everyone in front stopped. Fran turned to Gunter and asked, "What's going on?"

"Lemme find out, King," he responded, and then tapped a man of front of them.

"Hey," Gunter demanded, "What's the holdup, buddy?"

The man turned around and said, "It's the line for the latrine, but good luck with that. If you aren't in front, you probably won't get to go to the bathroom until after breakfast. We only have, like, ten minutes to get over to the chow hall and you definitely do not want to be late. Trust me on that."

The man who gave the warning stood up on his tiptoes and looked at the number of people in front of him, then looked at his watch and said, "Nah, you won't make it before breakfast. Better follow me to the chow hall."

"Fuck that," Bill said, speaking for all of them. "They can't deny us the right to piss. I gotta go."

"Whatever," the man in front replied. Then he added, "Don't say I didn't tell you so," before he got out of line and jogged off. Most of the other people were doing the same and suddenly the line for the latrines got a lot shorter.

Within a minute they were next in line. The person in the latrine before Fran came out, glanced at the short line with dismay and muttered, "Oh shit" before he sprinted away.

"Finally," Fran said, looking the others before going into the latrine. He took care of his business and met the others outside.

"Maybe we should hurry," Gunter said. The skinny man looked pale under his white hair.

Bill spoke up. "We're going now, we're fine. Stop worrying, you fucking Nancy,"

When they arrived everyone was already in formation in front of a large hut. The enticing scent of bacon wafted by. Fran saw the 'I' flag and led the men to the back of the formation. Sergeant Lopez was up front on a small wooden stand, reading from a sheet of paper. His voice was picked up by a wireless microphone and broadcast over speakers. "Charlie and Delta Flights are to report to Airfield Six..." The sergeant paused. "Just a moment everyone, we have late guests." He pointed to Fran and his men. "You four in the back that just showed up, front and center."

Hundreds of eyes turned back to stare at them. A lot of the eyes held sympathy. "What the fuck?" Bill asked. His voice carried in the quiet of the morning. "What's going on?"

"I won't say it again," Sergeant Lopez warned them. "Front. And. Center. On the double."

Deciding that things weren't going to get better by staying where they were, Fran led his men up to the front at a trot.

Turning to a large group of armed men, the sergeant told them, "These men are new personnel, sworn in to India Flight last night. They aren't familiar with what 'Obey all commands' means yet. Since it's their first day, they'll only get twenty. Proceed."

"What's this all about?" Fran said, stepping in front of the other three, his arms held out protectively.

His question was ignored, but the sergeant took note of the protective gesture. He pointed at Fran and said, "This one speaks for the others. Give him an extra ten for his effort." Addressing the formation Sergeant Lopez said, "Formation. Attention!" The noise of hundreds of boots clacking together could be heard as Fran and the others were led to a series of large wooden poles with cross-arms set up in front of the hut.

There were ten pairs of poles. The four men were forced to remove their shirts and were then zip tied to four poles near the center. Thick ropes with knots tied at the ends were retrieved from a small locker near the chow hall door and distributed out to four of the guards.

Fran's back was to the formation. The guards who were going to use the ropes stepped in front of the posts and did sets of warm up calisthenics, lubricating their muscles for the task ahead. They smiled and leered at Fran and the others to build up anticipation and dread while they performed their routines. When the guards were done they disappeared from view behind the tied up men and the sergeant ordered, "Formation. Begin count!"

"One, Sir!" the conscripts yelled, and Fran felt like a baseball had just been pitched into his right shoulder blade. His involuntary yelp accompanied the shrieks of the other three men and then blended in with the next count of, "Two, Sir!"

The next blow hit Fran at the base of his neck and he saw bolts of white in front of him. The impact was so forceful that he couldn't even emit a yell, he could only grunt. He disappeared into his misery and barely heard when the cry of, "Three, Sir!" came.

Fran thought that the man wielding the rope seemed particularly skilled at striking a new spot with every blow. The next several hits were placed strategically to his ribs, his buttocks and the back of his legs. His mind lost focus with the overwhelming pain. He only regained his senses when the blows stopped.

"That's twenty. Get the other three down and give this little group's leader his extra portion."

The bonds of the other three were cut and they slumped to the ground whimpering in pain. The soldiers yelled, "You're out of uniform! Get your shirts back on!" and Fran could hear his men scuffling, sniffling and grunting while they tried to comply as quickly as they could. The guards relentlessly harassed the three of them with slaps and kicks until they managed to escape, limping and hopping, to the back of the formation.

The sergeant waited until the formation was refilled and then simply said, "Continue." The beating resumed. Again, even as he suffered Fran noted the skill of his punisher. There was only one place left on the back of his body that hadn't been touched yet, held in reserve for the extra lashes.

The count started back up where it left off: "Twenty one, Sir!" and Fran's left calf exploded in agony. "Twenty two, Sir!" and it was his right calf this time. His calves took five blows each before the punishment was concluded. Fran was cut down without ceremony.

"All flights, fall in for chow," Sergeant Lopez ordered. "Section leaders stand by for the rest of your assignments. That is all."

Fran lay on the ground unable to move and was left there as everyone else filed by to eat. Someone clucked his tongue and said, "Told you so," and when Fran looked up, the man who had given the advice near the latrines earlier shook his head sadly as he went by. The last three people in the last flight to enter were Fran's men, and they came over to him and helped him up. They got him dressed, put his arms over their shoulders and assisted him into the hut. The nearby armed men didn't say anything; they just smoked cigarettes and joked amongst themselves or glared silently at the group as it limped by. Fran knew that one of them was the man who wielded the rope so brutally on his body. To watch them so carefree and unaffected by his misery gave him strength. Fran removed his arms from his men and made a show of walking under his own power. The guards ignored him, but his men noticed the gesture.

They went through the food line, which was empty. Most of the food was already gone so they had to make do with scraps. When they finally sat down at the long cafeteria table with the rest of their flight they were ignored by everyone else, treated as pariahs. Fran looked around but nobody would meet his eyes, pretending instead to concentrate on the food in front of them.

The four only had time for a few bites before a whistle blew over the loudspeaker and everyone in the mess hall stood as one. Since it was India Flight's first breakfast; they didn't realize right away what the whistle meant, and when they stood it wasn't as one unit. The slow, uncoordinated response drew the immediate attention of a dozen or so guards stationed near the front of the chow hall. They trotted down the line of the India Flight conscripts slamming rifle butts into their backs while screaming obscenities and instructions.

Fran and the others were fortunate to be the last seated because it put them on the opposite wall from the guards and saved them the misery of additional hits to their backs. Fran was especially sore but was quick to stand up. He had learned his lesson and in the future he would make sure that no one from his group drew any extra attention. As he filed out with the rest he thought back to what had just happened and added revenge to his plans. Fran and the others weren't just going to escape, they were also going to get retribution for the public beatings they took.

Outside, all of the conscripts reformed into their flights. India Flight was called to attention and the formation marched off. It took some time and the threat of physical abuse, but everyone learned to march in step. Initially, Fran was able to keep up without effort, but after a few minutes his back, ribs, and especially his calves starting firing off flares of agony to his brain. He suspected that his tormentor might have broken a couple of his ribs, or at least bruised them severely because every breath he sucked in was excruciating. Fran knew that if he stopped he would receive kicks, or worse, so he forced himself to go on.

Suddenly Fran remembered the painkillers in his pocket and he almost sobbed with relief. He surreptitiously slid his hand down and palmed several of them, but his sense of self-preservation kicked in and made him realize that taking too many at once would alert the guards to his improved well-being. He let all but three slip back down. He didn't know which pills he kept in his hand or the dosage, but he knew that if he didn't take them soon he would fall out. He pretended to cough and tossed all three in.

He was tempted to chew the pills but feared making a conspicuous crunching noise. He dry swallowed them instead and the medicinal, artificial taste of them made him gag slightly. The pills lodged halfway down his parched throat and caused him to have a coughing fit. Somehow Fran managed to not cough the drugs out, but the effort brought tears to his eyes and caused mucous to pool in his sinuses. He sniffled loudly and swallowed the pills all the way down along with his phlegm. The retching earned a few disgusted looks from the people in front of him but made Bill and Loomis chuckle under their breath.

Within minutes the pain eased and Fran could keep up with the others. Since he no longer had to concentrate on putting one foot in front of the other he was able to look around at where they were. It was a foggy morning and the unpaved road they were marching down had thick forest that pressed up on either side. Other than the sound of boots stepping in unison and the scratchy voice of one of the guards yelling cadence, it was eerily quiet.

Images of prison chain gangs came unbidden to Fran's mind. Even though what had happened to him and the others in the last day wasn't technically imprisonment, it was in effect the same thing. No one was free to go, they couldn't refuse an order, and they could be punished disproportionately for the smallest offense. Fran didn't appreciate the circumstances he had been forced into and now that he was feeling better he gave his thoughts of revenge more fuel. He imagined diabolical injuries to every military person on the base, but for that to happen he needed more resources than he currently had access to.

While Fran marched he further considered how to expand his army beyond the three converts he already had. If what had happened to him and his men before breakfast was a normal occurrence, he doubted it would be too hard to find new recruits, displaced people who felt like he did, but he definitely had to be careful. One spy, or one person wanting a 'meritorious' promotion would spoil everything. Fran's best bet to get more numbers was to send his three guys out. The problem with that was he didn't think Gunter or Loomis were capable or discrete enough to carry out the job the right way, which left only Bill. After they got back to the tent Fran would get together with the old man and discuss filling out the ranks with more discontents. He gave himself a timeline of three days to escape.

WORK DETAIL, WRIGHT-PATTERSON AIR FORCE BASE

India Flight arrived at their destination without incident. After leaving the shelter of the trees the formation marched for an additional fifteen minutes past airfields, hangers, and planes. They eventually ended up in a large open area that was part asphalt and part scrub weed. The only spot of color was a small red canopy tent and the guards went there to drop off their packs and take a rest. The conscripts stayed where they had halted, wondering what was next. With the punishment meted earlier that morning still fresh in their minds, none of them dared move without being told to do so.

Fran and his crew looked around surreptitiously but there wasn't much to see. An open-faced shack with construction tools stood off to one side and in the far distance another flight of conscripts breaking out of formation and moving about with purpose. Scattered at different intervals across the vast space were planes and other military vehicles, either parked or in motion. One of the guards relaxing with a soda under the canopy called the two section leaders over and gave them instructions before dismissing them with a flick of his hand. The section leaders returned and the man yelled, "Attention!"

The woman briefly outlined the flights tasks for the day, shouting to be heard over the airfield noise. Fran barely paid her any attention. He was seething inside at the personal humiliation he felt. The swearing in, the beating, and the impending slave labor under the sun out in the middle of a flight line were the only things he could focus on at the moment. Fists clenched at his sides, Fran made a concentrated attempt at getting his emotions under control. In his past he had invested a lot of time and effort into not feeling affected by what others did, but the accumulation and the rapidity of the injustices that he had to endure lately were straining his normal reserved nature. The irony that he routinely and intentionally subjected others to treatment similar to what he was experiencing was not lost on him, but he felt his lifetime spent victimizing others was his place in the world's natural order and his getting publicly whipped and ridiculed was not. To him, these idiotic, ignorant Air Force people were messing with Mother Nature herself.

The woman droned on. "Blah, blah, blah," and then finally: "Carry on!" The command broke Fran out of his reverie as the formation separated around him. Most of the conscripts, including Fran's men, went to the construction shed so Fran tagged along. He calmed down from having his moment and listened to Loomis quietly complaining about the work assignments.

"Fuck me. We have to clear this whole thing by hand? What about that backhoe over there?" Loomis said. "Why don't they use that? It could do the work in twenty minutes that'll take all of us the whole day to do."

Fran and Bill didn't think the question was worthy of answering, but Gunter did. "Dude, you got a lot to learn about the military. Nothing they do makes sense. Getting upset about it isn't going to make things any better. You just have to suck it up and deal with it."

"Deal with it my ass. My damn back's nearly broke from that whupping earlier and I got a fucking lump on the top of my head the size of my fist." He took off his cap and pointed to a spot on his head where a large hematic lump was visible through his hair.

Fran, Bill and Gunter all laughed, but they quickly choked it down lest they draw attention to themselves. Under his breath Bill asked, "Loomis, how the hell did you get hit on the top of your head?"

Shaking his head, trying to figure out how the others saw it as funny, Loomis told them, "I dunno. I think the guy swinging the rope might've done it on purpose."

His admission only served to cause a new outbreak, harder to stifle than the last. Most of the conscripts were giving Fran's group odd looks, and mindful of drawing the ire of the guards, made sure to distance themselves by a buffer of several feet. The other conscripts didn't want to be seen as part of the same group of men singled out earlier that morning for a brutal lashing. Bill, Gunter, and Loomis didn't notice the implied ostracism, but Fran did. He mentally noted who walked away and who stayed close and looked at the group with sympathy or curiosity. Those who were sympathetic were the potential recruits he was looking for. When he was able to, Fran caught their eyes and smiled at them. He received several smiles in return.

When it came to recruits Fran was a realist. He couldn't reasonably expect to find and build a whole army of people with the same dispositions and inclinations as the three he already had. In fact, doing so wouldn't make strategic sense. Not every situation required a human hammer. He wanted all types and would need to employ them depending on the task. He would just have to be careful not to let either himself or his men get carried away and feed from inside the group because that would lead to desertion, or worse.

Grabbing shovels and wheelbarrows and various other tools, the conscripts were directed to a large patch of grass and debris marked off with wooden stakes and orange plastic tape. The woman told everyone, "Our task is to dig ten inches deep, in a line, from rope-to-rope. We have to advance a minimum of four feet per hour. I'll show you where to dump your wheelbarrows." She looked at her watch. "It's a little after seven right now. We break for lunch at noon. That means we need to have twenty feet done by lunch and if we don't get twenty feet, we don't get fed."

The last statement incited loud murmurs of discontent from nearly everybody. Fran and his three were among the few who didn't grumble. Not only did it not bother Fran, who didn't care about a missed meal, but the stipulation worked in his favor. The angrier and malcontent the conscripts became, the easier they would be to convert. The woman spoke again. "Get started, you're wasting time. Move it!"

On the way to the line Fran quickly outlined his ideas to Bill and told him to start sending out feelers. Bill nodded. Fran made sure he picked a spot next to a few of the people who seemed receptive earlier. He was counting on the noise of the work to cover their whispered conversations.

The laborious process of tearing up earth and rubble began. No one spoke to each other at first but soon the monotony of swinging a pickaxe or scraping with a shovel led to muted talk. None of it carried to the section leaders or the armed guards, so soon everyone figured out that if they kept their voices under the radar they could communicate with each other and help pass the time.

Fran was about to initiate a feeler conversation with the person to his right, an auburn haired lady who had given him a sympathetic smile earlier, when she surprised him by speaking first. "Shame what they did to you, back there at the chow hall," she told Fran, giving him a small shake of head before she continued. "I can't stand bullies."

As a bully himself, Fran couldn't appreciate her mindset, but as a leader who needed to recruit as many people as possible, he could at least overlook it. He played it up a bit. "Yeah, I think they broke a couple of my ribs, which makes it really painful to do this kind of work." He winced and sucked air through his teeth, seeking additional sympathy for his injuries.

"Well, if you need anything, be sure to let me know. My name's Eileen."

"I will. Thank you, Eileen," he said, lathering on the charm. "I'm grateful to you. My name is King. It's a pleasure to meet someone as nice as you." She nodded at the introduction and the compliment.

He exchanged a little more small talk with her and let her know where his tent was if she wanted to talk about ways to make life better for them all back at camp, then found a reason to speak to the person on his left, a fit Hispanic man named Diego with short hair and glasses. Fran had a similar conversation with him, and throughout the morning he discretely wandered from person to person feeling out those he might persuade to his cause. He occasionally caught Bill doing the same work.

The conscripts barely made their twenty foot quota by twelve o'clock, but they did and were rewarded with a thirty minute break to eat. They lined up and took MRE's from open boxes set up on a table under the canopy. The guards paid no attention to the conscripts and it appeared that as long as the work crew made their goals they wouldn't get hassled.

When Fran sat down to eat, he was joined by a large group of people in addition to his core crew. Both Loomis and Gunter expressed concern and puzzlement when other people came over to sit with them and almost scared the newcomers away. Fran held a hand out and told them: "Hey! These people here are interested in learning more about what our plans are and you will extend to them the same courtesy that you give me."

They heeled with, "Yes, King," and "Sure thing, King."

The new recruits quickly introduced themselves and then everyone ate and used the restroom. Fran let it be known that there would be a meeting at the tent later and everyone was invited to come, so long as they did it covertly. He didn't let on that he was planning an escape. That would come later after he tested them a bit more and weeded out any potential weak links, moles, or people with cross-purposes.

After the short lunch the afternoon went much like the morning. Somehow the word had gotten around that Fran was a leader type or spokesman for the discontented and people found ways to get next to him instead of the other way around. By the time the conscripts reformed for the march back he estimated that close to two dozen people had been invited to the meeting later that night. Only five or six conscripts told Fran outright that they weren't interested in what he had to say, but that they wouldn't tell anyone that he approached them.

On the march back one of the weaker women, unaccustomed to hard labor, fell out of formation. She sat down on the pavement and announced that she couldn't go on. A guard at the rear called for a halt and she declared that she was too tired, her feet and hands hurt, and she needed water.

"Get up now!" he commanded, and she refused, stating simply, "I can't. I want to, but I can't. I'm too tired." He and the other armed men surrounded her and began kicking her in the legs and back, yelling for her to get to her feet and rejoin the march. She cried and shrieked and rolled around, trying to protect herself from the rain of blows.

The beating continued for a full minute. Finally a different guard told her: "I'll give you to the count five," and he began counting backwards. "Five, four, three..." and the woman still made no move to comply. "Two, one." The guard leaned over and asked the woman, "Getting up?" and she shook her head. He shrugged and calmly took his pistol out and shot her in the face, spraying bits of skull, brains and blood over half of the formation.

Some of the conscripts screamed, mostly the women, but everyone recoiled, even Fran and his men, who were standing relatively close and were peppered with globs and chunks. The sound of the raw meat pattering the road accompanied the outcry. A couple of the soldiers pulled the woman's body by the arms and dragged her to the side of the road. They tossed her into the weeds and then wiped their hands on the legs of their pants.

"There's always one," the man who shot the woman quipped, looking at the conscripts and grinning large, "but never two." The other soldiers laughed.

Several of the people Fran had approached met his eyes and nodded in confirmation. There were also some that had refused his offer earlier that in that moment became new converts to his cause. After he got over his initial shock and wiped the blood specks from his face, Fran was almost ecstatic. He couldn't have planned a better demonstration at a better time to further his purposes. He held back on thanking the soldiers for their assistance, though.

When the formation was dismissed back at the chow hall the conscripts were required to go back to their unit area. Public assembly was not allowed so Fran hung around inside the tent with Bill and sent the other two to stand guard at the entrance. While everyone one in his small group was a sadist, Fran only considered Bill and himself as highly functioning enough to control their urges. He didn't want to expose any potential recruits to the unpredictable and erratic Gunter and Loomis just yet; while he already had the bait, he still needed to set the hook and the two men might frighten people away.

People began arriving and coming into the tent. Fran and Bill screened them all with much more scrutiny than was possible earlier on the flight line. They probed for motivation, mindset, special skills and abilities, and so on. When they were done, out of all the candidates there were a few exceptionals, many averages, several marginal and a couple of them with little or no potential at all, even for menial roles. They also discovered one person, a skinny hipster sporting a patchy beard, that they suspected might be a plant by the Air Force. Both Fran and Bill came to the same conclusion almost simultaneously which sealed the thin man's fate. Bill restrained him while Fran got Gunter and Loomis from where they were holding the entrance and gave them their orders. It was dark by then. The two men spirited the mole somewhere distant, permanently silenced him, and then hid the body.

Fran asked the exceptionals back for a meeting after all of the interviews were done. Everyone knew that if they were discovered they could all face punishment so they kept their voices low. Sensing instinctively that it was too early to require the new group to swear allegiance to him, Fran nevertheless ensured their loyalty by ordering them to do dangerous tasks, missions with high risk and with the most chances of getting caught. Bill, Gunter and Loomis were introduced as his second-in-command and lieutenants.

Two of the three new people Fran thought had the most potential were nondescript, which in his mind made them perfect for scouting and raiding missions. The first was a man named Hank who could easily be mistaken for a plumber or a storekeeper, but who was actually a retired policeman. Hank intimated during his interview that he had been an oppressive and corrupt cop. Normally such a person was someone who only looked after himself, but Fran knew that if Hank was given both opportunity and license to do what he was naturally inclined to do, without condemnation, that the old man would follow orders well enough and be loyal. They signed him on and offered him a part in their enterprise.

The second person to come onboard was a woman. She was also bland and reminded Fran of his gym teacher from third grade. She wasn't pretty or ugly and probably rarely ever got noticed because she looked like no matter where she was, she belonged there. Her name was Helen and in her former life she ran a daycare center. She was a malicious creature and she didn't require much prodding to disclose her particular flavor of viciousness. At first she only hinted at her past exploits, but when she saw there would be no judgment forthcoming from either Fran or Bill she gave a full report. Fran's tastes didn't normally include small children because they lacked any kind of a reasonable challenge; they were in the same category as ants or roaches to him, but Bill seemed fascinated by Helen's exploits and pressed her relentlessly for more details. Fran finally grew bored enough of the conversation to stop the lurid interrogation and asked Helen to join them. She agreed eagerly.

The final person invited back was a sociopath named Clark, an extremely handsome man with a winning smile. Fran considered Clark the most lethal of the three because he didn't give off even a hint of a creepy vibe, which allowed him to mingle easily among normal people without triggering a negative response. Clark declined to state his previous occupation, but because he wore the mask of likeable and charismatic guy so well, Fran gave him a pass on his personal history and tasked him with the role of primary recruiter. Clark agreed. Fran was under no illusion that the man was doing it for him, but as long as Clark was effective the motivation behind the work didn't much matter.

After Clark departed the other two new recruits were given their assignments: Hank, along with Bill, was to figure out the issue of arranging transportation and disabling any remaining vehicles, while weapons acquisition was put to Helen and Gunter. Loomis was held in reserve, mostly because Fran didn't trust the muffintop with any complicated tasks.

Before retiring to their cots for some rest Fran talked the day over with Bill and the others. Their plan was well set and they expected things to happen relatively quickly. Fran guessed that because they were new conscripts their captors wouldn't expect a mutiny so early in the process of enculturalization, especially after the examples provided at the chow hall and during the march back from the airfield earlier. It was imperative that they strike quickly while they still had the element of surprise on their side.

Both scouting missions were planned to take place that very night. Fran was jostled awake by Bill at two in the morning. Fran worked the sleep out of his eyes and squinted into the near darkness and saw Helen, Hank, and Gunter crouched around him. All of them wore face paint and they were difficult to make out clearly.

Bill came over to Fran's rack and whispered, "Were all set, King. We should only be gone a couple of hours at the most."

"Okay," Fran whispered back. "Good luck and don't get caught." His vision was adjusting to the low light of the tent's interior and he could see the eagerness to please in Bill and Gunter's eyes. His newest recruits didn't have the same level of blind devotion to him yet, but they did have a firm set to their jaws as they nodded solemnly to him. That was all Fran could expect at the moment. If Helen and Hank returned from the night's scouting run successfully and in one piece, then he would invest the time and effort required to turn them completely.

Fran watched them leave and then lay back down on his cot. He could hear Loomis snoring from across the tent and the noise kept him awake. He wasn't really trying to go back to sleep anyway so he didn't mind; he needed to plan and he also wanted to be up when the two parties returned. He was pleased with how things were shaping up, with one small exception. Up to this point he was the preeminent and predisposed leader of his rebellious outfit. Fran reasoned that this was because he was a special kind of predator. He was not only highly intelligent, but he could control his urges and was aware enough to extend that control to others. He was also extremely patient when waiting for the right time to strike. In his mind no one else in the group came close to exercising the same restraint regarding their individual appetites. That is, except for Clark. And because of that, Fran reasoned, the recruiter was going to be a problem.

The handsome man was everything Fran was, and more. Clark was more personable, less intimidating, and better looking. Worse yet, Clark lived and preyed on others from within his own strata, the mainstream population. To exist and take from close proximity and to succeed at it took unusual talent and a shrewd confidence that Fran, who had always lived and hunted on the periphery of society, had little experience with. Fran took the easier road by only targeting the poor, the weak, and the unmissed.

But Fran knew Clark's type, which was also the man's weakness: Clark was a self-centered narcissist. Fran recalled a saying he had heard in the pen: 'That man has all the qualities of a dog, except loyalty,' and decided that Clark was too big a threat to keep in his growing army or among the living. Clark would only be loyal to himself and if the recruiter was allowed to stick around for any extended period of time he would eventually seek to supplant Fran.

"No." Fran whispered to the tent roof. "You're going to have to go, Clark, before you try and make me go."

Over the next hour Fran thought about how being in charge of a group had its difficulties. This recent problem with needing Clark and using him, but also having to dispose of the man at the right time and in the right way was a good example. Before the event Fran would have just killed Clark outright as competition, but now that he was in charge, killing one of his officers for no apparent reason would make the others distrustful of him and it might foment a rebellion. After mulling the problem over from many angles Fran decided to put it on the back burner for the time being. He grew sleepy.

He was dozing off when Gunter and Helen popped into the tent. Gunter scurried over to Fran's cot while Helen stayed at the entrance, peeking out and watching their back trail for anyone who might be following. Gunter's white pigtail flashed in the dim light of the tent as it swished back and forth with the thin man's frantic head movements. He was grinning wide and breathing hard with excitement.

"King!" he said, a little too loudly. "We hit the jackpot! Goddamn!"

"Shh," Helen admonished from the entrance, just as loud. "Keep it down you dumb bastard!"

"You shut up, you stupid fat bitch!" Gunter replied.

"Hey, hey, calm down you two, you're too loud," Fran admonished in a low voice, standing up and stepping in between them. He motioned for Gunter to follow him closer to the entrance. "Now tell me. Quietly," he warned Gunter.

"Sorry, King, it's just that we had a good night. And even though Helen here is meaner than a snake, she knows what she's doing," Gunter reported, indicating Helen with his thumb as he tossed out the off-handed compliment. "We found the armory without a problem right where the map said it would be. It's guarded, but only by a few guys. We were able to sneak right up to the back wall and if we wanted to take the guards out it would have been cake," he said, snapping his fingers for emphasis.

"What's your take, Helen?" Fran asked, turning to the frumpy woman. One corner of her mouth hung down in a permanent half-frown. Anyone who didn't know her would have looked at the woman's pasty-white, doughy face and made a snap assumption that Helen was a harmless hausfrau. That is, until they focused in and looked into her eyes. Helen's eyes radiated a feral intelligence and hinted at a remorseless soul. "Maybe she's crazy," Fran thought. He hoped so. He needed people like her: Ruthless, unfeeling and invisible. So he sought her input, and through that, her genuine buy-in to his leadership.

"He's right, King," she told him. "There's very little security. It won't be a problem to take the guards out, it's just that we can't know if they have the keys to the armory on them. If it was me that put them there, I wouldn't give them the keys. It'd be too easy for someone to kill them and then take the armory."

Fran nodded. "I agree. We'll have to hit the armory on the way out." He looked at both of them and asked, "What about the armory walls? Can we smash through one with a truck?"

"Hell yeah," Gunter said. "Easily."

"If you do that, it'll make a hell of a racket," Helen advised. "But yeah, like he said," she used her thumb to indicate Gunter, "smashing through the walls shouldn't be too difficult."

"Alright. Good work you two," Fran told them. "Now get some rest. The others will be back soon."

Helen waved and left. Gunter announced "I'm hungry," then walked over and sat on his cot. Fran heard him open an MRE and then the sounds of eating. The heavy smell of buffalo sauce permeated the tent and Loomis grunted awake.

"Mmmm, whatzat?" the fat man grumbled.

"Fucking chicken in sauce, dude," Gunter responded in a low voice, laughing through a mouth full of food.

"Yum," Loomis mumbled and sat up. Soon after that was the noise of another MRE being opened followed by the smell of tuna and the sounds of heavy chewing. The chomping and the mixture of smells were too much for Fran and he fled through the tent flap into the fresher air outdoors. He breathed in deeply of the clean night scent.

Maybe he just hadn't noticed it before but the air seemed to have a cleaner tinge to it. It had only been a few days since the event, but Fran was positive that he could tell the difference in air quality. The pollution generating factories and vehicles had barely hit a standstill but nature was already recuperating. Fran breathed deeply again; he couldn't remember a time when taking a breath had felt so exhilarating.

As he stood outside and enjoyed the night air, the sounds of eating coming from inside slowed in frequency and eventually stopped. Fran was ready to head back in when he caught something in his peripheral vision. He turned and focused. Two figures were lurking near a tent about thirty feet away. The figures were being discrete, sprinting hunched over from cover to cover in Fran's direction.

They must have spotted Fran in the ambient light because the figures halted suddenly and then quickly dipped between two of the tents. Fran waited for them to reappear, but by the time he figured out that they weren't going to, a hand slid around his face and covered his mouth. He felt a sharp prick in the middle of his back as a voice whispered, "Who are you?"

The hand was slapped away by the other person and Fran heard Bill whisper, "Shit, Hank, that's King!"

"Oh," was the former cop's only reply as he put the knife away.

The two men disappeared into the tent and Fran followed, wiping the feel of Hank's hand off of his upper lip. He didn't like to be touched, especially on his face, even though he understood why it had happened.

Inside, Bill was smart enough to keep his voice low as he gave his report. "We have good news and bad news, King," he started. "The good news is that we can get access to the military vehicles without a problem. They're just sitting there near the front gate and Hank here thinks he can hotwire them easy."

Loomis and Gunter slowly came awake. They sat up and listened in from their cots.

"Yeah," Hank said, and then built on Bill's statement. "All of the trucks are older technology, military-grade mechanics designed to be uncomplicated. I can get them started with just a screwdriver."

Fran nodded. "What's the bad news then?"

"The bad news is that we can't really disable all the vehicles," Bill said, shrugging and then spreading his hands out. "There are too many and they're spread out all over the place. It's too risky."

"We'll need to drive to the armory," Gunter spoke up from the edge of his cot. "We need to ram a wall down to get inside." In the light of the breaking dawn Gunter's pale face and white hair were highlighted against the military green of the tent side. Fran heard a grunt from Hank. The old man was nodding to himself, thinking it over.

"Maybe we can go in through the armory roof, then collect the guns and take them with us," Hank suggested.

Fran didn't like the idea. "That's no good because we won't have the time to try different ways in. We need to hit the armory and get right back out and off of the base. These military people will be on us too quickly for us to mess around."

"Okay," Hank conceded. "Then we should grab vehicles as close to the armory as possible and shave some time off. How many people are we bringing with us, King?" he asked.

"I don't know yet. Clark is going to get as many as he can, but he has to be careful. I would overshoot and say it could be as many as forty," Fran answered.

Bill spoke up. "That's two troop carriers then. Plus a vehicle just to ram the wall and leave behind. That's doable."

Everyone nodded at the way the plan was coming together, even Loomis who had been left out of the loop for the most part. Fran made a decision. "Good." he announced. "I don't see a reason why we can't step up the plan. We do it tonight instead of two days from now."

If anyone had doubts about the order, none of them voiced any. The seconds ticked by while the information was absorbed and processed. A noise from outside caused everyone to hunch down. Footsteps were heard outside. Whoever it was, they didn't pause as they went by. Then more steps, this time accompanied by voices. Bill went to the flap to peek out, then came back and reported to Fran.

"Looks like people are waking up, getting into the toilet line early," he said.

"Well, we aren't going to get anything else done this morning," Fran told them all. He turned to Hank. "Meet us back here after the work detail and we'll finalize the plans. Let Helen know."

Hank nodded and left and everyone followed the ex-cop out of the tent and walked to the end of the line at the porta-potties. It was already ten people deep.

"Shit, not again." Loomis wailed. His voice speaking at full volume seemed odd after the long night spent whispering.

Fran decided to exercise some of his newfound authority on the men. He turned to Bill and said, "Get us a spot up front."

Bill nodded and left the line, joined by Gunter and Loomis. There was some jostling up front and a few angry words, but the line shifted backwards into Fran. He saw Bill motion to him so he walked up and got in front of everyone as Gunter and Loomis held everyone back. He closed the door behind him to the sound of grumbling from the displaced people still in line. Fran dropped his pants, sat, and smiled. "I could get used to this," he thought.

FLIGHT LINE, ROYAL AIR FORCE STATION NORTHOLT

Walter and his team rolled up to the flight line for their departure stateside with four minutes to spare. He and Major Ackerman were ushered up the tail ramp of an Airbus A330 troop transport plane while the remainder of the team was shunted off and assigned to a separate flight. They were supposed to take the next plane out and would be following thirty minutes behind.

The major was talking loudly into Walter's ear in an effort to communicate over the noise of the twin Pratt and Whitney jets. They passed row after row of rearward facing seats. "Colonel, take your own row, there's plenty of room! This plane normally transports three hundred troops, so even with half of the seats ripped out for stowing gear there are still a lot left over!" Walter wasn't in a shouting mood, so he nodded back at the major and found an empty row near the middle of the plane. With all of this empty space he wondered why his team couldn't join him. He could have used the time in the air to gel with them and lean on their expertise of military communications.

Sighing and shaking his head in puzzlement at how the military managed to function despite making such nonsensical decisions, Walter tossed his small travel bag onto one of the seats. His bag held an Army-issued laptop and encrypted thumb drive, along with some notepads and his toilet kit. During his time embedded with the army in Afghanistan Walter had gotten into the habit of traveling light and being ready to move on short notice. He had enough time back at the barracks to shower and shave before donning his new uniform, which Walter was surprised to see already had his name embroidered on them. The clothes fit great, but they were still stiff and someone, maybe Major Ackerman, had made an effort to iron out the fold marks on them. He was wearing a green beret, which denoted that he belonged to the Adjutant General's Corps, and he looked passably like a real officer in the British Army. Walter almost felt like one too, but he also felt part imposter. He wondered what folks like Major Ackerman felt, having spent most of their adult life in the military making enormous personal sacrifices and actually earning their promotions, seeing Walter parading around in a Colonel's uniform with less than twenty four hours on the job. Oddly, if anyone was upset with him or thought him undeserving Walter didn't detect any hints of it.

From his seat facing aft Walter spent his time before takeoff watching the aircrew strap down the final pieces of gear brought onboard with forklifts. Pallets were stacked three high and crammed in so that there was only a narrow alley between them. In the short time since Walter's arrival the aircrew had brought onboard several equipment loads and secured them to the aircraft cargo hooks.

He admired the efficiency of the soldiers. They worked in silence for the most part, communicating with hand signals and nods. When they were finished, one of the aircrew did a final check on the tie-down straps while the rest took to their crew seats built into the plane's bulkhead. A few walked by Walter on their way back to stations forward and nodded respectfully to him, which made the feeling that he was an imposter resurface.

General Fells came aboard through an entrance on the airbus that Walter couldn't see; a pilot or crew man greeted him officially over the aircraft intercom: "Welcome aboard General. Time check is just three minutes past zero six hundred, London BST, and it's approximately twenty eight hundred nautical miles to Wright-Patterson Air Force Base. We'll be airborne a little over five hours and at a cruising speed of eight hundred and sixty kilometers per hour, which should put our landing in Dayton, Ohio shortly after zero five hundred Eastern Standard Time, local time. Sir, your cabin has been prepared. Please notify the flight crew if you require anything." The intercom clicked off, then clicked on again after about twenty seconds. "There will be a staff meeting in the General's cabin in three hours." Walter looked at his watch and set the digital alarm for half an hour prior to the meeting.

"Flight crew, prepare for takeoff," was announced and less than a minute later the plane was taxiing down the runway and lifting off. As the friction from the tires rolling on the tarmac waned and the airbus transitioned into flight, Walter's felt a sinking sensation and his stomach dropped into his seat momentarily before the lower pressure inside the cabin finally equalized. The feeling of falling forward eased as the angle of climb lessened, and Walter was finally able to lean back. The exhaustion of his long day coupled with the monotonous sound of the engine made his eyes droop. By the time the plane reached its cruising altitude of thirty five thousand feet, Walter was fast asleep.

He was startled awake by turbulence and was surprised to see that he was the only person who had been sleeping. Everyone else was sitting in small groups discussing things he could only guess at because he couldn't hear them over the aircraft noise. Feeling slightly guilty for his nap Walter checked his watch and saw that his catnap had only consumed a little over an hour.

Despite the short rest he felt rejuvenated and decided to do some work. He pulled out his laptop, booted it up, and found several alerts from Warrant Officer Smith and a few emails from Sergeant Kennet. Although his follow-on team had only been airborne for thirty minutes, they had been busy. Walter clicked on an email from Smith with the subject line 'Read Me First' and it opened up a composite intelligence summary of global geopolitics. Two article links were outlined in red and flashing so Walter clicked the top one and read it.

The repercussions of the event had finally reverberated to the opposite hemisphere with enough impact to disturb the longstanding equanimity of several nation states. Issue number one was that China had declared war on the former United States and had already deployed several flotillas from the People's Liberation Army Navy (PLAN) North, South and East fleets. It was still early in the analysis phase, but an estimated one hundred and seventy ships and an untold number of submarines had rendezvoused near the Korea Strait and were now steaming east out of the South China Sea. Ongoing analysis from the few intelligence sources still capable of producing data were determining the possibility that some of the vessels might remain behind for coastal defense, but it seemed more likely that an invasion of Taiwan was imminent, probably within the next twenty four hours. It was predicted that any ships that transited through the gap between Taiwan and the Philippines were an invasion force targeting Hawaii and the west coast of North America.

Walter broke out in a cold sweat. The realization that the world death toll was still spiking made him nauseous. What made it worse for him was that there was almost nothing anyone or any nation could do to stem or stop it. He continued reading, sure of more bad news.

The second red alert was closer to home. A Spanish naval task force was detected loitering in the vicinity of Longships, a group of islands off the coast of Cornwall. Spain was taking advantage of the event, and the United Kingdom's commitment to provide humanitarian relief and to defend American nuclear assets, to make a move for the islands. According to diplomatic sources, the Spanish government declared that it would only stand down once England surrendered its hold on the tiny territory of Gibraltar, otherwise Spain would be forced to invade Longships.

Every British citizen was familiar with the Gibraltar border conflict. It was an extremely old topic, but Walter was surprised that Spain was acting so opportunistically during such a grave time. He shook his head and moved on. The issue with Spain was only vaguely tangent to what he was concerned with and there were other forces in place to deal with the problem. Besides, he was headed in the opposite direction.

Several 'orange' items were next and Walter skimmed through them. He wasn't surprised to find several countries were now at war with each other. The Line of Control between India and Pakistan was breached in the Kashmir region, and India violated her own 'No First Use' policy by launching two Prithvi-I short range ballistic missiles into Kashmir and at least seven of the more advanced Agni-IV warheads into the city of Islamabad and surrounding areas. In retaliation, Pakistan's Black Spiders JF-17 fighter bomber squadron, eighteen subsonic aircraft strong and each equipped with a Ra'ad thirty five kiloton cruise missile, launched on Mumbai, Delhi, and several other populous Indian cities. The estimated death count from the combined nuclear strikes was put at eighty million people. More alarming were the residual losses. Deaths from radiation fallout, loss of infrastructure, and the subsequent privation were estimated to push the total to between one and one point two billion. Both countries were irrevocably erased from the planet. It took less than an hour to eradicate fifteen percent of the world's population and render over four million square miles of earth unusable.

Walter was having difficulty comprehending the misery of the event's secondary effects on the world at large. "Maybe the human mind is not meant to encompass the enormity of what was happening," he thought to himself. "Maybe in times such as these, we are only meant to ensure the survival of the race and to think not in terms of country, but in terms of humankind as a whole." Walter sat in his seat looking at his screen, at the report on the Indian subcontinent. He dreaded what might be next and debated on whether or not he wanted to read any more misery. After a minute of self-deliberation he decided he didn't want to, not at all, but if he was to do his part he must. He continued reading, absently rubbing his stiffening neck.

The next orange item dealt with the Korean Peninsula. In a surprise move, South Korea preempted an invasion by the north and swarmed over the DMZ. It was general knowledge that the buffer zone between the two countries was one of the most militarily enforced borders in human history. Walter read that South Korea infiltrated by sea, air, land, and even under the border, utilizing seventeen of the known tunnel systems dug by the north during the sixty year armistice between the two countries. Unfortunately for South Korea, members of the North Korean army staff were the craftier military strategists and had anticipated what the south would do.

The South Korean First Operational Command made the initial push with four corps of troops, over three hundred thousand strong, as well as conducting amphibious landings at several points along the North Korean coast. Twenty one hundred tanks, eleven thousand artillery positions, twenty four hundred combat aircraft, and twenty two ships comprised of destroyers, frigates and landing craft made a simultaneous crossing or infiltration into North Korea. Surprisingly, there was little or no resistance, so instead of pushing forward the southern army paused to consolidate forces and reposition reinforcements below the DMZ.

In normal times, Battle Damage Assessment of the subsequent massacre would have been regarded as the most disastrous and costly military failure in world history. North Korea had contracted all of its forces north to draw the South Koreans in, before ordering the People's Strategic Rocket Forces to launch a combination of artillery, anti-ship cruise missiles, and short and medium range ballistic missiles at its attackers, at southern critical infrastructure nodes, and at the South Korean capital of Seoul. Imagery analysts had difficulty counting the number of strikes due to the scale of destruction, but the early estimates placed it at over four hundred and eighty detonations.

The South Korean Air Force fared no better. The North Korean Integrated Air Defense System decimated ninety percent of the incoming combat aircraft, the majority of which were unable to execute their assigned strike packages before being shot down. Consequently, North Korea remained largely untouched and at full complement. The war on the peninsula was over in less than a day and Korea was once again unified after more than half a century of division. The population loss in South Korea was placed at fourteen million, most of which were civilians.

Walter kept reading. It was a similar scene between Israel and Palestine, and Russia was grabbing all it could of Eastern Europe. Africa was at war with itself, but Walter knew that in Africa that had almost always been the case anyway, just now nobody cared as much because they had their own problems to deal with. He sighed and put the laptop on the seat next to him and stood, stretching his arms and arching his back. He felt light headed and shook his head to clear it. Deep down he understood what was happening, but everything he had read had a surreal aspect to it. The feeling was very unpleasant and nauseatingly disorienting.

Without warning Walter hunched forward and projectile vomited. The contents of his stomach arced across the aisle in a greyish spray and covered four seats in the row across from him. He gagged but nothing else came up. He licked his lips and grimaced at the taste in his mouth and looked around.

Nobody seemed to have noticed what he just did. The people who were sitting in the nearby seats earlier had left, and it had all happened so quickly and the plane was so noisy that nobody saw or heard. Feeling guilty and embarrassed, Walter quickly grabbed his stuff and moved forward two rows. He sat down and arranged his gear as if he had always been there then feigned being sleep. Within moments he heard a woman's voice cry out "Ewww, gross!" followed by the sound of sympathetic vomiting.

Walter pretended to be asleep through the subsequent pandemonium and cleanup operation before being shaken awake by Major Ackerman.

"Colonel Doucet," the major said, jostling Walter slightly.

Playing his part Walter yawned awake. He stretched his arms over his head, careful not to overact, and sniffed. "What is that awful smell, Major?" he asked.

Grimacing, the major filled him in. "An airman got sick a few rows behind you, but it's been cleaned up. After the meeting we'll find you a better seat."

Nodding his thanks, Walter grabbed his laptop and allowed himself to be led away to General Fells' operational briefing. As he passed the now cleaned seats he saw what he thought must be the airman everyone else blamed for the vomit, a young Indian woman near the last row. She was receiving looks of disdain and she wore a hangdog expression. Walter felt sorry for her and enormously guilty, but in light of the human misery occurring all over the world, he conceded it was a relatively minor thing to dupe her and not take the loss of his esteem. As a concession, he avoided looking her in the eye as he passed.

Inside the General's well-apportioned cabin Walter saw the same people he met during the previous staff meetings. Since it was his first time in their presence in a military uniform, he received several double takes, but after that he was regarded as part of the regular staff. Their acceptance meant a lot to him and Walter relaxed enough to make small talk with them while they awaited the general's arrival.

Most of the conversations centered on what to expect after landing at Wright-Patterson. A few of the other officers had been there previously for training or joint operations, so everyone quieted down to hear what it was like there. The general consensus was that overall it wasn't a bad place to be, normally. As far as how the event had affected things there they could only speculate.

When General Fells finally made his appearance everyone stood and waited for the Lord High Steward to sit before resuming their seats. Even though the general had changed out of his dress uniform and wore the more practical combat uniform like everyone else, the man still carried the aura of authority around him. Walter wished he possessed a fraction of the general's self-confidence and presence. "Let's begin," he said. "General Vogel?"

General Ken Vogel was second in command of the newly established provisional government. The grizzled veteran had made a name for himself in the Falklands War, where he received a battlefield commission for bravery during the infamous Mount Kent offensive. Universally admired as a practical man, Walter reflected on how far General Vogel had come, from his roots as the son of a German immigrant fisherman to next in line of the British government. The general also had a reputation for being extremely likable and personable. Smiling, General Vogel said, "Yes, let's begin," and nodded to a colonel seated near the front. "S4? Your report, please."

Walter already knew the "S" numbers, which stood for different branches of the Army Staff. "S4" was logistics and he and his team belonged to "S2," which was the intelligence branch. Walter listened to the logistics colonel explain forward material positioning and other supply related details, but he soon lost track of the detailed listing of "tonnes of this and tonnes of that" being moved around and utilized.

Next up was S3, the operations branch. The S3 was a Brigadier, a rank above Walter. Everyone at the table perked up; the operations brief looked to be the most interesting brief as it involved every other branch in some manner. The Ophir Ridge plan for the North American continent was set up in stages, and the next stage was supposed to kick off once the British force landed stateside. The Brigadier outlined Phase One in detail, and after fifteen minutes of explaining slide after slide Walter's head was buzzing with troop dispositions, containment areas, force deconfliction, and spheres of influence.

He began to wonder how everyone else processed all of the information, especially the two generals who were responsible for assimilating every aspect of it, and once again he felt uncomfortably out of his element.

Looking over at Major Ackerman, Walter was glad to see that his aide was jotting things down. At least they would have notes of the meeting to study later. He took a peek to see what the major was writing down and almost shrieked in dismay when he saw that the page was filled with doodles. Walter nudged the major and gave the aide a look that said "What are you doing?" but the major only smiled sheepishly and put his pen down.

"Colonel Doucet, you're up," General Vogel said.

Giving Major Ackerman a final glance, Walter stood. Warrant Officer Smith had forwarded the necessary slides to whomever it was that compiled the brief and the first slide was the tiered intelligence summary he read over earlier. Looking out at stunned faces of his audience Walter sensed that for many of them, this was new information so he slowed down for the enormity of it to soak in. His last slide was a predictive analysis of interpolated human losses worldwide, with percentages of certitude laid out on a propagated time scale. Walter concluded his brief to the general with, "…as you can see, General Fells, even best case scenario is that less than half of the world's population will survive the coming year."

General Vogel spoke up, rubbing his hands together and General Fells was smiling. "Well, that's better than we thought. That's a spot of good news, at least. Thank you, Colonel Doucet."

Walter could only nod to General Vogel in disbelief as he sat back down. He sighed inwardly, sad that this is what things came to. Never in his right mind would he think a few days ago that not only would the news of the loss of almost four billion people be okay, but that it would be regarded as positive information.

A few of the other staff officers around the table gave Walter smiles or regarded him with mild jealousy at his being the deliverer of such good tidings. He smiled back wanly or ignored the others in turn, depending on their message. He scribbled a note to himself to have Mr. Smith forward him an electronic copy of the Ophir Ridge operational plans. He had to see it for himself.

The rest of the brief was filled with information on the remaining force-capable military units of the United States and other allies. All forward deployed forces survived, but initially they were without a command and control structure. The event placed the possibility of any such entity surviving in a functional capacity at zero percent. One of the first steps once Ophir Ridge was enacted was a world-wide broadcast to all allied units, directing them to initiate certain protocols, primarily that of coming under the control of the Ophir Ridge commander.

General Vogel gave the overview on allied force disposition. "I would love to say that this is the first slide of many, but it ain't so," the general began. "This is not to say that there aren't other functional allied units out there, there probably are, but the ones on this slide are the only ones that survived with a chain of command at a level high enough for us to contact. As you all may or may not know, NATO went out the door the moment the sun decided to spit radiation onto the western hemisphere and Ophir Ridge went into effect. As General Fells' second, I've been given the role of Supreme Allied Commander, to better coordinate efforts towards our strategic aim."

Picking up a lecture stick from the conference table and pointing at the slide, General Vogel asked the other officers seated around him, "Before I begin, any questions so far?" A two second pause where nobody spoke. "Good. Now where were we?" he asked, waving the pointer around and glancing at the slide, then back at everyone watching him. "Oh, yeah, now I remember where we are. We're on our own. Very little help coming." He shook his head. "Besides a fraction of the American naval forces and some U.K. and U.S. intelligence sites located in neutral countries, we have nothing. With no way to get them home, all of the blue troops in the Middle East including our own British forces are stuck there for the foreseeable future. We don't have the resources to split off of the North American priority."

The general put both palms on the table and looked everyone in the eye. "Both General Fells and I have looked at the predictions for blue force survivability in the sandbox, and I regret to inform everyone here that even if we dedicated every resource at attempting an extraction, our men and women there would be overrun before we made landfall. The deterrent is gone, and already the units there are falling to enemy action."

Indicating the slide again, General Vogel concluded. "All capable friendly naval forces are being recalled to protect Mother England and to support our Ophir Ridge overseas efforts. The same goes with the intel assets, which are working new missions." The general put the pointer down softly and looked over at his boss. "General Fells?"

"Thank you, Ken," General Fells said. He looked at his old friend, then at everyone else. "I won't keep you much longer. We'll be landing at Wright-Patterson within the hour. I expect a quick orientation and integration with the resident American troops. For the time being I wish to leave the Americans under the overall command of General Vogel, but we should all immediately begin working with purpose towards the same strategic aim. I don't think we'll have any difficulties in that regard, but we'll know more once we land. Keep in mind that the Americans should be shown compassion whenever possible. They have suffered gravely."

General Fells stood and the other officers hurried to their feet. "Thank you, that is all," he said to no one in particular, before exiting quietly with General Vogel in tow. After the two men left the other staff members began talking animatedly amongst themselves and Walter followed them out of the room, joined by Major Ackerman. On their way to new seats they grabbed Walter's belongings and some coffee from a station on the aircraft bulkhead.

Walter sipped his coffee and grimaced. "Awful," he muttered.

The major had no complaints. He actually smacked his lips contentedly after a deep sip, which made Walter wonder if they were both drinking the same coffee. Shaking his head he wondered if he would ever get used to being in the Army.

Major Ackerman handed Walter a small, heavy box and said, "I almost forgot, Colonel. Here's extra ammo for your Glock. I wanted to make sure you had it before we landed. Never know when you'll need it."

Walter thanked him as an announcement came over the speakers and instructed everyone to take their seats for the descent into Wright-Patterson. People settled in and a couple of minutes later the plane tilted forward and noticeably slowed. Walter had to pinch his nose and perform the Valsalva maneuver several times to meet the changes in air pressure before he suddenly felt the hard rubber tires hit the tarmac outside. The jets reversed direction and Walter's back became glued to the seat.

"Welcome to the former United States of America," the pilot announced, then added sarcastically, "Please enjoy your stay."

SUMMIT COUNTY JAIL DINING HALL

Josh, Finn, Ben and the other four men fired up the galley equipment and enjoyed a feast worthy of the end of the world. Josh got to know the remaining four men better while they ate. One of them, Bruce, a former trustee, used to cook the warden's meals. He knew the code to the freezer where the warden's favorite foods were kept and cooked up a special meal for everyone. Filet mignon and lobster bisque with red velvet cake for dessert.

The four men seated beside Finn and Ben were what Josh considered 'typical' prisoner stock, at least for the Summit County, Ohio area. They were all white and heavily tattooed. Bruce was tall and skinny. Brent was lithe, muscular, and sported a serious seventies porn moustache, and John-John was older and bald, with only three teeth and a heavy lisp. Last was someone who Josh already knew because of his reputation. In prison it's difficult to stand out unless you are physically different or are unusual in some other way. Ben was a huge black man who wore tiny glasses, so he was easy to remember but the last man earned his nickname and reputation by adopting a character, and Josh had to admit that even through the worst day in human history, he didn't see the guy break character once.

Josh said to him, "I already know who you are, Seagull. Everyone knows who you are."

"Why, thank you," the chubby man said, putting his hands together and bowing to Josh. He had a heavy squint and his black hair was pulled back in a ponytail. "If you need any lessons in hand to hand combat, just ask."

"Okay. I'll be sure to do that." Josh wanted to laugh but didn't want to hurt the guy's feelings.

After dinner everyone sat around for a while decompressing. They could occasionally hear whooping from the monsters trapped in the cell blocks and they discussed the need to take care of them. It was agreed that they should avoid more gunshots if possible to keep from alerting anything outside the prison. The only way to do that was to kill them manually.

"It's one thing to shoot into a crowd and let the bullets take the impact," Ben was lecturing, "but it's a whole other thing to stab up close and feel someone dying. Josh, I think that you and Finn should let the rest of us do that work. We've done it before."

Bruce and John-John nodded knowingly and Seagull bowed. “I can handle it,” Josh said.

“I want to be included, too,” Finn protested. “I need to learn how to kill sometime, why not tomorrow? Everyone needs to know that I can take care of myself, protect myself.”

“You’re right, Finn, everyone needs to pull their own weight,” Josh said before he added, “but tomorrow isn’t the time. We need you in Central. If something goes wrong, I know we can depend on you; you’re the only one besides me who knows what to do in there.”

Abashed, but smiling at the compliment, Finn answered. “Sure, Josh, whatever you need.”

“Great. Anyone have recommendations for quietly killing those things?” Josh asked.

“Aikido,” Seagull suggested.

“Okay. That’s one idea,” Josh said and Seagull beamed at being taken seriously. “Anyone else? Uh, please?”

John-John raised his hand and lisped out an answer. “Seems to me that poking them things through the bars ain’t much different than frog-gigging. Let’s just make us up some gigs and poke ‘em to death.” He put his hand back down, all out ideas.

“That’ll do,” Bruce said. “We have plenty of knives, duct tape and broom handles right here in the galley. I can make us up some spears before rack time.”

“I’ll help,” Finn volunteered.

“Great. And we can bunk in the CO quarters tonight.” Josh said to the cheers of the former inmates. “Bad news is that there aren’t cameras in there. I’ll need someone to go with me to clear it.”

“Want me to tag along?” Ben asked.

“Sure, if you don’t mind.” Then to everyone else he said, “You guys will like it in there, it has all the comforts of home. Clean sheets, showers, game systems, stuff like that.”

John-John, Brent and Seagull stayed behind to clean up the kitchen while the Bruce and Finn prepared the spears. After Josh and Ben found the CO quarters empty they went back to collect the others. Within the hour everything was secured, the spears were finished, and everyone was showered and wearing clean clothes from new guard issue.

The former inmates spent some time strutting around in CO uniforms and laughing at each other, rendering mock salutes and ordering each other to get against the wall and 'spread 'em'. Even Finn was laughing and despite the horrific events of the day, most of the men expressed a genuine improvement in their condition. After all, they weren't in cages anymore and the society that had condemned them to bondage was absent from the world. It wasn't long before they started yawning and getting sleepy. Normal prison routine had them conditioned to a certain schedule and they were way past 'lights out'. Even Ben, who seemed formidable otherwise, succumbed to the sandman and barely made it to his rack before passing out. Finn was the last one up besides Josh.

"Finn, I'm heading to Central to keep watch." Josh told him.

Fighting to keep his eyes open, Finn asked him, "Why? Nothing can get in here, just like no one can get out."

"I'll still feel better keeping an eye on things."

"Okay. Good night, Josh."

"Good night, Finn."

CONTROL CENTRAL

Josh settled into the chair in front of the monitors. It was the first time since he freed the inmates that he was alone and although he had spent many nights doing exactly what he was doing now, tonight felt different. He actually felt lonely. The new guys were okay and he liked them, but it wasn't company he was lonely for. He felt lonely for all of the people that were gone. His mother, his friends inside the prison and out, and all of the people he had never met and now never would. He sensed the emptiness that the world event had rendered into existence and sighed.

To pass the time, Josh flipped through the external cameras. Nothing. He switched to the cameras inside the blocks with the creatures still alive in them and saw that the creatures were either sleeping standing up or they were just standing there doing nothing. He couldn't tell which because it was mostly dark. It only took a few minutes to ascertain that for the time being everything was okay. Usually on watch he had a bunch of other things to keep him busy, stuff like admin tasks, buzzing other COs in and out of places, or studying for advancement-in-grade to the next promotion. None of that was necessary anymore and he grew bored. In the absence of anything else to do, he thought about his mother and the terrifying way she died, of how he had caused her death by calling her without realizing that the ringing phone would act as a beacon, drawing those monsters into her kitchen and destroying her.

He wept and generally felt sorry for himself. He bawled out loud and pounded his fists into the control board desk. This was the real reason he came to Central. It was to grieve. Crying in front of the men would only bring scorn, regardless of how well he might lead them through trouble. Some of the men might even turn on him. He took the opportunity to get everything out of his system so that he could appear strong and salvage something out of the mess that life was handing out to everyone.

Sometime during the night Josh fell asleep with his forehead on the console and awoke to the dawn light reflecting off of the glass from a corner guard tower. He sat up and winced at the crick in his neck and rocked it side-to-side while he scanned through all of the cameras. Nothing.

The sleep had rejuvenated him and allowed the previous day's disaster to settle firmly into his brain. Before heading back to the sleeping quarters he grabbed a pen and made a list of things that needed to be accomplished. He decided right then and there that he wanted to do more than survive. Life would never be the same but it was possible to make a bad situation better and that was exactly what he vowed to do.

To start off his list he wrote down the goal: "Do more than just survive." Then, "Save everybody I can, no matter who they are." Josh felt he had already made some progress on that one but rescuing the prisoners was just a start. "Hmmm," he contemplated. He tapped the eraser on his front teeth and looked out the window into the empty quad. "What else?"

Inspired, he muttered, "Ah. I think we should…" and then the cameras flickered and went out. Josh was taken aback and tapped the keyboard a few times but nothing happened. Then it hit him: Absolute silence. The power was out.

"Fuck. That sucks," he said into the quiet.

Grabbing his short list Josh left Central, careful to prop the door open on his way out with a binder. He wasn't sure if the locks still worked or not but he didn't want to take any chances in case he needed to get back in.

The walk back to the CO quarters felt eerie. His footsteps sounded unnaturally loud and deep down Josh knew that the prison had never been quiet and that it was never meant to. It was supposed to hum with activity and life. The thought spooked him and he quickened his pace.

Inside the overnight room the prisoners were still sleeping. Josh tried not to make any noise but it was difficult. Within minutes some of them were stirring and grumbling awake.

"Hungry," one of them complained and at the mention of food other eyes popped open and feet hit the floor. Yawns, moans, and farts resounded in the unashamed way men did when in trapped in each other's company for twenty three hours a day. Josh grimaced and opened the door wide to freshen the air, which brought puzzled glances from the veteran prisoners and a look of thanks from Finn, the newbie.

After they got dressed Josh led them out to the galley, explaining on the way that the power was out and they could no longer cook. A few of them complained but Ben told them to shut up.

"At least you assholes are alive," he reminded them.

The gripers clammed up, as much out of their fear of Ben as in agreement with what he said. Josh smiled. It was a good thing for him that Ben was there and on his side. He looked back at the big man and Ben gave him a wink.

They decided to use up as much of the food in the freezer as possible before it went bad, which meant cold slabs of ham chased by milk and orange juice. The meat restored everyone's good mood from the previous night and Josh brought out his list. The men listened to his ideas on working towards a productive life instead of just trying to get by and they pledged to work with him towards that goal. At the end of the meeting, Josh asked if he missed anything.

"Yeah," John-John spoke up. "You missed the most damn obvious thing, Josh. What about the women?"

At the mere mention of females the others chimed in with their approval. Talk quickly turned to different scenarios on how they could gather some up and have something other than 'man-gina' for the first time in years, at least for most of them. Finn was understandably mute on the subject.

"Alright, alright, I get the picture. You guys have obviously given this topic considerable thought. I'll tell you right now though, I won't have anyone forcing themselves on anyone," he warned them. "If that's what you guys are after, then I'm out. You can't rebuild by causing more misery."

"Nah, Josh, that ain't what they meant," Ben placated. "I won't stand for it either. They're just frustrated is all." He looked at them and asked, "Ain't that right, fellas?"

The men were quick to agree, but Josh could see that a few of them, John-John and Brent in particular, did not look like they were being sincere. He decided that he would shelve the issue for the time being, but would keep alert if they met up with any women.

"Okay, besides women, we have a few other things to take care of, namely the monsters still trapped in the cell blocks. We can't make this a permanent camp if there's a chance that they might get out somehow. Let's grab the spears and get to work. Finn, you might as well join us since Central's out of commission."

They returned to the CO quarters, grabbed their spears, and donned their tactical gear. Everyone laughed at how small the armor looked on Ben and how big it looked on Finn. Ben pretended he was wearing a kid's outfit, shambling around with stiff arms out to his sides squeaking, "Help me, Mommy, I'm stuck!"

Finally outfitted, they checked each other over. Along with helmets and boots, they all wore light body armor that covered chest, neck, arms, hands and shins. It was decided that the shields were unnecessary but that the shotguns would be slung on their backs and each would have a pistol in a leg holster in addition to their spears. Their waist belts carried some extra ammunition, tasers and riot control gear. Josh gave a quick demonstration on the last items. Most of the men had some limited experience with electroshock weapons, tear gas and pepper spray, but it was all on the receiving end.

They approached the first cell block with an easy confidence and some trepidation. They weren't really looking forward to stabbing hundreds of men in the face at close range even if those men weren't really human anymore. They still looked like people for the most part, even if they didn't act it.

The men could hear the beasts well before they could see them. There were grunts and yips that Josh considered complaining tones more than the rage he recalled from the day before.

Before the men came into view and hearing became difficult, Josh went over the plan again. "Ben is going to pry the sally port door open and then we attract their attention, drawing them to the inner door and dispatching them. Try to be economical in killing them. It's the humane thing to do, and you don't want to tire yourselves out. We'll be doing this all morning."

Everyone nodded their understanding and they crept to the sally port door. Ben's knees popped as he squatted and a few of them chuckled softly at the big man's grunts of pain. He glared and the men immediately shut up.

The crowbar Ben brought to pry the doors with clanked into the gap between the latch and receiver, and the reaction to the noise from the beasts inside was immediate and forceful. The monsters rushed towards the inner door as Ben leveraged the crowbar and the big black man jumped back in surprise when the door swung open easily. He looked back at the group, shook his head in disbelief and uttered, "Ah, shit. It's already open."

Beasts charged into the first sally port door and it slammed wide open. Ben's eyes flew wide open and the whites of them stuck out in stark contrast to the rest of his face as he screamed, "Run!"

They ran. No one had discussed a backup plan so everybody ran in different directions. The outer gate slammed open behind them and the monsters screamed in excitement and rage as they poured out of the sally port, into the quad, and began the chase.

Somehow Josh, Finn and Ben ended up running in the same direction, towards the corner guard tower from the day before. Josh was in the lead. He was the only person out of the whole group who had the ability to do daily runs and keep his cardio up. The other two were only slightly behind but Josh could tell by their bellowing gasps that Finn and Ben were running on pure adrenaline.

Josh got to the tower several seconds ahead of the other two, ripped the door open and waved them through before rushing in and using the manual lock to secure the door behind him. They all bent over to catch their breath as the door was assaulted by frustrated fists and kicks. Josh was the first to speak and talked while Ben and Finn continued breathing in short huffs, wheezing as they lay leaned exhaustedly against the tower wall. "We just lost the prison," he informed them over the noise.

The other two could only nod. Josh stepped past them and went up the stairs to look out through the glass enclosure at the top of the tower and what he saw deflated him. The quad was overrun by dozens of the monsters, the majority of which were clustered at the base of the tower he was standing on. Looking over at the CO quarters he saw that the door was wide open and the beasts were going in and out. There wasn't any doubt in his mind that the other men were dead. There wasn't any place for them to hide or any other possible way they could have escaped.

Ben and Finn finally recovered and joined him up in the tower. Besides their faces registering alarm at what was below and the obvious loss of the other men, neither of them said anything. The tower windows were designed to be transparent in only one direction to keep the prisoners unaware of what the guards were doing, so the things below couldn't see the men just a dozen feet above their heads.

Gathering the others close, Josh quietly told them, "There's no way the others survived. We made it to the only place those things can't get into. Hell, even if they are somehow alive, there's no way to rescue them. We have to abandon this place and go outside the walls. When I got up this morning, before the power went out I did a perimeter check and nothing was out there. All we need to do is get through the fence with that," and he pointed to the crowbar still grasped in Ben's big hand. The big prisoner looked shocked to see he still carried it.

The tower had a door leading to the top of the wall atop of which had a walkway for guards to do patrols. The three men draped over the side and hang-jumped the remaining six feet. The place they landed was as good as any and Ben went to work on the clamps holding the chain links to the support post. Within a few minutes the fence had enough give for them to crawl underneath. They repeated the process on the outer fence and were soon standing with their backs to the prison and looking out at the wide expanse of the jail perimeter's open fields. The land was intentionally flat and empty for over a mile in every direction to deny any escapees the benefit of cover.

Without the protection of the walls Josh felt exposed, but not nearly as exposed as his partners. At least Josh got to be outside every day when he wasn't at work, the other two had been confined to unnaturally small spaces for months or years. Ben seemed particularly affected.

"How long has it been since you two were outside?" Josh wanted to know.

"Two hundred and eighty six days," Finn answered without hesitation.

Ben took longer to answer. Finally, he said, "A little over eight fucking years. Shit. I've been trapped in there like an animal for eight fucking years."

Unexpectedly, Ben put his face in his left hand and wept. Ben and Finn looked away to give the big man his privacy. They both understood what it meant for him to lose control and show vulnerability, so they tried not to make it worse by watching him.

"I'm good," Ben said after about thirty seconds. He took a deep breath. "Let's go. We need to get out of the open."

Josh nodded and took off at a slow jog, making sure to set an easy pace. Until the others got their conditioning back he would have to be extra careful to keep out of situations that required aerobic exertion.

Primarily because the jail site was excluded, they didn't see or hear anything on their way to the tree line and once under cover Josh called for a rest. They sank down, grateful for the soft pine needles that carpeted the ground. The place they stopped was a lightly wooded copse of trees and brush, mostly evergreen. The sound of their breathing was the only noise that broke the morning's silence. Josh listened for noise in the direction of the prison but couldn't detect anything.

"I want to rip this fucking armor off, but I know it's for my own good. Makes it a fucker to breathe, though," Ben complained. "Can you believe I use to be a professional running back?"

"Huh? No," Finn said, looking puzzled. "What team?"

Ben waved him off. "It doesn't matter. None of that shit does anymore."

Finn sighed. "Well? What do we do now?"

"Still want to stay grouped up with me?" Josh answered Finn with a question of his own.

"Hell yeah," and "Of course," were the answers.

"In that case, nothing has changed. We're going to make new lives for ourselves, one that involves more than just mere survival. I don't know where your hearts are, but I want to help people. I want the men we just left behind to be the last ones killed by whatever the fuck those things are." Josh was standing now, his passion raising his voice.

Caught up in the moment, Finn stood too and proclaimed, "Hell yeah! We'll be like super fucking heroes!" He pumped his arm up and down and flexed dramatically.

Laughing softly, Ben touched their arms and brought them back to reality. "Okay Batman and Robin, you two need to settle down before we get heard." The young men looked shamefaced and had the good sense to drop the intensity.

"Where do we go from here?" Ben asked. "I have no idea what's out there. I'm not from this area."

"Me either," Finn volunteered.

"Well, there's not much near the prison," Josh explained. "Just a few farms and migrant communities. The closest actual town is Fairlawn, maybe three or so miles in that direction." He pointed west. "I think we should try for Fairlawn first and see if we can find out what happened, how bad things really are. I'm guessing it must be pretty bad because no one's been to the prison since everything happened." Josh tilted his head as he thought. "Yeah, if things weren't really bad the army or the government would have sent help by now."

"Do we have to walk all the way there?" Ben asked, already knowing the answer.

"Yep. Might as well get used to it unless you want a crew of those things chasing us and kicking our asses if we break down or need to stop. We'll stick to the trees as much as we can. I don't want to lose anyone else today." He started off in the direction he had pointed, and after a few paces the other two fell into step behind him, doing their best to keep up and stay quiet.

KLIMPS BREAK ROOM

Jim, Saul, Vickers, Megan and most of the Klimps group were seated around the table inside the break room. They had filled in the people who stayed behind on what had happened since they left, and despite coming back with the same number of people, there was a general mood of sadness because of the two who had perished on the rescue run. Cindy and Owen were the only two people not present at the meeting. Cindy was on watch up on the roof, and Owen was excused.

The young man was finally starting to process his sister's death. As soon as he was introduced to everyone and was handed a bottle of water, he went to the men's room and hadn't been out since. Jim went in to take a leak before the meeting and heard Owen weeping in one of the stalls. The sobbing made Jim feel uncomfortable and he left as quickly as he could, not even flushing the urinal.

When the subject of the little boy outside and his ability to control the goons came up, most of the people who hadn't witnessed it had a difficult time believing that it happened like the three men described it. Despite her complete trust in Jim and Vickers even Megan had her doubts.

"Maybe you saw something different," Ray said. "I mean, you guys just came back from a helluva run outside, seen two people get killed. Maybe your minds were playing tricks on you."

Saul shook his head. "That's bullshit, Ray." He indicated Jim and Vickers. "If it was just me, you maybe could say that. Maybe. But the fact is all three of us saw it."

Megan stood. "For the sake of argument, let's say that what you guys said happened actually happened," she proposed. "What's it mean? That there's some ten year old kid out there with superpowers? It doesn't make any sense. You guys have to see that it's a crazy story."

Vickers asked. "Ray, who was on watch up on the roof when we came back? They can verify what we saw."

"Sandy was," the old man answered.

Everyone at the table turned to Sandy and her eyes went wide at the attention. She shook her head slightly and said, "What?"

For the first time since Jim had met him, Vickers changed persona. They all knew he was a retired Army Sergeant, but he had never fully showed that side of himself. That is, until now. "You know what," Vickers said in a very direct manner, standing up and pointing his index finger directly at Sandy's face. "Tell us what you saw. Tell everyone about the boy."

Sandy was not very good under pressure. "I don't know!" she screamed. "I didn't see anything!"

Vickers was relentless. "What do you mean, you didn't see anything? You were supposed to cover our asses while we made it back to the base. We were coming in hot!"

Sandy began weeping, burying her face in her hands and mumbling. "I don't know. I didn't see anything."

Still in Army mode, Vickers turned to Ray. "What the fuck, Ray? Why was she up there when she's incompetent? Seriously, dude." Vickers sighed loudly. "Actually, never mind. I don't care that's she's incompetent, there are a lot of people like her and that's just the way it is, but the fact that she's incompetent and was on overwatch, supposedly protecting us, that is something I will not have."

Jim watched Vickers chew out Sandy and Ray. Initially he thought that maybe Megan would run over to Sandy and comfort her, or that Ray would defend himself or even that Saul would tell Vickers to stand down. When none of that happened Jim understood that the group dynamic had changed, and even though it wasn't formally announced, Vickers had assumed outright command. Thinking back on the last twenty four hours, Jim realized that Vickers had actually been leading from behind since even before they left on their expedition.

Silence around the table while Vickers let his admonishments sink in and for the group to ingest the overt power shift. When he finally spoke again it was with his friendly voice. Jim marveled at how the man could turn it on and off like it was on a switch. "Okay. Sorry about that. It's not a dig at you Ray, or you Sandy, but what it does show is that we have some holes in our setup that we need to fill. Not everyone is good at everything, but everyone can still have a purpose. What we need to focus on now are our priorities."

Turning to Saul, Vickers asked him, "Saul, what would you say our number one priority is?"

Taking the demotion to second-in-charge in stride, Saul answered, "Protection. Definitely. Protecting the store and protecting our folks."

"Exactly. That means we need more people. We need to gather in more people who can help us defend this place in exchange for being allowed to join us. The types of people who can contribute are people with combat experience, weapons training, or survival skills." Tapping his finger on the table for emphasis, Vickers told everyone, "That kid out there was weird and none of us can explain it. I don't like that. And because we don't know everything that's happening we need to be prepared for anything."

Megan was nodding, and so was Ray along with the rest of them sitting around the table, including Sandy who had stopped sobbing and was listening to Vickers explaining.

"There's only one good way to actively get more people," Megan said. "Advertise. A broadcast with either radio or television, billboards, stuff like that. There's no other way to do it that I can think of."

"Yeah," Ray spoke up. "We need to let folks know that we're here, and if they have the ability to get here they can join us."

"I think I like the idea of a broadcast," Vickers said, nodding his approval. "Only problem is it means that we have to go back out, hit a local radio or TV station." Looking around he asked, "Has anyone messed with the radio or television lately? Is anyone still broadcasting?"

Ray got up and went to his locker. "I checked the first afternoon but all the local TV stations are off the air, kaput. Same goes for the radio except for one station on the AM side. Last time I checked WEKT was still going. Problem is, it was only automated stuff, music playing through a looping song list." He pulled a small radio out of his locker, set it up on the table, and held out the cord. "Jack. Plug that in for me, will you? Thanks. Now let's see what's on." Ray turned the power on and country music blared out of the tiny speakers.

Everyone sat around and listened for a few minutes until a commercial came on for a local beauty salon. "Yep, no one there," Ray said, voicing the obvious. "If there was, there'd be someone talking."

"Spin the dial," Saul suggested.

Ray started to slowly scan through the spectrum, first up then down. He did it twice more. Besides the country station there was nothing else broadcasting. He flipped it to FM and began the process again. On the FM side there were several music stations on from Cleveland, Akron and Canton playing songs or ads. Ray paused on each one and each time everybody was hopeful that there would be a live person on. They were all disappointed when Ray finished a second run through without positive results.

"Damn," Jack whispered in the silence created after Ray clicked the radio off.

Megan echoed the sentiment. "Yeah, sucks,"

"We should check the radio regularly, see if anything changes," Vickers recommended. "In the meantime, we need to prepare a broadcast message, one that will gather more survivors to us." Walking up to the map Saul had hung earlier, Vickers asked, "Where is WEKT located?"

Everyone except Jim spoke up at once; apparently Jim was the only person besides Vickers that didn't know where the radio station was. In his case he hated country music, so he never even heard of the station even though it was local, and Vickers had only been traveling through.

Sandy, perhaps in an effort to restore herself in the group's good graces, went up and pointed to it on the map. "It's right here, downtown on Court and Liberty." When no one acknowledged her efforts and just ignored her, she sat back down, crossed her arms over her chest and sulked.

Vickers circled the location with a marker and studied the details of the area surrounding the station. "Well, that's not good," he said, frowning. "We can't get there on foot; the goons will be the thickest in that area."

Jim thought it through quickly and came up with an idea. "How about a pied piper kind of thing? One of us drives through there making a ton of noise and gets most of the goons to follow, clearing the area?"

"Hot damn, Jim, that's not a bad idea," Saul complimented, nodding and smiling. There were several other nods around the table and a few more smiles directed at Jim. Bettina squeezed his arm appreciatively and he blushed at the attention.

Vickers asked, "So, Jim, are you volunteering? It's your idea."

Put on the spot, Jim knew that the only answer he could give was a "yes," but before he could Jack spoke up.

"I'll do it," the young man volunteered. "I'm getting kind of sick of just sitting in here anyways. I want to go out, have some excitement. Plus I know this town like the back of my hand. There's no way the goons will trap me." For emphasis, Jack did a flex pose, as if to prove to everyone in the room that he was untouchable.

"Ah, the confidence of youth," Vickers responded before cautioning the young man: "You'll learn quickly that the excitement of running from the goons is extremely overrated and seeking it out is a good way to get killed." To the group: "We have our runner; now we need a team to get into the station and setup the broadcast."

After some debate, it was decided that Megan would record the broadcast which could be played on a loop. The team going in to get it running would be Vickers, Jim, Saul and Owen, although Owen didn't know it yet since he wasn't in the room. Megan would stay behind and oversee the defenses while Ray was relegated to keeping the store up and running.

The message they decided on was simple. All it would say is that a group of survivors were holding the Klimps store and were accepting other survivors, and that everyone was welcome. It gave the location, directions, and instructions on the best methods to get in without attracting too much attention. Finally, there was a warning that anyone seeking to take the store through attack or subversion would be terminated.

Once everyone was satisfied with the general gist of the message, Megan got on a laptop and recorded it. The computer would be taken to the station and left powered on, but for insurance purposes Vickers had four USB sticks made that contained the same message and handed them out to Jim and Saul. "You never know," he said.

The ex-Army sergeant announced that he was ready to go deal with Owen. "I'll fill him in on the plan; see if I can help him get back on track." He went into the bathroom and closed the door behind him. By the time he emerged with a dry-eyed but puffy-faced Owen nearly an hour later, dusk had arrived and Vickers declared the rest of the day a "wash." Jim admired how Vickers could give people orders without making it seem like he was bossing them around: "Let's get a watch schedule set up, Megan. Keep the girls, Ray and

Suresh off of it and let them know that since they won't be standing watch, they do all the cooking and cleaning."

Megan nodded. "You got it, Vickers."

Half an hour later a sheet was posted outside the break room with two schedules on it. One listed the times everyone had to go up on the roof and stand lookout and the other was the cooking and cleaning list. There were only six people who could stand watch, and they were set up in teams of two with four hours each. Jim was paired with Saul and was on from midnight to four in the morning. He groaned. The other two teams were Megan and Jack from eight to midnight and Vickers and Owen from four to eight in the morning. Since five of the six watch team members were going out on the radio station run, Megan picked Ray as a stopgap to stay up top with her while the group was gone.

Luckily the store carried night vision scopes that the lookouts could use to scan the area at night. Before heading up to the roof to relieve Cindy, Megan and Jack grabbed the scopes and the tools needed to attach them to the rifle scopes.

Cindy came down and seemed pleased to hear that she was no longer required to stand up on the roof for hours at a time, and Jim enjoyed watching her reaction when she was told that she would be doing the cooking and cleaning instead. She yelled, "I didn't vote on that! Where is Saul?" and then she stormed off. A few minutes later Jim heard her a few aisles over yelling at Saul, who redirected her to Vickers. She went silent and came right back. It was obvious to Jim she decided to drop the issue rather than confront Vickers, but she did not look at all happy about it. When she noticed Jim watching her and smiling she said, "What are you looking at, dumbass?"

He wanted to say something back, but everyone was watching the exchange. He just kept smiling, shrugged, and looked away. Bettina didn't like the way she spoke to Jim though, and glared angrily at the chubby blonde. Before he headed to the area set up for sleeping Jim asked Bettina for a favor. "I want you to make my food, not her. Okay?"

"Sure," she answered, grabbing and holding onto his arm. "You and me, both. I don't trust that bitch to not spit in either one of our meals."

Looking down at Bettina's hands wrapped around his arm, Jim smiled and decided that he could get used to having a pretty girl hanging on him. He was glad she wasn't expected to go out and possibly get hurt or killed and it gave him further incentive to come back in one piece. He yawned. "I need to get some shuteye," he told her. "I have to get up in a few hours to be on lookout."

After promising him some food when he got up, Bettina let him go. Jim used the restroom and then went to the sleeping area. Several memory foam pads were laid out along with brand new sleeping bags. He grabbed a sleeping bag, ripped the package open and laid it out. Jim normally slept in his underwear, but he briefly contemplated sleeping in his clothes because he was around people he had just met, then dismissed the idea. Sleeping fully clothed didn't sound very comfortable and besides, he would be covered by the bag. Shrugging, he kicked off his boots, dropped his pants and took off his shirt. Looking down at himself Jim was surprised to see that his belly was shrinking oh so slightly. He wasn't anything close to skinny, but the skin was no longer stretched as taut as it used to be.

Yawning again, he crawled into his bag and was asleep within minutes. He slept fitfully for a while, but then dreamed he was back in the pipe under the road near where Chuck was killed. Only now it wasn't a drainage pipe, it was a sewage pipe. It smelled like death and shit and in his dream Jim panicked and screamed and tried running away, but the stench followed him. Then all of a sudden lights appeared in front of him.

"Quiet down, you're waking everyone up!" Saul whispered angrily, still shaking Jim and shining a flashlight in his face.

Jim came fully awake and gasped in a full dose of Saul's rancid breath. "Oh my God," Jim whimpered, tears leaking from the corners of his eyes. "Please, Saul, get away from me!"

"Fuck you, man. I was just being helpful, getting you up."

Scurrying away on his hands and knees, trying to get out of the halitosis radius, Jim whimpered, "Fine, dude, whatever. I'm good. Appreciate it." He got to his feet and sprinted over the cold cement for some fresh air. It wasn't until he hit the end of the aisle that Jim remembered he was still in his underwear.

On his way back he passed Cindy in her sleeping bag. The interaction between the two men had woken her up and she had watched Jim go by, a look of distaste on her face. Out of spite he got dressed while standing right next to where she was lying on her mattress, making sure his package was in her line of sight the whole time. She surprised him by not turning away, and then she smirked at him when he shook his head, puzzled by her behavior.

He grunted and made his way to the roof. With the exception of Cindy, everyone was either asleep or on lookout, and Jim felt weird to be in the huge open space of the warehouse without any noise from human activity. When he passed by Bettina he could hear her snoring softly. He paused and looked down at her, wondering how such a pretty girl like her could feel any attraction towards a lummox like him. He noticed a small pocket of drool wet her pillow and it made him smile. Then she broke wind, a soft sound but loud in the absence of any other noise. Jim felt embarrassed to have heard it, especially when Cindy began laughing to herself a few rows away. He scurried off but the poofing sound and Cindy's subsequent laughter played over and over in his mind.

When he got to the roof he had to pause in the doorway because he couldn't see anything. It took a few minutes for his eyes to slowly adjust to the darkness. Eventually, what few lights still on in the city bled enough illumination for Jim to eventually make out three people standing near the far roof ledge and he ambled over to them. There was a soft breeze blowing and Jim made sure to be upwind of Saul when he joined them.

Megan was talking to Saul but stopped when she saw him. "Hey, Jim. I was just telling Saul that we've noticed something strange tonight." She handed him a rifle. "Look through the scope and locate the edge of the parking lot."

He did. "Okay, now what?"

"Pan to your right along the tree line and you should see it."

Jim slowly twisted right. He scanned slowly because he didn't know what he was looking for and didn't want to miss it, but when he did see it he knew that it would have been hard to miss. He did a quick intake of breath. A goon was squatting at the edge of the trees and it looked like it was staring right back at him.

Keeping the scope on the goon for half a minute or so to see what it did, Jim was baffled when the goon did nothing. It just watched, unmoving. From behind him Megan said, "If you think that's weird, then check this out: They're taking turns."

She must have sensed his puzzlement, because she repeated herself. "You heard that right, they're taking turns. Before that guy out there now, there was a woman, and a different guy before that."

"Why would they do that?" was all Jim could think to ask, but he knew the answer even before Megan said it. The goons were keeping a lookout as well.

CHOW HALL, WRIGHT-PATTERSON AIR FORCE BASE

Fran and his crew made it into morning formation with time to spare. His new converts made their way to him and either smiled or greeted him with "Good morning" before taking station around him. "What a difference a day makes," he thought to himself. Just twenty four hours ago he was publicly flogged and now he was surrounded by his core group and an additional buffer of about twenty five people. Clark had been busy.

A few moments later the flights were called to attention. Since India Flight was the last flight recruited they also went into the chow hall last, and even as he despised his current predicament, Fran looked forward to a warm breakfast prepared by someone else. His stomach grumbled and he frowned at having to wait for several hundred people to eat before he could even get inside. After a few minutes of being at attention without anyone moving into the chow hall, Fran wondered what was going on. "Why in the hell are we just standing here?" he asked Bill out of the corner of his mouth.

"Dunno, but I'm fucking hungry and getting pissed." Others around them overheard the exchange and grumbled their agreement.

For fifteen minutes the conscripts stood at attention and stared into the rising sun. Fran heard clattering and wondered what the noise was until someone a few rows up collapsed. A sergeant came over the speaker and said, "Stop locking your knees, people. That's only going to make you faint. The next person that falls out of formation gets flogged. Twenty lashes."

The announcement caused more complaints and the conscripts were starting to get louder, angrier. Fran feared that some of them might break and cause a problem with the guards, which would only make the guards more alert and complicate his plans. Before that happened, the chow hall door opened and several dozen officers in uniforms Fran didn't recognize came out. They weren't like the Air Force uniforms he was used to seeing. One of the officers was speaking loudly, and Fran overheard a British accent.

He was mulling this new development over when the door opened again and more people exited. This second group was much larger and it took a couple of minutes for them all to empty out. After they were gone the microphone came back on and said, "Alpha Flight, fall out for chow!"

Alpha Flight filed in, followed by the other flights in order. India Flight had to wait for more than six hundred people to get their food before being called. Then, when Fran eventually made it into line he found that breakfast was only an MRE and a bottle of water. Rumor passed from table to table that the British had arrived the night before and that they ate all of the hot food. Fran looked down at his tuna MRE and sat it down, uninterested. He passed the time instead discreetly studying the guards while everyone else ate.

The guards, a mixture of mostly young men and women, spent their time clustered together in the corner joking and laughing and paying little attention to the conscripts. The rifles they carried were either cradled loosely in the crooks of their arms or slung over their backs by a strap. Fran thought it a good sign that they acted as if they didn't expect any problems from the conscripts.

A few minutes later everyone was ordered back outside to stand in the sun. The manner in which the orders were passed, very impersonal and with the expectation of complete compliance, reminded Fran of his time spent in prison. His time in lockup was unpleasant, not for the usual reasons most people associate with incarceration, but because while he was in there, he was a just another predator in a small pond full of predators. With so much potential danger, what few prey there was kept their heads on a swivel, constantly on high alert and ever sensitive to the slightest, most subtle mood currents. So despite his success on the outside Fran had few opportunities to exercise his passions while in prison.

The conscripts were forced to stand again for many minutes. Loomis began grumbling along with some of the others but Bill shushed him. A small podium carried by two sweating conscripts was set up in front of the chow hall and still, they waited. Fran watched the guards scanning for anyone who might be ready to pass out and he recognized the behavior. The men and women watching over them had already become addicted to inflicting pain and were looking forward to more occasions of it.

Keeping the earlier threat of a flogging in mind, nobody faltered. Finally, Sergeant Lopez marched up and said, "Flights, at ease," into a small microphone built into the podium.

There was a collective sigh as everyone relaxed. Fran shook out his arms and legs to refresh the blood going to them and despite the ignominy the situation caused him, he took a lesson from the morning's activities. He learned that the threat of pain was more powerful than the actual infliction of it. As he looked left and right Fran saw the relief people felt when they realized that the threat of a flogging had been removed, albeit temporarily. Their relief actually caused them to forget their abject condition and feel a modicum of happiness.

Sergeant Lopez spoke again. "As many of you have probably figured out, the vanguard of the British forces arrived early this morning. They will be accorded the same courtesy and respect currently afforded our own service men and women. What that means is if they order you to do something, you will do it, immediately and without complaint." The sergeant shuffled some papers he was holding until he found the correct sheet. "We have done some preliminary digging on personnel from the last flight to arrive, India Flight." Looking up at Fran's group, he said, "I need the following people to step forward," and then he named five people, two men and three women.

Those that had their names called stepped out and went up front. Fran noticed that one of the women was someone he had talked to the day before while working on the flight line. He had asked her personally to join his cause. Had he been found out?

"These five," Sergeant Lopez began, "have verified prior military service and are now officially reactivated." Some light clapping from the sergeant and all of the guards. "They are no longer conscripts. You will obey an order from them as if they were never in your ranks."

Fran nearly cursed out loud. He tried to mentally calculate how long he and the others had before the woman reported on them. An hour, maybe two? The only thing he knew for sure was that he had to escape immediately and take as many people with him as he could.

"I have reports of late night shenanigans amongst the conscript encampment. We don't know who you are yet, but we have intelligence that says that some of you are leaving the encampment at night and roaming the base." Shaking his head as if disciplining a small child, he said, "We can't have that, it's too dangerous. So today, instead of working on the flight line, all of the flights will be assigned here. You will be building an enclosure around the encampment, which will be patrolled by dogs and armed guards starting tonight." Smiling, he told the group, "I hope that squashes your antics. If not, you will be caught and summarily executed."

Picking up his sheaf of papers from the podium, the sergeant walked away and into the chow hall. From off to the side came the order, "Flights, attention!" followed by, "Fall out to the encampment!"

Hundreds of people began shuffling back to the tents. As they walked, Fran's core group clustered around him, and without appearing conspicuous Helen, Clark and Hank made their way to him. A few others, probably new people recruited by Clark, hung on the periphery.

Just loud enough for everyone to hear, Bill asked, "What are we going to do now, King? They want to block us in."

Fran didn't like snap decisions. In the past he always planned out every detail meticulously before acting on a goal, but he was being pushed into a corner and his followers had to see him as decisive and quick thinking. "We go as soon as we get back," he told everyone. "On my signal we rush the guards and take them out, then take their guns. Bill, we need a vehicle to ram the fence."

Bill spoke up. "Leave it to me and Loomis."

"Good. Everyone else, stick together and wait for my signal."

As the conscripts neared the encampment, they naturally funneled into a gap between the porta potties and a small utility building. Fran spotted a small group of five guards smoking and talking to each other on the other side of the building.

Fran pointed and said, "Them."

The imminent violence gave the air a nervous energy. Fran felt it and he sensed that some of the others were tuned into it also, but the guards were oblivious. For the first time since his rescue, Fran felt fully alive. Inflicting pain and being in that moment was his natural element, and he was always more attuned to his environment when on the hunt: Movement slowed, smells became more vibrant, and he saw things with greater clarity. He came abreast of the guards and attacked.

Fran had no need for a weapon. He gripped the closest guard around her face from behind with his forearm and formed a claw with his other hand, digging into the woman's throat and burrowing in deep to get at the soft cartilage and ligaments beneath the skin. Her throat splashed thick arterial blood through his fingers as he grabbed the mass of tissue and tore it out.

The woman made an involuntary "urkk" noise before Fran cast her aside and went for a second guard.

The efficient violence that Fran visited on the first guard temporarily stunned everyone, including some of those in his own group. None of them had even suspected he possessed such an extreme familiarity with inflicting injury. It had only taken him a few seconds to disable the woman before he was already on the second guard, driving two stiffened fingers into the man's eye sockets up to the third knuckles.

His people recovered quickly and dispatched the remaining guards with less efficiency but equal vigor. The looted guns and knives were distributed to the conscripts before continuing on. Fran's brutality earned him a respectful radius from his own people and an even larger one from those conscripts who were not involved in the uprising but had witnessed his attack. Screams erupted from some of them, which melded with the sound of running feet and drowned out the noises made by the expiring guards. The newly armed conscripts trailed in the wake of those fleeing the violence.

The panic served as a screen of confusion. In the chaos of several hundred bodies running headlong in all directions Fran and his group easily dispatched all of the nearby groups of guards, only with knives this time instead of bare hands and booted feet. Not a shot was fired.

After all of the guards were either incapacitated or dead, Fran and the rest occupied an isolated pocket of the encampment. The noise of panic abated. Fran's group grew somewhat as those that were unwilling to stick around and be forced labor took advantage of the fracas and joined up. Alarms started on the base wide intercom system, blasting the location of the trouble and warning that that several of the conscripts were now armed and dangerous.

"Where the hell is Bill with the truck?" Gunter asked. Fran could see that as the arrival of the truck was delayed several of the potential escapees were rethinking their decision. A few even went so far as to lay down their weapons in anticipation of melting back into the crowd, when the noise of a large truck engine grew in the distance. Fran hoped it was Bill and Loomis and not the Air Force, but couldn't see over the tents. It was only when the truck drove over some of the tents and a few unfortunate standers-by that Fran knew for sure it was the rescue vehicle.

Bill slammed on the brakes and the truck slid to a stop less than six feet in front of Fran. The old man's hairy, skinny arm was draped over the ledge of the rolled down window and he was wearing a pair of aviator sunglasses. Tilting the glasses down over his nose, he yelled over the top of them: "You fellas need a ride?" Then he laughed, obviously enjoying himself.

The truck was a large cargo vehicle with an open bed and none of the conscripts wasted any time climbing in the back. Fran got in front first, followed by Loomis. Bill was watching the rear view mirror waiting for everyone to load up. No one wanted to get left behind and it only took a few moments for everyone to pile in.

Bill punched the gas and the truck lurched forward. Some of the more timid who didn't take a stand or hesitated now realized the better odds for an escape with the truck. Bill started to slow back down to let them in but Fran yelled at him go faster. "They had their chance, Bill! We don't have the time to pick up freeloaders and cowards."

The old man shrugged and said, "Okay, King," before speeding up and whipping the wheel to the left. The inertia tipped Fran over and pinned Loomis against the truck door. Loomis had his face flattened into the window and Fran heard the beefy man's front teeth crack from the pressure. When Bill completed the u-turn both passengers snapped back into the upright.

Loomis put his hand to his mouth and was dismayed to find that his front teeth were gone. He looked over at Fran with a puzzled expression and cried, "Where da fuck are my teef?" He lifted his upper lip to show Fran and Bill the damage and both men laughed at the half inch gap where they used to be. His two front teeth were snapped off at the base and were seeping blood.

Bill drove over a few more tents and several more people on the way out of the encampment. At first Fran was worried that hitting so many bodies would damage the truck until Bill, sensing his apprehension told him not to worry. "This truck is fucking solid. These people aren't hurting it none." To emphasize his point, Bill intentionally steered into a small crowd that was watching the goings-on. They tried to scatter when the truck changed direction but they couldn't disperse enough to outrun the bumper.

It didn't appear that Bill missed any and the truck jounced and jostled as it whoop-de-whooped over the unfortunate conscripts. All three of the men cab smacked their heads against the cab roof a couple of times and everything that was loose ended up on the floor.

Looking from the rearview mirror to Fran, Bill apologized. "Sorry, King. I guess we lost a few doing that. They bounced right out."

"Did we lose Gunter?"

"Can't say for sure. Maybe."

Elbowing Loomis, Fran told him, "Stick your head out and yell for Gunter."

"Thure King, no problem," Loomis lisped before he unrolled the window, leaned out and yelled, "Ith Gunter thill here?"

Gunter's face appeared next to the window as he poked it over the side of the truck bed. He looked at Loomis and laughed, "Yeth, I'm thill here. Dumbath!" before disappearing again.

"Great," Fran said. "Let's make some time, Bill."

"Head to the armory or off the base?"

Fran considered it for a moment before deciding. "Front gate. We don't have the element of surprise anymore. We'll have to get more guns from somewhere else. Anyway, we grabbed some weapons from the guards back at the encampment. It'll have to do for now."

The few Air Force personnel they saw only watched the truck speed by. They didn't know yet that some of conscripts were escaping using a troop transport truck, only that there was a problem back at the encampment. By the time they figured out that something was amiss, the truck was already past them, headed in the direction of the front gate.

Ninety seconds later the truck rounded the curve that led off the base and they saw that besides the fence, the exit was barricaded with thick metal stanchions, painted yellow and black, poking out of holes in the ground. In front of the barrier, three men in uniform were watching the truck approach. Bill floored the accelerator.

"Bill, what are you doing?" Fran yelled as the truck accelerated.

Fran knew there was no way the truck could pass through the steel barrier no matter how fast they went, and instead of trying to crash through it they needed to find a different way out. He braced himself for the inevitable collision when without warning Bill whipped the wheel hard twenty feet before the gate and they banked right, sliding sideways for a few feet before picking up traction and heading parallel to the base fence.

Bill looked contrite. "Sorry, King, I thought for a second maybe we could do it." When Fran didn't respond he looked to left and said, "Shit, there a big pit out there that follows the fence. I don't know how far it goes."

Someone in the back of the truck let off a few rounds, further annoying Fran by wasting their ammunition. He couldn't do anything about it at the moment, but once they stopped he would make it clear that the ammunition was precious.

A few seconds later Bill said, "The ditch is gone, we're clear," and the truck snapped left and crashed through the heavy security fence and off of the base to freedom. Bill checked the side view mirror and reported that LCBs were starting to pour onto the base through hole they had just made. Cheering could be heard from the back. Loomis joined in. "Woohoo, we did ith!"

"Not yet, Loomis," Fran cautioned. "Look around. We didn't think things through this far ahead and now we have to deal with these LCBs ourselves. We only exchanged our old troubles for a set of new ones."

Loomis dropped his smile as what Fran said registered. The truck drove down the street drawing LCBs out of side alleys and buildings and despite being in a vehicle, they were only barely able to keep ahead of the pursuers because the obstacles littering their path made the going slower than optimal. From up front, they could hear the people in back shooting at LCBs that came too close.

Turning to Bill, Fran asked. "How well do you know this area?"

"Only so-so."

Turning to Loomis, he repeated the question.

The fat man apologized with a shrug. "The thame. Only tho-tho."

"We can't stop or take the time to find a place to defend. We'll have to keep going until we get to where there are less of these LCBs." Fran instructed.

Bill nodded, concentrating on the street in front of him. The old timer knew the stakes if the truck crashed or got stuck on something. They would all perish within minutes, despite being moderately armed. A few times Bill had to smash small cars aside in order to evade a larger obstacle. Unfortunately, even when there weren't wrecks or abandoned cars, the road still had debris in it and Bill couldn't avoid all of it.

Speaking to the cab, Bill said, "At least the shit all over the street is slowing the LCBs down. If it wasn't for that, we'd be fucked for sure."

Just then he swerved to avoid a pile of dead bodies, electing to run over a small wooden box instead. His seemingly smart decision went awry when he ran over the box and whatever was inside blew two of the front tires out with a loud bang. The truck was built for extreme conditions and had three pairs of tires on each side, but the damage was severe enough to slow the vehicle down. Gunter leaned over the truck bed and yelled into the cab.

"You just blew two tires, Bill, one from each of the front pairs! You blow another and we're walking the rest of the way!"

Bill's only response was to tighten his mouth in resolve and slow down slightly. The slower speed allowed the LCBs to keep pace with the truck. Worse, fresher ones were still running out to give chase and a few of them made it to the cab doors. Bill acknowledged them by jerking the wheel left and right, slapping the LCBs into cars, light poles, and the sides of buildings. The pop-pop of gunfire from the back increased.

Weaponless and next to the window, Loomis began to stress at how close the beasts were getting to him before Bill was able to pinch them off. He screamed when an LCB hopped up onto the running board and slapped the window as it tried to get in.

"Jesus Christ! Shut the hell up, you fat asshole!" Bill yelled. "You scared the shit out of me."

Scared enough to go just a little faster even though it increased the odds of blowing another tire, Fran noted. Gradually over the next few minutes the road became less and less crowded with derelict automobiles and Bill was able to go even faster. Fran knew they were out of immediate danger when the group in the back cheered. He allowed himself a small smile.

AIRFIELD, WRIGHT-PATTERSON AIR FORCE BASE

After the plane landed at Wright-Patterson, Walter and the rest of the British were met by the installation commander, a colonel named Mark Slater. Introductions were made between the various staff members from both sides and although he seemed genuinely pleased at their arrival, Walter detected a slight rankling from the base commander when he was told he was now subordinate to General Vogel. It was only a slight faltering of his smile, but Walter read the American's eyes and knew the man had not anticipated the reduction of his position and authority.

The British contingent trailed behind the Americans as they were led to the base officer's quarters for a few minutes respite to drop off their bags and freshen up. Afterwards they were escorted to the base chow hall where Walter and Major Ackerman had their first meal on American soil, a breakfast consisting of bacon, eggs, pancakes, toast, and coffee. Everything was delicious and the portions were generous. While they ate the major filled Walter in on some of the rumors he had already heard.

"Colonel, did you know that the Americans have indentured some of the rescued civilians?"

"What? How do you know this?" Walter asked, puzzled. "We've only been here less than an hour."

"It's called the buzz. It's the undercurrent of all military units. You'll see. There's the official version, and then there's the buzz. Well, maybe not at your level, Colonel, I wouldn't know," Major Ackerman gave an innocent smirk and a shrug.

"No, nobody has filled me in on anything yet. But what do you mean, 'indentured'?"

"Well, apparently the Air Force blokes went out on rescue missions into the local populace and then forced all the able bodied ones they found to do labor. They have camps set up for them and everything."

"Was that some part of the Ophir Ridge Plan I don't know about?" Walter wondered, afraid he missed something.

"No, that's just it. Rescue people, yes. Shanghai them, no. What's worse is the other rumor," the major said, lowering his voice. "One of the American officers told me that after the rescue groups were divided up into useful and not so useful, the Air Force packed up the useless ones and drove them back outside the gates and forced them out of the trucks at gunpoint."

"General Fells won't like that," Walter ventured. "I'll let him know." Nodding at the food left on the plates, Walter asked, "Are you done eating? I want you to accompany me."

"Yes. Let's go."

Both men stood and made their way over to the general's table. General Fells and General Vogel were discussing something and Walter didn't want to intrude, so he just stood there with Major Ackerman.

General Vogel looked up, smiled, and asked, "Do you gentlemen need something?" At Walter's nod, the general indicated the empty seats across from them. "By all means have a seat and fill us in, gentlemen."

The two men sat. Before they could speak, General Fells told Walter, "As part of my senior staff, I don't require or expect you to stand on formality. You're here because I need frank and honest officers who'll tell me like it is. What's on your mind, Colonel?"

"Yes, sir. Thank you," Walter said, endeavoring to phrase things correctly despite what the more senior man had just told him. "I have it from reliable sources that the installation commander has imprisoned civilians and forced them into hard labor. In addition, he has repatriated others that he has determined to be of no use back off of the base. These were defenseless people that were driven out and dropped off into the midst of those creatures."

General Fells looked to his second in command and asked, "Did you know about this?"

"No, but if this is happening it contradicts what's called for in the Op Plan, which requires that all 'cognitives' are to be assimilated, not exploited or condemned to die."

Nodding in agreement, the general instructed, "Chase this down for me, Ken. Find out what's really going on. The next plane from London will be landing soon and I want to make sure I'm there. It's important everyone knows how vital their buy-in is if we're to be successful here." As an afterthought, he said, "Oh, and take Colonel Doucet with you. I'm sure you'll find his resourcefulness useful."

"Glad to, sir," General Vogel replied, standing up and straightening out his uniform.

General Fells stood also, and when he did the entire chow hall came to their feet and waited for him to depart before following him out. Walter and Major Ackerman stuck close to General Vogel. The older man kept a rapid pace and the two younger men had to half sprint to keep up with him.

The morning sun was unexpectedly bright and Walter shielded his eyes with the flat of his hand. When his eyes adjusted he saw row after row of soldiers in uniform standing in formation. It was only when he looked closer and saw the beards, bellies and general 'non-uniformity' of the troops that he recognized that they were probably the indentured civilians he had just found out about.

Walter noticed Major Ackerman look back towards the front of the building and frown. There were a series of half buried wooden poles set up in pairs. Walter asked, "What's wrong. What are those for?"

Shaking his head, the major sighed and replied, "I've only actually seen pictures of something like them. They're something the French Foreign Legion uses: Whipping posts."

"Well bugger me," Walter said in disbelief. "We won't win many hearts and minds with those devices."

As a group the British continued on, headed back to their berthing. Walter noticed some puzzled looks from the others when they saw what they initially thought were American Air Force personnel in ranks. Then the same rumor that the major had heard began circulating and the expressions changed from puzzlement to anger and confusion.

General Vogel beckoned Walter with a wave. "You're with me, Colonel." Major Ackerman saluted and said he would be at the barracks if he was needed as Walter veered off and accompanied the general to a waiting jeep. An American Air Force sergeant was standing by and she rendered a salute as they approached. "General Vogel, sir, my orders are to take you to the front gate to meet with the base security officer."

"So much saluting," Walter thought, musing at how often the military reinforced the pecking order. It occurred at every nearly encounter between them.

The general nodded and climbed into the front seat while Walter got in back.

"After I meet with security I'd like a tour of the base to inspect the facilities and logistics," General Vogel informed the sergeant as she clicked her seat belt on and pulled out onto the road.

"Yes, sir," she replied.

"We'll also check on that other thing," he said over his shoulder to Walter, alluding to the captives.

The base roads were empty of all other traffic and they made it to their destination within a few minutes. They were met by an Air Force officer, who saluted them all sharply and reported, "Good morning, General Vogel. I'm Second Lieutenant Cloyed, the base security officer. I've been instructed to brief our security protocols and to answer any questions you may have."

"Thank you, Lieutenant. Proceed."

"Yes, sir. If you gentlemen would follow me this way, please."

The two British officers trailed the man around as he showed them the security measures put in place after the event. Outside the fence a ditch had been dug about ten feet deep and four feet across that extended into the distance in each direction. The lieutenant explained, "As you can see, sir, we've had to make major modifications to our traditional defenses, which were built with terrorist attacks in mind, not an uprising-type scenario. The LCBs only come close when they see a cognitive, and for some reason they ignore the pit and fall right in. Then, every morning a team goes out, spears them, and takes them away for incineration."

"How did you keep the equipment operators safe while the digging the ditch and building the berm?" Walter asked. "From what we know, the LCBs go crazy at the sound of machinery."

"Oh, we didn't use machines. This was all done by hand." The lieutenant sensed that he might have said too much so he clammed up. The general pretended to ignore the slip up and they continued on the tour for another fifteen minutes before ending back at the jeep.

"An amazing effort, young man," the general complimented the security officer. "Especially considering that my reports say that only two thousand people survived the initial onslaught. That's only seven percent of the base population, give or take. Now tell me lieutenant, how were you able to accomplish all these modifications in such a short time and with limited manpower? Hmmm?"

Realizing he'd been caught in a trap, the lieutenant's mouth moved up and down without any words coming out except, "Dah, uh." Finally, he blurted out, "Perhaps that's a matter best explained by the installation commander, sir. It's way above my pay grade."

"That's the thing, Lieutenant Cloyed. I relieved Colonel Slater as the base commander an hour ago." The young man was given a reprieve from having to answer further when sirens came on over the base loudspeakers, followed by the announcement, "Alert, alert, all flight. Armed conscripts rebelling at the encampment. Emergency response team personnel are to report at once to the enlisted chow hall. Weapons free, weapons free." The sirens blared again and the message repeated.

The general froze with one foot in the jeep and listened to the announcement. He shook his head and yelled at Lieutenant Cloyed over the racket: "Tell me what's going on with these conscripts, son. I want the truth." When the junior officer balked, General Vogel pressed him. "Well? Spit it out."

"Um, yes sir, general. Uh, you see, we, I mean the Air Force rather, we uh…"

The garbled explanation was interrupted. First by the security officer's handheld squawking, "This is Robles at the conscript encampment. At least two dozen conscripts have escaped in a troop transport. They look like they're headed towards the front gate." Then a few seconds later, "Oh my God, they've killed all of the guards! All of them!"

A second distraction came from dozens of LCBs sprinting towards the perimeter fence, attracted by the loudspeaker broadcast. They screamed and grunted and Walter got his first look at a group of unrestrained LCBs. It was a sobering sight. The general grabbed the handheld from the lieutenant and yelled into it, "This is General Vogel, the new installation commander. Secure from announcements over the base loudspeakers! Now!"

Within seconds the siren was silenced and the speakers clicked off. The LCBs continued running towards the fence, towards the last man-made sounds they heard, until they hit the pit. Walter watched the ground swallow them up. He could still hear the grunts, whoops and odd screaming noises but the worst of it was absorbed by the wall of earth.

As he stared at the mass of LCBs wanting in he heard the sound of a large vehicle approaching at a high rate of speed. A line of trees and some buildings blocked it from view until it appeared around the corner only twenty five meters in front of them. The back of the truck was filled with armed men and women.

The truck sped up when the driver saw the defensive measures in place and Walter thought the man meant to smash through the metal poles with the truck. Then the tires squealed as the driver cut right, slid a meter or so, and continued along the fence line.

General Vogel turned to the young security officer and asked, "How far down along the fence do those ditches go, son?"

About a hundred and twenty feet, sir," the lieutenant answered and then ducked as someone in the back of truck let off a couple of rounds. Walter flinched and dodged as General Vogel leaned sideways on his left leg before tipping over completely onto the asphalt. The contents of the general's head spilled out, a pulpy reddish grey mass, followed immediately by an enormous gush of blood that pushed the soggy, gelatinous tissue farther away with the strength of its flow.

"Oh, boy," Lieutenant Cloyed said with a burp before retching all over the front of his uniform.

Having spent time in the Middle East, Walter wasn't as squeamish when it came to violent ends, but this was the first time he had ever been right next to someone when they were killed, and a general besides. He felt completely out of his element. He just stood there, watching as the truck got further away before it crashed through the fence in the distance and disappeared.

Coming out of his daze, Walter told Lieutenant Cloyed, "I need to report this to General Fells. Stay here and get things under control."

The lieutenant was still looking aghast at the general. The body was still twitching. He managed a weak, "Yes, sir." Walter hopped into the front seat of the jeep. Before the sergeant put the vehicle into gear, Walter told the security officer, "Get that hole in the fence patched up before this place is crawling with LCBs. And get the general's body off of the road."

The sergeant waited a few more seconds and when she was certain Walter was finished, sped off in a different direction from the one they took earlier. Exhaustion suddenly overtook Walter. The events of the last few days and the lack of sleep were taking a toll and watching the general's head disintegrate put the icing on the cake. He looked down at his hands and noticed that they were shaking. He used the pull down visor and saw that his eyes were red-rimmed and that there was blood speckled all over his face.

"Are you okay, sir?" the sergeant asked, looking at him with a mixture of pity and concern.

"I think so. Why do you ask, sergeant? I'm sorry, what's your name?"

"Sergeant Tate, Colonel."

"Okay, Sergeant Tate. Why do you ask? Do I look unwell to you? 'Off my rocker', as you Americans put it?"

"No, sir, sorry, sir," she answered and for the rest of the ride she didn't address Walter again. They arrived at a building with a sign out front that read, "Wright-Patterson Air Force Base - Installation Commander - Colonel Mark Slater, USAF." Jumping out, he told his driver, "Wait here," and jogged up wide stairs with an elaborate set of double doors at the top.

Four armed guards, two American and two British, flanked the entrance doors. An American made to intercept Walter, but a low, "Uh-uh," from one of the British guards stopped him. The airman stepped back in place and they all rendered a salute. Walter returned it sloppily and asked, "Is General Fells inside?"

"Yes, sir," one of the British responded, opening the door for him. "He's in the office at the end of the hall, sir."

Walter nodded and went in. Halfway down the hall he saw a door labeled 'Men' and he took a detour to take relieve himself and wash the blood off as best he could. At the sink he splashed cold water on his face and watched the return fall coalesce from single droplets into a dark pink stream before it disappeared down the drain. Staring at it, Walter realized that he was witnessing a part of someone vanish. He shivered and checked his face in the mirror for residual blood. It was relatively clean, but his uniform looked like he had walked through a red mist. "General Fells is not going to be happy with this," he said aloud to his reflection.

From behind him he heard, "I'm sorry, but why won't I be happy?"

Walter spun around but the general wasn't there. He looked down and noticed a pair of combat boots under one of the stall doors. "General Fells?" he ventured.

"Yes, it's me. Who is that out there? Is it you, Walter?"

"Yes, sir. I'll wait outside for you to finish."

"Don't bother, I'm finished in here anyway. Was dozing off actually. Stay where you are."

The sounds of pants going up, a zipper closing, and a military belt being clasped came from inside the stall. The toilet flushed and General Fells undid the lock on the door and swung it open. Unsure what the exact protocol was in this particular circumstance Walter looked up at a corner of the ceiling.

The general washed his hands and dried them before addressing Walter again. "Okay, now what is it you wanted to tell me, Walter?" he asked, leaning back against the sink.

"I'm afraid it's a bit of bad news, sir. There was an escape by a group of the civilian detainees about fifteen minutes ago. Their escape attempt led through the front gate, and when that failed…"

"Well, good for them," General Fells interrupted. "I was discussing this very issue with Colonel Slater, as a matter of fact. Was that what the base intercom was going on about?"

"It was, but that's not the bad news, sir." Walter knew how fond of his second in command General Fells was, and wasn't anxious to break the news. Thinking back to earlier and how he was told by the very man in front of him how much his candor was appreciated, he figured the best way to go was to get it over with. Besides, the general was starting to look impatient. "I'm sorry to have to tell you this, but General Vogel was shot in the head and killed by one of the escapees."

Several emotions showed on the general's face in quick succession. First was confusion, as if his brain couldn't comprehend the information, quickly followed by grief over the loss of his longtime friend. The last emotion, and the one that stayed, was a furious, angry resolve. Walter backed up a few steps when the general looked up at him. His brow was furrowed and his face was red. He nodded. "Thank you, Walter. That must have been difficult for you knowing my relationship to the general."

"Yes, sir. I'm very sorry, sir."

"It wasn't your fault. Colonel Slater holds the majority of the blame and I'll address that with him, but I'm going to ask you to once again go above and beyond for me."

It was Walter's turn to nod. He couldn't think of a different response, and wouldn't have done otherwise anyway. "Of course. Whatever you need, General."

"I want you to find whoever did this and bring them back. Alive, if possible, but I'll be happy the other way, too. Just bring them back. Use whatever resources you need."

"I'll get them, sir. You can count on me," Walter vowed.

Without another word, the general clapped him on the back and stomped out. On his way out, Walter noticed the slight slump in the general's bearing that hadn't been there before.

Walter's mind was spinning as he headed back down the hallway to the entrance. While he was knowledgeable in investigative journalism and tangentially, in finding people who didn't want to be found, he never had to find and then capture a violent person or persons before. He was going to need help with that part; his first order of business was to put together a team and get after the escapees before the trail got cold.

When he got outside, Walter was surprised to find the Air Force sergeant still parked at the curb. She was leaning against the hood smoking, but when she noticed him approaching quickly tossed the cigarette away and stood up straight.

They both got in the jeep. "Sergeant Tate, take me back to the front gate."

Her only reply was to put the jeep in gear and accelerate.

TWO MILES SOUTHWEST OF FAIRLAWN, OHIO

Josh, Finn, and Ben found the going easiest along the tree lines. The trees provided cover and protection on one side while the fields on the other side gave visibility for miles. None of them spoke as they concentrated on where to place their steps. By necessity their speed was kept to a slow walk and the three men were able to keep the pace without difficulty. Whenever they heard a noise from the woods they instinctively dropped to their bellies and waited for it to pass.

An hour later they were at the outskirts of Fairlawn, a medium sized town of less than ten thousand people. Josh had been to the town on many occasions, usually to grab something from one of the drive-thru fast food places, but he had also attended a retirement ceremony for a CO at one of the hotels near the town center. Josh called for a huddle. "Let's try and keep our voices low and communicate only when necessary," he reminded them. The other two nodded their understanding. "Cool. I know my way around the town a little, but to be honest, I really didn't have a plan beyond getting us here," Josh confessed. "I mean, I don't really know what the best move is. Do either of you two have any ideas?"

"If you want advice from someone who's spent years of his life in a cell, my advice is to watch and wait," Ben said. "Sometimes, when you don't have anything better to do, and if you're patient, an opportunity will present itself."

More confident now that he was out of the prison, Finn added, "I agree. It beats charging in there without knowing the lay of the land."

"Good. We check things out for a while. Let's find a better spot, though. We're out in the open here," Josh recommended. He led them a short ways away to a small shed and together they carried a small picnic table over to the back of it and quietly climbed up onto the roof. Crawling on their bellies they slunk up to the peak of the roof and peered over.

From their new, higher vantage point they got their first look at the abject scale of the disaster, something they could only appreciate by actually seeing it with their own eyes. Even the horrors back at the jail could not prepare them for it properly. It was horrific earlier, for certain, but jail was its own microcosm. It wasn't real, everyday life. More so, incarceration is specifically engineered to not be reflective of the outside world. Prison enculturalization is so effective that after a time every prisoner fantasizes about the outside so much that their ideal version of it is usually much rosier than the reality of it.

Even considering the understandable delta between the ideal and the real as it applied to the disaster, it was still quite a shock to the men. Less so for Josh, since he went home every day, but Ben and Finn took it especially hard. Finn wept outright and tears leaked down Ben's cheeks.

Bodies and pieces of bodies littered the streets. Some of the buildings were still smoldering from day old fires and cars were randomly scattered everywhere, most with their doors wide open. People hung over or poured out of car doors, from windows, and even trees. What upset Finn the most was seeing the burned and mutilated bodies of women and children, tragic loss caused by the seemingly casual indifference of the predators that savaged anyone they came into contact with.

The only living beings the three men spotted were the crazy ones, either standing in corners or huddled around carcasses, picking off bits of meat and eating it. To Josh the monsters seemed lethargic, as if resting after a huge expenditure of energy. It brought to mind a pride of lions sleeping off a huge meal of water buffalo.

"This is worse than I thought it would be," Ben rasped.

"Yeah," Josh answered dolefully. "I can't imagine that anyone could have survived all of that. But a few people must have, right? Because somehow we did."

Finn stopped weeping and dried his eyes on his shirt sleeve. He squeezed his nostrils shut with his thumb and forefinger and then absently wiped a long string of snot on one of the roof shingles. "Yeah, that's true. But how can we help anyone?"

Eyeing the mucous a foot away with a slight grimace of disgust, Josh answered him. "We stick to the plan, that's how. Be quiet and watch and wait."

Ben nodded in agreement and keeping his hand low, the big man pointed to the right side of the street. "Look over there. Someone hung a sign out."

The sign was clear in both its message and its urgency. Scrawled on a large sheet with red letters a foot high was a one word plea: 'HELP!' The sheet was pinned at the top corners by closed windows and it was occasionally perturbed by the wind. As Josh watched, the sheet crimped and the message changed to "HP!"

Looking in dismay at the long stretch of space between their hiding place and the building where the sheet hung, Finn shook his head. "That building might as well be on the moon. There's no way we'll make it that far without getting our asses kicked."

"You're right," Josh agreed. "We wouldn't get a hundred feet."

After a few minutes where nothing in front of them changed and no one spoke, Josh had an idea. "I think I've got it. So easy."

"What's easy?" Finn asked suspiciously.

"All we need is a distraction." Looking left and right between the two men, Josh saw the inkling of distrust on their faces for the first time so he was quick to allay their fears. "Relax, guys. I'm not asking anyone to do something I wouldn't do. Besides, both of you numbskulls are too far out of shape to do what I have planned."

His volunteering spirit coupled with the slight rebuke put the two former inmates back into a more receptive mood. Ben was quick to qualify things. "You had me worried there Josh. I thought you wanted to make me into two-legged bait." Finn nodded in agreement with the sentiment and added, "Yeah, same here."

"Nah, I wasn't trying any of that. I just wanted you guys to tell me what you thought."

Finn had a logical mind, honed through working with computers and writing very structured software code for many years. He did some mental calculations. "I don't think it's worth the risk, Josh," he said. "First of all, how were you planning to distract them? There are really only two ways to do that, and that's by running or driving and neither one works."

Josh tilted his head to the side. "Actually that was my plan. Running out and yelling, getting them to chase me," he admitted.

Ben jumped on the point Finn was making. He asked, "Okay, what then? Were you planning on outrunning them all and then magically popping up back here, free and clear?"

Josh frowned. "I see your point. I didn't really think it through that far."

"And for what?" Finn admonished him. "A stranger? Someone we don't even know? What if the person who put the sign out is dead? Or they already left? Even worse, what if we risk everything to go and rescue them and they turn out to be an asshole?" Finn was breathing hard after his whispered rant.

"Okay, okay, it was a bad idea. Jeez."

They all rested their chins on their hands and watched the activity in the street some more, trying to think of a foolproof and safe way to help any survivors. Josh couldn't help peeking over at Finn, who had obliviously placed his hand less than two inches from the snot string he had smeared earlier. Josh watched in rapt fascination as the mucous slowly meandered over the granular surface of the shingle towards the young man's hand.

When the shiny discharge closed to within a centimeter of touching Finn, Josh stopped paying attention to the street in anticipation of Finn's reaction. He mentally willed the snot rope on to greater speed. It made it to within a hair's distance of touching Finn's pinky when Ben suddenly said, "I got it."

Finn perked up, moving his hand further away in the process. Josh grimaced in frustration. He sighed and asked, "What were you thinking, Ben?"

"I was thinking 'fuck that guy'. Let's be realistic, we can't save everyone, not without maybe getting ourselves killed. My plan is if we want to save people, we need a fortified place to retreat to, we need better, silent weapons, and we need more information." The large black man turned and looked directly into Josh's eyes and added, "I'm not a dumbass, Josh. Just because I'm big doesn't mean there isn't a brain up here." Ben rapped his knuckles on his forehead for emphasis.

"I know that. Everyone knows that. Isn't that right, Finn," Josh asked, indicating the young man with his chin.

Finn nodded. "Yeah, everyone knows that. For sure." He quickly added, "By the way, I'm not just saying that because I'm scared of you, Ben. To be honest, I wish I was more like you. Smart. Strong. Respected."

"Thanks guys. I just want what I say to be taken seriously." He looked down the street at the sheet again. "And I seriously don't think we should try and rescue that person right now. Shit, we don't even know what's happening to everyone."

"I hear you," Josh told him. Turning, he asked, "What do you think, Finn? Do you agree?"

Finn disliked being put on the spot so he blurted out the last thing he heard just to get the attention off of himself. "I say 'fuck that guy' too. We should do what Ben said. It's safer."

Wanting to do the right thing Josh considered what the men had to say. He had never been in charge before. Before becoming a CO he led a normal life with normal responsibilities that were primarily centered on himself. He became a correctional officer for the heck of it after he applied through an ad in the paper looking for candidates. At the time Josh was two years out of high school and still working in a fast food place and he had no other plans beyond knowing that he didn't want to be stuck at a minimum wage job forever. He not only wanted a better future for himself, he also wanted to gauge whether or not he was wanted and accepted by others, especially by the adults. He took the tests, sat in for the interviews and completed the physical. When it looked like he would be hired he was glad because it meant he could get a place of his own and finally become a 'real man', but after meeting some of the COs and touring the Summit County Jail where he would be working if he accepted the job, Josh's motivation changed from his modest goals making a living to doing his best to be a better group member and contributing towards something greater than himself.

After the event, Josh accepted the role as the group's appointed leader voluntarily because it meant he could retain some meaning in his life. He felt that he worked best in a group, and if the best place for him in his current group was to lead it, then that was what he intended to do to the best of his ability. He mentally considered the characteristics of the two men with him, because who they were flavored their contributions to their little trio. Ben was smart, patient, and confident and if Josh wasn't around would probably have been selected as the leader. So far the big man seemed content to be Josh's second, to provide advice, and to act as a mentor.

Finn on the other hand was the nervous type and relied on the other two for approval and to make the decisions. The young man was smart and personable but he lacked self-confidence. Josh figured that what Finn endured during his time in jail robbed him of his belief in himself and was hopeful that in time the man's self-assurance would return. Until then Josh would include Finn in the discussions but would not overly depend on his judgment.

Deferring to Ben's reasoning, Josh reconsidered a rescue attempt for whoever it was that hung the sheet out of the widows. They didn't have the information or the resources to do it safely. He said, "Ben, you mentioned that we need a safe place to operate from and more details about what's going on, right?"

Ben nodded. "Yeah."

"Okay, then that's what we'll do, starting with a hideout. We need a place that those things can't get into, but that will let us go in and out without being seen or caught. What kind of place might that be?"

"A bank?" Finn ventured.

"No, too many windows. Plus, I think that's the bank right there, next to the building with the sheet on it. What else?" Josh asked.

"How about an industrial building or something like a factory?" Ben contributed.

"Yeah, that's the idea, something we have to climb to get into and can pull the rope or ladder up with us afterwards."

With Josh facilitating, the creative juices started flowing. Not every idea was a good one, but there were many with potential. The places that they weeded out had fundamental flaws, like stores and houses, that weren't built to withstand a determined siege. The good ones were places that were built with the intended purpose of keeping people out or limiting access somehow. They finally narrowed it down to factories, hotels, and government buildings, preferably those away from the town center.

Since they were already on the edge of town it made sense to start looking immediately. They quietly climbed down from their perch and headed north. The plan was to skirt the entire town until they found a likely candidate building.

Every little noise or suspicion of noise caused at least one of them to hit the deck and as soon as one of them dropped the others followed without hesitation. Josh was getting annoyed at the constant up and down and wanted to say something, but he suspected that if he told the other two to not jump at every imagined sound, the first time they questioned themselves would be the one time there was an actual crazy person and then they would all be in trouble. Eventually everyone got a little better at distinguishing what was forest noise and what was unnatural noise.

Even though the town had a small population, it was still large enough that it took the three men over an hour to get a quarter of the way around it before taking their first break. They had carefully surveilled every building they came across but didn't find any to suit their purposes. Most were houses and other places that couldn't be defended easily. As they squatted and talked, Josh noted that the other two men looked exhausted. They hadn't had to walk any real distance in a long time and the constant movement in full tactical gear since morning was starting to wear on them. He knew that even if they didn't find the perfect location soon, they still had to pass the night somewhere and might have to settle on a less than ideal spot. Josh did his best to rally them, but he could tell that even if they wanted to push on, Ben and Finn were close to the end of their rope. "How about this, guys? We make one more go to try and find a place for the night. We could all use the rest." Josh took their lack of protest as assent.

"I gotta piss before we go," Finn declared.

They waited for him to go and when he was ready they started off again. Josh hoped they had another hour in them, but knew that the others were exhausted when Finn tripped over something and went sprawling, instinctively yelling, "Shit!" on the way down.

Finn's shout was easily the loudest thing within a square mile of their location. Both Ben and Josh went prone immediately and Finn had the good sense to stay on the ground where he fell. At first, there was no reaction to the outburst and Josh let out a sigh of relief at the close call. Then he heard it: a racket of whoops and shrieks from all around them.

The men did their best to be as small as possible. The field they had been traversing had hip high growth on it but the plants were loosely spaced, limiting the amount of screening they provided. Anyone or anything within twenty feet would be able to spot them.

A few minutes passed. The crazy people were still looking for them and the whoops sounded closer than before and more concentrated. Keeping his head flat to the ground, Josh craned his head up and down and chanced a look. His heart almost exploded in his chest when he spotted one of them about fifteen feet away. It was a woman in a blue sundress and she had her back to them.

The woman turned her head slightly. Somehow she was still wearing her sunglasses, an overly large pair favored by Hollywood types. It was almost comical, a monster wearing fashion accessories, but there was nothing funny about the way she scanned the near-distance, trying to pinpoint where the scream had come from.

Luckily it was late in the afternoon and the shade from the trees and a nearby irrigation berm worked in their favor and broke up their body shapes, otherwise they would have been doomed. The crazy woman scanned in their direction but must not have detected them through her dark lenses because she suddenly whooped in excitement and sped off.

Gradually the whoops came fewer and farther away. Nobody made a move to get up and continue the search for shelter. Josh could see the sky from where he was laying and he watched it slowly sink into the horizon. He knew that if they didn't risk moving now they would have to stay where they were for the entire night. Stumbling around in the darkness or lying in the grass were not their safest options.

"Let's keep moving," he whispered as he came up to a low squat. He swiveled his head in every direction and made sure the fields around them were empty before continuing. He could hear Ben and Finn's steps behind him and noted that they had regained their earlier fear of noises. They were definitely stepping with exaggerated caution.

Josh had to admit to himself that he was also petrified. He expected a boogeyman to jump out from behind every tree, or to materialize up out of the ground at his feet, so when he felt a tap on his arm he nearly shrieked. He curtailed it just in time when he saw that it was only Ben trying to get his attention.

Sagging to his knees in relief and from the adrenaline dump, Josh heard Ben say something in a low voice he didn't quite get. "What? I didn't hear you."

Leaning in, Ben repeated it. "I said, that building over there looks like a school. You almost took us right past it."

Ben was right. Through a small screen of trees Josh saw what looked like a school in the distance. He also saw several yellow buses, which verified it. He put his hand on the big man's shoulder and matched Finn's happy grin. "It looks like our luck is improving, fellas."

They crept through the trees separating them from the school. On the far side was a large expanse of open ground that they would have to cross before they could go in. It was at least a hundred yards through a nearly empty parking lot and surrounding lawn and on top of that there was no way of knowing if the school was locked or who or what they would find once they got inside.

"Fuuuuck," Finn commiserated.

His sentiment was felt by the other two, but Josh wasn't ready to give up. "It might not be as bad as it looks guys. I mean, if we're careful like we have been, we should be okay."

Ben turned to face Josh, suddenly serious. In a low voice, almost a growl, he pointed at Josh's face and said, "Listen, Josh. I agreed to follow you, but you need to know that I don't like 'should be okay' when it comes to my life. This isn't a game. There aren't any do-overs here. Let's get it straight right now that we only take risks when there are no other options. Agreed?"

Feeling chastised and a little threatened by Ben's menace, Josh agreed reflexively. "Sure, sure, Ben, you're totally right. There's no reason to take unnecessary chances. I still think we should try and get into that school, though. Staying out here in the open overnight is taking a chance too, probably a bigger one."

"Yeah," Finn whispered. "What if those things see in the dark or something?"

"Okay, that's better," Ben concurred. "Thinking things out, not rushing out into the open and hoping things will be okay on the other side." A look of concern crossed Ben's face. "Do you really think those things can see in the dark?"

Getting down on his belly, Josh turned his head up and whispered, "Let's not find out. I want to get into that school before we learn the hard way." Then he began crawling the way soldiers did in the movies when they had to go under barbed wire.

Ben and Finn dropped down and followed his example. At the tail end of the odd procession, Finn did his best to keep up but it was hard work. It felt like he was swimming, except on gravel. He didn't dare raise his head too far off of the ground because he was scared it would be noticed, only lifting it occasionally and just far enough up to make sure he was still behind Ben.

In front Josh also found belly crawling across a gravel parking lot to be one of the more onerous tasks he had done in his life. The first few yards were easy, but then the stones began biting into his hands, forearms and elbows. Worse still, he had to crawl in a way that kept the tactical vest off of the ground because if he didn't, it made a loud scraping noise. His movement ended up being an ungainly sort of modified pushup crawl. Before making it even halfway across the lot Josh was exhausted. He started taking frequent breaks, laying his head down and sucking in large gulps of air. While he lay there gasping he marveled at the perspective he had from his low vantage point. He could see with clarity things he would never have paid attention to otherwise; bugs as they crawled by, cigarette butts and other trash were everywhere, and the horizon was skewed. Tilting his head up a little he saw the school in front of him. Somehow, it looked like it was farther away than when he started. "What the hell?" he thought, before gritting his teeth and doggedly crawling on.

The men finally made it to the lawn as dusk settled and Josh sighed with pleasure at the contrast between crawling across a gravel parking lot and the soft carpet of grass he was resting on. They rolled to their backs and put their arms out at the sides to better catch their breath. Whoops and screams began to emanate from multiple points in the distance as the daylight dimmed further. The men slowed their breathing while they tried to pinpoint where the cries were coming from and after a few minutes they determined that they hadn't been discovered yet. Without a word Josh flipped over and started crawling again.

Seeing the door to the school looming ever closer motivated Josh and he picked up the pace. Before he knew it he made it to the concrete pad of one of the side door entryways. He managed a few more feet to the shadow created by the door overhang and was able to stand without fear of being spotted. His head got light at the sudden transition and he had to put his hands on his knees to prevent himself from swaying over and falling back onto the ground. The moment passed and Ben and Finn joined him in the wall's lee. The former inmates were shaking with relief and from the exertion.

Before inspecting the doors, Josh checked on the others. Ben was sweating profusely and Finn looked positively ragged. The young man's face was haggard and he leaned heavily against the wall, panting. When he looked up he saw Josh studying him, he made a lazy thumbs up.

"I'm okay, Josh," he wheezed softly, smiling. "Just tired is all."

Ben reached out to put a comforting hand on Finn, which made the young man flinch before he caught himself. "Sorry," he said a little sheepishly. "Habit."

"I get it, little man," Ben whispered. "But nobody's going to touch you like that again. You have my word."

Josh watched the short exchange with approval before framing his face with his hands and looking through the glass door into the school interior. It was getting darker by the moment, which made it difficult to see very far down the hallway inside. Then, even though he was pretty sure that they would be locked, Josh tried the doors anyway. He turned back to the others and shook his head.

"Okay," he turned and said into the gathering darkness. "We're running out of options. I know we made it this far okay, but these doors are locked. Plus, it's dark inside and I have no idea…"

Josh never completed the sentence. The metal and glass door behind him suddenly exploded outward and smashed into his back and head. He was flung forward and out, landing on the grass in a daze. In a panic he tried to clear his head and crawl back into cover, but his body didn't seem to understand the commands he was giving it. His arms collapsed and his face smacked into the ground. He faintly heard sounds of a struggle before he was jerked to his feet and flung over a shoulder. It was a very broad shoulder, more like concrete than human flesh, and Josh jounced painfully up and down on it with his stomach.

Through his daze he heard his mouth eject "oomphs" every time his carrier took a running step, then the metallic click of a door shutting before Ben's voice told him, "Don't worry, Josh, I got you. You're okay."

He started coming around. He heard Finn ask in a whisper, "Is he dead?"

Josh tried to say, "I'm alive, I'm okay," but instead of words he made a moaning noise.

Muted bangs and thumps came from somewhere to Josh's left. Ben said, "Finn, shut that bitch up or we'll have visitors."

Finn muttered a hesitant and unconfident, "Uh, okay," before he headed over to the door to silence the brute pounding on it. The sound of Finn's retreating feet echoed off the narrow, locker lined hallway and Josh knew they had made it into the school somehow. He tried sitting up but could only make it part way. Ben reached down, grabbed him under the armpits, hefted him up, and settled him onto his butt. He still felt lightheaded but with his back against the wall it wasn't as bad as before.

Josh looked left and saw Finn outlined against the school's double doors. On the other side of the reinforced glass a bespectacled woman in a plain dress and sensible shoes growled and pounded her fists in frustration at her inability to get back in with them. Her fierce demeanor belied her boring teacher's attire and the bizarre disparity, coupled with the accumulation of the day's events rendered Finn immobile. Josh could tell from the young man's body language that the last thing Finn wanted to do was open the door and confront some savage facsimile of a docile third grade teacher.

"Be right back," Ben said, before striding purposefully towards the standoff at the door. When he got there, he gently nudged Finn aside while pulling out his spring baton. In one smooth motion Ben pushed the door open with his right hand while whipping his baton down on the woman's head with his left.

The result was as spectacular as it was effective. The vectors of acceleration and force, combined with Ben's brute strength, caved the top of the woman's head in all the way to her jaw and the concussion severed her spinal column at the base of her neck. She slumped to the ground bonelessly and all at once, and her dead weight forced her upper body backwards and her feet sideways. The twin noises of her knee muscles snapping could be heard over the sound of her crumpling to the cement. It was sickening to hear.

Ben let the pneumatic door assist slowly ease the entrance door shut, only intervening at the last moment to make sure the latch caught silently. Finn looked morose, still standing off to the side where Ben had guided him a few moments before. He muttered an apology but Ben just shrugged and said, "No problem. Let's see how Josh is doing."

The two men approached and watched Josh struggle to his feet. He was improving by the second and his dizziness was just about gone. He eyed the doorway they entered through with trepidation, expecting it to be filled at any moment by the frantic bodies of those transformed, lured by the dead woman's siren call and eager to get in and maul them. The doorway remained empty and after half a minute Josh was able to take his focus off of it.

He turned to find both Ben and Finn regarding him with questioning looks. "Thanks. You guys really saved my bacon there."

"It was Finn's quick thinking, really," Ben admitted. "When that lady came barreling through the door and sent you flying, it caught me by surprise. Finn was able to grab the door before it could close again. All I did was pick you up and carry you in."

"Is that all?" Josh quipped good-naturedly. "Just picked up a full grown man and sprinted twenty feet? What a slacker."

The small joke relieved the tension of the last several hours. When he laughed, the movement caused Josh to wince in pain and when he felt the back of his head his hand came away bloody. There was also a good-sized lump where the door frame cracked into the back of his skull. "We should probably find the nurse's office. Hopefully that lady out there," and Josh indicated the dead woman at the door with his chin, "was the only one in here."

"We can't assume that," Ben cautioned. "But if there were any running around loose, our noise would have brought them running by now. Still might be some in the rooms though. You never know."

"I don't feel comfortable wandering around these hallways," Finn said close to Josh's ear. "I can't see shit."

Night had finally fallen. "Okay. We'll wait here until morning and we can see what we're dealing with. Try and get some rest."

KLIMPS MEGA STORE

Technically, while he was on watch Jim was supposed to keep an eye on everything in all directions. At first he did just that, making slow patrols around the rooftop while scanning the darkness with his night vision scope. He went clockwise while Saul went counter-clockwise, neither one of them particularly interested in interacting with the other. After his third rotation of not seeing anything noteworthy except for the squatting goon, Jim spent the majority of his time on that side of the roof observing it.

Even though the goon barely moved except to scratch the odd itch, Jim was fascinated by it. For the last couple of days the only time he had seen a goon stay still was when it was facing a corner or a wall aestivating. The goon at the tree line wasn't dormant like that and was clearly alert, but since it didn't follow his movements, Jim was pretty certain that it couldn't see in the dark. Noise was altogether different. If Jim made even the slightest sound the goon's head would turn and lock onto the disturbance and stay focused on that location until it became distracted again by something else. The first few times it happened it gave Jim goose bumps; the goon's eyes radiated a hot white in the subtle green background of the night scope's light amplification.

After a while even trifling with the goon by making small sounds became boring, so Jim decided to wait for Saul to get to the other side of the roof and then chucked a spare bullet into the brush near the goon to get a reaction. He couldn't look through the scope and throw at the same time, so he marked the goon's location, adjusted left a little, leaned the rifle quietly against the roof wall, and whipped the bullet as hard as he could. He quickly brought the scope up and refocused just as the bullet landed.

If Jim was a gambling man, he wouldn't have bet on himself in a million years to hit where he was actually aiming, and he would have been smart not to. Instead of the brush near the goon, the bullet sliced ten feet to the right and hit the beast in the teeth.

Whatever made the goons what they were reduced their vocabulary to a few distinct sounds, and so far Jim had only heard variations of grunts, whoops and shrieks, depending on their mood. His throw introduced a new sound; a chortling, wet warble akin to a baby goat's bleating that indicated surprise, shock, and bodily damage. Before it turned and bolted, Jim watched through the scope as the goon's face blossomed white from the copious amount of spewing blood. Keeping it in his sights as best he could, Jim followed its run through the trees. It tripped several times over roots and bushes but kept shambling to its feet until it disappeared from Jim's view.

Saul was at his side. "What the fuck just happened?" the little man whispered fiercely.

In no mood to confess, especially to the little man with a big man syndrome, Jim lied. "Beats me, but I think something spooked that goon."

"No way, dude. Those things don't spook. Tell me what you did," Saul insisted.

"Seriously, Saul, get off my ass. How could I have done anything from up here?" Normally Jim didn't like to use his size to intimidate people, but Saul was really getting on his nerves. Puffing up and looming over the smaller man, Jim poked him in the chest with a forefinger, thumping it down on Saul's sternum with every word. "Back the fuck off, Saul."

Saul backed up but didn't stop whispering his accusations. "Listen you stupid shit. You saw what happened yesterday with that kid. Why the hell would you screw around with them? I heard you grunt, like you threw something. You don't have to admit to it, but I know." Walking away, Saul threw a warning behind him. "If something happens because of what you just did, it's all on you. Ass!"

For the first time in a long while Jim got angry. He grew up as a fat kid attending public schools so he was no stranger to intimidation and confrontation. Over the years he had learned to swallow down his anger in order to stay out of trouble, but the extreme range of emotions he had endured since the event had eaten away at his limits and he felt a red-hot rage building. Jim stood there, shoulders bunched and eyes narrowed as the swell of emotion bubbled up and compelled him to move.

He wanted to beat the hell out of the bearded bastard, make him choke on his own foul breath. Deep down Jim knew it was a bad idea, yet he found his feet moving him in Saul's direction. First one step, then two. He committed on the third step; surrendering to his violent urge felt just and right, and Saul deserved what was coming to him.

"Stop right there, you big fucking dummy," Saul growled from right in front of him.

Caught by surprise, Jim came up short just as the barrel of Saul's rifle poked him in the belly. He squinted into the darkness and could see that Saul had been watching him through the night vision scope the whole time.

The rage that had threatened to overwhelm Jim disappeared in an instant, replaced by a deep conviction that he might die in the next few moments. Time slowed and several thoughts flashed through his mind. For instance, the notion that he had survived incredible odds to make it far as he had, only to die at the hands of a man with awful dental hygiene and only at half his size. Or that he finally landed a decent looking girlfriend who might be the real deal if he played his cards right, or that Vickers and Megan wouldn't like it one bit if Saul shot him and might even avenge him. These images and dozens more played out in only a matter of a few moments and left Jim stupefied. Because he was at a loss at what to do, he did nothing.

Saul was not so conflicted. He jabbed the rifle barrel into Jim's stomach and as a comeuppance, emphasized his words with barrel pokes instead of using his finger. The hard barrel drove Jim back a step every time it prodded him. "Now how about you back the fuck off?"

Feeling the three foot high roof ledge behind his knees, Jim stopped. Saul kept the pressure tight against his midsection, then leaned in and said in a more friendly tone, "If you come at me again Mr. Big Boy, I'll shoot you in the face and throw you off the roof. Then I'll celebrate by banging your little sweetie downstairs. Comprende? I'm getting sick of your shit already." With a final shove that almost made Jim lose his balance and fall backwards, Saul let the gun drop and moseyed back to his side of the roof.

For the next several minutes it was all Jim could do to get his breathing under control. His whole body shook and he got chills as the sweat that broke out on his body during the confrontation evaporated in the cool night air.

Even after he stopped shaking Jim still felt slightly ill. Deep introspection normally wasn't his thing and hadn't been for many years, but as he stewed over the altercation with Saul, what had happened over the past few days, and even further back, the previous decade of his miserable existence, he realized that he had been experiencing life through a fog. His old comfortable routines and his pathetic, perpetual loneliness were symptoms of his inadequacies at coping with a colossal, modern, and impersonal world. He was fed up.

Jim's shame at being bullied brought about a revelation. Who he was before the change was not who he was meant to be or could be. The reason Saul felt confident enough to push him around was because he gave off a victim mentality. Jim didn't want to be that person anymore. Getting chased from his front yard in his bathrobe was a metamorphic trigger, the rebirth of a man who was tuned into his surroundings, who acted instead of reacted, and who possessed a self-confidence that was evident on his countenance and brooked no argument.

Jim's epiphany was so powerful that for a moment he expected to levitate from the rooftop through sheer force of will, or for wings to sprout from his back and the clothes on his body to disintegrate from the inability to contain the awesomeness that was in him. While that didn't happen, there were minute changes to his persona; standing taller with chest out and shoulders back, formerly downcast eyes now projected straight ahead in silent challenge, lips that normally drooped in a near frown were now steadfastly set in a firm line.

Turning his back on Saul, he ignored the potential for escalating their battle of wills. Jim was through with the little man's pettiness. If Saul decided he wanted things to continue, he would learn of Jim's metamorphosis with painful lesson in humility.

A sound from the direction of the woods interrupted Jim's self-analysis. The noise was blatant, meant to attract attention. Jim snapped the scope up and peered through it, the rifle tip wavering as he tried to locate the noise through the small round glass. A false dawn was breaking, which made it harder to see with the night vision since things took on a faint aura. Jim was expecting an adult sized target as he scanned and he initially disregarded a smaller shape because it wasn't big enough. His mind sensed something odd though and almost of its own volition it backtracked the scope. There. Just at the edge of the woods and right in the open was the boy from earlier. He seemed to be staring right back at Jim. Odder still, although he was just a kid, the way the boy stood silent, motionless and unafraid and with his head craned up towards the roof top creeped Jim out.

"Hey, Saul," Jim tried to whisper, wanting to share what he was witnessing. Except when he tried to open his mouth, he couldn't. Instead, he felt a compulsion to join the boy down there on the ground, to be near him and bathe in his warmth and protection. To Jim it felt like staying where he was on the roof, being so far away from the boy, was denying a promise of comfort, a yearning that required immediate mollification. He started shuffling forward.

A hand grabbed him and Jim yelled his surprise, jerking back and flinging his rifle into the air.

"Shit!" Vickers yelled, ducking down and covering his head. A moment later the gun landed behind them with a loud clatter and discharged. A man screamed and Jim was tackled hard into the cinderblock parapet and restrained by Vickers, who sat on top of him and pinned his wrists to the roof surface.

"What the hell, Jim!" Vickers shouted, then softer and closer into Jim's ear: "This isn't good for us, buddy."

For a few more seconds Jim just lay there. He didn't struggle or speak, he just stared at the wall hoping to reestablish contact with the boy on the lawn, but the connection was severed and the thread was fading. He slowly came out of his paramnesic state and when he looked up at Vickers, he had tears leaking down his face into his ears and he could hear crying.

"What happened?" he asked Vickers, confused. Morning was dawning and Jim looked up in the weak light to see a concerned looking Vickers frowning down on him. "And who's crying?"

"I don't know what happened, Jim. You tell me. And Owen is crying because you just shot him."

"What?" Jim said unbelievingly. "Is he okay?" He tried to sit up but Vickers wouldn't let him.

"Stay down there for a second, Jim. Tell me what's going on."

Others starting pour out onto the roof, concerned about the gunshot and the screams. Someone approached that Jim couldn't see. Vickers looked up and shook his head. "Give us a sec, Megan. Okay?"

Jim heard her respond with, "Sure. I'll be over there taking care of Owen if you need me."

Turning back to Jim, Vickers asked again, "What happened?"

Jim vaguely remembered what occurred but it had the substance of a dream. What was stronger was the disquieting sense of loss he was still feeling, a lingering sadness. He couldn't place what it was that he felt was missing.

Vickers didn't press him for more, but he didn't let him up either. Eventually the pangs stopped, leaving behind a wispy memory. "The boy!" Jim uttered. "The boy from earlier, he was calling to me."

A sound of running footsteps approaching made Vickers look to his left, and then the Army sergeant leapt to his feet and met a hurtling Saul just as the angry man was launching a kick at Jim's head. Jim felt a puff of air on his cheek as the bottom of Saul's boot sailed by less than an inch away.

"You piece of shit!" Saul yelled and jabbed his finger at Jim around the bear hug Vickers was giving him. Vickers was slowly forcing the angry man back and away. Jim took advantage of the space to sit and then stand up.

"You're dangerous and useless!" Saul continued yelling. "You don't belong here!"

Looking around, Jim saw that almost everyone had made it up to the roof. They were standing at a safe distance from the altercation and staring at him as he stood there looking confused. Even Bettina was up top. She was giving Jim a dirty look while cradling Owen in her arms, soothing the back of his head with soft caresses. Owen had a bloody bandana wrapped around his hand.

In that moment Jim made a decision to leave the group. He didn't belong with these people and clearly wasn't wanted here any longer. He started for the roof exit when Vickers put up an intercepting hand. "Wait, Jim." To the others gathered around in a half circle he said, "Everyone just wait a second."

Vickers let go of Saul and made a warning gesture, as if to say "Don't you move," then joined Jim near the roof edge. "I know you guys are angry with Jim right now, but you're all making a mistake." There were a few guffaws and Saul said, "Bullshit! Just look at him. The guy's a loose cannon."

"Just hear him out. Jim's put his life on the line for everyone here over the last couple of days, so we owe him that. And what happened to Owen was an accident." Turning to Jim, Vickers gave the 'they're all yours', indication.

Nine pairs of eyes stared at Jim expectantly. Even with the intervention Vickers just provided, he was still tempted to say "fuck it," and leave. The old Jim would have done it without a backwards glance, but Jim's eyes had been opened earlier and despite the annoyance of having to explain himself to people who seemed willing to give up on him too easily, he knew the best move he could make was to stand up for himself.

He looked over at Owen to apologize for accidently shooting him, but when he saw how the tall athlete was hamming it up for Bettina's attention, he scowled and changed his mind. He made a general apology instead. "Sorry for waking everyone up and probably scaring the hell out of you guys. I know what this looks like, and it doesn't put me in the best light, throwing my rifle into the air and screaming, shooting Owen in the hand."

Shuffling over to the roof edge, Jim timidly peeked over at the spot at the edge of the grass where the boy had been but he didn't see anyone there. Turning back, he told them, "The truth is, I don't really know what happened, exactly. I have a vague recollection of the little boy calling to me from the woods over there," he pointed towards the woods with his thumb. "I think I was about to jump off of the roof when Vickers startled me then and all of this happened." Jim shrugged.

Even though he was still angry, Jim's story grabbed Saul's attention. "You saw the boy? Why didn't you call me?"

"I tried, but the boy wouldn't let me."

This time Ray spoke up and came forward, working himself up. "Bullshit. I'm with Saul on this one. You're too dangerous and I think you should leave before you get someone killed." The fat man's hands were clenched impotently down at his sides and his teeth were set in a grim line as he stared directly into Jim's eyes, daring him to disagree.

Unexpectedly, Saul came to Jim's defense. He put a hand out and gently shoved Ray back. "Hold on. You didn't see what we saw earlier, Ray. The little boy and the strange way the goons were acting. I'm telling you, something weird is going on." Pointing at Jim, Saul said, "This guy may not be my favorite person but I believe he's telling us the truth. We can't ignore it." Saul's speech made the others curious and they wandered over to the side of the roof and looked towards the woods, maybe expecting to see the boy standing there. Even Owen was up, cradling his arm and giving a dramatic impression of being in great pain. Jim was glad to see that Bettina wasn't buying the act and had abandoned her role as his nursemaid.

She came over to stand next to Jim, grabbing his hand and looking up at him sheepishly. She gave him a coy look and mouthed the word, "Hi," with a flirty smile. Jim had been prepared to be angry at her for showing another man some attention, but he had never had such a cute girl hanging on to him like she was doing and his resolution came undone in a less than a second.

"Hi," he said back, grinning from ear to ear and blushing. He looked around and saw almost everyone was watching the little exchange and his cheeks got warm and colored even redder. He looked down at the ground, willing people to look away. For a guy who had been virtually invisible for most of his life, he was getting more than his fair share of attention and he was at a loss at how to handle it.

Vickers came to his rescue. "Alright, Jim, show us where you saw the boy."

Happy for the reprieve, Jim studied the tree line and pointed in the general direction of where the boy was standing. "He was right about there, watching me, although to be honest it was dark and all of trees look the same through the night vision scope. But I'm sure it was in that area."

Still skeptical, Ray asked, "Well, if it was dark, how did he see you?" The old man grinned triumphantly at the corner he just painted Jim into.

Jim shrugged. "How should I know? But he knew I was here, he looked right at me. So how about next time you stand watch while I sleep and you see how you like it when he mind fucks you?" The new, more confident Jim met Ray's glare without flinching, and to Jim's surprise the older man dropped his eyes first, and once again the pecking order of the small group shuffled, only this time in Jim's favor.

"Alright boys, pissing contest is over," Megan announced, inserting her body in between the two men. "Let's try and be productive. And since everyone is up here, we might as well have a meeting and talk about how this changes things. We have to go after the boy, figure out what's going on."

"Don't you white people know anything?" Owen spoke up from off to the side, toying with the bandage on his injured hand. "You are never, ever, supposed to chase crazy shit into the woods. As the only black man here, I have to refuse out of principle!" He grinned to show he was just trying to lighten the mood and it worked. Everyone gave a laugh or a chuckle, even Jim, although he stopped short when he noticed that when Owen moved the bandana around, there was only a shallow scratch on his hand that had barely bled. Jim and Owen locked eyes, and Owen gave a 'eh' smile and a raised eyebrow in Bettina's direction as if to say, "Hey, I tried."

Vickers waited for the laughter to die down before getting them back to business. The group needed to decompress; it was good for morale. "Megan's right," he said. "We need to figure out what happened to Jim because if it can happen to him, it can happen to any one of us. Still, I don't want us to get overloaded with competing priorities. First things first, we need to follow up with our plan to get to the radio station and begin recruiting. We can shelve the issue with the goons and the boy until we get back. The team leaves after Owen and I finish our shift at eight o'clock and we hold a quick planning meeting. I need the rest of you to get your meals and make sure all of the gear is prepped before then."

Glad to finally leave the roof top Jim barreled towards the stairwell door, Bettina dragging behind him with her hands still gripping his bicep. Sandy and Cindy backed out of his way to let the two pass before trailing them down the stairs. Everyone began chattering at once and the stairwell echoed with the voices of several people trying to be heard over the others. Jim picked up snatches of their conversations and almost all of them were discussing him and his strange behavior.

"Lucky I didn't kick his ass," Owen was saying, followed by a giggle from Sandy and a more serious reply from Cindy on how she wished he would have. Saul was telling Ray, "The fucker threw down on me. Can you believe it?" Megan and Jack were more pensive: "He's such a nice person and it's too bad things like this keep happening to him," she said, and Jack replied with, "Yeah, that's why I volunteered to drive the truck later, to give the guy a break. He seems cool." To which she replied, "Yeah, he is. He saved my life."

The comments from Megan and Jack made Jim beam. What the others were saying concerned him a little but he understood why they were being said. Bettina squeezed his arm and whispered, "Don't worry about them. I'll watch out for you," and that made him feel a whole lot better. He got a spring to his step and practically skipped down the rest of the stairs.

The next few hours were spent resupplying and redoing the backpacks, wrapping the laptop up with bubble wrap and stowing it with Vickers' gear, and getting a quick bite to eat. Jim surprised himself by only needing a cereal bar and some coffee for breakfast. His appetite was decreasing and he didn't feel the physical hunger pangs he normally felt. Also absent was the psychological need to stuff his face.

Once the preparations were complete Jim showered and changed. Afterwards, he was at the sink brushing his teeth when Saul walked in wearing only a towel and carrying a small toiletry kit. Jim tensed up, expecting Saul to toss out a rude comment or possibly even try and continue what was started earlier, but nothing happened so he relaxed.

Saul hung his towel on a hook and hopped under the shower and for the next few minutes the only sounds were Jim's brushing and Saul's scrubbing. Jim finished first and was walking out when Saul announced over the sound of spraying water, "You know, Jim, we don't have to be enemies. I mean, I was prepared to make friends but for some reason you took an instant dislike to me. Mind telling me why?"

Jim hesitated in the doorway. He started to say something, stopped, and then almost said it again before he reached into his kit and pulled his wet toothbrush and his tube of toothpaste. With a peek to make sure Saul wasn't watching, Jim put it on the sink counter and eased out of the bathroom, hoping Saul took the hint. He closed the door on Saul still talking. "Jim? Did you hear me? Are you still…"

He made his way back towards the entrance and could hear Bettina's voice. She was telling someone, "I don't know, I just thought that maybe this was a good idea. On the first day when this all started I saw a lady running from one of those goon people. She would have gotten away too, except she had a long ponytail and it was bouncing behind her as she ran. The goon person grabbed her hair and snapped her right down. It was right then I decided that…"

She stopped talking when Jim rounded the aisle and she saw him do a double take at her new look. She had shaved off all of her hair. She laughed at his reaction and made duck lips. "Do you like?" The dazed look on his face made her laugh again, but once he got over the initial shock Jim knew that no matter what Bettina did to her hair she was still a very attractive girl.

He stammered out a weak, "Uh, um," before Megan jumped in.

"Cat got your tongue, Jim?" she asked. "You know, what she did to her hair makes a ton of sense, so I asked her to cut mine the same way," and as Megan said it she flipped her hair up to show Jim her new, shorter locks. "No more social pressure to look a certain way so we might as well be practical."

Still checking Bettina out, Jim was only half paying attention to the former nurse. He nodded and said, "Yeah, it makes sense I guess."

Jim figured that Bettina must of taken a shower too, because the old makeup and grime from earlier was gone, replaced by pink glowing skin. She had also taken the opportunity to dress practical like everyone else by exchanging her street clothes for camouflage and boots. She reminded Jim of G.I. Jane and he was instantly even more attracted to her. He desperately hoped that he didn't screw things up with her, or that she wouldn't die horribly anytime soon.

The girls started blabbing to each other again, so he tuned out and wandered away. Then, because Owen and Vickers were supposed to be up on the roof for at least a few more hours, Jim did something he had very little practice at: He exercised some initiative. Using the map in the break room to study the roads, buildings, and area surrounding the radio station and searching the WEKT website with the laptop set up in the break room for pictures of the inside of the building, Jim drew on what he had learned about goon behavior so far and mentally rehearsed getting to and traveling through the building, imagining where he might meet resistance or danger and mentally plotting escape routes and defendable positions to counter it.

While he went over the logistics of the day ahead Jim knew that now more than ever he wanted to live. Maybe it was Bettina or maybe it was just that he had uncovered a dormant part of himself, something deep-seated that made him look to the future and see possibilities instead of a depressing void, but he wanted to live. He was leaning back in his chair ruminating on his life when he heard people approaching.

"Well, look who's here, studying up." It was Vickers, accompanied by Saul, Owen, and Jack.

"I thought you guys were going to be up on the roof for a while longer," Jim said.

"Nah, Megan and Ray spelled us," Vickers explained. "It gives us a chance to head out earlier in case things go longer than planned. I'm pretty sure none of us wants to be trapped out there overnight again." The others nodded their agreement, including Jack who hadn't even logged any real time outside yet. Vickers pointed to the map. "Show us what you figured out so far, buddy."

Even though he wasn't prepared to brief everyone, Jim gave it a shot. "Sure, but I might not have thought of everything." He expected a derisive snort from Saul, but the little man didn't say anything, he just looked at the map attentively.

Jim pressed on. "I looked at the map from two different points of view, from both an on foot perspective and from a driving perspective. Since we need Jack to lead the goons out and keep them away if possible, he needs a destination that will trap them in place."

He pointed to a spot on the map. "Look here. If he takes Route 3 just past the Broadway Creek Bridge, on the right is that industrial park where they make dentures. It's fenced off, so I was thinking he could drive in there and loop around, then lock it back up on the way out. It would keep the ones that followed him inside.

"Hey, hey, wait a minute now," Jack interrupted, standing up. "I didn't sign up to do a suicide mission. No way am I hopping out to lock the gate with those things chasing me. And what if it's locked and I can't get in?" Jack furrowed his eyebrows at Jim and shook his head. "Dude, you need to come up with a better plan."

Before Saul or Vickers could say something, Jim beat them to it. "Relax, 'Dude', I already thought of that. I'll be going with you. We'll bring lock cutters, an extra lock and some chain. You drive and I'll navigate. In fact, you won't even have to get out of the truck. I can handle the gate solo."

"Jim, if you go and something happens, we'll lose two of you. That's a huge risk," Vickers cautioned.

Jack's hackles came back up. "Wait, what you're saying is that it's okay for me to die because it's just me, but it's not cool if Jim dies?"

"Shut up and sit down, you stupid shit." Saul stalked over to the taller, younger man and got in his face. "That's not what he's saying. He's just saying you guys have to be careful." Turning to Vickers, he asked, "Isn't that right?"

"Yeah, sure, that's exactly what I meant," Vickers replied half-heartedly, not caring if Jack was offended or not. He joined Jim up at the map. "What else do have for us?"

"For the rest of you guys that are on foot," Jim said, pointing at some spots on the map and circling them, "I would avoid these areas here and here. They're parks and are too open, so don't even go past them. Also try and avoid going down these paths," he told them, crossing out a few streets with a large 'X', "because they aren't roads, they're narrow alleys and it would be too easy to get stuck in there." Taking the marker Jim drew the route he thought was best, then asked Jack, "You said you knew the area like the back of your hand. Did I miss anything?"

Still a little put off by Saul's earlier chastisement Jack scratched his head. "I wish I knew, but I've been in this building practically the whole time. I don't know, to be honest."

"It's a good start," Saul added, stunning Jim with the unexpected compliment. "We can work with that and adjust it as we go along."

Nodding at Saul, Jim added, "One last thing. I checked the radio station's website and they have a bunch of pictures of the inside of the building and the location of the broadcasting studio. The good news is you guys won't have to clear a bunch of floors to get to it because it's on the ground floor, but the bad news is the station was broadcasting when the change happened and it was probably full of people. Worse, according to the pictures there was a cubicle farm outside of the studio, meaning no hallways or rooms but all free roaming goons."

The room went silent as everyone processed the last bit of information. Vickers thanked Jim and said, "If anyone has any questions now is the time to ask them."

No one had any and the group broke up and began filing out. Jim decided to stay behind and make maps for everyone that showed the routes and the hazards. While he was sitting there, Vickers walked in and sat with him. Speaking in a low voice, he asked, "I like how you're stepping up, Jim. It shows good initiative and builds the confidence others have in you. I noticed that even Saul threw you a compliment." They both laughed at that. "I just have a quick question, and I want you to think about it," he continued.

"What's that," Jim wondered. He had no idea what Vickers was getting to.

"How do you think you'll do next time things get crazy? Remember the ditch outside the drainpipe, how you froze? I don't want that to happen to you again when I'm not around," Vickers explained.

If it was anybody else besides Vickers asking, Jim would have immediately denied feeling apprehensive, but because he trusted Vickers he gave it some thought. He didn't feel scared or nervous like he did yesterday, and the day before, even less so. He gave Vickers an honest answer. "I won't lie. Anytime I'm out there I'm scared something bad is going to happen. But over the last two days or so I've been able to think things through a little better each time we run into trouble. I used to be scared of the goons themselves, but now I'm just scared I'll be caught without options." Jim looked Vickers directly in the eyes. "So I guess the answer is no, I don't think I'll freeze up next time. I'll act instead."

Vickers clapped him on the back. "You made it, Jim. In the military we call what you're describing as 'having the bubble', and it means you have a three hundred and sixty degree sense of situational awareness. The bubble improves with practice so the more you use it, the better it gets. It's also good to hear you admit that you're scared. Always respect those things out there, Jim. The moment you stop fearing them is the day you take too many chances and don't make it home." Standing, Vickers told him, "Don't take this the wrong way buddy, but I'm proud of you."

Jim grinned from ear to ear at such high praise from someone he had already developed a deep respect for. After Vickers walked out, Jim felt a renewed sense of motivation and quickly finished up the maps. He was getting up to go when he had a compulsion to double check them. Even though they all checked out fine, the reassurance made him feel better. He went out to join the others, mentally checking off the last few things he needed before they left.

INTERSTATE 70, VICINITY OF SOUTH VIENNA, OHIO

Fran and his gang were zipping along I-70 past Springfield, having left Dayton and the city's large number of LCBs behind. The road was mostly clear of cars and Bill felt safe enough to go faster than they had been. Within an hour of crashing through the fence at Wright-Patterson they had already skirted around the medium sized town of Springfield and were halfway to Columbus.

Bill looked down at the gas gauge and knuckled it. "We're running low, King. We either need to stop and gas up or get a new truck."

The comment interrupted Fran's thoughts on their destination. He used to live in Columbus and he knew it was a much bigger city than Dayton, probably ten times the size, which meant ten times the number of LCBs. If what they just went through was only a small taste of what they could expect in Columbus, they needed to make as wide a detour around the city as they could. But first they needed fuel. "Pull over at the next gas station we come to."

Bill nodded and drove for a few minutes until he saw an exit sign that advertised gas. He veered right and took the ramp, slowing down but not stopping at the top. The stop lights were out but even if they weren't the odds of running into cross traffic were nearly nil. They hadn't seen another moving vehicle since Dayton.

A large multi-pump gas station was visible just over top of some trees to the right and Bill headed that way, avoiding the few abandoned cars parked askew on the road. Gunter leaned forward and looked into the window at Loomis. "What's going on? Why are we here?"

"Gath," Loomis told him. "We're running low."

"K."

Gunter's head disappeared and Fran could hear him talking to the people in back, probably letting them know the reason for the detour. "We need a map, too," Fran mentioned to Bill, who nodded in reply before coasting the truck into the gas station.

Only a few cars littered the small parking area and none of them were blocking the pumps. Bill pulled up next to one and gave a quick look. "No power, King," he said. "These pumps won't work without juice."

"Can we get to the underground tanks somehow?" Fran wondered.

"I never thought about it so I couldn't say, but maybe one of the new people in the back know how it's done," Bill replied before turning the ignition off and popping his door open. The door creaked stiffly and he had to kick it to get it wide open. "I must have hit something the wrong way," he smirked before hopping to the ground. "Don't call the cops on me."

Fran gave Bill a flat smile, then nudged Loomis and pointed to the passenger side door handle. The tap spooked the fat man and he jumped to comply. Loomis had been nervously staring into the woods since they arrived and after he got out he resumed his scanning. His twitchy behavior was starting to annoy Fran.

"Do you see something, Loomis?" he pried. The only reply Loomis gave was a small head shake. Fran was about to tell him to stop acting so panicky, but relented when he saw how pathetic the man looked with his two front teeth gone and his fu manchu beard matted with dried blood. Instead, Fran told him, "Okay. Do me a favor and keep an eye out," before heading to the rear of the truck where everyone else was disembarking. Loomis perked up at the small amount of responsibility and trust Fran had just given him and his face took on the demeanor of someone intent on doing a very important job well.

After a quick head count Fran found that including his original team of four their group now numbered eighteen. Hank and Helen were among those that made it but Clark was missing.

Helen spoke up before Fran could ask. "Clark and a few others got bounced out of the back when we crashed through the fence. We lost one more when she got pulled out by an LCB after we slowed down." Fran nodded. "She dropped her weapon though, so it wasn't a total loss," the old woman added.

"Lemons from lemonade," Bill proclaimed inaccurately and was rewarded with a seductive smile from the former day care owner.

Ignoring the two Fran introduced himself to the newest members of his group, delivering a speech he had tried to mentally rehearse over the last few minutes. Public speaking wasn't one of his skills so he made it curt. Standing up straight and licking his lips, he addressed everyone: "I'm King. I want to make one thing clear. I'm in charge. That is not up for dispute." He paused for effect. "This isn't a democracy but it's not a prison camp either like back at the base. Anyone who doesn't like how I run things is free to go, but if you stay, you listen to me. Is anyone not clear on that?" Silence. "Fine. I've already selected my second-in-command, which is Bill," he pointed to the older man. "I also have four others that will assist me in running things." He pointed to Gunter, Loomis, Helen and Hank. "If you have a problem, you go to them, not to me." Here Fran was improvising, taking a cue from Colonel Slater back at Wright-Patterson. The man had many layers between him and the regular troops. "You never come to me directly, you always go through them," he reiterated, and without waiting for a response, Fran turned around and went to the front of the truck, pleased with his performance.

Bill and Helen were talking in back of the truck but Fran wasn't focused on what they were saying. Instead, he spent a few minutes looking around, squinting into the trees surrounding the parking lot or trying to see through the glass of the gas station's small convenience store. Like Loomis, he was uneasy, but it was mostly because he was more of an urban predator. Wide open spaces like where they were now were only places to pass through, not stop. The afternoon quiet seemed unnatural to Fran.

Bill and Hank joined him in leaning up against the front bumper. "I have some good news, King. Hank knows how to get gas out of the underground tanks."

Hank took over. "Yep. A few years ago I worked a case where some convenience store employees figured out how to steal fuel." The older man laughed. "Dumb kids got greedy and got caught. While I was investigating I learned how they did it. Once we clear the store I can set it up."

"Can you two handle it?" Fran asked.

They answered with, "Sure," and "No problem," and disappeared back towards the rear of the truck. Fran heard Bill say, "I need some volunteers…" as the 'Major' started rounding people up. With nothing else to do Fran watched Loomis use his grimy fingers to worry at the new gap in his mouth.

Hank rejoined Fran at the front of the truck as Bill, Gunter and half a dozen others went by on their way to the store entrance. The former cop didn't speak and Fran was grateful for his silence. They both watched as Bill ordered two men to pick up a newspaper machine and hurl it through the front door.

"Oh no, no, no," Loomis yelled, expecting the glass to shatter loudly and bring goons running to their location, but all that happened was that the glass spider-webbed and bowed in and the newspaper machine thunked to the ground. The loudest noise ended up being shrieks that Loomis made when he got scared. One of the men that had tried to break the glass gave Loomis a look that said, "And we're supposed to listen to that guy?" and a few women laughed outright.

Gunter began kicking at the reinforced window but it wouldn't collapse so he beckoned two others to join him. Soon the hammering of booted feet began echoing across the parking lot. Hank told Fran, "Just a sec," and walked over to join the gang at the door.

The ex-cop grabbed people by the scruff of their uniforms and pulled them away from the door and the din stopped. "What?" Gunter protested. "We were almost inside."

"No you weren't. These convenience store windows have a chemical epoxy in them that will deform forever. It's designed to keep meatheads like you out. Have you tried the door yet?"

"No."

Hank pulled the handle and the door opened outward, stopping only when it bumped into the discarded newspaper machine. Hank gave the hand signal for 'after you', and Gunter clucked his tongue before signaling the others to follow him into the store. They quickly swept the small interior, making sure to check the stock room, freezers and restrooms.

"All clear," someone announced. Hank walked in and Fran decided to go in too and see how the tanks were accessed. He found Hank working at something under the cash register counter and squatted down to watch.

When Hank saw Fran there, he explained what he was doing as he worked. "State law requires an interlock on all underground petroleum containers for emergency secondary access," the old man lectured. "It has to be separate from the power grid in case of natural disaster. I guess what happened to us qualifies, so..." Hank twisted a wire affixed with a circular seal off of a small metal box and then pried the cover open. "They put these seals on to keep the employees honest, otherwise it'd be too easy to pilfer gas." Then: "A-ha, here we go."

Fran bent down and saw a small electronic panel and some toggle switches. He told Hank, "Looks like it's powered down."

"Yeah, that's because it really only needs juice in an emergency. Could you do me a favor and grab some 'AA' batteries from the display case over there?"

Fran grabbed a package of ten and handed them down to Hank, who used his teeth to rip the paper and plastic apart, then pried out two of the batteries and plugged them into a receptacle next to the circuit board. The board powered on and lit up with digital readouts of 'CLOSED' displayed next to all of the toggle switches. After Hank zipped his hand down and flicked all of the switches over, the readouts changed to 'OPEN'.

"We're in business," Hank exclaimed matter-of-factly as he crawled out from under the counter. Fran backed up to give him room, curious how what Hank had just done gave them access to the gas in the underground tanks. He was about to ask when Hank explained it to him. "Somewhere in the back room should be a manually powered suction hose." He beckoned and Fran followed him through a set of double doors and into the stockroom.

The room was dark but had already been cleared as safe. Out front others from the truck joined the group inside the store and were busy ransacking the shelves for food and other supplies. Fran waited just inside the stockroom door.

"Got it," he heard from the darkness and then Hank was marching back out with a coil of large diameter hose hoisted over his shoulder and carrying some metal fittings. He passed by Fran and continued through the doors leading outside, and Fran felt compelled to follow. A few others, curious as to what was going on, joined the procession.

Out past the gas pumps there were several small metal caps painted green, yellow, white and orange built inset into the ground. Hank went to the green one and lifted the cover. The ex-cop didn't seem to mind that there were now several people crowded around him watching the procedure. The only acknowledgment he made that he noticed them was to speak loud enough for everyone to hear.

"The green tank covers means 'diesel'. Once the panel inside is powered up, the covers outside here are released, and the circuit preventing access to this special hose fitting here," he said, pointing to the coil and metal fittings on the ground next to him, "is opened."

He dragged one end of the hose over to the open cover and snapped it into a receptacle inside, and then looked up at the others with a smirk, "Technically, this is illegal, so don't let me catch any of you guys doing this." A few of them gave tepid chuckles at his attempt at levity. Then: "Can I get one of you to drive the truck over here?"

One of the women detached and went over to the truck, turned it over, and pulled it up next to Hank, who moved aside so she could get close. When the truck was in place he removed the gas cap and attached one of the metal fittings to the free end of the hose, then stuck it in to the truck's fuel receptacle. "Now I need two more volunteers." Two men raised their hands and stepped up.

The hose had two small grip mechanisms. Hank showed them to his two helpers and briefly explained their purpose while he demonstrated. "These bellows suction the fuel out, but they're a bitch to start because the fuel is about twenty feet below ground level." When his helpers took over the older man began recounting a story from his days as a cop to anyone who would listen. Fran walked away. He had seen and heard enough.

While the truck was fueling others were conveying the contents of the store into the stake body and securing it with bungee cords and string. Bill wandered out with a map and waved it at Fran.

"King, do you want to go over the route?"

Fran nodded and Bill unfolded the map on the truck hood. They studied it and it only took a moment for both of them to come to the same conclusion. Bill stated the obvious. "Looks like Route 42 lets us bypass Columbus and avoid the interstate."

"Then that's the route we'll take," Fran replied. "Let's wrap things up and get out of here. I don't know why the LCBs aren't all over us here and I don't care, but I don't like being exposed like this."

"Okay, King." Bill said and walked away, grabbing people and nudging them towards the truck. Hank came up to him and announced that the truck was refueled and ready to go, but that he would like to take the time to fill some extra gas tanks just in case.

"It's less than two hundred miles to Cleveland," Fran replied. "Will a full tank get us there?"

Hank did the mental calculations in his head. "I guess, but I can't say for sure. I don't know what kind of mileage these things get," he slapped the truck's hood with palm.

"Forget it, it doesn't matter. I want to get out of here. Something isn't right; we haven't seen an LCB since we got here. Give Bill some help getting everyone in the truck so we can leave."

"What about the tires? We should change the flats."

After a quick look at the tires, Fran decided it could wait also. "We'll change them later. Let's get going."

"You got it, boss."

Fran was starting to get an appreciation for what it took to be the leader of a bunch of people and he was finding the whole deal extremely distasteful. Dealing with individuals, and having to know each of their distinct personalities, strengths, weaknesses and needs was draining him. Fran thought back to the genesis of his idea to carve a personal, self-serving Kingdom of Fran out of the chaos of the largest cataclysmic event in human history and surmised that so far, it was not really turning out the way he had envisioned.

Of course, he mused, he never thought he would get as far as he had. He had his round table of hand-picked deviants, a small gaggle of followers, and he was poised to get even more. Fran hoped that if he continued to put in the work that in the not too distant future he would get what he wanted; an army at his beck and call, a herd of victims from which to choose from, and the impunity to do whatever it was he wished to do to them. His final thought made him smile to himself, but he had to be careful to hide his mouth behind his hand. Fran knew that when people saw him smile at things that gave him the greatest pleasure, it had the effect of freezing them in their tracks out of instinctual fear. He didn't want his new recruits to see it and scare them off.

"We're all set, King," Bill came up and reported. "We're just waiting on you."

Taking a last look around the parking lot and at the ransacked store, Fran nodded and got in the truck. Loomis piled in afterwards and slammed the door shut. Within seconds they were back on the road.

FRONT GATE, WRIGHT-PATTERSON AIR FORCE BASE

When Walter got back to the front gate he noted that someone had covered General Vogel with a blanket but hadn't moved his body from where it fell. Knowing that at some point General Fells was going to show up and not want to see the body of his best friend left like roadkill on the asphalt, Walter figured he would save the young security officer a severe ass chewing or worse and reminded him to get the body inside. In the distance Walter spied several troops patching the break in the fence where the escapees had punched through earlier. A medium sized pile of bodies blocked the front of the hole, a testament to the battle that must have been fought to retain control of the breach.

While several men were dispatched to take care of the general's corpse, Walter organized the pursuit of the people that killed him. Had they only escaped Walter would have wished them the best of luck. After all, they were serving involuntarily under deplorable conditions. If he himself had been pressed into service instead of given a choice, he would have done the same thing. Unfortunately, they had accidently shot the second highest ranking military officer of the entire country in the head and so there must be consequences. He was almost certain that those consequences would be death, and although Walter wasn't sure he could just execute the escapees when he caught them, he knew he couldn't come back without them, even if that meant their eventual execution by other hands.

He called the Lieutenant over. "Is there somewhere that we can talk?" he asked.

"Yes, sir. My office is this way."

It was easy to tell that the security officer spent a great deal of time at his post because his office was a mess of dirty clothes, empty takeout containers, and scattered paperwork. "Sorry about the disorder, Colonel," he apologized. "Since everything went to hell, the normal routine is a little screwy."

Walter waved it off although the office had obviously gone without a cleaning for at least several weeks. "Understandable, but I'm not here for an inspection. I need your assistance. I've been tasked with pursuing and bringing in those responsible for General Vogel's murder. Obviously, none of us Brits are familiar with the area, and beyond what little we've seen of the LCBs, we lack practical experience there as well. With me so far?"

The lieutenant was nodding his head so Walter continued. "What I need from you is a small team to assist me in bringing the escapees back for justice. I'll be bringing one of my own men, and I'll need a few Americans who know the area well."

"I can help out personally if you have no objections, sir. I'd like to volunteer for the job. I'm just spinning my wheels here at the gate."

When Lieutenant Cloyed saw Walter thinking it over, he pressed his case. "I'm originally from here so I know the area well, and I'm also probably the most familiar with the LCBs of anyone I could get to go with you. After all, I deal with them all day long."

Walter only needed a moment to decide. He was in a hurry and wanted to get going before it got dark. "I need you ready to go within the hour. I'll leave it to you to arrange for proper transportation and travel supplies."

"Roger that. And thank you, Colonel Doucet. I appreciate the opportunity."

Walter was already walking away. "I'll meet you back here in forty five minutes." Once in the jeep he told the driver to take him to officer billeting. She nodded and sped away from the security gate.

During the five minute drive to the barracks, Walter didn't say a word. Instead, he closed his eyes and leaned his head back against the seat rest and concentrated on the details of what was next. He would take Major Ackerman, of course. Since the two of them had met they had established an excellent rapport with each other. Walter had a good feeling about the man's abilities; he was a proper military man with over a dozen years of service, most of them in combat areas. Walter admitted a little guiltily to himself that there was one other reason he wanted the man along. Major Ackerman was British, and while he had no concrete reason to distrust the Americans, having a countryman along would give Walter some peace of mind.

He opened his eyes after the jeep came to a stop in front of the officer's quarters. Asking the sergeant to wait a few minutes, he hopped out and headed up to Major Ackerman's room. It took several knocks before the bleary-eyed officer opened the door, but when he saw Walter he came fully awake and asked, "Hello, sir. What can I do for you?"

Without preamble, Walter quickly explained what had happened and what he needed. It amazed him that the major didn't so much as ask a single question, only letting Walter know that he would be down as soon as he was dressed.

The room next door to the major's quarters was Walter's and upon entering it he realized that he hadn't even had a chance to unpack. He also hadn't slept in a couple of days either other than snatching a few hours on the plane. Walter sighed. Sleep was likely to elude him for the foreseeable future. The longer he and the others wasted preparing to leave, the further away his quarry fled.

Since everything he owned on the continent was already in his bag, Walter took a quick bathroom break and headed back downstairs. He was happy to see that Major Ackerman had preceded him and was standing by at the jeep.

The major gave Walter a salute and took his bag from him, adding it to the major's own in the rear storage compartment. Within minutes they were back at the front gate. Lieutenant Cloyed was there, climbing in and out of an unusual vehicle Walter had never seen before. "What's that?" Walter asked the major.

"I couldn't say, sir. I've never seen it before."

To Walter it looked similar in size to a Foxhound, the British Army's lightly armored patrol vehicle, something Walter had ridden in many times while in the Middle East, but what he was looking at carried much more reinforced armor. The armor looked capable of repelling large caliber bullets.

The major whistled appreciably, which made Lieutenant Cloyed grin. "She's a beaut, isn't she?" He suddenly remembered that he hadn't saluted yet and immediately rendered the proper honors.

"I think that's something we can dispense with for now," Walter lightly admonished, not even bothering to return the salute. "We have bigger things to worry about." He quickly introduced the major and lieutenant to each other and then asked about the vehicle. "Just what is this anyway? I've never seen one."

"Well, Colonel, let me introduce you to fifteen tons of American badass." The lieutenant bowed with a flourish. "This is the Grizzly APC six by six, built by Blackwater for urban combat." He patted the side and quoted some of the specifications: "She's constructed entirely of AR500 steel, with EXO Scale anti-EFP appliqué armor and ArmorThane tactical coating to reduce spall probability. Inside is a fully enclosed Caterpillar drivetrain, and she's armed with a remotely operated 12.7mm ring mounted turret machine gun." He paused to catch his breath. "The reason you've never seen one is because there are only two of these in existence. Blackwater was getting ready to ship this one over to Pakistan for the Army to conduct vehicle trials. I don't know where the other one is, but this baby was actually strapped down in one of our Globemasters, ready to go, when the shit hit the fan. Another six hours and it would've been gone, lost to us forever."

Major Ackerman rubbed the side of the APC, admiring its imposing strength and power. Walter looked it over also before wondering aloud, "We need to overtake fugitives doing their best to get away from here as far and as fast as they can. Will this even catch up to them?"

"Oh, Colonel, she's fast, don't worry on that account. Even though today was the first time I've driven it, I watched my old boss, Major Nelson, drive her around the flight line. He wouldn't let me have a go though, said 'RHIP'. You know, rank has its privileges." The younger man shrugged and his face grew serious. "I didn't like him much, but he didn't deserve to turn into an LCB."

"Wait a minute. You saw it happen?" Walter asked.

"Yes sir. It was right here at this post, inside the security building office. We were going over some paperwork and in the middle of a sentence he just stopped talking. When I looked up, he was standing straight up, twitching a little and his mouth looked like he bit into a lemon." Lieutenant Cloyed did a rough imitation of what he saw, standing loosely at attention, shaking and putting on a sour face. "Then, just like that," he continued, snapping his fingers, "the major just changed."

"Changed how? How could you tell?" Major Ackerman prompted, intrigued.

"He made a chimp face, which at first I thought was funny. I mean, you have to understand, Major Nelson was not a 'funny' guy, ever. He was always Mr. Proper. 'Lieutenant this, Lieutenant that', call me 'sir,' blah, blah, blah. So at first I thought he was goofing me. Then he let out this damn scream right in my face and right away I knew something was wrong." The lieutenant used his hands to help explain what happened next. "We were standing on opposite sides of the desk when he roared and starts chasing me around it. He wasn't messing around either, he definitely meant to kill me. I was finally able to get to the door and shut it behind me, but it was a close call."

Walter had asked because he wanted to understand what it was he was dealing with a little better, but decided that it was time to get moving. "Well, that certainly sounds frightening, Lieutenant. Thank you for sharing that with us but we need to leave now if we plan to make up any distance before it gets dark. I hope to have an idea where they're headed to before then."

"Let me show you two how to get in. In case you didn't notice, the Grizzly doesn't have doors. The only way in is through these two window hatches."

They watched the younger and more nimble American leap up and slither through the small opening near the top of the APC. They followed, albeit slower. The major showed Walter where small covered climbing aids were built into the armor plating, activated by pressing on cover flaps. Soon they were all inside and the British men got their first glimpse of the byzantine dashboard.

Lieutenant Cloyed saw the confused looks and reassured them. "Don't worry, the cockpit looks much more complicated than it really is. While my boss was out joyriding this thing, I was busy studying the operator's manual." He sat down and began clicking various toggle switches and the Grizzly thrummed to life. "Check this out," he said. "It doesn't have a normal steering wheel; it uses the same setup as a fighter jet. Everything is controlled by this yoke: Gas, brakes, and steering."

There were supplies stacked around the back of the cabin. The Grizzly was stocked with food, weapons and extra fuel. "Everything looks ready. If there's nothing else, let's roll out."

"Alright, sir, moving out." Looking back Lieutenant Cloyed said, "Better grab your seats, gentlemen, it's about to get rough," and with that, he signaled two security personnel manning the front gate. The six solid steel stanchions used as vehicle barriers were pneumatically lowered and the first set of gates retracted open on mechanical rollers.

The APC rolled forward into the no man's land between the fences and the gate behind them rolled shut. Several LCBs were pressed up against the chain links of the second gate that led to the city beyond. Walter watched the LCBs twitch and smoke before they fell to the ground, dead.

"We electrified the outside fence yesterday," Lieutenant Cloyed said with a grin. "LCBs charge it anyway, even when they see others dying from it. They have a one track mind." The second gate rolled open and the lieutenant pulled forward and ran over the fresh corpses. Walter expected to be jostled out of his seat so he held on, but the Grizzly's suspension dealt with the bodies easily, barely rocking the APC's body. Noticing the tight grip Walter had on his seat bottom the younger man laughed and patted the dashboard. "Heavy duty suspension. The manual describes anything less than eighteen inches high as 'surmountable objects'."

A quick look out of the rear view mirror, which was actually an LCD screen attached to an external camera, showed Walter that the second gate was closing behind them. He experienced a short moment of dread at the thought of being outside the sanctuary of the base. It was no longer academic, something seen vicariously through the distance of the television or from the safety of an auditorium seat, and until he made it back with the escapees his likelihood of dying horribly were heightened significantly. Walter was able to calm himself some when he took a look around at the interior of the Grizzly. If ever there was a safe place to be when on the move outside the base's fence line, it was the inside of a vehicle designed to deflect armor-piercing bullets and withstand IED blasts.

The Grizzly afforded a near three sixty degree of vision and Walter stared in shock. In a matter of a few days Dayton went from what must have been a normal, civilized city to a place of appalling devastation. Bodies littered the streets, buildings still smoked or burned outright, and cars were scattered everywhere. As they passed the protective ditch Walter got an even worse jolt; LCBs poured out of alleyways, shops, and wrecked vehicles or jumped out of trees and off of low roofs to converge on them.

Major Ackerman urged the lieutenant to greater speed. "Go, man, go!"

Despite his confidence in the APCs abilities, the young security officer fed off of the major's vibe and didn't hesitate to comply. The Grizzly surged forward but it lacked the acceleration responsiveness of a lighter vehicle. It was soon mounted by a few dozen LCBs who proceeded to pound on the windows in their attempts to break in.

It was a great surprise to everyone that the mass of LCBs had no apparent effect on the Grizzly, which continued to accelerate despite carrying a couple tons of unwanted passengers. Better yet, the sound of screaming and the pounding of angry fists could barely be heard through the thick armored glass and steel plating.

Major Ackerman looked at Walter and nodded appreciably.

Walter gave a smile back in acknowledgement before climbing past the major and sliding into the Grizzly's passenger seat. He had been worried that tracking a single vehicle through the post-apocalyptic mess would be difficult at best, but looking forward he could easily see the trail forged earlier by the large military transport vehicle by the pushed aside vehicles and the crushed bodies of LCBs that it left in its wake.

Looking at the broken bodies Walter mused, "The dead ones don't look like LCBs at all, do they?"

The lieutenant's eyes never left the road ahead, but he acknowledged Walter's question with a sad shake of his head and a small sigh. Walter alternated between watching the young man drive, and working the controls while scanning the road ahead of them. He was quickly developing a fond respect for the security officer, similar to how he felt for the major. He wasn't sure why it was so because in his past he rarely made attachments. His frequent travel and hectic professional life left little time for personal relationships of any kind. "Maybe because each life is more valuable now my mind is instinctively reacting to it," he thought to himself. "It subconsciously wants the nearness of others."

On impulse he decided to become friends with the two men he was travelling with instead of just working with them. He turned to the lieutenant. "What's your given name?"

"Me?" the young man asked.

"Yes, you." Then over his shoulder: "You too, major. Can I have your given name?"

"Mycroft," came from the back, followed by "Lincoln," from the driver's seat.

"I want you guys to call me Walter."

The lieutenant looked uncertain. What he and the major were being asked to do was unorthodox and went against everything they had been conditioned to do. Finally the major shrugged and spoke for the both of them. "Roger that."

Except for the muffled pounding of fists from the LCBs outside, the APC interior went quiet as the men inside imbibed their thoughts. After a few moments of this, Walter broke their reveries by asking, "Lincoln. Based on the direction we're heading and if you were the fugitives, where would you go?"

"Hmm, where would I go?" Lincoln sucked some air in between his teeth as he contemplated the question. "The road we're on right now leads to Route 70, which goes through Springfield and then Columbus. That could be where they're headed. It's hard to say though because they could just be going this way for lack of any other options or because they picked it at random and are trying to get away from the LCBs. I mean, they were in an open bed troop carrier, and judging by the horde they had to bust through and the number of cars they had to smash aside, just getting out of the city alive had to be their number one priority."

Mycroft was peering between the two front seats and evaluating the road ahead. "If the trail stays like this, we'll have no problem following them."

"I don't think it will." Walter opined. "Already there are fewer LCBs and cars and it's getting harder to tell that they've been this way. We must be leaving the city boundaries."

"We are," Lincoln said. "I think we should keep going in this direction unless we see some indication they turned."

The other two men agreed, and as predicted the road cleared up and became relatively free of both obstacles and attackers. Lincoln offered to show Walter the driving controls and instruments while Mycroft stood up and practiced with the roof mounted turret. The sounds of the turret's servo-assists carried up to the front as the veteran soldier spun the sights back and forth, testing the barrel's spin rate and maneuverability.

Even with alternating his attention between the instructions he was getting and the road ahead, Walter was able to learn the basics of operating the Grizzly within a few minutes. When he was done, he asked Mycroft to switch places with him. He wanted a go at checking out the powerful gun.

During his many deployments to Iraq, Afghanistan, and Eastern Europe embedded with different troop units Walter had never been allowed to man any of the military's armaments, except once when a NATO soldier from Hungary let him pose for a picture in an old M2 Infantry Fighting Vehicle. The rusty relic was a U.S. Army castoff from the 1980's that Walter doubted was even operational. Still, even knowing that the demi-tank was old and defunct didn't dampen his interest one bit, even when the Hungarian made a big show out of 'letting' him stand at the gun's pedestal. There was something about being enveloped by tons of metal, crafted solely for the purpose of war and destruction, that resonated with Walter; it almost made him wish he had joined the Army instead of pursuing a career with the press.

When Walter hopped into the Grizzly's gunner position he knew instantly that he was in a completely different category of offensive firepower technology than the M2. He popped his head up into the turret enclosure and was met with an unobstructed three hundred and sixty degree view of the outside. Gripping the joysticks of the machine gun his index fingers instinctively curled around the built-in ergonomic triggers. He couldn't help but smile.

Lincoln was snatching glances in the rear view mirror and caught Walter's joyful expression at manning the guns. "How do you like it, Walter?" he asked, already knowing the answer.

"It's exhilarating."

"If you like I can stop and hand the controls over to Mycroft. I can show you some of the advanced capabilities of the turret and Mycroft can get some practice driving the grizzly," Lincoln suggested.

"Sounds great to me."

Lincoln and Mycroft exchanged knowing smirks at Walter's enthusiasm, knowing that he had caught the 'bug' that eventually infected all military personnel sooner or later. It was the thrill of being at the tip of spear and knowing that what they were doing had the weight and power of an entire nation's support. Even if that nation was now defunct, the impressive might represented by the military hardware surrounding them was hard to ignore. Now that Walter was given an unfiltered taste of it, both Mycroft and Lincoln knew he was hooked for good.

"Okay. In case you were worried, the glass dome you're looking out of is an advanced version of the 'Save a Gunner' turret, or SAG. It uses the newest nanotech armor capable of stopping fifty caliber rounds. It also rotates one full revolution in less than four seconds…" Lincoln continued explaining the capabilities to Walter for the next fifteen minutes as the APC traveled east on Route 70.

Walter was beginning to feel very comfortable with things when the Grizzly suddenly stopped. "What's going on," he asked, while at the same time looking forward through the turret glass.

"LCB convention," Mycroft announced at the same time Walter saw them. At least a hundred LCBs filled their lane, heading east in pursuit of someone or something.

At the sound of the Grizzly's diesel engine throttling behind them, some of the LCBs turned and reversed course, sprinting back towards the APC. Lincoln went forward and jumped in the copilot seat.

"What's our plan, Walter?" Mycroft asked, surprisingly calm considering that even more, at least two or three dozen, had turned and were headed back their way.

Knowing that they had to act, and act quickly, Walter said, "Let's try and go around and get ahead of them. They were chasing something and my guess it was the group we're after."

"Roger that." The Grizzly surged forward and to the left, dipping down into a shallow ditch before hitting the median. To the passengers inside the vehicle the maneuver barely registered. The advanced traction and shock system easily compensated for the uneven terrain.

From the window up top Walter saw the LCBs adjust course to follow them. He was slightly surprised, alarmed even, when a few in front actually led them, deciding on a course that would intersect the Grizzly's path further down the road.

Lincoln noticed it, too. "That's not good," he muttered.

It was Walter's intention to avoid firing the machine gun if they could. He didn't want to alert the escapees to their presence. But he was getting worried; fully half or more of the large LCB horde were now focused on the Grizzly, with more turning back every second. The LCBs up front were spilling over the median and would block the road before the Grizzly could drive by.

"I'm going to have to shoot if you can't make it past them," Walter decided.

"Hang on," Mycroft said, and accelerated up the incline to power into the opposite lane. The large vehicle went airborne and bounced back onto the tarmac. This time because of the speed and severe angle, the suspension couldn't smooth out the rough transition and Walter was jostled to the deck. His cheekbone hit the corner of one of the wheel covers and split open. He reached up and felt his face. There was a large gash under his eye and his hand come away coated in blood. Walter looked at the blood in wonder and muttered, "Oh, hell," before his eyes rolled back and he blacked out.

FIRESTONE HIGH SCHOOL, FAIRLAWN, OHIO

Josh, Finn and Ben sat with their backs against the lockers and whispered their plan to clear the school. Despite several good ideas being voiced, in the end it was decided that conducting any kind of room-to-room tactics in a school with an unknown layout and done in complete darkness was just too risky. The men settled down for an uncomfortable night on the cold tile floor of the school's main hallway to wait it out until daylight.

None of them slept well. The intermittent screams from outside were unsettling enough, but sometime in the early morning hours someone ran up to the same school doors that the men used to get in and pounded on the door, screaming, "Please, help me! Let me in, they're coming for me!" It was a man's voice. At first, Josh was apathetic, groggy from several hours of restlessness, but when he realized that he wasn't dreaming the incident he hopped right up.

Before he could get to the door a pickup truck with a loud exhaust pulled into view. An adjustable spotlight wavered erratically around the area of the closed doors before finally settling on the outline of a panicked old man slapping on the door's reinforced glass. There were several people in the truck bed outlined by the dawn light and as Josh watched one of them raised a bow and fired a bolt into the old man's back.

Ben came up from behind Josh on all fours and beckoned him to get down, which he did just in time. The man outside sunk to the ground and had Josh not ducked he would have been caught in the beam of the spotlight. To avoid the risk of discovery, Josh and the other men had to listen impotently as the old man's urgent pleas for help were replaced by groans and cries of agony.

A figure disembarked from the bed of the truck accompanied by the sound of cheering and laughter. A silhouette passed in between the light and the door and a few seconds later the person arrived at the concrete entryway still armed with a bow and bent down to retrieve the arrow from the man's back. Ripping the bolt out caused a renewed outcry from the victim, whose screams had mercifully died down to a pitiful mewling sound. Josh heard the old man beg his assailant for mercy; a soft, almost intimate pleading.

When the person bent down, Josh could tell from the profile that she was a woman. She put her face down close to the man's and caressed his cheek with the back of her hand. Josh was almost relieved by the apparent act of kindness. Maybe the old man had been shot by accident and having realized her mistake she was comforting him. Or, maybe she felt remorse about what she had done.

It came as a shock when the woman shifted and kneeled on the man's head to hold him down while she retrieved a large knife from a hip sheath. She held the blade in front of the old man's eyes, twisting it so that he could see what she was holding, before she slowly brought it to his face and gently pushed it into his eye, burying the blade deep into the socket and twisting it.

With his head held flat to the ground by the pressure of the woman's knee, the only movement the man was capable of was a rapid kicking of his feet. The heels of his shoes rapped out a soft staccato on the pavement. After the man stopped moving the woman ripped her blade free and wiped it on his shirt. She unbent and stood back up, looking back towards the pickup truck. None of the men inside had moved as the drama unfolded mere feet from them while they lay prone and out of sight. For a brief moment Josh was worried that the woman might get curious and look inside. If she did, there was no doubt that she would see them there and then call in the others from the truck. He breathed a huge sigh of relief when it didn't happen; the woman didn't appear to have any interest in the school or who or what might be inside it.

The three men inside watched her walk slowly and sensuously back to her group, her lithe body outlined in silhouette by the spotlight, which tracked her movement. Within seconds she was back in the truck and it squealed out of the parking lot. The whole incident had taken place in less than two minutes. Almost anticlimactically a small crowd of the crazy people burst forth from the woods and gave chase after the truck. Josh saw the figures sprinting after the vehicle and hoped that somewhere down the road the crazy people would catch up to the murderers and take them out. What he had just witnessed went against everything he had resolved to do and Josh felt partly responsible for the old man's death because he had done nothing to stop it.

Finn was the first to speak. "Did you guys see that?"

Normally Josh would have rebuked anyone who had asked something so obvious but the incident had left him saddened enough to ignore it. Instead, Josh told him, "Yeah, dude, we saw it."

"That was some fucked up shit," Ben added. "What happened to women while I was away? What did I miss?" he asked rhetorically.

There were now two bodies blocking the entrance door; the woman Ben had killed the previous night and the old man. Josh figured anybody looking at the bodies might think the two people were trying to get inside because something inside was worth getting to. "We need to clear the door," he said. "It has to look like nothing happened here." Going up to the door he gave a push, but it eventually took the efforts of all three of them to shove the combined dead weight of the bodies out far enough to slip through to the outside. Ben was the last out and Josh hissed at the man to catch door before it clicked shut.

Ben made an 'O' face when he saw he was about to lock them out and he caught the door with a few inches to spare. To make sure it didn't lock behind them he stuck his baton in the gap.

It was chilly out. Finn rubbed his arms and whispered, "Let's do this quick. I feel naked out here," and the others grunted their agreement. They dragged the bodies behind some low hedges to the right of the entrance.

After retreating back inside Josh looked at where the bodies had been. They hadn't completely removed any signs that the bodies were there because anybody at the door would be able to tell by the bloody trail that bodies had been cleared away, but he hoped that at least it wouldn't be obvious to anyone from a distance. It was the best they could do.

A noise from behind made Josh turn around. Finn was taking practice swipes with his baton. Any effort at trying to get more rest was forgotten, and Ben and Finn were prepping themselves for the room to room clearing that had to take place before they could declare the school building safe.

"Hey little man," Ben coached, "You have to snap the wrist and let the baton do the work. Don't swing it around crazy like that." To illustrate Ben whipped his baton down a few times, demonstrating the correct method. "Did you see how I caved that crazy bitch's head in last night?" he bragged. "I used a wrist snap on her."

Finn mimicked the bigger man's technique and got a nod of approval for his quick skill adoption. Josh joined them in taking practice swings and for the next minute the hallway was filled with the sound of whistling noises caused by the batons whipping to and fro.

After their warm up they discussed what came next and agreed that Finn would keep watch out in the hallway and provide backup while Josh and Ben took care of whatever might be in the rooms.

Standing outside the first door they came to Josh got a slight case of the shivers. He was nervous and briefly considered chickening out until Ben said, "Don't you worry, Josh. I got your back." That was all the encouragement he needed. After a few more steadying breaths he slowly pulled the door open and stopped, listening for any signs of movement, mentally prepared if one of the monsters sprang out at him. When nothing like that happened and the only thing to be heard was the beating of his own heart, he chanced a look in.

Everything was in order. For some reason Josh envisioned the room in chaotic disarray similar to the cell blocks at the prison; he expected papers strewn everywhere, abandoned backpacks, and definitely some bodies. But desk chairs were pushed neatly in, the floor was spotless, and there wasn't a soul, living or otherwise, inside.

Ben peeked in and shrugged. "I guess no news is good news."

They left the door open and moved on to the next room and found it to be in the same condition as the first. By the time the trio made it to the end of one side of the hallway, it was evident that the school had been closed during the time of the change, even though it had occurred on a weekday. Finn solved the mystery by finding a bulletin board flier that stated that school was cancelled that day for some sort of teacher training event.

"Hmmm," Ben said. "That explains the empty rooms. Wonder where the rest of the teachers are then?"

"Teacher's lounge?" Finn offered up.

"Maybe," Josh answered. "Or maybe the gym or the auditorium." He located the sign for the gym on the wall of a branching hallway and they headed that way. When they arrived the double doors were propped open. A quick glance confirmed gym was empty.

Without a word they continued on. Another branch in the hallway led them past the cafeteria with its tables topped by chairs moved up there to clean the floor. A long wall of lit vending machines stood on the far side.

Ben frowned. "Man, when did kids start getting vending machines in school?" he whispered.

"How old are you, anyway?" Finn asked, looking sideways at the big man.

"Never mind," Ben snorted and they pressed on.

At the end of the hallway was a set of double doors and they could hear chaos coming from inside them at fifty feet out. Grunts, shrieks and screams echoed down off of the lockers that lined the walls. Mixed in with the sound of maniacs was a faint cry for help. Josh picked up the pace, eager to come to the aid of whoever was screaming. The other two rushed after him.

The sign over the doors said 'Auditorium' and there a padlocked chain wrapped around the door handles. Nearby, in a classroom entry way, was a body wearing a janitor's outfit lying in a pool of dried blood. Ten feet further on what was obviously the janitor's head was resting at an angle underneath a water fountain. The eyes and mouth were open and the man's swollen tongue protruded.

A few days ago such a scene would have been traumatic for any of them, but now the only emotion elicited was wry humor as Finn pointed out, "Holy cow, that guy still has his glasses on. What are the chances?" The other two shook their heads and Josh said, "Astronomical."

"I bet the woman I took out last night did him in," Ben figured.

Turning back to the doors Josh tugged experimentally on the chain. The noise of metal on metal carried into the auditorium and the small, narrow wire mesh windows built into the twin doors were instantly filled with snarling faces. Josh jumped back but after he saw that the crazy people were trapped inside he put his face up to one of the windows to see if he could locate whoever was screaming for help.

"Goddamn it, move out of the way. I can't see," he chastised the dozen or so faces blocking his view, not at all surprised when they didn't comply.

"You aren't thinking of going in there, are you?" Ben asked.

"Yeah," Finn agreed. "They're all locked up in there nice and tight. I vote we should let them stay in there and rot."

"C'mon, you two," Josh pleaded. "What good is saving someone if we only do it when it's easy or convenient? Whoever is in there can use our help. Just think about if it was you. No, wait. Never mind, cancel that because it was you. It was both of you guys back at the prison. What if I had just walked away then because it was easier, huh?" Josh was no longer pleading now, but was instead pointed his finger at his two partners. "I told you guys earlier that this is what I wanted to do and you both said you were good with it. Are you going back on your word?"

"No, you're right," Ben said, followed by an enthusiastic, "Hell no!" Finn. Josh bro-hugged them both and said, "That's the spirit. Let's get this done!"

Newly motivated, Ben and Finn looked to Josh for their orders but he didn't have any. "Okay, uh, I'm not sure how to do this," he admitted sheepishly.

The three wandered over to the door. It was bumping in and out an inch or so as the savages on the other side intermittently surged forward. Finn grabbed the chain and inspected the lock. "Damn, it's a combo. I thought maybe four-eyes over there might have a key on him, but it doesn't matter now. Not sure we want to open that door anyway; no telling how many are built up waiting to get out."

"I have to agree with him, Josh," Ben added. "We won't be doing anyone any good by dying out here trying to rescue them."

The disturbance the three men were causing at the door by their talking brought additional attention. From inside they could now hear rational shouts from the people trapped inside. Yells of "Help," and "Get us out of here," were among the pleas. The voices were both male and female.

Finn tried yelling back to let the people inside know that help was coming, but either they didn't hear or were too scared to do anything but repeat the same things as before. "Shit," Finn said dejectedly.

A phone rang nearby. The men looked at each other, confused. The last thing they expected was to hear a phone. It was coming from an office a few doors down and they trotted over to it. The glass on the door read "Principal's Office" and the light on the desk phone inside was blinking with every ring.

Ben tried the door and it was unlocked. He rushed in and picked up the handset. "Hello?" Then "Yes," and "That's right."

An impatient Finn was whispering, "Who is it?" and Ben shushed the young man with an upheld hand. Undeterred, Finn turned to Josh and asked, "Who do you think it is?"

Josh shrugged. "I don't know. I'm guessing maybe the people trapped in the auditorium?"

"Yeah, that makes sense, I guess. What do you think they want?"

"C'mon, man," Josh sighed, exasperated. He wanted to hear Ben's conversation. "What do you think they want?"

"Okay, okay. Sorry."

Hanging up the phone, Ben filled them in. "There are two of them in there and they're trapped up in the balcony seats. I spoke to a man, but there's also a woman in there with him, his secretary. He said there are seventeen of those things running loose inside."

"That's too many," Finn said, stating the obvious.

"Maybe not. He told me we can open the roof access above them and they'll be able to climb out. The roof stairwell is at the end of this hall."

"Which end," Josh asked.

"He didn't say."

"Okay," Finn told Josh and Ben before he sprinted down the hallway. "I'll check the right side, you guys check the left."

Josh and Ben looked at the back of the retreating man and shook their heads. Ben muttered, "He needs to calm down. He's too damn excitable."

"Yeah," Josh answered and began to walk with the large black man to the left end of the hallway. "I think that he thinks he's being helpful."

A yell from behind them brought them up short. It was Finn yelling from the other end of the hall. "Hey guys, it's down this way."

"Wish he would hold it down," Ben murmured.

"I'll talk to him. I think he's been suppressing stuff for a while and now he's finally coming out of his shell."

"Yeah, maybe, but if he doesn't come out his shell with less volume he's going to get us killed."

By the time they made it to the stairwell door, Finn had already disappeared. They could hear him clomping up the steps a few flights up. There was a sign on the wall that read 'Roof Access' with an arrow pointing up. The two men went up the stairs at a more measured pace.

Ben looked around and commented on the lack of graffiti and general cleanliness. "Man, I wish when I was a kid back in the day my school was this nice. Things might have turned out different for me."

"Where did you go to school?"

"Detroit. Henry Ford High, class of '85."

"I never heard of it. Was it pretty bad?"

"My school was so bad that they had a police station inside the school; I'm not talking one or two policemen, it was a full-on police station full of cops. The only reason I got a football scholarship is because the two guys in front of me couldn't go. One got shot and one went to prison. Guess I got lucky," Ben admitted.

"You were one of the good guys, huh?" Josh asked. He liked Ben and had come to respect the big man immensely over the past few days.

"Ha! I didn't say I was one of the good guys, my friend. I just never got caught."

Both men were chuckling as they got to the top floor. There was a small ladder built into the wall and Finn had already ascended it and was up on the roof. His head popped into view at the access hole. "Found where they are," he yelled down, "but the cover's too heavy for me to lift by myself."

Ben went up followed by Josh. Once on the roof they saw Finn standing by a square roof hatch and they joined him. Small thumps and muted voices could be heard on the other side. "See?" Finn asked. "This is the one."

"Stand back, young buck," Ben said, spreading his hands wide to clear some space before squatting down and gripping the hatch opening from underneath the far lip. He grunted and pulled upward. His arms bulged, threatening to split his sleeves, and thick veins stood out on his face and neck. He exhaled and let go. "I think its rusted shut," he declared, wiping his hands on the front of his trousers. "It barely budged." He showed them his hands. "Plus, that metal is sharp as shit. I almost cut my damn fingers."

"Let's all three try," Josh suggested. The noise from the people trapped below continued unabated.

They all squatted down and pulled their cuffs down over their fingers to dampen the edge of the hatch. When they were situated Ben counted down: "Three, two, one, pull!"

The cover gave suddenly and flipped over. The men gagged as shrieks, grunts, and a foul, miasmic stench roiled out of the opening. Before they could recover and peek down, a chubby, hairy hand bedecked with thick rings appeared over the edge, quickly followed by another. Soon a flabby, shorn-headed curmudgeon wearing spectacles with a cracked lens joined them up on the roof. He was followed by an attractive but somewhat disheveled woman. Ben asked, "Just you two, right?' and at the woman's nod he slammed the hatch cover shut. The noises from below waned and the light breeze carried most of the smells away.

"Oh my God, thank you guys so much for saving our lives," the woman said, putting both hands to her heart and weeping a little. She was wearing a floral print dress and functional shoes. Her makeup was smudged from sweat and tears but her teeth were straight and white and her haircut was sensible yet becoming.

The man nodded and echoed her. "Yes, I want to thank you fellas for helping us out of a very, very tight spot." He was squinting from the sunlight and judging from the pale look of him Josh figured that the man didn't spend much time out of doors. For some reason the fact that the man still wore a tie cinched tightly up to the top button of his shirt struck Josh as odd. After all, who cared about appearances anymore after what had happened? The man extended a hand. "I'm Principal Dean Morgan, and this young lady is my secretary, Miss Olivia Stanton. Feel free to call me Dean."

The three men shook the proffered hand and introduced themselves. The woman meekly asked to be called Livvy instead of Olivia. "Nobody calls me Olivia," she explained. "Even my mother calls me Livvy." She kept snatching glances at Dean as if seeking his consent.

It didn't take the three men long to figure out the relationship between the two. All three of them had just come out of an environment where non-verbal communication was even more relevant than the spoken word. Finn was particularly sensitive to the woman's behavior, as it mirrored his own coping mechanisms, learned from being locked up twenty three hours a day with sadistic beasts, and he was the one to interject: "In case you two didn't know, the world has changed over the last couple of days. More than just what's down there in the auditorium. There are no more school principals or teachers, and no students, police, or government either, for that matter, as far as we can tell." Finn directed his gaze at Dean, who wilted under the intense stare and dropped his eyes.

Livvy perked up at the news. "Do you mean that what's down there," and she pointed through the roof to the auditorium below, "has happened everywhere?" All three men nodded. She turned to her former boss and said, "Did you hear that, 'Dean'?"

The former principal kept looking down, not willing to meet her eyes, which meant his gaze was perfectly positioned to see her foot arcing towards his crotch. Unfortunately for him, he was too slow to react. The dull thud of her leather encased toes connecting with his scrotum resonated with all four of the men but was felt most acutely by Dean. He gurgled and small spit bubbles formed at the corners of his mouth before he fell over into the fetal position and began retching violently onto the asphalt rooftop. Josh, Ben and Finn looked a little peaked, but Livvy ignored them and began raining insults and additional kicks at the hapless man.

"You piece of shit son of a bitch! How's it feel to be the victim, huh? Can't threaten me with my job now, can you?" She reared her foot back for a kick to his face when Josh grabbed her around the waist and pulled her back. She struggled momentarily before going limp. "You don't understand," she cried. "He used me. He threatened me and then took advantage of me." She yelled some more, reenergized and struggling fiercely in Josh's arms to have another go at the injured principal. "I was a virgin!"

"Shh. It's okay, Livvy. You're safe now," Josh consoled her. He carried her over to the far side of the roof, followed by a concerned Ben. "He won't bother you anymore, I promise you," Josh whispered in her ear. "You see that big guy right there?" and he pointed at Ben. She nodded. "He won't let anything happen to you. Isn't that right, Ben?"

The big muscular man shook his head solemnly. His glasses caught the sunlight with every shake and flashed the sun's reflection back at Josh and

Livvy. "Nope," Ben declared, "he won't touch you again. That's a guarantee."

"Oh, shit," Josh said, releasing Livvy. The other two turned, but before anyone could stop him or even say anything, Finn tossed Dean off of the roof. The principal screamed in horror on his way down, and a few seconds later the wet smack of his body hitting the asphalt four stories below carried back up to them. They watched as Finn wiped his palms together, mission accomplished style before heading towards them.

Ben couldn't resist. "See? Didn't I tell you he wouldn't bother you again?" he asked, which caused all three of them to laugh out loud. When Finn rejoined them Livvy stood up on her tiptoes and kissed him on the cheek.

"Thank you," she said to the brightly blushing young man, surprising him with his first kiss from a female in over a year.

They headed back downstairs to the cafeteria and after Ben quickly verified that it was safe, Livvy excused herself and went into the woman's locker room. The others were busy stuffing their faces with fare from the cafeteria stockroom. Tuna straight from the can, chips, soda, microwaved tater tots and a dozen other foods that looked appetizing at first but soon had the men groaning from the pain of their distended bellies and the nutrient overload.

As he lay across one of the cafeteria tables trying to digest his meal, Josh considered what Finn had done up on the roof. He wasn't sure if hurling a man to his death, regardless of the reason, was something that needed to be addressed or if it should just be brushed under the rug. Last week his reaction would have been much different. If it had happened then, Josh wouldn't have debated it for a second, but the world had changed, and Josh wasn't sure which parts of his morality should brought along and which parts should be left in the past. Ultimately, he decided that for the time being he should put his actions and the actions of others into two categories: things that could get him hurt or killed and things that wouldn't. When he weighed what Finn had done against that very broad criterion, it clearly fell into the range of something that didn't matter.

Sounds of snoring came from the next table over. Josh glanced over to see Ben passed out in a food coma. The big man let a gasser rip that momentarily startled himself awake before he zonked out again. Finn giggled, which made Josh smile.

Soon the cafeteria was quiet and peaceful again and Josh drifted off to sleep. The previous forty eight hours were a whirlwind of frightful actions and near-death confrontations and up until now he hadn't felt safe enough to allow himself to relax. The meal and the safe environment both contributed to his feeling of well-being and contentment and he was couldn't resist.

When Josh opened his eyes again it was early afternoon. He sat up and looked around. Ben was still flat on his back snoring but Finn was missing from where he was sitting earlier at the next table over from Ben. Alarmed, Josh hopped up to go look for him. So far Finn had shown an impetuousness that needed to be monitored and controlled. Josh didn't have to go far, however. Finn and Livvy were curled up together on the tile floor. They had found a blanket from somewhere and had made a little bed between two of the tables.

Finn cracked an eye open and noticed Josh staring at them. He gave Josh a huge grin, as if to say "Look at what I did." Josh smiled back and gave a thumbs up before wandering over to the boy's locker room. He went in and flicked the lights on, prepared for anything, but the room was empty. Everything was neat: the lockers were all shut and the floor was mopped and smelled like pine cleaner. Fresh towels were in a laundry bin near the door and Josh grabbed one and hit the showers. The nap and hot water did wonders for his constitution. By the time he redressed he felt incredibly refreshed. He hunted through a few lockers until he found one with some deodorant in it and he swiped his underarms before getting redressed in his tactical gear.

The noise from the showers must have woken the others because when he exited the locker room everyone else was sitting around one of the tables talking quietly. He rejoined them and listened in. They were talking about what had happened since the event and what was next for them.

Livvy had shed her secretary's attire and was now wearing a tracksuit and sneakers. To Josh, that demonstrated that she was resourceful and practical. He also noticed that the shock of being trapped in the auditorium by both the monsters and a sadistic, rapist boss was wearing off, an adaptive trait which further demonstrated her potential usefulness to the group.

She clearly favored Finn. The two of them were sitting so close to each other that their legs were touching, and they constantly gave overlong looks to one another. Josh understood that both of them had suffered through similar circumstances and the bond they were developing could only be good for both of them.

All of them had seen and done horrific things over the previous few days. Livvy was telling her story and relating it to what had happened to the men. "Just like you guys, the change caught me by surprise. Of course, anything like what went down would be a shock, but I always figured that the end of the world would be a slower process, like SARS or some kind of fuel shortage or war." She collected her thoughts before continuing. "This was like," and she snapped her fingers, "Bam! Instant."

"How did you survive?" Finn asked.

"It's funny, actually. I never would have made it if it wasn't for Principal Morgan. We were up in the balcony watching a presentation given by one of the teacher's advocates. The only reason we were up there was because that lecherous prick wanted to grope me while everyone else was down below." Livvy's tone got an edge to it. "He got off on that kind of stuff, abusing me while everyone else was oblivious to what was happening. He was always threatening to fire me or file false charges against me and send me to jail unless I did what he asked." She sighed. "I suppose I should be grateful, though. If I was down below with the others I would have died. It happened so quickly; one second the woman at the podium was droning on and on about union issues and the next second people were screaming."

She looked up at everyone seated around her at the table intently listening to her tale. There were no looks of judgment on their faces, which encouraged her to finish. "It was awful. I didn't see what it was that made everyone go crazy. I was kind of in my la-la zone where I went while I was being touched, so at first I thought people were yelling because they discovered us and were angry. I was mortified, but the truth was way worse. I peeked over the ledge and saw that a few of the people stayed normal. You know, like us now." She circled her index finger to indicate herself and the three men. "The normal people didn't last long. The others jumped over the seats or ran down the aisles and pulled them apart. Literally pulled them apart and jumped up and down on the pieces."

Continuing, Livvy said, "The only way out of the balcony was through a door on the auditorium level and there was no way we were going down there. So we huddled towards the back row of seats where they couldn't see us. The people below never left, though. That's why we were still up there when you guys showed up."

"The janitor chained the doors shut," Ben told her. "You wouldn't have been able to get out that way anyway, so it's a good thing you didn't try."

"Oh, Dmitri. The janitor. Where is he?" Livvy asked, perplexed.

"One of the crazy people, a woman, was loose inside the school when we got here. Unfortunately for Dmitri she found him." Finn explained. He didn't give additional details but Livvy understood and frowned.

"That's sucks. He was kind to me," she said, then explained: "I think he knew what was happening to me and was looking for a way to help me out of my predicament. I also got the feeling that Principal Morgan was bullying him too, so he had to be careful with what he could do."

They all talked a little more. Josh explained to Livvy that the three of them wanted to set up a safe place for survivors to regroup and start pushing back, and then asked her if she wanted to join them. She gratefully accepted the invitation and the group grew by one more.

She wanted to start right away but Josh calmed her down. "I understand. Really, I do," he told her. "But you haven't been out there yet and we have. I think that it's best if we rest up here first and come up with a plan, do things in an orderly way. Plus, now that we're here, we should try and reach out and see if we can find more information on what's happening."

"We can use the computer lab," she suggested. "The power is still on and everything should still work, right?" They nodded.

She stood up. "Follow me. I'll take you guys there."

They trekked after her down more hallways to a room filled with tables that had laptops set up on them. Josh and Finn sat down and immediately started plugging away, hitting all of the major news websites. None of the sites had any content dated after the time of the change. Livvy sat down next to Finn and watched him surf while Ben went to the large screen television mounted to the front wall and flipped through the channels.

"Looks like there's nothing out there," Ben said, echoing Josh's exact thoughts.

"Not so fast, guys," Finn told them. "Even though there isn't anything out there on the bigger news sites that doesn't mean there isn't anything out there. Give me few more minutes and let me see if I can find something." The young man's fingers were racing over the keyboard. After a minute or so, he said, "See?" He pointed at his screen. "There's actually a lot of stuff out there, but all of it is from personal blogs and shit from overseas." Finn motioned everyone to take a seat. "Everyone get a browser up and type 'worldwide event' and 'catastrophe' into the search engine. Put a filter on it for forty eight hours and you'll get what I have.

After Josh typed in the keywords and filtered the results his screen was full of hits. "We need to go through this and try and make sense of it all."

Neither Ben nor Livvy knew how to filter so Finn showed them. After that, the room grew quiet as everyone became absorbed in researching the different pieces of information out on the internet. Josh went for the bigger picture first and discovered, mostly from British sources, what must have happened, the extent of the disaster, and what it portended for the world at large. It was almost too much for him to comprehend so he switched to seeking out information that could help him and the others understand their own personal situation better.

Using a free mapping website Josh was pleased to discover that live aerial information was still being downloaded from satellites and getting processed. He zoomed in on the small town of Fairlawn and found the school they were in. The legend on the screen said that the data was only a little over seventeen hours old.

"Hey everyone. Check this out," Josh said. "We can do some prep from right here." He turned his monitor and presented it. "We have a sky-high view of everything."

The others crowded around and they agreed they should scan the areas around the school and see if they could find survivors. The mood in the room perked up considerably, both from the feeling of camaraderie between the four of them and from the positive feeling of doing something that moved them forward.

Over the next couple of hours they had created a rough map of the town on the classroom white board, centered on the school. There were marks where signs for help were hung or painted on roof tops and where large clusters of what they figured were former humans were gathered. Also plotted were locations of stores where they could get supplies and food, and other places like car dealerships and gun shops.

Ben was at the board drawing a skull at a location in the woods to the east of town. It designated what looked like a tall pyramid of bodies. At least to Josh and Livvy it looked like a tall mound of corpses. The other two weren't so sure. The trees and the angle of the overhead view made it hard to say with absolute certainty. Ben and Finn thought it might be a dump site for trash, but everyone agreed that until they knew for sure, the area should be marked dangerous.

Last, by laboriously looking for the pickup truck Finn discovered the encampment of the killers from the night before. From the satellite view they could count twenty two people set up in a factory courtyard blocked off with tractor trailers. The courtyard had sectioned off areas for sleeping quarters, restrooms, and eating. They studied the encampment, marked with a gun symbol, and found a few disturbing things. For instance, two people were kicking a soccer ball around near some makeshift lynch posts where several bodies hung. There were also cages that held living people, and the factory perimeter was ringed with hundreds of bodies. The photographic evidence combined with what they had already seen firsthand convinced them that sooner than later the violent group was going to have to be dealt with if they intended on staying at the school.

It was getting towards dusk and Josh determined that there were still things they needed to accomplish to better their situation before night fell and it got too dark. His job at the prison made him rely heavily on security cameras, so he asked Livvy if the school had any. She nodded and told him the feeds were in the main office. Josh sent her and Finn there to see if the feeds could be forwarded to the computer room, which Josh had semi-formally dubbed the "Command Center." The two former prisoners groaned good-humoredly at the use of the official sounding vernacular. It reminded them of prison, but they let it pass after a show of being mock angry at Josh.

While the pair went to check on the cameras, Josh partnered up with Ben to make rounds inside the school and make sure that all of the external doors were locked. Josh wanted to chain the doors shut but Ben made him renege on his idea. "If we put chains on from the inside everyone will know that someone is in here. It's better to let people think that the school is empty."

"I didn't think of that," Josh acquiesced. "That means we also have to leave the shades up too, or that would look suspicious. Good thing the Command Center is in a room without windows."

"Yeah."

During their sweep they confirmed that all of the doors were locked and decided to head back when a loud alarm sound blasted from somewhere close by. Josh and Ben hit the deck. The noises repeated and while Josh was looking around for what it might be Ben started laughing. It was the handheld radio chirping; Josh had forgotten all about them.

Grabbing the radio from his belt clip Ben answered, "This is Ben. Go ahead."

"Hi Ben, it's me, Livvy. Finn wanted me to tell you guys that he was able to send the cameras to the computer lab. We're back in there now and we were wondering what happened to you two."

"We'll be there in a few minutes. We were just checking the doors, making sure they were locked."

"Okay. See you in a bit."

Ben clipped the radio back onto his belt, stood up, and helped Josh to his feet. Chuckling, the pair walked into the computer lab a few minutes later and saw that Finn and Livvy had reorganized the desks into sections. One section showed live feeds from the external cameras, one had laptops open to the various pages they had found that displayed information and news, and the last was being used for mapping. Finn had also appropriated some more comfortable chairs from somewhere and stashed all of the student chairs in a different room.

"Wow," Josh smiled and nodded. "This looks like the real deal here. Thanks."

"No problem." Finn answered. "I'd forgotten how much I missed computers and being around them. I feel like I'm back in my element now." Finn looked at Livvy and smiled. "Plus, I can't take all the credit. Liv helped out with everything."

Turning to her Josh saw that Livvy was actually blushing at the positive attention. To put her at ease he threw his up hand and said, "Thanks!" She laughed and completed the high five.

Indicating the mapping table, Finn explained, "If everything stays functional, the satellite maps are supposed to update daily. Hopefully, the next pass will be downloaded and processed sometime tonight"

"Great. I was thinking that Ben and I should go out tomorrow and see if we can help a few of the people in the easiest places to get to."

Finn looked dejected. "What about Livvy and me?"

"We'll need someone here to hold down the fort and supply us with information, like directions and stuff, which is your area of expertise. Livvy can stay and help you out."

Livvy nodded her assent, and in turn Finn said, "Okay. We'll stay here and man home base"

Ben chimed in. "Plus, we can move faster and easier if it's just the two of us." The implication was that Finn was a liability. Even though Ben and Josh never discussed it, the way Finn had acted the last few days, like being careless, or overreacting and throwing people off of roofs, showed that the young man needed some tempering before he could be fully trusted again, particularly when it came to putting their lives in his hands.

If Finn recognized the mild rebuke he didn't show it. Josh guessed that staying inside and out of danger was Finn's preference anyway. He probably only protested because he thought he might look weak in front of his new girlfriend if he didn't.

Livvy announced she would be back in a little bit and left the room. Shortly afterwards they heard the door to the girl's locker room shut and Ben and Josh took the opportunity to razz Finn. Ben punched him lightly on the arm and asked, "So, did you hit that yet?"

Josh laughed at Finn's blushing and further teased his new friend. "Looks like someone's ready to wife up in here."

"Cut it out guys," Finn said, blushing deeply. "She's nice. I like her."

Josh was curious. "Yeah, she is nice and we like her too. I was wondering what you told her about us."

"Yeah, what does she know?" Ben asked, suddenly serious.

"Well, I hope you don't get mad Ben, but I told her the truth. I didn't want to lie to her, especially after everything she's been through. I wanted her to trust us."

Ben was surprised at the confession. "What did she say?"

"She didn't care. She told me that because we rescued her, and for what I did to that Dean dude, that it was all she needed to know about us to know that we're the good guys." At the mention of his pitching the school principal over the side, Finn caught the look that passed between Josh and Ben. "I know what you guys are thinking and I want to apologize for that. I shouldn't have done that like I did, but I was just so angry that he felt like he owned her that I couldn't help myself. It won't happen again. I promise."

Speaking for the both of them, Ben told him, "I know you have some issues about what you went through and no one blames you for feeling that way, but we need to be sure that you can keep your head. You can't keep tweaking out on us like that. Just because I like you doesn't mean I want to die because you can't control your emotions."

Finn sounded despondent. "I get it, and I'm really, really sorry."

The locker room door opened and they heard Livvy walking back, so they shut up. She walked in dragging some gym mats and saw all three of them looking at her like they were hiding something. A look of concern crossed her face. "What is it?" she asked. "Did I do something wrong?" The men were quick to deny it, but they could tell she was still uneasy.

Finn couldn't handle seeing her in distress. "They were just teasing me Liv, helping me cope with all of this shit that's been happening. I swear it has nothing to do with you."

"Do you swear?"

"Yeah, I swear. They were chewing me out a little and they didn't want you to hear."

Livvy looked to Ben and Josh and they were both nodding their consensus. "Okay, if you swear, I believe you." She finished dragging the mats the rest of the way onto the room. "I grabbed these from the gym. I figured that just because we have to sleep in here doesn't mean we have to sleep on the hard floor."

The men thanked her and grabbed a mat apiece before making space in different areas of the room. After they made makeshift beds for themselves they all hopped back on their computers for another hour or so.

Even though all of the information he was reading was useful and interesting, Josh found himself nodding off. He kept yawning and rubbing his eyes but sleep was winning out. "I need to rest my eyes. Can one of you guys take first shift?"

"I configured the audible alarm on the camera system," Finn said. "If anything trips it we'll get a warning in here. I mean, we can still have someone stay up, but all of the entrances are monitored by infrared and the cameras can see better in the dark than we can."

Thinking it over, Josh wanted Ben's input. He turned to the big black man and asked "What do you think?"

"We should have someone stay up. I'm not betting my life on a machine. No offense, Finn."

"No, I get what you're saying. You guys go ahead and grab some Z's. I had a good nap this afternoon so I'll stay up until I get too tired and then I'll wake one of you up."

Eying the mats he and Ben had laid out off by themselves, Josh looked at the cozy setup Livvy had set up for her and Finn and said half-jokingly, "Stay focused my friend."

"Oh, jeez," Livvy laughed, turning out most of the overhead lights. "Don't worry, he'll be fine. Get some sleep."

Within minutes after laying down and closing his eyes, Josh did just that.

NORTH COMMERCE DRIVE, OUTSKIRTS OF MEDINA, OHIO

Jim, Vickers, Owen, Saul and Jack made it without any incident to where they had abandoned the pickup the day before. Jim was worried the whole time they travelled there that the boy or the goons were going to show up in force, but his small group didn't see a single living being. It was unnervingly quiet.

The finalized plan was to drive as close as they safely could to the city of Medina and drop off the three men going to the radio station. Then, after Jim and Jack trapped as many of the goons as they could at the denture factory, the pair would drive around in a holding pattern until contacted to pick the others up for the trip back to Klimps.

They piled into the truck. Jack was the driver, Jim sat next to him in the front, and the others filled the back seat. Jack did a U-turn and sped off while Jim checked his backpack once more to make sure he still had the chains, the padlock, and the bolt cutters needed to break into and relock the factory gate.

Within seconds Saul's foul breath wafted up from the rear seats and permeated the entire interior of the truck. In response Jim lowered his window and breathed deep of the fresh air outside, asking himself how the man could be so clueless as to how bad it really was. Jim kept his face close to the window and surveyed the world outside. Like the woods on the way out, the road and the fields flanking it were empty of goons. Jim said something about it aloud and Vickers answered from the back.

"It might be they migrated closer to the city. Relatively speaking, there's much more activity around there than here."

Saul jumped in. "That makes zero sense. I mean, how do they know where the city is? It's not like they have a map. If they wander out here, what are the chances that they then all wander away, especially back to one place? Shit's spooky if you ask me." He went quiet for a moment before saying something he had said multiple times over the last few hours: "Come to think of it, I didn't see any of the bodies from yesterday that we killed. Has something to do with that kid, I bet."

No one argued with Saul's line of thinking. Personally, Jim felt the same way, but the others didn't have the same strength of conviction that he and Saul shared; Vickers had a wait and see attitude, Owen wasn't sure, and Jack simply didn't care or have an opinion because he hadn't seen very much of the outside world since the change had happened. Jim bet that by the end of the day Jack would have a much different perspective than the one he had now, plus more appreciation for how lucky he was to have survived as long as he had. Assuming, of course, that he lived through their excursion.

Jack turned left on Patriots Way and sped up. From the back seat Owen said, "A-ha, there's some, left side."

Jim looked past the front of Jack as those in the back seat craned their heads to peek out of the rear seat window. In the distance a small pack of four goons were giving chase after the truck. Jim shook his head at how stupid the goons were; they had no hope of catching the much faster vehicle, yet they still pursued it. Only when Vickers spoke up from the backseat did he realize he had failed to see the goons weren't as stupid as they seemed.

"Would you look at that?" Vickers said in an awed voice. "Those things can't turn a doorknob, but somehow they can calculate angles of pursuit well enough to lead us."

"Lead us?" Owen piped up. "Lead us where? How the fuck do they know where we're going?"

The off-hand comment had an unexpected result: Jim heard Saul laugh for the first time since meeting him.

"Oh my God!" he gasped between cackles. "Haven't you ever hunted? Leading means to figure our destination based on which direction we're traveling, not take us somewhere, you dumbass."

Apparently Saul's explanation didn't clarify things enough for Owen because he still looked confused. "I'm not a dumbass," he muttered.

Vickers stepped in and put it in simpler terms. "Owen, do you see how the goons aren't running directly at us?" Owen nodded. "Somehow they can reason out the correct angle, based on our speed and direction, to meet us at a point down the road that intersects with us."

Understanding lit up Owen's face. "No shit?"

"Of course they'll never catch us," Saul rejoined. "But it does show how fucking dangerous they are."

The truck was nearing the end of Patriots Way and closing in on Marks Road, near where the drainpipe was that they had hidden in the day before. The truck noise continued to draw additional small groups of goons. Jim watched their weird high-stepping lope as they crossed fields and ran along the road in frenzied pursuit.

Jack took a right on Marks Road, heading in the direction of West Liberty Street. A quarter mile later he slowed to negotiate a path around a car on the road parked slantwise, blocking the way. The roof of the car was flattened almost to the top of the door panels. Glass littered the road and the legs of a man wearing sneakers were sticking out from under it. Jack didn't want to run over the legs so he swerved wide to get around them and in doing so drove dangerously close to the ditch on Jim's side of the road.

Jim was looking down. He watched as the asphalt disappeared under the car and the ditch loomed large. He could see a culvert fifteen feet down and was about to reach over and jerk the steering wheel away from the ditch when Owen yelled out from the back.

"Wait! Stop! I thought I saw someone in there. Someone poked their arm out of the window gap!"

Jack jerked the car to a stop. "Where?" he asked. "I didn't see anything."

But Owen wasn't going to waste time with explanations. He reached over Saul's lap and pulled the door latch and was about to crawl over Saul to get out when Saul slapped him on the back of his neck.

"The fuck? Get off me!"

"Shit, I see it too," Vickers said. "Look."

The others turned to where he was pointing. When Jim finally saw it, he was amazed that Owen was able to spot such a small target from a moving car. It was a woman's hand, and she was reaching out through a small gap in the crushed metal carcass. Her hand only stuck out as far her wrist but Jim could tell it was a girl because underneath all of the blood sunlight reflected off of a shiny diamond bracelet. Her fingers wiggled slightly.

Everyone scrambled out and rushed over to the car. Owen grabbed the woman's hand and Jack and Saul leaned in to ask her how she was doing, and to let her know they were going to help her. Vickers stayed back slightly to monitor the goons and Jim helped the former sergeant keep a lookout.

The three men at the door were trying to extract the woman by prying up on the crushed roof panel and pulling on the door handle and frame but the heavy gauge metal was crimped so badly that nothing budged. Soft crying began from inside the cramped interior when the woman saw she couldn't be freed immediately.

It didn't take long for the goons to begin to catch up to the small group now that they were stopped. Worse, the creatures were coming from all sides instead of just chasing from behind. Jim and Vickers reported seeing incoming at the same time.

"No time guys, we have to move," Vickers decided. "We'll come back for her."

The woman heard the announcement and began crying louder, begging the men not to leave her. Her hand withdrew and teeth and gums framed by bloody lips appeared at the opening. "Please," she pleaded. "Please don't leave me. Get me out. I don't want to die." But Vickers was adamant and began pulling Jack, Owen and Saul away from the disabled car and pushing them in the direction of the truck. He reached into his pack and pulled out a bottle of water and a protein bar and slid them into the gap where her mouth was busy sobbing, then leaned in close and told her sternly: "We can't get you out right now, but I promise you we'll come back. But you need to be quiet. Those things are right behind us and if you make any noise they'll find a way to get you out before we get back." As an afterthought Vickers reached back into his bag, pulled out another protein bar and pushed it in after the other. As a final warning before getting into the truck he cautioned her: "Be smart. If you stay quiet you'll live."

Although she had no choice, Jim was still surprised when she acquiesced with a weak, "Okay," before her lips withdrew from the hole and she hid. Vickers hopped in the truck and slammed his door shut as Jack squealed the tires in a rush to get moving.

Once again they led the goons on. Owen kept a lookout behind them to make sure that the goons didn't stop at the disabled car. He reported that they went right past it. "Don't worry, Owen," Vickers told him. "We'll come back for her as soon as we finish what we came out here to do." Owen nodded in reply. Vickers tapped Jack on the arm. "Slow down a little. We want to keep them on our tail."

The truck slowed as they drove past a large apartment complex on the left. Jim watched the largest pack of goons yet turn away from one of the apartment buildings and sprint after them.

When Saul saw the charging beasts he barked, "Would you look at that. There must be hundreds of them!"

High above the goons, a small group of people were frantically waving towels and hands and jumping up and down, desperately trying to get noticed. There were five or six people all crowded together on a small fifth story balcony.

"That explains why there are so many goons," Vickers observed, then he directed Saul to fire off three rounds. "To let them know we see them," he explained.

Nodding, Saul leaned out of the passenger door window and fired off three shots in measured succession into the air. The frantic waving from the balcony turned to excited cheering. "That building is going to be a bitch to clear," he pointed out dourly.

Jim hoped that it wouldn't come to that. He had enough of risking his neck for other people, especially for strangers. "Maybe they'll hear the broadcast and make it on their own."

"Yeah, that'd be the best option," Saul replied. On that point at least Saul and Jim agreed.

As the number of goons that noticed the truck and came after it increased, so did the noise level. Hundreds of whooping throats made an astonishingly loud racket, even inside the truck. The majority of the pack was still behind them, but looking ahead Jim could see that the whoops seemed to carry farther than the truck's engine noise because goons were converging on them from well into the distance in front and from both sides.

"We need to pinch them off somewhere soon or I'll never be able to shake enough of them for you guys to get out," Jack yelled from the front seat. Even with yelling it was getting hard to hear each other and for the first time since they started out that morning Jim was beginning to worry; there were many more goons being drawn to the truck than any of them ever anticipated. A small number had actually made it to within ten feet of the truck and Vickers told everyone to start picking them off.

Since Jack was driving he was the only one who couldn't safely shoot. The rest of them leaned out of windows, or in Owen's case aimed out of the sliding rear window, and fired at the closest pursuers. It wasn't necessary to score a head shot or even something fatal since disabling a goon was good enough, at least as long as the truck kept moving. With this in mind, the occupants were able to create a safe cordon to drive the truck through. Goons that fell tripped scores more that weren't able to negotiate the obstacle, especially with the large number of them pushing forward from behind.

"Left turn coming up, hang on!" and the truck jerked hard. As soon as he completed the turn, Jack stepped on the gas and pulled ahead of the main group on their tail. At the next corner he went right and then left. "Get ready to hop out," he warned, then went left again and slammed on the brakes.

Knowing they had just a tiny window to leave the truck unseen, Vickers, Owen, and Saul hurriedly hopped out and slammed the doors. Jack accelerated away and took the next right, ending up on the main street they had just left. Jim saw the large herd of goons standing in the middle of the road a few blocks behind them. Several hundred of them were milling around confusedly, having lost track of their prey.

"They really are stupid, aren't they?" Jack asked rhetorically and tooted the horn. The goons refocused on the truck and the chase began anew.

"Now we just have to make sure we don't get trapped," Jim warned, looking at the jumbled mass of cars along the street caused by people changing during the event.

"Nah, we're good." To emphasize his point, Jack jumped up onto the sidewalk to avoid a dense cluster of vehicles log jamming the road. Chairs and small outdoor tables from cafes and coffee shops pinged off the front bumper or flipped over the truck roof. Jim expected Jack to shy away from the many bodies littering the sidewalk but the younger man didn't seem to have the same squeamish reservations about plowing over corpses that Jim would have had if he were doing the driving. Actually, to Jim it looked like the opposite. Jack appeared to be enjoying himself immensely.

"It's like real life GTA, dude," he told Jim with a slap on the arm. "All of the mayhem and none of the consequences," he chortled. He intentionally swerved into a curious goon that had come out of a doorway ahead of them to investigate the din. The truck smeared the goon into paste on the building's brick façade. "Woo-hoo! One hundred points!"

"Dude, you're enjoying this shit way too much," Jim remarked. "You need to take these things seriously. And get off the sidewalk."

Laughter from Jack, then: "Dude yourself, bitch! I'm having a blast."

Looking in the side view mirror at the number of goons chasing them, Jim felt a chill. They now filled the street curb to curb. "It won't be fun if they catch us because you're fucking around. If this truck catches a flat I'll beat your ass before they get a chance to."

"Okay, okay. Chill, bro." The pickup bounced back out onto the street. On their way through the city center Jack surged or slowed down depending on how easily the goons were keeping up. Jim spent the time staring out of the back window, studying them. He noticed that the thinner, faster ones were pushing the fat and obese goons to the side in some bizarre real world survival of the fittest contest. When Jim looked down at his own belly he saw a smaller version of himself than he had seen in years. A week ago he would have killed for the motivation to be on such an effective diet and exercise regimen. "Oh, well," he thought to himself. "Just being alive is a victory now. The weight loss is just bonus."

They were nearing a more open portion of downtown that was comprised of mostly churches, apartment buildings and larger businesses. On the plus side the roads widened out and the going was easier, but it was also more populated. Ahead of them Jim watched small 'squads' of goons go on the alert and mobilize to cut the truck off. The next minute was nightmarish. It marked the first instance that a large group of them had gathered in their path of travel, and despite his recent admonishments to Jack, Jim was grateful afterwards for the zeal the young man had in the application of his tasks.

The heavy truck surged forward and bodies were flung in all directions, crushed beneath the large off-road tires, or crumpled onto the hood, up the windshield and over the roof. Blood, hair, and flesh exploded and squirted all over the hood and windows. As pieces of goon bumped and thumped their way down the side and over the truck it felt to Jim like being in the world's grisliest carwash.

The entire time they were plowing through the crowds, Jack was laughing maniacally at the carnage he was causing. A few times he pointed out exceptional grisly details; for instance, when a female goon tried to prevent herself from sliding off of the hood by grabbing a male goon's hair, only to have the hair come off in a clump. Jim had to admit that the woman's look of confusion at the toupee in her hand as she disappeared under the front of the truck was actually pretty funny. It just wasn't lunatic funny.

After they cleared the cluster and met with open road again Jack's cackling simmered down to light giggling. "Oh, shit, Jim that was awesome. I almost peed in my pants."

"Heh. I can't believe we made it."

Jack peered into the rearview mirror. "Dude, check out what we did."

Jim glanced through the back window and was blown away at the slaughter. At least eighty feet of road was paved with meat. The cars lining the street looked like someone splashed through deep puddles formed after a bloody rainstorm. It was impressive and devastating, but didn't dampen the eagerness of the goons one bit. The bodies of the fallen didn't register to them at all. They still pursued the truck. The sound of the wipers brought Jim back around. It took several squirts of the washer fluid onto the drying viscera to squeegee the glass clean.

The road ahead was relatively clear and Jack began his slow down, speed up tease routine to keep the goons interested enough to continue following. Suddenly the phone in Jim's pocket vibrated. At the same time Jack jumped in his seat and blurted, "What the hell?"

Pulling out his cell Jim saw that he had a text that read "Turn on radio to WEKT." He clicked the radio on and tuned it in. Megan's voice rang out: "…a safe and secure location looking for other survivors. We have ample food, water and medicine. Our location is…"

"Woot, it worked! We're done," Jack yipped.

Jim quickly texted back: "Loud n clr. Keep going?" and hit the "Send" button.

A few seconds later his phone rang so he turned the radio down. "This is Jim," he said.

"It's Vickers. Were finished up here but I want you guys to keep going and lock up as many goons as you can in the enclosure. I don't want to have to go through this shit every time we need to go into town."

"Got it. I'll let you know when we're heading back your way." Jim hung up and told Jack, "That was Vickers. He said to go through with the original plan."

"Really? We did what we came for already. Why can't we just swing back around and pick them up?"

"Just keep going. It's not a request; he's our leader so we listen to him and do what he says."

Jack was churlish. "Well I didn't fucking vote for him so I'm not risking my ass for no reason."

Thoroughly annoyed, Jim tried to be patient and explain why they needed to keep going. "Vickers said locking them up will make it easier next time we're here, so how about you just do what he says."

"Nope, I'm not doing it."

The truck jerked sideways. Jack executed a sharp u-turn between two parked cars and hopped back onto the sidewalk, causing the goons running after them to readjust their course. The goons now numbered at least a thousand, their ranks swollen by fresh additions.

Jim was at a loss. Not only were they headed in the wrong direction, they were going to have to drive over more goons just to get clear. In desperation Jim reached over to grab the steering wheel, but Jack saw the move out of the corner of his eye and punched Jim in the face, a hard blow to the upper jaw. The blow smashed Jim's soft inner cheek flesh into his teeth and brought tears to his eyes.

Jack pointed and screamed at him. "Don't fuck with me, you dick, or I swear I'll kick you the fuck out right here!"

Blood filled Jim's mouth and he spit it out onto the dashboard. He was still dazed. He couldn't remember ever being punched in the face. It hurt and he decided he didn't want another.

A second later the truck slammed into the goons and lost most of its forward momentum. When they came through the first time the goons weren't bunched up yet, but this time around they were massed compactly about thirty or forty deep. Every second they became more bogged down. Jim had never ridden through a tank of molasses but he imagined that it would be similar to what he was experiencing now.

Jack switched the truck into four wheel drive and they were able to torque through a few more ranks before slowing down again. The goons were following alongside the truck, punching the windows and truck body, climbing into the bed and piling onto the hood. The rear tires spun in place and kicked a red rooster tail fifty feet long behind them, blinding dozens of the goons with a thick coating of their brethren. Then the truck stalled and came to a complete stop.

Jim shook his head in disbelief. A minute ago he was in the clear and now he was surrounded, covered in goons, very nearly buried in tons of meat trying to punch, jump or kick their way in and rip him apart. He recognized that he only had seconds left to live.

ROUTE 42 AND I-70 INTERCHANGE, EAST OF COLUMBUS, OHIO

Ten miles before they hit Columbus, the large stake body truck driven by Bill took the Route 42 exit off of Interstate 70. In the thirteen miles since leaving the gas station they had seen very little activity, LCB or otherwise. The long stretch between Springfield and the exit was mostly agricultural and any houses they saw were set off into the distance. The only person Fran saw was a man in the distance running through a field, but he couldn't tell whether the man was running from something or chasing something. With little else to do Fran counted the few abandoned vehicles they passed. He only counted nine so far.

Loomis followed their progress on the map, and the crinkling of the paper as the man constantly adjusted and refolded it was irritating and angering Fran, and hearing the mileage readout out every tenth of a mile was even worse. Fran began to fantasize taking a pair of pliers and slowly removing the rest of Loomis's teeth when Bill pointed off to the left.

"King, check it out."

They were approaching a small strip mall with a Waffle House and small shops. Fran didn't see what Bill meant. "What am I checking out, Bill?"

"No, not the mall. There."

Past the mall was a large RV dealership. The sign for it read: 'Midwest RV sales' and beneath that was the motto 'Where the fun begins!'. Fran immediately recognized the potential. "Pull in," he ordered.

The fenced lot held thirty or forty of the large luxury vehicles. Bill braked to a stop just inside the entrance and everyone in the back hopped down. A couple of them ran over to close the large rolling gate. Fran followed Loomis out, stretched, and did a quick survey of the lot. The RVs were parked in rows off to the side of some buildings and an eight foot high perimeter fence enclosed everything. The protection and the location's relative isolation made it an ideal place to spend the night and would give them the breather they needed to take stock and reorganize. It was also a chance to ditch the distinctive looking army truck by acquiring a few of the RVs.

The left side of the lot contained three collocated buildings, with signs in large block lettering marking them as 'Sales', 'Garage', and 'Maintenance'. The garage was in the middle and was the largest structure. It had a customer entrance and twin garage doors were pulled down with a placard on each that read 'Beep for entry'. To the left of the garage and farthest away was a small maintenance building. Fran figured that it was most likely unoccupied, unlike the sales office, which was closest to where the truck was parked. Stretched out in front of the open office door were several mutilated and decomposing corpses, probably what was left of the sales staff.

Bill, Hank and Gunter quietly took charge of making sure the lot was safe. Fran watched them round up the others, separate into three groups, and dole out tasks. Bill and Helen took one group towards the garage, Gunter took a few people towards the sales office, and Hank took the biggest group towards the large gravel area where the RVs were parked. Besides Fran, the only person who stayed behind at the truck was Loomis. Either no one wanted him along or they thought Fran wanted him to stay close.

With the exception of his handpicked core group, Fran was struck at how generally inept everyone looked as they went about clearing the lot. Some were either holding their rifles pointed at the backs of those in front of them or else pointed up in the air. A few also seemed fidgety and skittish, flinching at imaginary noises or jerking their heads about nervously. Not that Fran could blame them. The hazards in what they were doing were genuine and was one of the reasons Fran enlisted a group of people to do his bidding in the first place. In any case, the likelihood of finding LCBs was slim. When they arrived the sales office door and the lot's main gate were open, so unless any happened to be trapped in the garage or among the vehicles there probably wouldn't be any LCBs to worry about.

The first group to finish their checks was Gunter's group. After a few minutes they returned to where Fran and Loomis were waiting by the truck and Gunter reported in.

"Sales Office is empty, King," the skinny man grinned. "Well, actually, there are more bodies in there, but nothing alive."

Fran nodded and awaited the return of the others. Minutes passed and low idle chatter started up. A few of the new people studied Fran when they thought he wasn't looking, but he had a sixth sense for when he was being observed and always managed to catch the stares, swiveling his head quickly to lock eyes with whoever it was. They dropped their gaze every time in deference. Gunter snuck up behind Loomis and thumped him on the ear, causing the others to chuckle. Fran ignored the horseplay and looked for Hank and his team. He found them near the back of the lot as they looped around the last row of RVs and quickly disappeared from view again. There was no sign of Bill and Helen's squad yet.

Fran had a thought and beckoned Gunter closer. "Were there any cell phones in there?"

Gunter shrugged. "I didn't look. I'll go check the bodies." He tagged Loomis on the shoulder and both men walked over towards the bodies and began ransacking them.

One of the garage doors clattered up and Bill, Helen and the rest of their group came out dragging a struggling young woman. Her mouth was covered with tape, and whoever taped her to keep her from screaming didn't bother moving her long blonde hair out of the way first, they just wrapped tape around her whole head several times, hair and all.

She was feisty. Despite having her hands tied behind her back, she still tried kicking and head-butting the man and woman pulling her forward. After one of her bare feet connected with the man's thigh, he stopped long enough to punch her in the stomach. The blow calmed her down but elicited a few negative comments from some of the new people: "What the hell? That's a girl!" and "This isn't what I signed up for, abusing women."

Without appearing to Fran took note of which people complained or had sour looks in response to the abuse. He also paid attention to who was indifferent or seemed excited. There wasn't any room in his organization for the weak, the timid, or the sympathetic and as far as he was concerned those types of people were victims and belonged in the prey pool. To fulfil his vision of the future, he needed to surround himself with the ruthless, the sadistic and the resilient, with the only qualification being that their appetites must be controllable and further his aims for conquest.

Hank and his team finished their sweep and headed back. The garage team arrived back at the truck first. The pair holding the blonde girl threw her onto the ground at Fran's feet and he idly watched her try to catch her breath as she struggled with her bonds. One of the women gave an exasperated snort and in an act of pity ran over to the girl. She cradled the girl's head in her lap and cooed something comforting.

Thinking that there was no time like the present to teach a lesson, Fran signaled a throat slashing motion to Bill. Nodding, the older man hurriedly complied. He walked over to the woman comforting the girl, snapped her head back and pulled a knife across her throat, drenching the bound girl in a viscous crimson fan that walked across her face from one side to the other, before transitioning into a fountainous pulsing jet that arced out onto the asphalt.

If the girl's struggles were spirited before, now they were positively crazed. With her mouth covered she could only breathe through her nose, which was where gravity drained some of the blood. She gagged, her eyes opened impossibly wide, and with a great snort she expelled as much of the coppery flow out of her sinus cavity as she could.

The sound of struggling and retching was lost as some of the new people reacted to the violence. The woman with the slit throat slumped sideways and convulsed. Her head jerked crazily and her hands slapped and grabbed futilely at the pavement. Four of the new recruits, two women and two men, either ran away from the brutal act, screamed in anguish, or sank down crying. The rest of them reacted like they were comfortable with the violence or were too jaded from all that had happened recently to care much.

The man who ran was rolling the parking lot gate open. Hank shot him in the back. The other man sat against one of the truck tires shaking and sobbing with his face in his hands. Fran pointed to a severe looking woman who seemed to be enjoying the show. "Shoot the crybaby," he ordered, indicating the weeping man. Shrugging, she leveled her rifle at the man's head and dispatched him.

The sound of the gunshots echoed and died away. The only sounds, besides the girl struggling to expel the last of the blood from her nose, was the moaning of the two women overwhelmed with shock at the acts of violence. In the absence of other noise they sensed they were the focus of attention and desperately tried to get themselves under control. It was too late.

"Tie them up and tape their mouths shut," Fran said offhandedly, nodding in the general direction of the two women. The others hurried to comply. Turning to Bill and pointing to the blonde girl, Fran asked, "What's her story?"

"Bitch jumped out of the shadows and grabbed Helen around the throat."

"Is she an LCB?"

Bill shrugged and then addressed the girl. "Hey you, can you understand what I'm saying?"

Her eyes darted from Bill to Fran and back again before she tentatively nodded. Seeing her comprehension, Fran gave the order to release her. "Untie her. She's a fighter, which is more than I can say for those two." He glanced at the women who showed weakness. They were tied up and on their knees.

Since he had everyone's attention anyway, he decided to give a quick pep talk. "The old ways are gone and like it or not, the world has changed. I am your leader, your warlord, and there isn't any room in my army for soft, for mercy, or for kindness. Those traits used to let you get along, but now they'll get you killed. If not put down by me or one of my officers, then by the LCBs." Fran pointed at the two kneeling women. They had abandoned the façade of not being petrified and openly wept and begged for mercy with their bulging, frantic eyes. "The only thing these two kneeling before me deserve is contempt and they're just the first of many that will serve us."

Fran hopped up onto the truck bed and scanned the remainder of his group, now only a dozen strong, not including the new girl. She was standing off by herself giving everyone, especially Fran, wary looks as she gingerly tried to work the tape from her hair. "This isn't a democracy," he continued. "I decide where we go and what we do. I even say who lives and who dies." Now that he had their undivided attention, he smiled benevolently. "With that out of the way, you'll see that I'm a generous and giving leader. Stay strong and together we will carve our own order out of this mess. We will rebuild it into something where the strong rule over the weak and the weak serve the strong."

From their reactions, Fran knew that he had them. Many of the newcomers hadn't yet come to the realization that what had happened to the world presented opportunities to go along with the setbacks. He marveled that in just a few days ordinary people were able to regress to the point where they were ready to accept and embrace a new existence where the old rules no longer applied and the only limits to one's desires were what they were willing to do to get them. "Are there any questions?"

One of the troops, a man, raised his hand and spoke up. "What's next, King?"

"After we rest up for the night, we head for Cleveland. It's far enough away from the base that we shouldn't be bothered by the military, at least not until we're ready for them. Once we get there I plan to take over the city. And all of you will rule it with me."

The man nodded and smiled. The others began smiling too, contemplating the possibilities. Before the change they were just regular people, law abiding citizens forced to obey the rules. But now they had the chance to be more than that. With the obviation of social mores and the protection the group offered, they had the chance to have anything and everything they ever wished for. Fran watched that dawning awareness kick in and suddenly the mood was lighter. They began cheering him, chanting his name: "King! King! King!"

This was what Fran wanted, what he had been trying to achieve. Hearing his small group praise him made the abuses and annoyances he'd had to deal with over the past couple of days almost worth it. The only thing that robbed him of experiencing total satisfaction was the knowledge that he still had to actually deliver on what he promised. Still, that challenge would come later, so he pushed it back into the recesses of his mind. For moment he wanted to enjoy the adulation.

The impromptu celebration was shattered by the ping of a bullet ricocheting off the metal body of the truck bed. A metal shard sliced across Fran's forehead and he was propelled over the side of the truck and onto the ground six feet below. He landed with a grunt as the others yelled, ducked or ran from the hidden shooter. The impact from the fall knocked the air from Fran's lungs but he was able to get up on his elbows and crawl behind one of the tires for cover. Blood poured out of his wound, over his face, and onto the asphalt.

More shots rang out and a woman's scream was cut off abruptly as a bullet thumped into her side with a meaty slap. Fran heard hissing and noticed that the truck was slowly sinking as the remaining tires on the far side were deliberately punctured by the hidden sniper. He wiped his face and tried to take stock of what was happening but the blood ran back down into his eyes and impeded his vision.

"It's coming from the road!" Hank yelled, popping off a few rounds. "Everyone start firing towards the road!"

More shots from others in Fran's group joined Hank's return fire and the sniper momentarily stopped his assault, giving Fran the opportunity to stand and get to a better position. He ran towards the sales office, ordering everyone to follow him. He passed the woman who had been screaming, her head deformed by the impact of a large caliber bullet. A few others were down, crying or moaning and leaking blood.

"Come on, let's go!" he yelled, and led everyone that could still move under their own power into the relative protection of the building. He waited until they all went in before he did, not out of some chivalrous gesture but as a needed demonstration that he was not afraid, even though he was. Just before Fran went in another shot rang out and he was able to pinpoint the location of the sniper by the rifle flash.

"I saw where he is," he exclaimed breathlessly to nobody in particular. He used his shirtsleeve to mop the blood from his brow, but it still leaked heavily.

"If he's smart, he won't stay there for long. I wouldn't," Hank said matter-of-factly.

Fran nodded in agreement. Hank made sense.

Bill looked around. "Loomis isn't here." He went to the window and peeked out from the side of it. "He's still out there. I see him rolling around."

The blonde girl spoke up: "The fat guy got shot in the foot. I saw it."

"Shit." Bill looked over to Fran. "Do we go get him?"

"Heh," Fran almost laughed. "Maybe when it gets completely dark. Whoever was shooting at us knows how to shoot. Another half inch and he would've shot me in the head instead of hitting the truck rail." Suddenly Fran felt woozy and sat in one of the desk chairs. The others were silent, watching him. One of the new men handed him a towel from a small washroom in the back of the office. "Thanks," Fran muttered gratefully.

The window shattered as the assault followed them into the building. Nobody was standing in the line of fire and the only damage was a shattered picture hanging on the opposite wall.

"That shot didn't come from across the road," Helen observed.

"Nope," Hank agreed. "Plus, it didn't sound like the same gun. The crossfire means we can't stay in here. They may already have us surrounded."

"So much for regrouping," Gunter muttered. "What's the plan, King?"

More shots rang out. Loomis began screaming and Bill peeked out again. He turned back to the room. "Uh, Loomis won't be coming with us."

Fran craned his head forward to look outside but couldn't see what Bill meant so he sat back down, not curious enough to expose himself any further. He decided to just take Bill's word for it that Loomis was a goner. Instead, he consulted his core group. "I haven't heard any shots from behind us yet. Think it's safe to go out the back window?"

"Better than the front window," was the only response besides some resigned shrugs. Hank was the one who had spoken up. The others, including the girl, nodded in agreement.

Fran tied the towel around his head and got up, careful to stay low and against the wall, out of any angle of shot afforded by the large opening the window provided. The others began following him, imitating his tactics. The light was slowly dying as dusk approached but it was still bright enough for anyone trying to look in to possibly see what was happening.

Several holes appeared in the thin building walls as more shots were fired into the interior of the office. Helen grunted as a bullet entered her calf. Fran kept going, increasing his speed, actually scared that at any moment one of the indiscriminately fired bullets would find him. He was about to stand and open the window when Hank, who was right behind him, grabbed his arm.

"Just a sec, King. Let me try something first."

The old man rolled onto his back and kicked legs out at the lower wall. His first kick pushed the corner of the wall outwards a small amount. Realizing what Hank was about, Fran joined him and on their third kick together they bent the thin wallboard out enough to crawl out without being exposed. Fran's head pounded from the kicking and rolling about.

There were only nine of them left. In just fifteen minutes Fran had gone from jubilant to losing a decent portion of his ever shrinking army. On top of that, he was reduced to scurrying behind buildings and hugging the ground or risk getting shot. Fran was an optimist though, or at least he always tried to turn a bad situation around. "Hank!" he whispered loudly, "Were there keys in any of the RVs?"

More bullets impacted the wall they had their backs against and Hank winced before he answered. "Don't know. We didn't look inside. I figured we could do that later." He ducked again as glass shattered inside and something heavy fell over. "But I guess not."

"We can't stay here," Bill stated the obvious.

"I know a way."

Everyone turned to the blonde girl with the dried blood coating her face. They all knew it was only a matter of time before their assailants changed vantage points or did something else drastic, so they were desperate. Fran wasn't used to trusting people he had just met, especially someone who had been abused so recently by his group and had every reason to exact revenge, but he was running out of options and decided it might be worth it to take a calculated risk. In the few moments he took to mull it over the shooting slowed and then stopped. The gunmen were up to something.

"Okay. But if you screw us, you die. Badly," he whispered.

The girl nodded. "I understand. Just follow me and keep low."

She crouched and ran into the gathering dark towards the side of the garage. Fran went next, followed by Bill, Helen, Hank, Gunter and the last of the recruits from the base. Although they did their best to keep quiet, the sound of their feet crunching over gravel seemed absurdly loud to Fran.

The girl ran right past a side entrance to the garage which puzzled Fran for a moment, but he figured the door was locked or the girl had some other reason for passing it up. He was proven correct when she rounded the front of the building, stood up and sprinted away, waving her arms and screaming, "Help! Help me! They're going to kill me!"

Fran roared his frustration and several of the others in his group brought their guns up to take the girl down when a spotlight snapped on and momentarily blinded them. The light was followed by concentrated gunfire, rapid shots fired from a machine gun. With Fran and his group bunched up the shooters were much more successful than earlier and most of the rounds struck true.

Turning away towards the darkness Fran saw Bill's left ear magically separate and spin off into the air as Helen's head disintegrated into a pink mist. Gunter grunted and his shoulder jerked back from a bullet's impact. Somehow Fran made it out of the glare of the spotlight unscathed and he was quick to put his followers between himself and the source of the shots. He could see shadows elongating and dancing in front of him as everyone tried to scatter or flopped around in pain.

Within seconds he was at the back wall of the garage. He waited for half a minute for the others to arrive but none of them did. After the shots stopped again Fran considered his options. He was on his own again. He only had one weapon, no spare bullets, and he was trapped by a well-equipped and competent group of people intent on killing him. Fran didn't hesitate. He sprinted to the fence, scaled it, and fled into the field beyond, cursing under his breath at whomever it was that ruined everything he had worked so hard at putting together.

VICINITY OF MIDWEST RV SALES, JUST NORTH OF THE ROUTE 42 INTERCHANGE

When Walter came to the first thing he noticed was that he hurt unimaginably. He thought his face might be on fire. The pain pounded in sync with his heartbeat and the deep throbbing in his orbital bone took his breath away with every pulse. When he reached up to touch his injuries he felt a thick bandage there and his memory of what happened came rushing back. Walter looked up with one eye at the faces of Lincoln and Mycroft outlined in the dim interior of the Grizzly, and croaked out a weak "Ow, this hurts."

"Ow is right, Walter," Mycroft answered back, handing over some pills. "It's aspirin and painkillers." He also handed over a bottle of water before continuing. "You had us both worried when we found you. You scared our young friend Lincoln." Lincoln smiled crookedly but didn't speak.

Walter took a moment to swallow the pills down with a large gulp of the water. "Uhgg, my goodness. Where are we?"

"Thanks to Lincoln's driving we outran those buggers chasing us back there. After we made it free and clear we looked back and found you swimming in your own blood. We thought you were dead."

"Oh, I wish I were. This is abominable."

"Well, this should cheer you up. We found them."

"Found who? The fugitives?"

"That's right. It looks like they don't suspect anyone went after them because they decided to bivouac for the night in a camper lot nearby."

"They'll know we're here, we have to get them." Walter bolted upright and immediately regretted it when the blood dumped out of his brain and the pain in his face intensified. He felt lightheaded. Mycroft put a restraining hand on Walter's chest and eased him back down.

"Easy, sir. They don't have a clue we're here," Mycroft told him. "After we got away from that last group Lincoln put the Grizzly on battery power, hoping to run silent for a few miles and lose the bastards permanently."

Lincoln finally spoke up. "That's when we spotted them. I backed up before they saw me and here we are. They're right over the hill in front of us."

The news that they had caught up so quickly went a long way towards improving Walter's disposition. He smiled. "That's fantastic. Now help me up."

The two men cradled Walter behind his back and eased him into a sitting position. After another minute the pain medication kicked in and he felt restored enough to stand. His two friends watched him closely to make sure he didn't relapse. "Don't take this the wrong way, Walter, but you look like shit warmed over."

"Why thank you, Mycroft. Despite that, we still need to finish what we came out here for." He began gathering up supplies and putting them in a rucksack. When nobody else moved he waved his hands at them. "Well, you two aren't going to make me go out there by myself, are you?"

The other two men reluctantly packed for a mission outside of the Grizzly. In addition to the side arms they all carried they armed themselves with long guns from the gun locker in the back of the vehicle. Lincoln decided on a SCAR-H Mk-17 battle rifle, Walter grabbed a Mossberg M590 pump-action shotgun and Mycroft grabbed a .338 Lapua Magnum sniper rifle. After a moment of hesitation, Mycroft grabbed a SCAR-H as well. When Mycroft noticed Walter looking at the two rifles, he shrugged and said, "I'm greedy, and I like them both." All three of them chuckled at the admission.

Once outside Walter indicated that Mycroft should take the lead and they headed out in a column. They walked over to the shoulder of the road opposite the fugitives and down into the drainage ditch. When they were perpendicular to the RV lot Mycroft dropped his rucksack and the other two did the same before crawling on their bellies back onto the road. Using their binoculars they watched the groups below return from scouting the buildings and the vehicles. It wasn't until the group slit a woman's throat that Mycroft crawled back to get the sniper rifle.

While he was gone Walter and Lincoln watched the drama unfold below. Two men, one who tried to escape and one weeping with his back to the military truck's tire, were both put down at the instruction by one man. Mycroft rushed back after he heard the gunshots and arrived back alongside out of breath.

"What happened?"

"See that man on the truck giving a speech?" Walter asked. "He's obviously the leader. He just ordered the execution of two more of his own men."

"Is he the one we came for?" Lincoln wanted to know.

"I suspect he is," Walter replied. "But I doubt he'll come along peacefully. And as much as I hate to contribute to all the death and killing, I don't think there's any way around it."

"I won't disagree with you," Mycroft sighed. "No sense trying to do this the old, lawful way, especially with dishonorable people like them." With that, he raised his Lapua, sighted in and pressed the trigger.

The sound of the shot was followed by a metallic clang and man standing on the truck rag-dolled over the opposite rail and disappeared. The blood bloom caused by the kinetic energy of the Lapua's 70mm supersonic bullet when it ricocheted off the railing and then the man's unprotected flesh was visible even two hundred meters away. Before the atomized corpuscles dispersed completely, Lincoln had his assault rifle up and was firing off rounds at the other members of the gang.

Walter watched a few of them drop through a pair of high powered binoculars but within seconds anyone in the parking lot not disabled had clambered behind the protection of the truck. Mycroft and Lincoln began shooting at the tires and the truck body hoping to flush them out. One of the injured ones, a fat man, was rolling around in the open. With nothing else to shoot at Mycroft began targeting the man's arms and legs, which pulped and flopped loosely whenever a bullet touched them. Watching the man limbs limply wave and hearing his piercing screams of pain were not something Walter enjoyed experiencing.

Down at the truck the group's leaders must have regained their wits and organized a counterattack because without warning bullets were directed back towards the road, causing all three of them to drop their heads defensively. For ten seconds the return fire was heavy and furious before it stopped completely.

Walter risked poking his head up to take a peek with his binoculars and noticed a few people running into the rightmost building marked 'Sales'. "They went inside that small office down there," he reported.

“Roger,” Mycroft answered. “Lincoln, mind taking a flanking position and see if you can engage them from the side?”

“Sure.”

The young officer departed at a trot via the ditch. Instead of waiting for him to take up his new position, Mycroft continued firing with the Lapua. “Those walls they’re hiding behind won’t stop these rounds. All they accomplished by going in there was trap themselves,” he said for Walter’s benefit, in between placing his shots. “Still, we need to get them all before it gets completely dark out or they’ll just get away again. If any get away they won’t be so careless next time.”

Walter continued observing while he listened. “One of them is peeking out of the window.”

A shot rang out next to him, followed by Mycroft’s humorless chuckle. The head disappeared from view. “Thanks. I’m guessing now they’ll think twice about peeking out again.

They knew when Lincoln found a good perch by the sounds of gunfire coming from the right side of the lot near where the RVs were. With the crossfire established Mycroft asked Walter to go back down the road and drive the Grizzly up. He also gave a short warning: “Be careful, Walter. All of this noise is bound to be attracting any LCBs in the area.”

Happy to feel useful Walter nodded and trotted along the ditch back to the Grizzly. He got in and started it up. The powerful diesel roared to life and seemed to lunge against the brakes and gears keeping it in check. Walter gave it its head and thirty seconds later he drove past Mycroft and closer to the lot’s main gate. He shut it down and hopped into the turret mount, opting to use the machine gun in manual mode versus using the computer assist, which he didn’t know how to use anyway. In the waning light he focused on the building the fugitives had taken refuge in and waited for the other two men to force them out.

He was so intent on the building and its windows that he didn’t notice the group making their way between the office and the garage until a woman screamed. The servos assisted his swivel left and he was barely able to make out a girl running from the others, waving her hands above her head and pleading for help.

In his many tours into conflict zones embedded with combat troops Walter had often considered if he could take a life, particularly the life of a stranger, somebody who hadn't done him any personal harm. He usually concluded that he wouldn't be able to, but on occasion, when he was feeling very lucid or very drunk, he was honest with himself and admitted that deep down the truth was he didn't, couldn't know for sure. As a civilian, he wanted the answer to be a resounding no, because that would be murder, and good, decent people didn't commit murder.

It was a testament to how quickly the world, and Walter, had changed that he never hesitated to fire into the group clustered next to the garage, most of whom had their rifles up ready to shoot the fleeing woman in the back. He was pretty sure they had no idea he was there until they started collapsing.

Walter watched those that didn't drop scatter in every direction but he didn't bother to chase them with bullets. He wasn't the best shot and didn't want to accidently hit the girl who had screamed. Mycroft didn't have the same reservations; the major's barrel jerked left and rights as he aimed and fired off several more rounds, trying his best to eliminate all surviving fugitives. The crackle of gunfire also came from Lincoln's direction.

It was all over in less than a minute. Silence reigned momentarily before Walter picked up on sounds of pain and anguish coming from inside the lot. He got out of the Grizzly and walked over to Mycroft, who was getting up and brushing the dirt off the knees of his uniform while simultaneously keeping an eye out for fugitive activity. Mycroft spoke up: "You should probably lock the Grizzly before we head down there to secure the site. Some of them got away and I don't relish a taste of our own medicine or the long walk back to base."

Walter clicked the remote lock. "Good point. I saw firsthand what that turret can do."

Mycroft reached down and grabbed Walter's shotgun. He handed it over and complimented Walter's shooting. "That was good work."

Grabbing the offered gun, Walter could only eke out a weak, "Thanks, I guess."

The major gave him a quizzical look. "Was that your first time?"

"Yeah, and even though they had it coming I'm not feeling too great about it."

The sound of running footsteps caused both men to spin around and bring their guns up to the ready.

"Wait, don't shoot. It's me. Lincoln." The young lieutenant rejoined them, breathless from the jog back. He gave a short fist pump and reported in. "We did some damage. I'm pretty sure we got most if not all of them. Are we going to wait here until daylight or try and finish things up tonight?"

While he was in charge, technically speaking, Walter deferred the decision to Mycroft. The man had conducted real-world combat operations and was the logical choice to lead the operational side of things. Even so, the major still waited for Walter to give the official nod and gesture indicating he was passing the torch. Once that happened, Mycroft went into full-blown take charge mode.

"The way I see it," Mycroft summarized, "if we wait here we'll never get them. They'll be miles away by the time daylight arrives, which means we're going to have to take some small risks and end it now." Turning to Lincoln, Mycroft asked, "Are there any NVGs in the Grizzly?"

"I doubt it. We only get night vision equipment issued to us based on operational need. They're too expensive for general issue."

"What about the rifles? I'm sure they're also expensive," Walter questioned.

"I had one of my men put those in the Grizzly. I never thought to bring NVGs, even if there was time to before we left."

"We go in regardless, weapons-free," Mycroft said, unfazed, nodding grimly in the day's dying light. "That's that then. Be the Best."

"Huh?"

"Oh. Sorry, young Lincoln. It's the motto of the British Army. You know, like 'Aim High' and all that harrup-rup."

"Okay, sure. Let's go get 'em!"

"Wait," Walter interrupted. "Before we head in there, there was a girl screaming and running from them. I'm pretty sure she wasn't with them."

"Okay, I take back weapons-free. It's now weapons-hold, everyone." Turning to Walter, Mycroft quickly explained: "That means only shoot in self-defense or if I give the order."

Walter nodded and they set out in the last remnants of daylight to creep up on the fugitive's holdout.

COMPUTER LAB, FIRESTONE HIGH SCHOOL

Josh awoke to a hand lightly shaking him and surprised himself by knowing exactly where he was. Ben's big hand let go when he saw Josh's eye's pop open.

"Ahghh. What time is it?" Josh asked between yawns. He sat up and stretched his arms.

"It's four in the morning. Almost time for roll call, Boss."

Both men chuckled at the use of the prison lingo. Josh rubbed at his face and hair in an attempt to rouse himself to full alertness. Ben handed him a bottle of water and he chugged half of it. "Anything happening?"

"Nope. Not a thing, at least not on the cameras. I tried searching with the computer some but I have to confess that computers were new when I went into the joint. Shit, I never even seen one until we started getting them in the prison library, and even then we weren't allowed to connect up to the outside world. I spent most of the night looking at the cameras and the maps, plus the live broadcasts Finn found out of England."

"Did you learn anything that we didn't already work out?"

Ben was about to answer when Livvy murmured restlessly in her sleep and without a word they walked further away so as not to disturb her. After they reset Ben resumed their conversation. "Things are worse than we thought. Besides half the world being dead or changed, the other half is at war with each other. The news says China and Russia are headed this way to take over what's left of the country."

"No shit?" The news brought Josh more fully awake. Now in addition to fighting for his life and the life of his friends, he had to worry about a foreign invasion force. "That's not good. I'll read up on it while you catch some shuteye and we'll go over it again when you wake up."

Ben nodded and wandered over to his mat while Josh sat down in front of the monitors and checked out the camera feeds; even with the infrared setting nothing showed on any of the dozen or so views.

Ben's snoring soon filled the room and Josh did his best to tune it out while he switched to reviewing the news from overseas. Finn had preloaded different web pages of the available new agencies on each computer. Josh checked Reuters first and clicked on the scrolling chyron link that went directly to breaking news on China.

Most of the information was sketchy but the gist of it was that China was making moves on Taiwan and some of the other nearby Asian countries. Without the deterrent of the American military forces keeping the Chinese in check, they had already blockaded Taiwan and Japan and captured several U.S. Navy ships. The pundits predicted that both Taiwan and Japan would be in Chinese hands within the next forty eight to seventy two hours, and once that occurred Hawaii and North America would be the next targets.

Since Ben had also mentioned Russia, Josh read up on the reports from that country next. Unlike China, which was pushing out of its land borders and conducting operations on the open seas, Russia was attempting to subjugate Western Europe, particularly Poland, Ukraine and lower Finland through land invasion. This meant that information on what was happening was more restrictive and less reliable, with the majority of the information unverified or only being reported by a single source. What Josh got out of the reading was that the Russian invasion of the United States was only a rumor so far, based on the supposition and postulation of military and political analysts. China stood as the biggest threat.

The Guardian, Sky News and the British Broadcasting Corporation were all reporting that a British military contingent had already made its way stateside, forward deployed to Wright-Patterson Air Force Base in Dayton as part of something called 'Operation Ophir Ridge'. There was a lot of information on this plan and Josh spent almost an hour reading through highlights of it and trying to situate everything in his mind. There was almost too much information for him to process in one go and in the end he decided that he and the others should concentrate on their immediate safety while trying to save as many other people as they could. Perhaps later, when things were safer, they could all make the trek to Dayton and seek the protection of the military.

Somebody, probably Livvy, had laid snacks out on the table. Josh unwrapped a large chocolate chip cookie and absently chewed on it while he went through the camera feeds once more. None of the displays showed any changes since his last look except that breaking daylight was causing the infrared setting to wash out the displays. He clicked the cameras back to normal mode.

The thought of a new day motivated Josh to stand, stretch and walk over to the door and open it. He poked his head out and looked left and right; the hallways were quiet. Bored, he sniffed at his armpits and winced, then cupped his hand over his mouth and huffed in his own breath. The smell made him gag and he abruptly felt itchy. He was in desperate need of a shower and a vigorous tooth brushing. He vowed to himself to take care of it as soon as the others were up and about.

Eventually the other three members of the group yawned awake and ambled over to the table with the food on it. Ben and Finn picked at a few of the items but Livvy ignored everything to come over and stand next to Josh.

"Any good news?"

"No, not really, but there's nothing we can do about any of it right now. Ben and I need to get ready to head out soon. Are you and Finn clear on what you're supposed to do?"

"Yes. Keep in communication with you guys, monitor things as best we can using the computers, and make sure that nobody gets in here that hasn't been cleared."

Josh was impressed. "Awesome. It's reassuring, knowing that you guys will be on top of things in here."

"You can rely on me. And Finn. I mean both of us."

"I know." Josh smiled. "I'm going to wash up real quick." He pointed to Ben and told him. "I'll just be a minute. Once I get the funk off me I'll feel human again."

Ben followed him out. "I'll go with you. I'm starting to get a rash."

Both men hit the showers and afterwards they put their prison tactical uniforms and body armor back on over athletic gear they found in a large laundry cart marked 'clean'.

Ben sighed and said, "I feel like a million bucks."

"Yeah, me too. I'm ready to take on the world. Let's grab a bite and roll out."

Back in the lab, Finn and Livvy were absorbed with the information on their computer screens. Without turning Finn told them: "We're going over the updated mapping information. It's super-fresh."

"Is there anything different from last night?" Josh asked.

Livvy turned and she was visibly upset. "Finn and I noticed something and it's not good. Two of the help signs are down. Not missing, but pulled down. And it looks like whoever pulled them down was using the signs to locate survivors and kill them." She turned her screen so that Josh and Ben could look over her shoulder while Finn looked on from his chair. "I couldn't figure it out at first," she continued, "but after we zoomed in you can see bodies laid out on the sheet, here."

She pointed at a view of a decapitated man and woman. The bodies were deliberately arranged to show a sexual act. "It's one of the 'X's we put on the whiteboard near Crystal Lake Road."

"Shit. I remember that one," Ben said. "That sheet was on someone's lawn last night."

"It actually gets worse," Finn cut in. "The house where the sheet was is less than a mile from here as the crow flies. Whoever did that to those people is nearby, or was."

Immediately some of Josh's academy training kicked in. Tools with terms like 'risk analysis', 'situation assessment', and 'prioritizing mission objectives'. He mentally went through all of the known factors and listed them out loud: "So what we know is that the primary dangers are from the changed people and from at least one, maybe more groups of unchanged. We also know that anybody advertising for help is being targeted by the unchanged. What else?" he asked.

"We have a general idea of where everything is," Ben added. "Survivors, the changed, the unchanged, and where the supplies are, or at least where they were."

Josh began hastily listing things on the whiteboard in an awkward scrawl. "Okay. Give me more. Keep them coming." Three columns were written out and underlined: 'Threats', 'Needs', and 'Assets'.

"We have this lab and all the tools in it, especially the computers," Finn volunteered.

Josh added the computers under 'Assets'.

Nobody said anything as they mentally reviewed the content on the whiteboard. Ben was studying the map they had roughed out the night before when they studied the satellite imagery. He looked up. "We already know what we need. Everything we circled last night: Weapons, food, and supplies."

Nodding, Josh added the items to the list, under 'Needs'. "Anything else right now?" he asked.

Again, nobody spoke. Josh added the changed, the unchanged and a '?' under threats. "We have enough here to come up with a solid plan, at least for today. When Ben and I get back we can modify it if we need to."

"How do you know how to do this stuff?" Livvy asked. "Organize and plan, I mean."

"Heh, I can't take credit for it. They teach this stuff at the Academy. Or used to, anyway." Josh shrugged. "To be honest, I hated learning this stuff at the time and complained about it to my mother. I called it 'useless junk', but now I'm glad they forced it on me."

Leading the discussion, Josh and the others came up with a plan to visit three places with help signs out, but only the ones with signs on the roof or ones that wouldn't be visible from street level. Josh explained that the people that had been attacked so far were the people who hung signs that were easily seen from ground level and reasoned that whomever was hunting survivors down wasn't using the internet. They planned their route to pass by a gun shop, a home goods store, and a food market.

"Why the grocery store?" Finn asked. "We have plenty of food right here."

"Tater tots and cookies aren't going to sustain us for very long, at least not in a healthy way," Josh explained. "Besides, we don't know how long the electricity will stay on. We need dry goods."

"Oh."

Between them, Josh and Ben decided on outfitting themselves with just the body armor, the whip batons, and the walkie-talkies. They wanted to travel light and if they needed to, fight silently.

The first stop along their route was a gun store, and even though they both suspected it had already been raided they needed to check it anyway. If there were still weapons Josh wanted to grab them and hide them somewhere to pick up on the way back. The same principle applied to the grocery and home goods stores. Plus, if everything went well they would be bringing a few people with them that could help lug the loot back.

Fairlawn was a small city covering less than five square miles, split by one major roadway, Route 18, that connected it with Akron to the southeast and Medina to the west. A few years back Josh had briefly dated a girl from the same school they were now using as their impromptu headquarters, so he was somewhat familiar with the city. His fond memories of taking his date out for ice cream and watching the fourth of July fireworks from the knolls of Croghan Park didn't jibe with Fairlawn's current state and it saddened him a little.

Brushing off his maudlin thoughts he followed Ben out into the hallway, trailed by Livvy and Finn. The couple saw them to the door and wished them luck before making sure it was locked tight behind them. After the click of the lock, the two men stood in the doorway for a minute, listening and watching. Ben looked down at the dried blood that stained the concrete, sighed, and muttered, "Didn't take long for the whole world to go to hell, did it?"

"Nope." Then: "Ready?"

Ben nodded and they set off.

Neither of them was anxious to leave the false safety of the school's brick wall and crossing the parking lot fully exposed, but once they reached the end of the building they had to. Josh took point and steered them along the fence, his head on a swivel. The thick grass boundary between the asphalt of the parking lot muffled their footsteps. The only sounds they heard were the chirping of birds and the slight metallic jangle of a nearby chain link fence as the slight breeze sieved through it.

It was almost a wonder to the both of them when they hit the tree line without incident. A large exhalation came from behind and Josh turned to see Ben bent over with his hands on his knees, hyperventilating.

Ben put up his index finger signifying 'wait', so Josh kept an eye out while the big man got his breath back. After half a minute Ben nodded and whispered, "Sorry. I forgot to breathe while we walked over here but I'm okay now."

Without a word Josh tapped Ben on the shoulder and moved into the trees. He didn't bother to make sure Ben was following because like the day before, Ben made a decent racket trudging over obstacles, kicking sticks, and slapping at branches. Without wanting to, Josh found the former inmate's attempt at stealth more amusing than annoying.

When the three of them made their way to the school a few days ago, to Josh it had seemed like they had traveled for a long time and covered a great distance to get there. He was surprised to find himself back near the main street less than twenty minutes later, at the same spot they had seen the sign asking for help on the sheet and where they debated whether or not to rescue whoever had put it up.

The sheet was gone, replaced with a headless body hanging by a rope tied around its feet. The body was stripped and faced the building, and it looked like someone had cruelly tortured the person before delivering the coup de grace; it was flayed from the neck to the knees.

"I bet that's hard work right there, skinning somebody," Ben said softly. "Whoever did that must enjoy it."

"Sucks," Josh answered, turning away from the sight. "We knew this though. Hopefully the ones that were still there this morning when we looked will still be alive when we find them. Let's keep going."

Without another word the two men continued on their way. There was a noticeable lack of crazy people. Just a few days ago they were rampant but so far this morning they hadn't seen a single one, alive or dead. Josh tried to mentally work through why that was, but decided he didn't have enough information to make a good guess. He led them through a back service alley that serviced several businesses that included the gun store marked on their list. They passed several dumpsters belonging to restaurants and that smelled overripe, but in general the air was crisp and invigorating. The only thing that belied the illusion of a beautiful, lazy day brought about by the combination of warm weather and serene quiet was the presence a few bodies scattered about.

The gun store was nestled between a burrito shop and a coin laundry. The sign over the rear door read: 'Don DeSantis Gun Shop' and below that a set of crossed rifles under a skull with the motto 'Buy Them Cheap, Bury Them Deep'. The door was slightly ajar.

The snick of Ben's baton being extended prompted Josh to do the same and both men approached the door ready to snap their weapons down if something came rushing out. Ben used his free arm to guide Josh behind him and took the lead. Josh took in Ben's large and imposing muscularity blocking the doorway and his view and decided not to object; after all, if the large man was good enough to have played professional football, he was certainly better capable of handling any normal sized crazy person than Josh was.

Using just his fingertips, Ben slowly further eased the door open. The sunlight gradually crept in and illuminated a short, empty hallway that ended in a busy showroom, with rifles and pistols lining the walls in orderly rows and showcases littering the open area. They didn't hear a sound or spy anything alive so they advanced down the hallway. Josh eased the door almost closed behind them.

To the left an open door revealed a cluttered desk and some filing cabinets, but the office was otherwise empty. Ben turned back and raised his eyebrows questioningly and Josh shrugged: It was apparent to both of them that the gun store was empty and threat-free so they lowered their batons and went into the showroom.

As he passed the register counter Ben jumped back then immediately relaxed. He used his baton to indicate that something was on the floor. Peeking down Josh saw a body there. It was a man. Judging from the lividity the body had been there at least a day, maybe two. The man wore a holster with a pistol in it so Josh figured that he wasn't one of the crazy ones, assuming the man didn't normally go armed. Someone had ripped the corpse's shirt open and used a knife to carve the unfinished word 'Assho' with the letter 'o' only halfway completed. Josh briefly wondered why the person didn't finish the message, but whether the person doing it got bored, scared, or otherwise, ultimately it really didn't matter so he concentrated on what else was in the store.

The glass in some of the gun cases was smashed in and guns were obviously missing, but there were still plenty, several dozen at least, left in the shop.

Josh saw other useful items, too, like tactical gear, tasers, communication devices, and binoculars. He began methodically pulling things out and placing them in a pile in the hallway. Since cost was no object, he selected only the most expensive items and the best brand-name gear. Ben was also grabbing whatever caught his eye and adding it to Josh's pile. Ten minutes later the men took a break and looked at what they had collectively gathered. It was obvious that the amount of stuff in the pile was too much to take with them.

"Let's hide it somewhere," Ben said.

"Okay, but we have to hurry. We still have a lot of stuff to get done."

They left the same way they came in and scouted around the back alley some more. It was Ben's idea to hide the gear out in the open, in a place nobody would think to search. "If we try and hide it someplace difficult, the next person trying to hide something is going to find it."

"I guess," Josh acknowledged, trying to follow Ben's reasoning without success. He decided to go along anyway. "What's your idea?"

"Think about a place we would never look for anything useful. That's where we'll put the stuff."

On impulse, Josh pointed at the big metal container behind the taco shop. "You mean like that dumpster over there?"

Ben nodded. "Perfect. I like how you think."

They adjourned back in the gun shop hallway and separated the gear into two piles. In the smaller pile of things were the items they would carry with them now: Tasers, portable hydration packs, zip tie restraints, Glock 19 pistols with holsters and extra ammo, folding tanto knives, binoculars, and small Maglites. All of the items except the pistols fit easily into the cargo pockets of their pants.

The larger pile held shotguns, rifles, and more pistols, as well as several thousand rounds for each. There were also six boxes of freeze-dried ration packs, several cleaning kits for the guns, survival wear like belts and vests, tactical radios, portable GPS units and charging stations. Josh pulled some large gun bags from a shelf and they loaded the remaining gear into them. Taking three trips they carried the bags outside and placed them in the dumpster. As an extra precaution Ben pulled some rotten smelling trash bags over the top of their cache. Neither of them thought anyone would be investigating the contents of a dumpster, but in the rare event that someone did, that person would have to be an exceptionally curious and determined individual to rustle through putrescent garbage without cause.

Feeling good about their haul, Josh pulled a small-hand drawn map out of his pocket and showed it to Ben. "Our next stop is here, this house near the Bicentennial Park where somebody painted on their roof asking for help. I was thinking that since we haven't seen anything so far, maybe we should use the streets. It'd be faster and easier."

"C'mon, man. You know that these days easier doesn't mean better. Easier gets us killed. Let's stick to your plan, hug the buildings, and arrive alive."

Feeling slightly ashamed, Josh nodded. "You're totally right. Stick with the plan."

"You got it." Then: "What do you think happened since yesterday? This area should be crawling with those crazy fucks."

Shrugging, Josh looked around before he answered. "It's been bothering me too. I wish I knew."

They went down the alley the same way they came in. At the end they took a left past a liquor store parking lot before crossing a small side street into a residential area.

The neighborhood they were in had seen better days and Josh figured that it probably looked uninviting even before the change. Now the setting was positively eerie. Decrepit row homes lined each side of the litter strewn street. Some were boarded over and others were in obvious disrepair. Dead bodies were scattered about in various states of dress and mutilation. Based on what he and Ben lived through at the prison, they knew by looking at the corpses that not everyone died at the hands of the crazy people. The ones that were shot, neatly dismembered, or tied up were done in by other humans using tools and weapons, and the bodies that were trampled near into paste, rudely decapitated or partially eaten came from the opposite camp.

There was nothing in sight that evidenced anything living. At the least, Josh expected to see stray or abandoned pets or hear birdsong, but nothing moved or made a peep. The smell was another matter; the presence of stench was very much evident. It was rich and cloying and the lack of any kind of breeze gave it an almost physical heaviness that burrowed into their clothes and made everything around them seem close and enveloping. Forging ahead despite his disgust and his trepidations, Josh ignored the sidewalks and cut left, navigating across front yards utilizing the cover of porches, plants and the occasional car left in a driveway. Ben followed close behind and like Josh, kept his baton extended and at the ready.

They were almost to the end of the street when they heard the first man made sound since leaving the school that wasn't generated by them: Gunshots. First a single pop, then a pause followed by two more pops. Josh figured it came from a few blocks over.

Both men froze in place when the first gunshot sounded and stayed like that until well after the last. "Think we should investigate?" Josh asked.

"No. I think we should stick with the plan."

Josh nodded and kept going. Before they crossed the next side street they reconnoitered in every direction. Whoever fired the shots and whatever it was they were shooting at didn't make an appearance.

They crossed the street at a running crouch and continued their slow way down the next block, which ended at Bicentennial Park. The house they were looking for was on the other side from where they were. Josh called for a break and they sat with their backs against the side of the last house. There was an unobstructed view of the park and they looked out at it while munching on energy bars Ben had pocketed from the gun store. The park looked normal, not a corpse or a crazy person to be seen. If Josh hadn't known better, the serene, if litter-strewn, setting of paved pathways, shaded benches and a children's playground would never have hinted at a world gone crazy. But he did know, and he also knew that crossing the open expanse was fraught with deadly risks.

"I'm fucking sore as hell," Ben said between bites. The big man bit into his energy bar again, chewed, and swallowed. "I haven't moved around this much in years. My damn ass is killing me, like, for real. I'm afraid to take a shit because clenching my cheeks hurts too much."

"Bah. You're the toughest person I know, Ben. Don't go soft on me now, I need your help. We need to figure out a way to cross that park without dying." Josh showed him the map and pointed to a large brick house on the other side. "I think that's the house over there."

"Yeah, it looks like it. But now that we're here, I'm not sure we can get there without taking some chances. Is that something we really want to do? Risk our lives for complete strangers?"

The questions exasperated Josh and he began to lose his temper. "Dude, this isn't the time or place to rethink things! You gave me your word."

"Chill, Josh. My word is good. I just wanted to check and make sure you were still solid."

"Well, I am."

"All right then. Let's cross this motherfucker and save us some people."

DOWNTOWN MEDINA, OHIO

Trapped, Jim and Jack watched in dismay as goons continued to dogpile onto the truck. Jack began bawling uncontrollably, hunkered in the middle of the bench seat, and tried his best to hide from the angry, growling faces at the windows. Jim looked at the kid scathingly; the fearless maniacal Jack of one minute ago was gone, replaced by a frightened kid, and as illogical as it was considering their current troubles, Jim took the opportunity to pay Jack back for punching him earlier. He ignored the threats outside and came up with a plan to get even with the little shit. Jumping into the back seat he reached over and locked his arm around Jack's throat. He yanked back hard, pulling the crying man over the seat rest and into the back with him.

Confused, Jack protested through his blubbering. "What the fuck, dude? What are you doing? Those things are gonna get us!" Jim uttered, "Yep, and it's all your fault," then increased his arm pressure. Jack shut up with a gurgle. With his free hand Jim unlatched and opened the rear sliding window that led to the truck bed.

Three things happened immediately: The noise from outside intensified, Jack's struggles grew frantic, and grasping hands began reaching into the truck body through the small window opening. Twisting his hips and arching his back with effort, Jim rolled Jack closer to the hands and fed the guy to the dozens of wriggling, questing fingers. It didn't take long before the fingers became handholds, seizing hold of Jack's shirt and hair. The goons took over, inexorably dragging their mewling package closer so that even more hands could take hold. Jim let go and watched incredulously as a screaming Jack was squeezed through an opening only ten inches wide.

The screaming served as a lure, enticing all the other goons to swarm towards the truck bed for their share. Bones snapped and blood sprayed. The goons tore into Jack with remarkable enthusiasm and inexorable force. The parts of Jack's body that couldn't make the transition through the small opening flayed off and ribboned onto the truck seat in small wet piles before oozing into the cracks at the juncture of the back rest.

Jim watched in sick fascination, unable to turn away until the entirety of Jack's body slithered out of the window. The last bit, the heel of the Jack's left shoe, caught on the window frame and the goon's yanked a final time, causing the shoe to pop off and smack Jim in the forehead. The blow brought Jim back to his senses. He shook off his fugue and looked around. Almost every goon that had been covering the truck had rushed to the rear for a chance at Jack. The distraction gave Jim a tiny window of opportunity to escape.

Still, he hesitated. He was scared to open the door and give the goons a fresher target, but Jim knew that if he stayed where he was it would only be a matter of time before they broke through the windows anyway. Even now, a few of the goons were fighting over the opportunity to squeeze in through the opening Jack had recently vacated and Jim could hear the boundary glass cracking as the metal framing bordering the sliding windows bent inward.

He had to do something. He knew that because the mantra in his head kept telling him to "move dumbass, move". Again, Jim's hand refused to obey his mind's command to reach over and grab the door handle. Worse, he felt a panic attack coming on.

Jim cursed his own body when the phone in his pocket vibrated and reached down to grab it out of his pocket without a second thought. He felt his hand, his betrayer hand that had refused to open the door and allow him to escape, reach down of its own volition and finagle the phone out of his pants.

"Damn you hand," Jim whispered as the offending appendage flipped the phone up to show him the screen. Vickers was calling. Jim clicked the green accept icon and said, "Hello?"

"Jim, where the hell are you? We're waiting for you guys! And what's all that noise?"

"Dude, I'm fucking trapped in the truck. I'm surrounded by goo… Aaaah!"

Jim dropped the phone and dove to the floor as a large tongue of flame licked over the hood. The elated whoops of the goons reducing Jack's body to biopulp and the frustrated shrieks of the ones trying to climb into the truck all turned unanimously to cries of fear and panic. Above the noise the goons made while running away was the tremulous farting whoosh of pressurized aerosol put to flame.

Looking up through the windshield Jim could see a thick stream of fire waving back and forth as the person wielding it aimed it at the remaining goons. A voice yelled out: "Well? Are you just going to sit there or don't you want to be rescued? I can't do this all day."

With a grunt, Jim scrabbled onto his elbows up to the front seat. He looked around and saw that the flames had cleared everything around the truck; he also perceived that the goons keeping a respectful distance were working on overcoming their fear of the flames. That was all the encouragement Jim needed. He grabbed the phone from the floor and his backpack from the front seat and darted out of the door. Standing in front of the truck was a man in a firefighter outfit, wearing a large canister strapped to his back attached to a gun-shaped device. Without another word, the man beckoned for Jim to follow him.

From the phone in his hand came a weak "Jim? Jim? You still there?" so Jim put the phone to his ear and said, "Yeah, I'm still here. Some dude with a fucking flamethrower just saved me and he's taking me somewhere."

A short silence on the other end and then Jim could hear Vickers passing on the new information to Saul and Owen before asking: "So I'm assuming the truck is a wash?"

"Yeah, it's gone. But I can't be too far from you guys. We were actually driving back your way when we got surrounded." Jim's rescuer arrived at a brick building and started up a portable fire escape. It was made out of metal rungs attached to chains and the top of it was hooked over the windowsill of a second story apartment.

"Where is Jack, by the way?"

"Uh, Jack didn't make it. Listen, let me call you back in a minute and I'll explain. I have to put the phone away and climb."

"Okay, we'll stay here until you call back."

Jim hung up and stuck the phone back in his pocket and looked back the way he had just come. The goons were regaining their nerve and they were starting to close on him. With a final rattle of the ladder chains the man above disappeared over the sill.

A few seconds later he leaned back out and steadied the chains so Jim could go up easier, motioning impatiently for Jim to hurry up. The moment Jim began his ascent the goons abandoned all caution and rushed him. The grunts and whoops intensified and Jim didn't even need to look back to know they were coming. He knew he only had seconds to outclimb their reach.

The ladder rungs were only a few inches deep and they rested flush against the bricks. Jim couldn't get his feet in deep enough to support his weight. He had been talking to Vickers and not paying attention to the man in the fire suit's climbing technique. Once, twice, then three times he tried but his foot kept slipping off the bottom rung and kicking down into empty air. The only thing keeping him on the ladder was the grip he had around the chains, but the chains were digging into his fingers and palms and he knew he couldn't hang on for much longer.

In a fit of rage, Jim wasted the last few seconds of his life screaming out his frustration at the shitty narrow ladder rungs and his innate lack of athletic ability. "Aye-eye-eye-aye!"

A hand tapped his foot and Jim kicked at it. The movement swung him around to face outward and he was afforded a heart-stopping look at how many goons were clustered at the base of the ladder. They were hundreds deep and they all seemed eager to grab hold of Jim and wipe him from existence. Frustrated at his impending death while on the cusp of a rescue, Jim started crying when all at once he was yanked upward. Another lurch nearly caused him to lose his hold on the ladder. His vantage point changed; he was rising into the air. Jim craned his head up and saw the man who rescued him pulling up on the ladder and winching him to safety.

It was an unbelievable sight. Somehow the man was dead pulling Jim's substantial bulk up twenty feet of wall using only arm strength. The man's clenched teeth were visible through the tinted visor as he grunted, wrestled the ladder up a foot at a time and reset until Jim's chin was parallel with the windowsill and the two of them were helmet-to-face. The man held Jim in place and said in a muffled and wavering voice, "Well, sweetheart, are you going to come in or do you want me to drop you back down? I can't hold you up here forever."

Jim noted the man's trembling, white-knuckled grip and knew he only had a moment to act. With an effort he lunged for the window sill with both hands at the same time the man let go of the chains, but he wasn't prepared for the sudden transfer of his bodyweight from the ladder. His feet dropped out from under him and there was nothing inside the window for him to grab. Screaming, Jim's hands did a scrabbling dance to find something, anything, to hold onto, and then he was slipping out of the window opening. He almost dropped back down into the waiting arms of the goons below, but at the last moment Jim's rescuer grabbed the back of his shirt and heaved him inside, flinging him onto the apartment floor.

Jim hit hard, rolled a few times and cracked his head against a table leg. For a long moment neither man spoke and the interior of the apartment was filled with gasps for air and groans of pain. Jim mustered up the strength to come up to one elbow and look around.

The apartment Jim was in was small and judging from the posters on the wall the man who lived there had a strange fetish: Amazons. Posters of scantily clad women bodybuilders posing and flexing were everywhere, and even though it wasn't Jim's cup of tea, he wasn't one to judge, particularly when that someone had saved his life three times in as many minutes. It was only when he saw several shelves lined with trophies did he realize he had it all wrong.

The sound of a zipper behind him made him turn. The firefighter removed her helmet shook out her blonde, straw-like hair. Jim stared. Even knowing she was a woman he still had trouble identifying her as such. Her face and neck were all angles and her brow was decidedly ridged and thick.

"Close your mouth, asshole. Your jaw is hanging open," she snapped. "If I had known you lacked manners I would have left you down there to figure things out for yourself."

Now that her voice wasn't muffled by her helmet and covered up by the whooping goons, Jim noticed that it had a slight feminine lilt to it. He didn't want to be rude to her though. She had taken a great personal risk to rescue a complete stranger and he owed her the courtesy of accepting her as she was.

"I'm sorry. I didn't mean anything by it. I thought you were a man. I mean, you know, you're so strong." He cleared his throat. "Anyway, I want to thank you for saving my life. I was a goner for sure." Sticking out his hand, he introduced himself: "I'm Jim."

She took his hand and shook it. "I'm Jayelle Bjorn. My friends used to call me Re-born, because I was saving up to get my operation." She made a scissor snipping motion with her index and middle finger. "You know, to rearrange some things." Jim wasn't sure that he did know, but he let it pass.

Re-born stood and unsnapped the firefighter suspenders. When she stepped out and stretched Jim got a good look at why she was able to haul him up two stories using only her upper body. She had phenomenal, striated musculature.

Veiny hands and forearms morphed into thick upper arms joined to wide shoulders, and a narrow waist tapered down into massive thighs and up into a powerfully sculpted chest. She allowed Jim to stare for a bit before she smiled and asked, “Are you impressed?”

“Oh, yeah. Definitely.”

She closed the window and the sound from the masses below eased to a low din. Turning to Jim, she asked: “So tell me. What were you thinking driving like a madman up and down Court Street? In case you missed it, it’s the end of days and our friends out there aren’t happy to see us. You got your friend killed.”

“First off, I wasn’t driving, the other guy was. Second, it was not my idea to cruise up and down Crazy Street out there, it was his. He flipped out on me. Third, he wasn’t my friend and it wasn’t a joyride. I’m part of a bunch of people holed up in the Klimps Mega Store out on Commerce Drive. We made a run for the radio station to transmit a broadcast, looking for more survivors.” He indicated Re-born with a tilt of his chin. “We’re looking for people like you, actually: Tough, capable, useful.”

Her face got serious, the muscles in her jaw clenching in a remarkable display of masticular definition. “Thanks but no thanks. I’m fine right here. I have zero interest in joining a suicide squad.”

If Re-born was determined to stay Jim had no chance of making her leave, even if he was inclined to do so, which he wasn’t. “Fine, but for the record, Jack, the guy that was driving, he couldn’t handle what was happening. But the rest of us can.” He stood. “I suppose that means you won’t help me get to my friends ether, then.”

She shrugged. “Sorry, pal.”

Grabbing his phone he texted a quick message to the others. “Sry. Jack dead & trck gone. Hd help but stuck here.”

“Where r u?” came from Saul.

Jim asked Re-born, “Where are we exactly? What’s the name of this apartment building?”

“Bishop Towers.” Clearly Re-born had nothing better to do because she was leaning against the wall watching him.

He passed it on. "Apart #?" came the response.

Jim sighed. "They want to know your apartment number. I think they're coming to get me."

She laughed. "Who are they? Family?"

"No." Jim looked at her confused. "People I met since all of this started. Why?"

She shook her head in disbelief. "Why would people you just met risk their lives to come and get you? That doesn't make any sense."

Now it was Jim's turn to be shocked. "Seriously? At least I know them. You just went all World War Two on those goons out there to rescue me, and I'm a complete stranger. Why would you do that?"

"Goons? Wait, never mind, I guess I see your point. I can't say for sure why I rescued you though. Maybe to deny those things out there, those "goons" as you call them, the satisfaction of taking someone else."

Jim gave her a sideways look. "Are you sure you don't want to come with us? The end of the world is a lot easier with company."

She hesitated before giving a long, loud sigh. "Okay, I'll join up with you guys. Beats staying here staring out the window, I suppose. But tell your friends not to come here. I know a better way to get to them."

The positive turn of events put Jim in a good mood. He put his hand up: "High five, Re-born."

"Nope. I don't high five. That shit is lame."

Left hanging, Jim dropped his hand and texted the group that he and a friend were on their way to the radio station. Re-born was throwing things into a hiker's backpack: Big heavy bottles of muscle mass powder, prescription bottles, and clothing. Jim waited patiently and went through his own backpack. He ripped open a protein bar and munched on it while he looked around the small apartment. He noticed the flamethrower apparatus leaning against the wall near the window they came in. It was constructed of mostly canvas and PVC piping.

"Where did you get that?" he asked between bites. "It's pretty badass."

"It belonged to the guy next door. He was some kind of home defense nut and he was sweet on me, so one day he brought it over for some show and tell. It's illegal as hell and it scared the shit out of me that he was next door making and buying all this survivalist paraphernalia." She pulled it away from the wall and looked it over. "After things went bad I broke into his apartment and grabbed it, just in case. I'm not sure about all the mechanics of it, but it's easy to use. You just pull the trigger and aim it. There's an igniter built into the handle."

"Are we taking it with us?"

"If you feel like lugging it around, be my guest sweetie. But it's heavy and it'll slow us down."

Jim considered it but decided to leave it. It was more important to travel light than risk having a pack of goons catch him because he was lugging a flamethrower on his back. He had regrets though, because he imagined how cool he would look to Bettina with a flamethrower strapped on while blazing out some goons.

Throwing on her pack, Re-born asked if he was ready to go.

"Yep."

"Good, then follow me." She led the way out into the hallway and walked to a closed staircase at the end of it. She eased the door open and listened a few moments before going in. Jim went next and closed the door quietly behind him.

They crept up the stairs; up and up until Jim starting to breath heavy. He wasn't used to so much exertion. At each landing the floor number was stenciled onto the wall and when the number hit fourteen Jim tapped Re-born on her calf and signaled for her to wait.

"Sec," he gasped.

She looked down at him with amused disdain then sat next to him on the stairs so they could talk low. She leaned in: "How did you get so out of shape, Jim?"

He gave her a dirty sidelong look. "Maybe I should get 'roided. Man up and pump iron like you."

The slap was quick and painful. It rocked his head back into the steel railing and the impact of his head against it made a deep metallic 'thwang' that reverberated throughout the stairwell.

"What the fuck?" Jim grimaced, reaching back to feel his head. There was a large knot there and his hand came away bloody.

Re-born loomed over him and stuck a thick finger in his face. Her eyes were bulging. "Listen you rude bitch. If you got a problem with me or the way I look, you're welcome to get to your friends on your own."

Jim felt instinctively that the safest course of action was to apologize immediately and emphatically; it was the only conflict resolution strategy that had ever worked for him, so that's what he did. After several seconds Re-born's eyes deflated and she dropped her finger. "Apology accepted. Now let's go, we're almost there."

The roof exit was only five more floors up and it was unlocked. Re-born stuck a dead pigeon in the door frame to prevent the door from closing behind them and led the way towards the roof ledge. Jim shuffled behind her alternately massaging his legs and the back of his head and joined her in looking over at the adjacent rooftop a few stories below where they were standing. The gap between the buildings was at least ten feet and when Jim looked straight down and saw how small the trash cans in the service alley below looked, he backed up slightly.

"Are you scared of heights, Jim?"

"It's more like I'm not a fan of falling off of high roofs."

"That's too bad because that's our way to where your friends are." She pointed to the adjacent rooftop.

"How are we supposed to get over there? Jump? It's too far. We'll break our legs."

"Trust me, it's very doable, even for you. Watch how I do it."

She tossed her backpack over to the other side with a grunt. It landed about forty feet away and the impact caused it to open spill some of its contents out. When Jim looked at her with a 'See?' expression she stuck her tongue between her lips and, "pfttt'ed" him. "No worries, Princess. Piece of cake."

Backing up a couple dozen feet and dropping into a track runner's starting stance, Re-born lunged forward into a dead sprint. She pumped her arms and exhaled through gritted teeth as she sprinted past Jim. Six inches from the edge her feet propelled her upward and out. As she launched herself into the air, the forward tip of her right sneaker made the tiniest contact with the decorative roof ledge, causing her body to cant minutely in midair and changing her angle of trajectory.

She very nearly made it. The difference in momentum caused by her sneaker touching the ledge wouldn't have mattered in a shorter jump, but the distance between the roofs was too much for Re-born to compensate for correctly even if she hadn't panicked and flailed her arms wildly. From Jim's perspective it appeared as if she was trying to flap wings she didn't possess.

The sound of her body hitting a dumpster cover far below barely carried up to where Jim stood looking down. He looked over at the other building and noted how close Re-born had come to clearing the opposite ledge; a foot from the top there was a red splotch on the wall with a few blonde hairs wedged in the rough interstices of the brick facing, stuck there from the impact of her head cramming into it.

"Shit." Jim grabbed his phone and texted "ok to call?" A few seconds later the reply came back "Yep." He dialed Vickers and explained what just happened.

Vickers sighed heavily. "Let me get back to you after we figure something out. Seriously, this isn't something we planned for. I'll buzz you in a bit."

After hanging up Jim stayed up on the roof. It was a safe enough haven provided he didn't do anything crazy, like try and jump over to the next building. He walked up to the front ledge and peered down at all of the goons milling around in the street below. He located the truck he escaped from earlier. It was easy to find with the ring of dead and burnt bodies lying around it.

Vickers still hadn't called back when it started raining a few minutes later. Jim cursed. He was about to head back to the stairwell to stay dry when something below caught his eye. The goons were scattering, waving their arms and whooping in alarm. Curious, Jim tried to spot what spooked them because besides the flamethrower he had never seen the goons run from anything before. Whatever it was they were afraid of Jim didn't see it. He ran to the corners and looked down the road in each direction.

"Hmm, nothing. So weird."

While they were oblivious to his presence he studied their behavior some more. They were no longer running; they were huddled in doorways or under trees. Then he had an epiphany: The goons had an aversion to being wet. Similar to a cat in a bathtub, except more acute.

The rain became a downpour and Jim admitted that the feeling of getting rained on was indeed very unpleasant, so he decided to finally go into the stairwell. Halfway there his phone buzzed. It was Vickers again.

"I have bad news, Jim. We don't have a way to come and get you. Matter of fact, we're stranded here ourselves and were hoping that you might be able to rescue us. Is there a parking garage under that apartment building?"

"Dunno, but I don't think so. I can try and check though."

"Okay, do that and get back to me."

"Sure. But first, I saw something just now that was a little strange." Jim explained the goons and the effect the downpour had on them. Vickers wasn't sure if it was helpful information but said he would let the others know about it.

"Okay. I'll call you back after I check for a garage."

They hung up and Jim went back downstairs. His first stop was Re-born's apartment to pick up the flamethrower. He had a feeling that it was going to come in handy.

VICINITY OF ROUTE 42 AND I-70 INTERCHANGE, EAST OF COLUMBUS, OHIO

After the sound of barking gunshots to Fran's rear died out he stopped in some tall grass for a breather and squatted to present less of a target. Fran debated whether or not he should leave the area of the RV dealership and the carnage caused by the mysterious gunmen; he knew he was lucky to have escaped unharmed and he should take advantage of that and start over someplace else. For one thing, he had no idea how to link back up with his officers or his followers. Once the machine gun began mowing them down it was every man and woman for themselves, and even if some of them had survived the attack, they were scattered. Second, going back to where an unknown number of armed men, probably bandits but more likely personnel from the military base, were out to kill him was crazy. They were better armed, better trained and had the advantage of numbers and position. Last, all of the stuff Fran and his group had collected and scrounged; the food, the guns, the truck, now belonged to the attackers. If they didn't take the supplies for themselves, they would certainly destroy anything left behind because that's what Fran would do if he were in their place.

In the end, Fran determined that logically it made sense to cut his losses, except that the more he thought about what had happened the more his ego stung. What finally made him turn back was the knowledge that someone had gotten the better of him. Fran was the alpha, the hunter, the super predator, and the cowards who snuck up and sniped from hiding were unworthy of getting the best of him. Fran vowed that by the time he was finished with them, they will have learned that lesson.

His decision made and his confidence restored, Fran headed back in the direction of the RV lot, careful to tread silently. Although he still had a fully loaded pistol and extra ammo, a firearm was not Fran's weapon of choice. It was a loud and distant killing tool. What Fran preferred was the blade; it was intimate and silent and allowed Fran to see in his victim's eyes the pain and the fear of knowing that death was looming. He pulled his knife out and held it in a fighter's grip as he stalked.

A few minutes later he was alongside the RV lot. Judging by the number of disembodied flashlight beams that were waving around, Fran figured that he and his group were set upon by only three attackers. He crept closer to the front gate where he had an unobstructed view of the aftermath of the attack.

One person was rifling through the contents in the back of the truck, quietly rearranging things into piles. The other two were near the garage doors, interrogating survivors. Fran patiently watched and waited for the entire scenario to arrange itself through the play of the flashlight beams.

Three of his group that survived had been captured: Hank, Bill, and one of the new followers, a man. They were on their knees in front of the garage ungagged but with their hands secured behind their backs. All three were bloody but Fran couldn't tell from his vantage point if they were injured or if it was someone else's blood. Their captors eventually illuminated enough of the scene for Fran to piece together the full picture of what was happening.

The attackers wore military-type uniforms so Fran assumed they were sent from the base. The blonde girl who had led them all into the trap was now free and helping the man in the truck with the supplies. She didn't have a flashlight.

One of the uniformed men squatted down and said something to Bill, who shook his head. Apparently it wasn't the answer the man wanted because he punched Bill in the stomach, causing him to double over and vomit. Even from the distance Fran was watching from he could tell that the vomit was bloody. The man moved on to the follower and the two had a conversation that lasted a few minutes.

Eventually the questioner gestured to his partner who walked over and freed the prisoner. Bill was still doubled over and coughing occasionally, which left Hank as the only person left to interrogate. Fran knew that Hank was an opportunist and that the man's loyalty was to himself first, an attitude Fran held dear and couldn't disparage. In any case whatever information Hank might give up had little value. The losses suffered during the attack shattered any plans the group had. In fact, there wasn't even a group anymore.

A concussive whump came from the area in back of the truck. The third man and the blonde girl had doused the pile of supplies they didn't want in gasoline and lit it. The flames reached fifty feet up into the sky and the light momentarily exposed Fran. Luckily nobody was watching for him; all eyes were on the impressive fire column.

While the men were distracted Hank made a run for it. Fran saw the whole episode and it was almost comical. Hank was old. Maybe the retired police sergeant was fleet of foot in his heyday, but injured and with his hands behind his back he had no hope of escaping.

The freed follower shouted a warning about the escape attempt and the man who had been doing the questioning reacted by shooting Hank in the back of the head. The other military man protested briefly and went over to check on the body, but Hank was obviously dead.

Bill coughed once very forcefully and lay still and like that Fran had nobody left. Fran considered his lieutenant's death a sign that he was always meant to remain a solitary predator. He went over the options left to him. Overall, he was slightly better off than he had been when he was trapped in the apartment building back in Dayton. At least the area around the RV lot wasn't crawling with LCBs. There hadn't been a single sighting of one since they arrived earlier that afternoon.

With the prisoners gone and the supplies ransacked or destroyed, the men inside the lot regrouped near the sales office door. Fran couldn't hear what they were talking about, but after a minute the man who had burned the supplies separated and departed at a run. He went to the gate, rolled it open, and drove an imposing military vehicle in and parked it. The blonde girl ran up and rolled the gate closed behind him.

Half an hour later the follower who the military men freed was escorted to the gate and shoved out. The gate rolled shut behind him and his protests at being left to the LCBs fell on deaf ears. The other four ignored him as they went about their tasks. Using the man's shouts as cover Fran quickly made his way over to him and approached silently from behind.

Eventually the man accepted that he wasn't going to be readmitted and with a loud sigh turned to leave. He jumped when he saw Fran there and his scream was cut off by a mortal act: Jab, jab, slash, jab and twist. Fran punctured the man's voice box, his left eye, severed his throat and punched the blade forward a final time into the man's right eye, twisting it clockwise before he withdrew it.

The knife did its dance so fast the wounds didn't even bleed until the body collapsed backwards onto the road. Fran crouched low and watched to see if any of the group inside the fence noticed, but the small sounds of the body falling and its death throes didn't register with them. They all seemed occupied with setting up a camp near the sales office.

There was nothing else left for Fran to accomplish outside the fence. If he wanted to exact revenge on the people who shot him, killed his crew, and destroyed his supplies he needed to get in without being detected, and the best spot for that was in the back of the buildings. He started making his way back towards there when one of the attackers, the younger man, separated from the others and made for the fence line. It looked like he was headed directly for Fran.

Fran backpedaled until he was sure he was out of the periphery light and then he dropped to his stomach. He brought his gun up to the ready, not wanting to but prepared to shoot if he had to. The other two men appeared more dangerous and Fran didn't want them to know he had escaped. His specialty wasn't in direct confrontation; it was in stealth and subterfuge and he knew that in a straight conflict with them that he would end up dead.

It became obvious that the young man was walking the fence perimeter as a security measure and not in response to something Fran did, but the instant the corpse outside the gate came into view the man sprinted back to the others, yelling the alarm.

Using the distraction as an opportunity to get to a better hide, Fran dashed back to his spot behind the RVs, and while the three men opened the gate and examined his kill, he continued on towards the rear of the lot. At the fence behind the buildings he climbed as quietly as he could back inside and crawled through the hole he and Hank had kicked out in the wall of the sales office. He crept up to the smashed window and watched the group at the gate. Fran was disappointed to see that they had the girl with them because he hoped that he might be able to snatch and abscond with her while she was separated from the others.

Eventually they rolled the gate shut and came back towards the sales office, forcing Fran to slither back out the way he came in. He stayed close to the outside of the hole in order to hear their conversation. One of the men asked the girl, "Are you sure you don't know who did that?"

"No, I told you, I wasn't with them for long. They caught me inside the garage and then I was a prisoner for most of the time." Even from his position outside and not seeing her non-verbal cues, Fran could tell by the tone of her voice that she was annoyed. "How many times do I have to tell you? I used to work here. My desk is right in there. I had nothing to do with those people before they showed up."

"Leave her alone, Mycroft. I believe her. All of the people that escaped the base were wearing military uniforms. Besides, she was the one who helped us get rid of them." Fran had assumed that the man who did the interrogating was in charge, but now it was evident by the mild rebuke that the man who just spoke was the group's leader. The conversation also confirmed that the men were from Wright-Patterson, sent to capture or kill him and his group.

It didn't make sense to Fran that the military would go through such great lengths to pursue a bunch of conscripts. Not only was it dangerous to leave the base, but letting them go would have cost nothing except a truck and some cheap, replaceable labor.

"I thought we got them all, but the body outside the gate says otherwise," the interrogator spoke. "Which means that there's at least one we missed."

"Let me look at the bodies again," the girl said. "I'll take a better look this time. It's just that it's hard to tell who is who with them all mushed up like that. Some of their faces are gone."

The four walked away towards the site of the slaughter and their voices faded. Fran didn't want to risk leaving his hiding spot to follow them so he was unable to hear the rest of what they said. Instead, he used the time to reflect on his predicament. What happened to place him where he was now instead of where he envisioned himself being?

After a few minutes alone with his thoughts, Fran began traipsing into unfamiliar territory: Self-doubt, immediately followed by anger. He knew intrinsically that neither of the emotions were beneficial to his survival and he fought hard to dampen them, or at least channel them into something more productive.

Blood began seeping out of the wound on his face and he felt a few drops patter softly onto his shirt. He took a deep breath, relaxed and consciously erased the furrows in his cheeks. The leak slowed and then stopped and once again Fran was in control of his emotions. His mind went back to work. It came to Fran that although the world had changed, he hadn't changed with it enough, hadn't matched it stride for stride and that restraint was going to get him killed. He was holding on to the old paradigm where there was a state monopoly on the use of force. The men who attacked him and his group were trying to reinstitute and reinforce that model, and didn't yet realize that the power now belonged to those who were willing to do whatever it took to grab it and hold onto it; former fringe people, once labeled as monsters, devoid of mercy and practiced in brutality and ruthlessness.

Fran resolved immediately that he would no longer just pay lip service to the new ways where there were no rules or restrictions. He would commit to it fully, embrace it with his entire being. The insight lifted his mood and became almost a physical sensation; Fran could feel his brain rewiring itself with its new doctrine. The new, expanding rule set was eye-opening and possibilities previously hidden or only hinted at became exposed.

All of this happened in the blink of an eye, but much changed for Fran in that instant. He evolved from a very skilled super predator into something else, someone else that only held pity for his previous being, contempt at self-imposed limits, and lack of vision and scope. Fran almost laughed aloud at his infantile goals of before, of coercing men and women into an army, a kingdom of subjects cajoled into doing his bidding. The new Fran didn't need to ask anyone for anything. He would take what he wanted because the subjugation of others was his right, as befitting someone as gifted and as special as he was.

The voices from out front returned and broke Fran out of his reverie. He was so entranced with his newfound capacities that he was disappointed to leave off of it just to listen to what the people out in front were saying. After a few seconds the euphoria he was feeling waned and plateaued at a stable but reassuring state of buoyant confidence. Fran was confident that he only had to reach out with his mind to tap into his renewed sense of self-righteousness and he was free to revisit it at will, to draw strength and purpose from it.

From up front: "So you're sure, Claire? Two of them are missing?" the interrogator asked.

"Yeah, I'm positive. The one that you guys shot first, he's the leader, and the other missing man was one of his 'officers'. That's what the one in charge said, anyway." A loud feminine sigh carried back to Fran's hiding spot. "That's all I really know, except that the leader was scary and dangerous looking. I wish I could help more but I spent most of the time duct taped and scared out of my mind."

Fran grinned to himself at the unanticipated compliment: He was indeed scary and extremely dangerous. They would all realize that fact soon enough. Fran was also pleased to learn that Gunter was still alive. Maybe when he was finished with his fun he would try and locate the man. He no longer had a need for lieutenants, but his new vision called for something in the same vein: He needed disciples.

BICENTENNIAL PARK, FAIRLAWN, OHIO

Despite his earlier bravado Josh was having second thoughts about crossing lawns between where he and Ben were sitting and the location of the possible survivors in the house on the opposite side. They had discussed several plans but no matter what angle they looked at it from there was no safe or easy way to get there. Cars were too loud, running attracted too much attention, and there wasn't much cover to sneak through.

"I know you said you wanted to help, Ben, but I also know that you didn't sign on to be part of a suicide squad. I'm the one that decided to be some weird guardian angel." After a brief pause Josh shook his head and said, "I want you to stay here. There's no sense in both of us dying when I'm the one with the savior complex."

"That's not the way it's going to happen, Boss," Ben argued. "Either both of us go or neither of us do. I'm a big boy. I knew the risks when I shook your hand back at the prison."

Josh was tempted to debate some more but the look in his friend's eyes showed no give. Instead, he smiled and asked, "So which bad plan do you want: drive, run, or sneak?"

"Sneak, in any direction except through the middle of the park. House to house is the best way."

"Okay," Josh relented. He looked at his watch. "We need to start now if we plan on getting over there and back to the school before it gets dark."

The men went around the left side for no other reason than it was the side of the street they were already on. They made it around to the side of the park and were half way to their goal when something struck Ben in the back of his head. The large man let out a strangled yelp and put his hand up to the wound as a large bowling trophy clanged onto the sidewalk and rolled onto the lawn of the house they were skirting.

Josh looked back at the noise and saw Ben's eyes go wide in anger, surprise, and pain. Both of them ducked for cover and scouted around for the person who threw it. The sound of someone shooing them drew their eyes up to an open second story window. A fat man in glasses yelled, "Fuck off! Get out of here!" down at them, making shooing motions with his hands.

Josh knew that Ben was strong, the size of the man's muscular bulk testified to that; Ben was a former pro football player who had dedicated several years of prison time pumping iron in the yard. It wasn't until Josh jumped on Ben's back to prevent him from charging into the fat man's house that the former prison guard developed a sincere appreciation for exactly how strong his friend was. Josh might as well have been a fly for all the apparent effect it had on slowing Ben's quest for retaliation, and Josh clocked in at just under two hundred pounds. When the fat man saw Ben coming for him he retreated from the window. Sounds of a door being slammed shut and furniture being tipped over came from inside the house.

"Dude, calm down, calm down," Josh pleaded with Ben. "He's not worth getting killed over." None of his words had any apparent effect. Josh despaired that he and Ben were going to meet their end while doing a piggy back shuffle in the middle of someone's front yard, when he got the great idea to hop off and punch Ben in the ass.

It got the desired result of bringing Ben back to his senses. The big man deflated immediately.

"Ooooo, shit, sorry man I lost my cool," Ben said, massaging his rear end. "That asshole up there chucked a trophy at my head for no reason!"

"I know. We're in trouble, though. It was loud."

Neither of them spoke as they canted their heads, hoping that in spite of the noise they made that it went unnoticed. The fat man's house was silent, but in the distance a rising crescendo of cries from the crazy people was building. The open space of the park and the proximity of the houses made it difficult for Josh to tell which direction the cries were coming from and they seemed to come from anywhere and everywhere, including the insides of some of the houses. He grabbed Ben's arm.

"We need to hide. Now."

The only house Josh was certain of that contained no monsters was the fat man's house. He ran onto the porch and tried the front door but it was locked. From inside: "Go away! Leave me alone!"

"Let us in," Josh demanded.

Ben tried to push him out of the way in order to force the door open, but Josh stopped him. "We can't break the door," he said in a low voice. "We need to be able to close it behind us. Look for a key."

They looked under the door mat and above the door, everywhere they could think of. The whoops were getting closer and Josh saw a few of the changed people popping out from between houses, scanning for them.

Ben found a key under a flowerpot on the top stair of the porch. "Josh!" he whispered. "I got it!"

Ben rushed over and put the key in. Josh was pretty sure it would work, but even so, relief poured out of every one of his pores as the key turned and the door popped open. When Ben swung it wide, an ear shattering alarm erupted from a box just inside the entrance.

"Fuck! That's just great." Josh groaned. He pushed Ben into the house and followed him in, shutting the door behind them. The alarm continued its "Blahnt! Blahnt! Blahnt!" while they tried to disable it. The digital readout above a small keypad read: 'Enter disable code:'

"They know we're here," Ben said calmly. He had the front door curtain pulled slightly to the side and was watching the front of the house. "A few of them are headed this way."

"It needs a code and I don't know it."

Ben shrugged and swung a heavy fist into the alarm console, shattering it. The dichotomy of the loud alarm and the sudden silence was echoed in the emotions of pure relief followed by an extreme sense of urgency. They knew that the crazy people were going to continue in the direction of the last noise they heard, which meant that trouble was coming.

Josh looked through the sheer curtains of the front window. Correction: Trouble wasn't coming, it was already there. Three goons were climbing over the porch railing and several more were approaching the front yard at a run. Ben pulled him close and whispered in his ear. "I have an idea." Josh turned and followed the big man further into the house. He knew they had very little time before the monsters got in and overwhelmed them, so he hoped that Ben's idea was a good one, otherwise they were dead men.

Ben raced up the stairs and started opening doors on the second floor. All of them swung open except the one at the end of the hall. When Ben felt the resistance, he leaned his upper body back and did a front kick at the wood next to the handle. The door shattered and flew open, scattering some furniture piled up against the other side. The fat man was hunkered down against the far window, threatening them with another trophy. In two seconds Ben was across the room. He batted the trophy aside and backhanded the man in the face.

"Oh owowow!" the man wailed, putting sausage-like fingers up to his cheek to probe for damage and to protect it from another blow.

"How is slapping this guy a plan?" Josh asked.

Ben turned to Josh and gave him a wink. "Trust me," he said, smiling with a mouthful of teeth before reaching down and grabbing the man under his armpits and lifting him into a bear hug. He manhandled the struggling and protesting man across the room, through the door and back downstairs.

"Please," the man begged shrilly, "Put me down. I'm sorry! I'm so sorry! I'm scared!"

The pleas fell on deaf ears. Josh was actually starting to feel sorry for the man, but Ben gave him a look that brooked no dissention. Through the curtains Josh could see that the front porch was full of milling, angry creeps. Luckily the sun was at such an angle that they couldn't see into the house without cupping their hands and blocking the light, and Josh knew they were incapable of that type of rational act. Still, they were blockading the house and if any of them accidently bumped into the window and broke it, the aftermath would be devastating.

Ben hauled his catch over to a side window and clamped a meaty hand over the fat man's mouth. He indicated the window to Josh by pointing his chin at it. As quietly as possible, Josh slid the window all the way up and got out of the way. The whoops and shrieks from the front of the house increased in volume and the fat man's struggles to release himself from Ben's grip become more desperate. He spewed gobs of snot out of his nose and made pathetic whimpering noises.

Some of the gelatinous spittle landed on Ben's hand and with a look of disgust Ben tossed his burden head first out of the window. A loud cry accompanied the six foot drop, immediately followed by a disturbance from the front porch as the things crowded outside sensed a victim had dropped into their midst.

"C'mon," Ben urged, leading the way to the kitchen at the back of the house while wiping his hand off on a throw pillow that read 'I Beat Anorexia'. He did a quick check through the curtain, found the back yard to be free and clear, and fled outside. Josh didn't need any additional prompting and slid out after him. As the two of them hopped over the back fence into the yard on the other side, the noise behind them diminished except for one loud scream of pain and terror that ended abruptly.

It wasn't lost on Josh that so far he and Ben had done the exact opposite of what they set out that morning to accomplish; instead of rescuing people, they actually aided in someone's death. He decided that for now he would concentrate on getting back to the school safely and to process what had just occurred later. He knew there had to be a better way to help other survivors than to sacrifice them as bait while he and Ben escaped.

The rest of the journey back was unremarkable. They were able to gather and relocate to the command center all of the guns and supplies they had liberated from the gun shop and stashed in the dumpster. Finn and Livvy suspected that something had gone wrong but sensed by their sullen moods not to press the returning duo about their trip outside. Instead, Finn gave an update of what he and Livvy learned through their web crawling and survivor searching.

"We can tell that you guys had a rough day, but we have a bit of good news: We found another group of survivors. They're holed up in a superstore about five miles west of here, in Medina."

MIDWEST RV SALES

Walter hoped that the body of the renegade group's leader would be among the pile of corpses near the garage and was disappointed when it wasn't. That meant that he, Mycroft, and Lincoln would have to continue the pursuit, only they didn't have the benefit of trailing a loud, noisy group of unsuspecting people. The man they were after now held all of the advantages and Walter had no idea how to proceed. He discussed it with the others.

"Everything you say is true," Mycroft admitted. "Our task is much more difficult now."

"Can't we radio back to the air base and ask for instructions?" Lincoln asked.

"No, not really." Walter answered. "I can't call the leader of the free world and ask to call off the hunt for his best friend's killer just because it's difficult."

"Can't you just go back and say you took care of it?" the blonde girl wondered aloud. "I doubt the guy is going to go back to the base and turn himself in. No one will ever know."

"It's not that easy, Claire" Mycroft told her. "It's not even as simple as not getting caught telling a lie. You said yourself that the guy was ruthless and crazy, that he talked about setting up a private army and enslaving others. Letting him go is the wrong thing to do. First thing tomorrow, we head back out to find him."

Claire nodded. "Okay. I want to thank you guys again for taking me with you. I was scared I was going to die here."

Lincoln touched her forearm reassuringly. "Get some shuteye," he advised. "We have an early day tomorrow."

She nodded and crawled into a sleeping bag laid out on the ground. "Night," she said.

The three men smiled the way men do when they are providing a young, pretty girl with comfort and protection.

"I'll take first watch," Mycroft volunteered, picking up his rifle and standing up. "Then it's you, Walter, and then Lincoln."

The others nodded and got in their own sleeping bags. None of them suspected that the man they chased away earlier was back, listening to every word they spoke and learning their intentions. They would have been chilled to see the anticipation of their deaths in his dead eyes and grim smile.

DOWNTOWN MEDINA, OHIO

It felt strange to walk back into Re-born's apartment. When he was last in there, and it wasn't very long ago, Re-born had been alive and well and confident. She had survived what were probably the worst days of the change, alone and not knowing what had happened. After she rescued Jim from the truck she had the opportunity to reconnect with others and be to a part of something positive. Then, with one tiny miscalculation combined with a dash of hubris, she was transformed from live human potential into a twisted lump of flesh, forever married to the top of an alleyway trash dumpster.

It should have bothered him. A week ago, a front row seat to a woman's plunge from twenty floors up would have ranked at the top of his list of life's worst experiences, but after what he had endured lately the incident was almost comical. He decided not to dwell on it and got back to the work at hand.

He grabbed the flamethrower from its spot against the wall. Liquid splashed around inside the fuel tank making it unwieldy. It was much heavier than Jim anticipated, so he left it there for the time being and decided to see if there was anything else he could use. Then he recalled Re-born telling him about her next-door neighbor and how much of a crazy prepper the guy was.

Out in the hallway Jim had no idea which side the guy lived on so he turned right to the next apartment over and tried the door. It swung open onto a darkened room that held a slightly funky odor; it reminded Jim of old shoes or dirty laundry and he was almost embarrassed that he recognized the identities of the smells so easily because his own apartment reeked identically like it. The small amount of light let in from the hallway let Jim see only about eight feet in. He tried the light switch but the power was out or a circuit was tripped somewhere. Jim stood in the doorway and contemplated leaving; darkened rooms held more threats than usual these days. A clock somewhere deeper in the room ticked off the number of seconds that he stood there weighing his options.

Eventually Jim gathered his nerves and stepped into the room. He walked along the sink, opened some curtains and found himself in a tiny kitchenette. The daylight exposed an apartment similar to Re-born's only much more cluttered. Shelves lined every wall from floor to ceiling, and were stuffed with all manner of items: gas masks, bladed weapons, guns, ammunition and other various military-looking items.

Jim already had a pistol, a knife and enough supplies to get him back to the store. He thought about grabbing another gun, but he knew that firing a weapon only served as a goon beacon and would definitely bring more than he had ammunition to dispatch them with. After considering everything presented in front of him, the only item Jim decided to take was a long-handled tomahawk. It was a silent weapon like his knife but better at keeping the goons at a distance. It came with a quick-release sheath that attached to his belt and Jim practiced reaching down for the weapon without looking, getting used to the placement on his hip and how the release snapped open.

The phone in Jim's pocket buzzed. There was a text message from Vickers that read: "Well? Parking garbage?!!?" Jim was tempted to tease the autocorrect blunder, except for the exclamation points on the message that indicated that Vickers was showing signs of duress. He texted back a short "Omw", went back to Re-born's place for the flamethrower and strapped it on.

Taking the same stairwell that took him to the roof earlier, Jim headed down this time and found the parking level at the bottom. The door into the garage had a narrow security window that let Jim peek out. There were a few cars parked in spaces assigned by apartment number. He would need to get keys so he looked for spots assigned to lower floors first. The flamethrower was starting to cause his back to ache and the less he needed to go up and down stairs for keys the better.

Since he didn't have a pen he only tried to remember three apartment numbers: "3A, 4C, 6A." He began chanting the numbers like a mantra, "3A, 4C, 6A, 3A, 4C, 6A…" as he ran up the stairs to the third floor. Jim passed the second floor landing and in his hurry tripped on a stair, smashing his outstretched hands into the concrete and knocking the air out of him. While he lay there trying to get a full breath the phone in his pocket buzzed. It was Vickers again with a terse "??".

Glad for the distraction and for the chance to pass on good news, Jim texted back "Yes. Lking for keys. 5 mins".

"Hry up, geting bad hear".

"K".

With a groan Jim got back to his feet, then began the mantra again: "3C, 4A, 6C…wait…3B, 4C, 6A…fuck!" He growled and retraced his steps all the way back down and memorized the apartment numbers again. This time he took it easy rounding the stairway corners and arrived at door 3A without incident. He was panting heavily.

Reaching down to his hip, Jim pulled out the tomahawk and readied it. The door was already ajar and he used his blade to push it all the way open. There was a small bowl on a stand right inside the door with keys in it. Jim grabbed them and was glad to see that one of them was a car key. Without bothering to check the rest of the apartment, he did an about face and went back downstairs. Once back at the parking garage door he did another check and it still appeared safe.

He popped the door open and raced to spot 3A. The remote had a keyless entry and he "blurp blurped" it, the noise bouncing around and off tons of concrete. He winced and redoubled his speed. When he got to the door, he ripped it open and dove in, only to gag when the flamethrower enclosure got caught on the door frame and pulled the harness straps tight against his throat. He coughed, backed out and looked around, expecting a flood of goons to come pouring out from somewhere and pounce on him. It didn't happen.

"Calm down, Jim, you big dipshit," he admonished himself. "You'll give yourself a heart attack." He took a deep breath, calmly removed the flamethrower, placed it securely in the trunk, and got back behind the wheel. The car started on the first try.

Grabbing the phone from his pocket he texted that he was "Gtg so B rdy." Then he backed out and gunned for the exit. Jim didn't expect that the exit was around the first left turn he took and he nearly collided with a metal security grate. The grate explained why the garage was goon-free. Through the metal bars Jim could see that the rain outside had stopped.

Because of the noise Jim was making it didn't take long for goons on the other side of the grate to start congregating and screeching their anger and frustration. There was a small pedestal set up with a large red 'Exit' push button on it so Jim pulled up next to it, rolled down his window and slapped at it. The gate rolled up while he hurried to roll up the car window.

The time it took for the gate to open enough space to clear the car felt like an eternity. The whoops and shrieks from the goons already at the grate brought more even running and they quickly formed a crowd. Some of them clamped onto the horizontal bars and shook the grate, but they lacked the intelligence to know to let go and four or five of them were pulled screaming into the door covering, bursting like bloated ticks or falling writhing onto the ground absent hands or arms. A few, by luck more than design, rolled under the grate and rushed the car. Even with the windows rolled up, the noise they generated from their throats and their banging fists and kicks deafened and frightened Jim.

"C'mon! What the fuck is this, the world's slowest garage door?" he bellowed at the goons, to himself, and at the world in general.

The clearance was three feet, then became three and a half. More goons were ducking under and coming at the car. When the gap widened to four feet, a few made it to the roof of the car and began jumping up and down, caving the top down and shrinking the interior. Jim had to duck his head and crane his neck to see out of the windshield as hairline cracks appeared in all of the windows. Off to the right, Jim saw a middle-aged woman squat and defecate. Even in his harried state he was still able to marvel at how stupid the goons were. They didn't even know enough to drop their pants before taking a crap!

The area in front of the garage was filled edge to edge with goons before Jim decided he had enough room to squeeze under. He pressed the gas pedal all the way to the floor, expecting to accelerate under the gate, but the weight of more than a dozen goons bogged him down. He crawled forward in slow motion. It was only when he scraped the ones on the roof off on the bottom of the grate that Jim was able to generate some speed. He nudged a bunch aside with the bumper and he was suddenly in the clear.

It seemed to Jim that over the last several hours he was continually going from one bad predicament into a worse one, so despite having a little running room he wasn't optimistic that his good luck would remain. What he desperately wanted was to reunite with the others and share some of the burden of survival with them. He was getting a headache from the constant tension. He relieved some of it by punching up on the roof and fixing the indentation.

At the third side street Jim cut right and headed in the direction of the radio station. He was relieved to see that compared to when he and Jack had come through earlier, the streets were nearly clear. A few straggling goons tried to attack or chase the car, but he was able to bump them out of the way or swerve around them.

Finally, the radio station loomed up ahead. Jim clenched his fist and said a whispered, "Yes!" He saw that his celebration was premature when he got closer; the front door was packed ten or twelve deep in goons climbing over each other to get at the humans inside. Jim didn't know of any other way for the guys inside to get out, so he gritted his teeth, increased his speed, and barreled into the goons doing an impressive sixty five miles per hour.

Earlier, when Jim and Jack had run into the massed goons with the truck, the front of the vehicle was a large, flat surface that compressed bodies into each other and made each foot of forward momentum gained more difficult than the last, but the car was a different story altogether. It had an aerodynamic front end designed to maximize airflow over the top and beyond. Jim was ecstatic when the car treated the goons like it did the air, shoveling underneath them and jetting them up into the air or over the car roof.

From just inside the doors of the radio station the others watched their rescuer barrel through the goon pack from the side. One second the goons were trying to get through the tempered glass of the entrance doors, the next there was a sheet of blood coating those same windows that dripped down to reveal their best opportunity to escape.

Saul was the first out of the door. He popped the rear door of the car open, ushered Owen and Vickers inside and jumped up front. The goons were already beginning to recover, although most of them were incapable of standing due to shattered legs, broken hips or other catastrophic damage.

Jim started moving before the door slammed shut. Even so, that didn't keep Saul from yelling, "Go! Go! Go!" or for Owen to bellow "What took you so long?" several times. All of the noise was unsettling to Jim until he realized what he had accomplished. Once more he had donned the mantle of rescuer and he was starting to enjoy the fit. He was no longer the outcast, the loner; he was a vital part of his group, so much so that he right now was the only reason the others were alive and well. As a lifelong gamer, Jim subconsciously measured his life achievements by 'levels'; he swelled with pride knowing that he had just leveled up in his social and rescuer abilities.

The goons thinned out the further they got from downtown and so did the volume of the yelling. Within minutes the hectic shouts generated from being near death were replaced with acclamations of gratitude for Jim's brave and heroic actions. They patted his back and shoulders and proclaimed him man of the hour.

Jim grinned and concentrated on the road, wending his way around the smaller groups of goons while Saul tuned the car radio to their broadcast. Megan's voice blasted out of the speakers.

"Success!" the little man announced unnecessarily.

Soon they were back at the damaged car with the woman inside. The area of it looked goon-free and the only immediate threat was the goon groups they had outrun, approaching from the rear at least a mile away. Jim stopped and Vickers instructed him to pop the trunk.

Everyone hopped out. Jim went with Vickers the retrieve the jack while Owen and Saul went over to talk to the woman. She was crying with gratitude and clasping Saul's hand.

"Thank you for coming back for me. I was afraid you were going to leave me here to die. Oh, my God, I'm so, so grateful."

"Back up, Miss," Vickers told her. Her hand disappeared and he jammed the scissor mechanism into the small gap between the top of the door and the crushed roof frame. It barely fit.

Jim looked around. The goons were gaining from behind but they were also converging from all around. He figured they had less than a minute. "We need to hurry."

"Duh," was Saul's typically dismissive response, but Jim could tell that behind the beard the short man was also nervous and anxious. There had been too many close calls since that morning.

Vickers directed Owen to hold the jack in place and stuck the metal arm into the receiver that operated the screw mechanism. "Here goes."

The roof rose immediately and kept rising with every twist of the jack's internal screw. The popping and cracking of the deformed metal was accompanied by the screams and whoops of the encroaching goons.

"We're not gonna make it," Saul said. "Everyone, get back in the car."

"No!" the girl inside shrieked. "Don't leave me!"

The two men operating the jack ignored Saul's command to get back in the car as Vickers increased his already frantic pace. Jim did a quick peek and was alarmed at how close the goons were. They were now at a full on sprint at less than a quarter mile away.

"C'mon, Vickers, that should be good," Owen pleaded, looking around frantically.

Shrugging, Vickers reversed directions with the screw and the jack lowered enough for him to pull it out and toss it onto the ground. He pointed at Jim and Saul. "Get over here you two and grab one of her arms."

Saul was already seated in the passenger seat, ready to go. With a show of reluctance he got back out and joined Jim in grabbing one of the girl's outthrust arms. Vickers and Owen grabbed the other.

"Hurry!" the girl pleaded.

Vickers did a quick countdown. "Three, two, one, pull!"

The men strained and the girl's head and shoulders slid out of the gap. She was stuck on something inside. "Wait!" she shrieked, but Saul ignored her and yelled, "Pull!"

A cry of abysmal pain came from the girl as she spurted out and was accidently dropped onto the asphalt. Her time in the car and the damage she took during the rescue left her without the strength to stand and she lay on the ground crying.

"Get her and let's go!" Saul shouted, running around to the driver's seat. Jim and Owen grabbed the girl under her arms, shoved her into the backseat, and piled in after her. Vickers hopped in front and Saul accelerated, mowing over a few of the closest goons and maneuvering around the rest.

Once they were clear again Owen quipped, "Man, those things remind me of dogs chasing cars," and then laughed loudly at his own joke for a few seconds before he shut up. No one else thought it was funny, but Jim kind of understood why Owen cracked wise; the guy was nervous and letting off steam.

"How is she?" Vickers asked, turning towards the back seat.

Jim looked at her and tried to assess her condition. She was skinny, with greasy brown hair and a bad case of acne. Her eyes were closed and her hands were folded tightly across her chest. Plus she was moaning softly and panting as if internalizing pain. "Not good, I think," he ventured.

"That's it? Not good?" Saul spit back, catching Jim's eyes in the rear view mirror.

"Eat a dick, Saul. Do I look like a fucking doctor?"

The eyes in the mirror narrowed. "That's it! After we get back, you and I are going to dance. Goddamn Baby Huey piece of shit."

"Boohoo you're hurting my feelings, you funky motherfu…"

"Cut it out you two," Vickers said sternly, looking at both of them in turn. "Save your breath because it looks like we're going to have to carry her back from the road. And by 'we', I mean the two of you who can't seem to realize that we're a team."

Disappointing Vickers bothered Jim more than knowing he and Saul were going to get into some fisticuffs later. Almost without meaning to, he mumbled out a, "Sorry, Vickers."

Everyone went quiet until the car came to a stop a few minutes later at their staging spot on the side of the road. The goons in pursuit had fallen back into the distance and were no longer visible. The girl continued to cry and moan in pain and she yelped when they pulled her out of the backseat.

A more contrite Saul asked, "What's wrong with her anyway? She was fine when she was stuck in that car."

Without looking back, Vickers was already crossing the road into the field leading into the woods. "We'll figure it out back at the store," was all he said.

Forced to work together, Jim and Saul ducked under the girl's outstretched arms and performed a two person drag, lugging her toward the field. She offered little assistance beyond mincing steps that only half allowed her to keep up. When Jim saw Saul grab her belt, he did likewise and together and with a lot of effort they were able to keep up with the unencumbered Vickers and Owen.

It surprised Jim to hear Saul using words of encouragement to entice the girl into helping them in dragging her back, wheedling her with promises and light-hearted threats: "C'mon girl, we have everything you need back at the store; a soft bed, good food, and a hot shower. All you have to do is help us get you there," and, "I don't know if we can keep carrying you. We might have to leave you here if you don't try and walk on your own." She moaned a little louder when he mentioned leaving her, but it made her try harder and the going became a little easier.

In between glances at the ground to make sure he didn't trip, Jim kept his head in constant motion, scanning in all directions. As much as he felt sorry for the girl he was helping, he would leave her in a second if circumstances dictated choosing between her and himself. In any case, just like on the way out earlier that morning, the area was deserted. The only things Jim heard were the soft footsteps of his group and leaves and grass rustling in the slight breeze. Likewise, the only things he saw were the types of harmless things that were supposed to be there; trees, the sky, dragonflies, and the other members of his group.

Even though he didn't detect any goons at the moment, the anticipation of an attack was wearing on Jim's nerves. He didn't believe in luck but there wasn't any reason he could think of that would explain why the goons were absent. He wondered again about the boy that seemed to be in control of the area. Was he the reason they had safe passage? And if the little boy was in charge of the resident goons, how did he do it? These types of thoughts occupied Jim until they emerged from the woods near the Klimps store.

Vickers was already on the phone reporting their return to Megan or Ray while the group waited near the tree line for the go ahead to dash inside. The 'click' of the door release carried over to them and they double-timed for the safety of the building. With the goal of promised safety in sight the girl powered through the home stretch and they made the store without incident.

As the door shut behind them the girl sunk to the ground crying, but Jim couldn't tell whether it was from pain, relief, or a mixture of the two. He found he didn't care either way; he was tired from lugging her through the woods all the way from the car and was glad to be shed of her. Relieved of his responsibility for the girl's safety, Jim suddenly realized he had forgotten his flamethrower in the trunk of the car and made a mental note to tell Vickers about it later.

Megan and Bettina were inside the entrance to meet the returnees. Jim was pleasantly surprised when Bettina squealed, jumped into his arms, and hugged him around the neck. "Eww, you stink," she said, wrinkling her nose and hopping down.

"Ha! Thanks. It's been a long day." He didn't take her comment personally because even though he couldn't smell a stench on himself he didn't doubt that it was there. Instead, he pointed to the sobbing girl sitting on the ground: "Something's wrong with her. We found her trapped in a car outside of town and I think she's injured."

Megan overheard and followed Bettina over to the girl. Both women kneeled down and began talking to the new woman in low tones. Jim heard, "My goodness!" from Megan and, "Can we even do anything about that?" from Bettina. The conversation only made the girl cry harder which made Jim uncomfortable. He walked away and went for the showers.

Vickers joined up with him about halfway to the bathroom and neither of them spoke. Still, Jim appreciated his friend's presence as he wondered where Saul might be. Although he wasn't exactly afraid of the smaller man, he didn't relish another confrontation so soon after all he had already endured since daybreak. Having Vickers with him was a guarantee that he would at least be able to shower in peace.

They stopped off in the clothing department for new clothes. So far they didn't need to worry about laundry, and as the only 'husky' man over six feet tall, Jim was pretty sure he would have his whole size selection to himself. Besides, by the time he ran out someone else will have already figured something out.

During his shower Jim reflected on the many close calls he had survived so far and tried to think of ways he could minimize future risks. If he kept gambling on luck or other people to bail him out, eventually he was going to come up short. He asked Vickers in the next shower stall, making sure to speak loud enough to be heard over the noise of the two nozzles. "Hey Vickers, have you thought about how the goons can tell us normal people apart from other goons? I'm still trying to figure that out. I mean, I think we look the same, right? If we figure that out there may to be a way to trick them into leaving us alone."

"I have to confess that I haven't devoted a ton of time to that particular question, but what you're saying makes sense. Besides recognizable human noise like cars or talking, they must use senses other than hearing. They can tell you're there sometimes even when you're quiet."

"Yeah. And I don't think its smell either because they ran right by the girl trapped in the car."

"Which leaves taste and touch and those can't be it," Vickers said. He turned off his shower and stepped out. "I'll mention it to the others and see if they have any ideas."

"Okay."

Jim waited until Vickers left and then he quickly rubbed one out. Privacy was scarce nowadays and in the rare times he was by himself he was either running scared or under some other kind of duress. Jim never would have thought in the before times that one of the things he would have to worry about after the apocalypse was alone time. He pushed those thoughts away and concentrated on the task at hand and when he was done he rinsed off a final time and stepped out of the shower, almost colliding with Saul.

"Jesus Christ!" Jim yelled, embarrassed. "Are you fucking creeping up on me?"

"Relax, wankboy, I'm only here to grab a shower. I heard you going at it so I waited for you to finish your business. I was being polite."

"Whatever. How about next time you come back later instead of listening outside the shower curtain?" Jim yelled, then grabbed his clothes and hurriedly dressed himself before fleeing the bathroom.

As Jim was leaving Saul shouted a last dig from the shower stall: "Looks like I'm gonna have to announce my presence from now on!" Then he laughed and whistled the theme from movie "Jaws" towards the closing door.

Jim could hear muffled guffaws as he shuffled away. He was really getting tired of Saul's shit and vowed that very soon he was going to settle things with him once and for all. He cursed under his breath and went looking for his new girlfriend.

REAR OF SALES OFFICE, RV LOT

Sitting behind the sales office, the rush of energy Fran gained from his earlier enthusiasm waned, replaced with impatience and some mild agony from his facial wound. He wasn't sure what he had expected, but it certainly wasn't his plan to hide out all night listening to a bunch of boring chit chat. One of them, the interrogator, stood watch and walked around occasionally, but in the main they all sat around near the office entrance talking about their lives before the change.

He yawned and winced and remembered the pain medication he carried in his pocket. He reached down and grabbed a few pills out, dismayed that most of them had spilled out during the firefight and subsequent scramble to escape. Fran couldn't see what he held in his hand, but there was no reason to remain in pain while he waited for his future victims to fall asleep. He dry swallowed three of the horrible tasting pills.

Soon after the light throbbing in his face muted enough for him to ignore it. Fran felt the drug trying to take further hold on him but he fought it; he never intended to dull his senses, only his pain. A few minutes later it slipped his mind that he was supposed to be fighting the euphoria and his will weakened until he surrendered to it. Fran relaxed and his eyes closed of their own volition. Before he slipped under he had a brief conversation with himself, a short conversation that warned of the loss of self-control and a counter-point that urged tranquility and healing. Neither of the voices held any interest for him and he dismissed them both with a gentle flick of his mind. The voices were replaced with a blank nothing.

RV LOT, SALES OFFICE ENTRANCE

Walter was listening in while Lincoln tried his hand at impressing Claire, something about a yellow belt in Karate, when he heard it: It sounded like mating crickets or some other ambiguous wilderness noise. He almost dismissed it but then the tone deepened and he shushed the others. After a few moments of concentrating he heard it again. It was the sound of a person snoring and it was coming from behind the building where they set up their camp.

"What the…" Lincoln began.

"Shh," Walter cautioned. He leaned over to the young lieutenant and whispered, "Go get Mycroft. Be quick." Lincoln got up and soft-footed it in the direction of the major, who was off inspecting the Grizzly. Walter glanced at Claire. Her face was a mixture of curiosity, fear, and bemusement. He gestured for her to stay where she was before he stood up and grabbed his shotgun from its resting place against the wall.

Thirty seconds later Lincoln returned with Mycroft in tow and Walter pointed in the direction of the snoring. Mycroft heard it too and nodded before he indicated he would circle around to the left and the other two men should follow along the right side towards the back. Everyone signaled their agreement, even the supine Claire who had no active role in what was about to happen.

Gingerly, the three men made their circuit and met at the rear wall. Inconceivable as it was, the man they were after was slumped on his side fast asleep. Even though the snoozing fugitive didn't look threatening or scary, Walter was still determined to be as careful as possible, mindful of any tricks or traps that might have been set. "It couldn't possibly be this easy," he thought to himself. "Could it?"

On the other side of the wall Mycroft held up his hand and began a countdown with his fingers. Walter nudged the lieutenant to make sure he was looking: "Five, four, three, two, one…" and then Mycroft stepped forward and nudged his SCAR-H into the side of the sleeper's throat. In in his best command voice he said, "Get up you murdering bastard! Nice and slow!"

The man stirred but continued snoring, so Mycroft bonked the man on the forehead with the barrel of his rifle. There was no response. "Fella is having a good kip, looks like. Lincoln, would you mind grabbing a bit of rope so we can tie this tosser up?"

Nodding, Lincoln disappeared. While they waited, Walter asked, "What do you think he's doing here?"

"I imagine he came back to do us in, then got tired of waiting. He looks more passed out than asleep, actually."

"Unless he's faking it," Walter offered as Lincoln returned with some rope and handed it over to Mycroft.

"If he is, he's the biggest idiot I've ever seen. But just in case…" The major flipped his gun over one-handed and stamped the barrel down hard on the sleeping man's forehead. The man's body went limp and the loud snores were replaced by low moans. Mycroft bent and bound the unconscious man hand and foot. "Help me carry him back."

Walter and Lincoln hurried to comply, each gripping under an arm while the major took the legs. They dropped their unwieldy package three times during the short trip because of the dead weight and awkwardness of maneuvering a full grown man in half darkness.

Claire was waiting for them when they got around to the front, anxious to see who had been captured. When she saw who it was she said excitedly, "Wow! You got him. That's the leader guy." Blood was running from the man's head and pooling onto the ground. She pointed at it. "Um, is he dead?"

"I don't think so. I only gave him a little tap on the head. Most of that damage was already there."

They dumped their package unceremoniously onto the gravel, causing a large flap of loose skin on his face to flip over. Underneath, raw flesh and exposed bone leaked a constant flow of blood into his hair, ear and onto the ground. There was also a golf ball-sized hematoma on the man's forehead that belied Mycroft's claim of just a 'tap'.

"Well, we might as well do what we can for him and keep him from bleeding out," Walter suggested, nudging Lincoln. "Grab the first aid kit and we'll patch him up. The general will be disappointed if the guy dies on us before they've had a chance to meet."

"Roger that." Lincoln left to go root around in the Grizzly.

In the interim, Claire asked, "What about that swollen bump on his head? Do we pop it?"

"You're not supposed to," Mycroft said. "If you do it might get infected. Not that it will matter with this guy because he won't live out the week anyway, most like." When Claire looked at the major quizzically, he added by way of explanation: "With martial law in effect and the crimes he committed means he'll probably be executed soon after we get back."

"You're bringing him back just to kill him?"

Walter intervened. "I'm afraid so. I know it sounds barbaric, but in the grand scheme of things, it's a pretty minor atrocity. The general needs to punish offenders to establish his authority or he'll appear weak and make things worse."

Claire was about to protest some more but Lincoln returned and laid out bandages, medical tape, suturing material, and other gear from the medical kit onto the ground. He began threading a needle with thin black line, holding it up close to the battery powered lantern. "I need someone to hold his head down, wash and then keep the skin flap in place while I stitch him up. Be liberal with the antiseptic."

Mycroft made to assist, but Walter said, "I'll do it. I need to get some real field experience. If you hold his head, I'll do the rough stuff." The major smiled his approval and bent to put a heavy knee on the man's chest and a hand on his forehead. Walter donned latex surgical gloves and inspected the wound. Unlike some of his fellow reporters broadcasting from the front lines, Walter was never one to chase after and showcase the grisly battlefield casualties. Standing by watching people in agony always made him slightly nauseous and uncomfortable, something of a sadistic Peeping Tom getting off on pain and misery.

Grimacing, Walter gripped the piece of loose, floppy skin. It was roughly the size and shape of a small pancake and had a spongy, slippery texture. Before he lost his nerve, he poured some antiseptic into and around the cut and massaged it in with his thumb.

The man's eyes flew open and he screamed directly into Walter's face. If Mycroft hadn't anticipated the frenzied, bucking contortions that followed, Walter might have injured the man further. As it was, Mycroft punched the man in the belly and said menacingly, "Calm down, mate, or I'll really hurt you."

Through gasps for air, the man looked directly at Mycroft and nodded his understanding. After a few seconds Walter flipped the piece of skin back up and maneuvered it into place. The man's only complaints were the sucking of air through gritted teeth and glares promising retribution directed at everyone gathered around watching the ordeal.

"I'm not enjoying this either," Walter told his patient. "You may as well stop the evil eye routine." He asked Lincoln: "Are you ready?"

The lieutenant nodded and showed the curved stitching needle to the injured man. "I won't lie, this is going to hurt. A lot," and without further preamble Lincoln hooked the needle through both sides of the wound and pulled the suture through. The man on the ground gasped but didn't offer any further protests. Lincoln made to cut the thread but Mycroft stopped him with a curt admonishment.

"Just keep sewing, Lincoln. We aren't worried about scars with this one."

"You got it."

A minute later Lincoln snipped and tied the single, uninterrupted suture off and taped a large bandage over the site. Then he glanced at Walter's similar bandage covering the cheek wound received inside the bouncing Grizzly and laughed. "With all the practice I'm getting I should become a doctor."

Clair and Walter smiled but Mycroft was all business. "If you're done, I want to have a talk with our new friend." He kicked the prisoner in the leg. "Sit up!"

The man struggled to sit up but was having trouble because his hands were tied behind his back. Lincoln tried to lend assistance but Mycroft held a hand out. "Let him be! Don't let this man fool you into thinking he's helpless." The major kicked the man's leg a few more times until he sat up, then squatted down to get face-to-face. "You're a crafty one, aren't you?" No response. "What's your name?" No response. "Have it your way. Doesn't matter anyhow, you'll be dead by this time tomorrow." The threat elicited a malevolent glare from the prisoner, directed first at Mycroft, then at Claire. They all watched him grin at her before he licked his lips.

"You and I are going to have some fun later," the man said with smooth sincerity, winking at her. Claire's eyes grew frightful. She backed up slightly at the unexpected attention.

The threat earned the man a right cross from Mycroft, followed immediately by a left. The impact bounced the bound man's head off the wood exterior of the sales office. Blood spotting began to appear on the pristine white of his bandage, but the damage didn't erase the leer he wore. He recovered quickly and focused back in on Claire.

Uncomfortable with how things were escalating, Walter grabbed the bandage roll from the ground and wrapped it several times around the dazed man's head and eyes, blindfolding him. "No need to beat the guy anymore, he'll face proper justice when we return him to Wright-Patterson tomorrow."

"Justice?" the man laughed, looking around sightlessly. "Is that what you think you're doing, bringing me back for a good old-fashioned, legal seeing-to? If that's so, you're all deluded."

"Shut up," Mycroft warned.

"Or what? You'll beat me some more? I didn't do anything to any of you."

"You murdered General Vogel."

"No I didn't. I don't even know who that is, but I'm guessing it doesn't matter. I won't get a fair trial anyway."

"If you didn't murder him, you murdered others. Claire heard you order one your people to execute another and Colonel Doucet saw you. Face it, you're a killer."

"In case you haven't noticed, there's a lot of killing happening lately. What makes me so special that I deserve to be brought back and executed in cold blood? Do you know that the military is keeping a bunch of people prisoner at the base against their will? That they're beating and killing them with impunity?"

Despite the man's crimes, he made a compelling case; Walter, Lincoln, and Claire were watching the exchange of words with interest. What the man posited even gave Mycroft pause, but in the end, the major fell back on his military conditioning and said, "It really doesn't matter, we have our orders."

"So it's okay for you to do what you have to do because you have "orders", but it's not okay for me?"

"Since you're so talkative, how about you tell us your name?"

"How's about you tell me yours?"

"Okay. I'm Major Ackerman of the British Army and with me is my immediate superior, Colonel Doucet. The man who stitched you up is Lieutenant Cloyed of your own Air Force, and the young lady you terrorized is Claire. Now it's your turn."

The man laughed. "Terrorized her? I helped her, but okay." Then: "Call me King, if you have to have a name. I'm only telling you because I want you to know who to beg for mercy when our positions are reversed. There won't be any mercy, though, for any of you."

Whatever sympathy and pity the man had engendered using his arguments dissipated with the issuance of his threats. "It's getting late," Walter sighed. "Gag him and stick him in the office. We can deal with him in the morning."

The major and the lieutenant rose and grabbed King and dragged him into the damaged building. His protests and threats at being manhandled were cut off by one of the others muzzling him with some more of the bandages. The last thing King managed to utter was "…kill all of you, you'll wish you never…" and even though the man was tied, blinded, and silenced, Walter didn't doubt for a moment that given the chance, King would do exactly what he threatened, and more besides.

COMPUTER LAB, FIRESTONE HIGH SCHOOL

The news that there was another group of survivors nearby and that they were coordinated enough to broadcast a radio message did much to lift Josh and Ben's spirits, enough for them to put aside for the time being the disappointing events at the fat man's house.

"Tell us more. What did the message say exactly?" Josh asked.

Finn grinned while Livvy said, "We can do you one better. You can listen to it yourselves." She reached over and clicked the mouse attached to a nearby computer, raising the volume.

"…in addition, we are well armed and will defend it to the last man before detonating them. Message repeats. Hailing all survivors! We are a well-established, well-equipped group set up in a safe and secure location and looking for other survivors. We have ample food, water, and medicine. Our location is the Klimps store in Medina, Ohio. If you can make it to our location we will take you in. After taking necessary precautions, we would like to integrate you with our existing group for mutual defense, survival, and rebuilding. We must warn all who are listening to this broadcast, however, that if you seek to take our location or resources by force, sabotage, or subterfuge then we will respond without compassion to eliminate any threat, perceived or otherwise. In the event you succeed, our location is rigged with remote explosives, and in addition, we are well armed and will defend it to the last man before detonating them. Message repeats. Hailing all…"

Livvy decreased the volume. "It's the same message over and over."

Ben was grinning ear-to-ear and Finn and Livvy were smiling back. Josh also couldn't help the elation he felt. "Well, looks like we have a new plan," he chuckled. "That is, unless any of you guys want to stay here?"

Laughter filled the room, a sound none of them suspected they would hear so soon, considering the recent circumstances. Backs were clapped and hugs were exchanged until the mood died down to a sober level.

"Whew, that's a good bit of news," Ben said again before he asked something Josh was also wondering: "How did you guys find that message without a radio?"

"We didn't find it. Well not exactly," Finn explained. "Livvy actually found out about it from one of the forums we were on. Everyone is talking about it."

"What's a 'forum'?"

"Oh, yeah, I keep forgetting you've been locked up a while, Ben. A forum is kind of like an internet meeting site where people can discuss topics they're interested in. And as you probably guessed, what happened is the number one trending topic worldwide. I'll show you after, although I recommend you stay out of the forums that talk about sad shit. It's damn depressing."

"Okay. Sure…" Ben said unconvincingly. What the internet had become still eluded him. "Is everyone sure that's the best option, to meet up with the people who put that message out?"

"Well, our vote is for Medina," Livvy piped up, grabbing Finn's hand and raising it over her head. "The more people there are, the safer we'll be."

Josh almost laughed aloud that Finn was letting Livvy do the talking for the both of them; he had a feeling Finn would agree with whatever Livvy suggested, regardless of what it was. Turning to Ben, Josh raised his eyebrows: "And you?"

"After what happened today I say we go. It's not like we were having much luck rescuing people anyway."

The admission reminded Josh of how they got out of their tight spot earlier, by sacrificing the man in the house as live bait so they could flee like cowards out the back door. "Yeah, that," he said. "You're probably right. If we want to rescue people, and I for one absolutely still do, it makes sense to join up with a larger group that's better equipped. So that means I'm in, too." He kicked the bags they brought back with them and added, "We should leave at first light to make sure we don't have to spend the night out in the open. That gives us the rest of the day today and tonight to go through this stuff and separate what to bring with us, and to plan our route there. Let's get busy."

Everyone got to work emptying out the duffel bags and placing stuff in piles: Weapons, foodstuffs, and auxiliary gear. Josh made the decision to travel as light as possible while still being well-armed. Each person would only carry enough food for two days, which was twice as long as he anticipated as the worst-case scenario travel time. For guns, everyone got a Glock with two hundred rounds of hollow-point ammunition. There were other pistols in the haul, but Josh reasoned that having interchangeable ammo was more of a benefit than customizing each person's pistol loadout with individual preferences. Besides, the Glock was reliable, easy to use, and it didn't have a manual safety to worry about.

No one in the group besides Josh had any long gun experience so Josh went with the pump action shotguns. For one thing, he was more concerned with personal defense than taking out targets at long range, and second, a shotgun was very effective even in the hands of an inexperienced shooter, particularly against the type of swarming behavior the enemy utilized. Josh only held back on giving Livvy a shotgun, explaining to her that the kickback would do her more harm than any help her added firepower might bring to the group. She didn't protest.

There was enough of the other gear for each of them. Ben distributed tactical vests and belts while Finn handed out fixed-blade tanto knives, hydration packs, Maglites, and tasers. There were only two pairs of compact binoculars and without being told Finn added them to the piles reserved for Josh and Ben.

For the next hour Josh went over all of the equipment with the others: Safety, use, storage and with the guns, loading, aiming and deployment. He drilled into their heads over and over the dangers of rushing, panicking, and shooting past each other. He made them all practice unholstering their pistols and getting into shooting stances. He didn't call a halt to the lessons until he was reasonably confident that they wouldn't be a threat to themselves or each other.

"Finn, before we hit the sack I want you to map out a few routes to the Klimps store for us to study. Stay away from any dense population areas and spots we already marked as dangerous, and if you can, try and steer us past places where there might be survivors. I'd like to help people along the way if possible."

"Already did that," Finn beamed, pleased that he had anticipated the group's needs.

"No shit?"

"No shit."

"Alright, little man," Ben complimented. "I knew there was a reason we kept you around."

"Not so quick. I hate to say it, but there aren't any direct routes that take us past survivors. If you want, I can look for more tonight on the computer just in case."

Ben and Josh exchanged a look. "Nah, never mind," Josh said. "Just so long as we keep our eyes open. I don't want to go out of our way to find trouble. From what Ben and I learned today, trouble will probably find a way to come to us."

KLIMPS MEGA STORE, MEDINA, OHIO

After getting dressed Jim found Bettina and most of the others clustered around one of the tables set up for group meals. When he got close enough, he saw that they were gathered around the girl they had rescued. She lay still and Jim was glad that she wasn't moaning anymore. It was annoying.

"What's up with her?" he said as he walked up and squeezed in next to Bettina, indicating the girl with his thumb.

Bettina turned to him with tears in her eyes and sobbed, "She's dead."

"Dead? Dead how?"

From the other side of the table, Megan shrugged and said, "I'm pretty sure it was anaphylactic shock. When you guys pulled her out, you ruptured both of her breast implants and released silicone into her system."

"You can die from that?" Jim asked.

"Not usually, unless you happen to be allergic to it which I guess she was. Even if she wasn't, without a doctor the silicone poisoning would have kept her in severe chronic pain."

Looking around at the others, Jim sensed from their expressions that nobody felt him responsible, except maybe for Sandy and Cindy who by default were always busy giving him the evil eye, and as far as Jim was concerned they didn't count anyway. Out of habit he tried deflecting anyway. "Oh. We didn't do it on purpose. The goons were coming too fast and we had to hurry."

"No one is to blame," Vickers declared. "We did what we had to do. If we hadn't come upon her she would have died anyway."

"So that's your excuse?" Cindy suddenly screeched in frustration. "She would have died anyway? You and Jim have been nothing but trouble ever since you two came here. You both fucking suck!" The heavyset woman began crying. Sandy reached over and tried comforting her but Cindy shrugged off her sister's embrace. "You guys killed Zoe, Chuck, and Jack, and now you killed this poor girl!" she sobbed, "Did any of you even bother getting her name before you murdered her?"

Jim half expected everyone to jump on the bandwagon and pile on more abuse towards him and Vickers but was surprised when they simply walked away. Jim gave the sisters a sarcastic pouty face and followed Bettina, Megan, Owen, Vickers and Ray upstairs to the old break room. Cindy's outburst was forgotten as they settled around the table and held an impromptu team meeting.

Ray spoke first. "It might surprise those of you that just returned that we've already been contacted by a few folks, calling in to verify that our broadcast wasn't a hoax or a trap."

The news lifted the spirits of everyone who had gone out on the last mission and smiles and high fives were exchanged. Vickers asked, "Did any of them say they were coming here?"

"Yeah, all of them did. Well, all three of them that called," Megan interjected.

Vickers nodded and thought aloud, "If three called, we can likely expect a lot more than that. I have a feeling things are about to get real interesting around here."

No one around the table doubted it for a second.

ALL YOUR STATES ARE BELONG TO US

BOOK TWO OF THE OPHIR RIDGE SAGA

COMING IN 2015

Made in the USA
Middletown, DE
24 October 2020